JOHN RICHARDSON (1796-1852) was the first man in the Canadas who attempted to live on the monetary rewards of creative writing. He wrote a considerable amount of non-fiction, some poetry, and several novels. The most famous, *Wacousta; or, The Prophecy: A Tale of the Canadas*, an historical romance set in the Detroit-Amherstburg area, made effective use of the 'conspiracy' of Pontiac, the Indian uprising of 1763.

CARL F. KLINCK is Professor Emeritus of English, University of Western Ontario, co-editor of the *Canadian Anthology*, and general editor of the *Literary History of Canada*.

The Canadian Brothers combines all the excitement of a sentimental wilderness romance – mysterious and surprising occurrences, terrors by night and day, deadly combats, haunted minds, consuming passions – with an account of first-hand experiences during the War of 1812.

Originally published in 1840, it is a sequel to *Wacousta* and takes up the family history about fifty years later. As a young man, John Richardson took part in much of the military action described in the book, including the shelling of Frenchtown and the defeat of the British at Moraviantown. His account of the misery of the prisoners captured there by the Americans also reflects personal experience. General Brock, Captain Barclay, and Tecumseh are gloriously themselves and are accorded respectful tributes.

Carl Klinck's introduction places the novel in the contexts of the events of *Wacousta* and of the author's life, and traces its history, discussing briefly the differences between the original version and the Americanized edition, retitled *Matilda Montgomerie* (1851).

Literature of Canada

Poetry and Prose in Reprint

Douglas Lochhead, General Editor

The Canadian Brothers; or,

The Prophecy Fulfilled:

A Tale of the Late American War

John Richardson

Introduction by Carl F. Klinck

UNIVERSITY OF TORONTO PRESS
TORONTO AND BUFFALO

Toronto and Buffalo
Printed in Canada
Reprinted in 2018

Library of Congress Cataloging in Publication Data

Richardson, John, 1796-1852.
The Canadian brothers.

(Literature of Canada, poetry and prose in reprint 18)
Sequel to Wacousta.
Reprint of the 1840 ed. published in Montreal.
Includes bibliographical references.
1. United States – History – War of 1812 – Fiction.
I. Title. II. Title: The prophecy fulfilled.
PZ3.R394Can3 [PR9199.2.R53] 813'.2 76-11733
ISBN 0-8020-2179-4
ISBN 978-0-8020-6264-2 (paper)

This book has been published with the assistance of grants from the Ontario Arts Council and the McLean Foundation. Copies of the books from which the reprint was made were provided by Special Collections, Douglas Library, Queen's University.

The Canadian Brothers; or, The Prophecy Fulfilled was originally published in 1840 by Armour & Ramsay, Montreal.

Preface

Yes, there is a Canadian literature. It does exist. Part of the evidence to support these statements is presented in the form of reprints of the poetry and prose of the authors included in this series. Much of this literature has been long out of print. If the country's culture and traditions are to be sampled and measured, both in terms of past and present-day conditions, then the major works of both our well-known and our lesser-known writers should be available for all to buy and read. The Literature of Canada series aims to meet this need. It shares with its companion series, The Social History of Canada, the purpose of making the documents of the country's heritage accessible to an increasingly large national and international public, a public which is anxious to acquaint itself with Canadian literature – the writing itself – and also to become intimate with the times in which it grew.

DL

John Richardson, 1796-1852

Carl F. Klinck

Introduction

The Canadian Brothers of Major John Richardson was published in Montreal in 1840 in two volumes. Since few copies of this original edition were sold, whether as two books or as a pair within a single cover, the sequel to *Wacousta* has had a limited circulation among Canadian readers during more than a hundred and thirty years. This publication in 1976 is the second Canadian edition.

In 1851 buyers of De Witt and Davenport's paperbound books in the United States were offered an 'Americanized' version of *The Canadian Brothers* under the entirely new title of *Matilda Montgomerie.* Six additional reissues, bearing dates between 1851 and 1888, have been discovered and described by William F.E. Morley in *A Bibliographical Study of Major John Richardson.*[1] The story is now being repatriated with the original text and title of *The Canadian Brothers.*

John Richardson (1796-1852) was a professional soldier and by inclination a professional author, the first man in the Canadas who attempted to live on the monetary rewards to be gained by creative writing. There is no better introduction to his early environment than *The Canadian Brothers.* It is set in the scenes of his boyhood and of his first military experiences. His mother was a daughter of John Askin, a prosperous trader with the Indians and the garrisons of the Michigan area; his father was Dr Robert Richardson, a surgeon of the Queen's Rangers stationed at various points of the western border which had been established in 1795 between Canada and the United States by Jay's Treaty. Their son John was born at Queenston on the Niagara River, a little village overshadowed by the famous Heights where the forces of General Brock defeated the Americans in the last battle described in *The Canadian Brothers* (and, incidentally, glossed over in *Matilda Montgomerie*).

As a young boy John was taken to live at Amherstburg (Malden) on the Detroit River, where he learned the history of Canada's Old Northwest and especially of that region in 1760, when Major Robert Rogers took over the French fort at Detroit for the British army. Three years later the uprising of Pontiac and his Indians placed the garrison under siege. Around this 'Conspiracy' (so called by Francis Parkman in 1851) Richardson would before 1832 build the fiction of his first Canadian novel, *Wacousta.*

In his youth he had his own harsh experience of war, which would form the historical basis of *The Canadian Brothers*, the sequel to *Wacousta.* When John was fifteen and his favourite brother Robert only fourteen, the British-American-Canadian war of 1812-14 began with military action on the vulnerable frontier of the Detroit River. The boys became 'gentlemen volunteers,' John as an ensign in the 41st Regiment, and Robert as a midshipman in the small British naval force whose base was being established a few yards from their home in Amherstburg.

With some concessions to fiction, the experiences in war of Gerald and Henry Grantham are based on what the Richardson brothers saw and did in the border battles of 1812 and 1813. John was 'a constant participator' with the 41st in General Brock's capture of Detroit, and in the engagements at Frenchtown, the Miami, Fort Stephenson on the Sandusky, and Moraviantown. John was captured during the decisive defeat on the Thames and suffered with other British officers who became prisoners of war in Ohio and Kentucky. His memories of a full year as a captive in the United States are the source of vivid detail in many pages of *The Canadian Brothers.* His brother Robert, although under orders to remain behind, contrived to join the attacking forces landed at Frenchtown, and was seriously wounded when still fourteen years of age. He died in 1819.

Readers of this book, however, must know that, for purposes of fiction, the author does not describe the wartime experiences of Gerald and Henry Grantham precisely as they happened in real life to himself and Robert. In the book Gerald is the midshipman and performs in most of the military actions as Ensign John Richardson had actually done, and Ensign Henry Grantham plays a minor part as Midshipman Robert Richardson had done because of delayed naval activity and his own serious wounds.

Richardson also freely portrayed characters based upon people he had known on the Border; these were not drawn with the exactness which he lavished upon geographical and military details. He was a novelist as well as a historian. Yet one may see something of his father in Major Grantham (I, 105-6), and of his uncle, or more probably his grandfather John Askin, in Colonel D'Egville. Captains Molineux, St Clair, Cranstoun, and Granville, and lieutenants Raymond, Villiers, and Middlemore are fictional representations of certain officers of the infantry, engineers, militia, and navy assembled at Amherstburg. Lieutenant Middlemore, the punster, and Captain Cranstoun, the Scot, are unfortunate caricatures.

Some of the experiences attributed to Gerald Grantham (as commander of a ship) belonged in the War to naval lieutenants Rolette and Irvine. The great heroes, General Brock, Captain

Barclay, and Tecumseh are gloriously themselves, and are accorded respectful tributes similar to those in the author's poetic *Tecumseh* (1828) and in *War of 1812*, his textbook history of the operations of the Right Division of the Canadian Army. With this document in hand, further experiments in identifying Richardson's fictional officers of the British-Canadian and American forces may be carried on at the will of the reader. He will find little praise for General Procter of the 41st or for General Hull, American commander of the fort at Detroit.

Desborough and Gattrie are frontiersmen of American origin who have had to choose sides in the Border war. Desborough, like the traitor described in Richardson's later novel *Westbrook*,[2] took on the role of an outlaw avenging himself and the American cause upon the British settlers and their British protectors. On the other hand, Sampson Gattrie was Simon Girty, excellently portrayed as Amherstburg knew him in his old age, a 'loyalist' settler on the Canadian side near McKee and Elliott, infamous among the Americans because of his remarkable early career as an 'irregular' British Ranger in the territories south of the Lakes during the Indian and Revolutionary wars (I, 100-15).[3]

Lest references to Richardson's various writings become confusing, it is appropriate to trace his entry into the world of letters. When he was released from captivity in Kentucky in October 1814, he proceeded to England: he was on the Atlantic when the battle of Waterloo was fought. Attached at that time to the 8th, or King's, Regiment of Foot, but on half pay, he sought a commission with sufficient emolument to give him status in Britain – and indeed on the continent. The record of his early journalistic efforts is still obscure, although, if one interprets the evidence of his first two novels, *Ecarté* (1829) and the recently discovered *Frascati's* (1830), he succeeded in getting enough money to become acquainted with a gambling set in Paris.

After a spell of poetic experiments (romantic heroics in *Tecumseh* and satire in *Kensington Gardens in 1830*), Richardson returned to fiction: the Parisian phase was followed by a Canadian one, resulting in *Wacousta* (1832) and the beginning of work on *The Canadian Brothers.* Indeed, he had never entirely neglected Canadian material: *The New Monthly Magazine* in London, England, had published in 1826 and 1827 his series of 'A Canadian Campaign, By A British Officer,' which fifteen years later became his documented history book, *War of 1812.*

There was an interruption of literary activity in 1835, when, as a captain of the 22nd Regiment, Richardson fought with the British Auxiliary Legion of Lieutenant-General De Lacy Evans in supporting the Regent Christina of Spain against Don Carlos, who claimed the throne. Participation in this venture involved Richardson in military politics and three books of controversy and memoirs. Still dedicated to politics, he came to Canada in 1838 as a writer for the London *Times.* Thus began the experiences recorded in his *Eight Years in Canada* (1847), in which one may find accounts of his sojourns in Amherstburg and Sandwich during the late 1830s.

In *The Canadian Brothers* one notes the error of placing the battle of Queenston Heights in 1813, rather than, as it happened, in 1812. A man so well stocked with knowledge of military history, as Richardson was, must have had strong reasons for this anachronism. In his work of fiction he undoubtedly required the battle for a spectacular climax, and probably for the satisfaction of concluding with a British-Canadian triumph. His 'preface' to the novel shows that he took such understanding for granted on the part of the reader, who would also be grateful for the introduction of Tecumseh into the narrative 'somewhat earlier than the strict facts will justify.' It is easier to forgive Richardson for these manipulations than for inventing speeches in atrocious 'imperfect Scotch' by Captain Cranstoun, for which even an apology seems inadequate. Middleton's puns are indeed miserable, and the odd speech of the lovable Sambo is quite enough for the reader to bear.

The subtitle of *The Canadian Brothers*, *The Prophecy Fulfilled*, is a reminder that one should know what was reported in *Wacousta; or, The Prophecy* regarding the major characters of the early 1760s. *The Canadian Brothers* takes up family history in 1812, about fifty years later. The gap in our knowledge of those intervening years is not filled until Volume II, pages 32 to 40. The genealogical summary and chart on page xiii may bring together the scattered details.

Several decades before he had become colonel of the Detroit garrison in the early 1760s, de Haldimar had broken faith (in Scotland) with his friend Reginald Morton and had stolen and married Morton's fiancée, Clara Beverley. In *Wacousta*'s opening scene in Detroit during 'Pontiac's War,' Morton (disguised, and called 'Wacousta') appears among the Indians attacking the fort. With terrible strength and ferocity Wacousta uses the occasion for revenge, especially after his nephew (known as Halloway) is coldly executed by orders of the colonel.

Halloway's wife Ellen utters a curse and prophesies the destruction of the de Haldimar line in these words: 'if there be spared one branch of thy detested family may it be only that

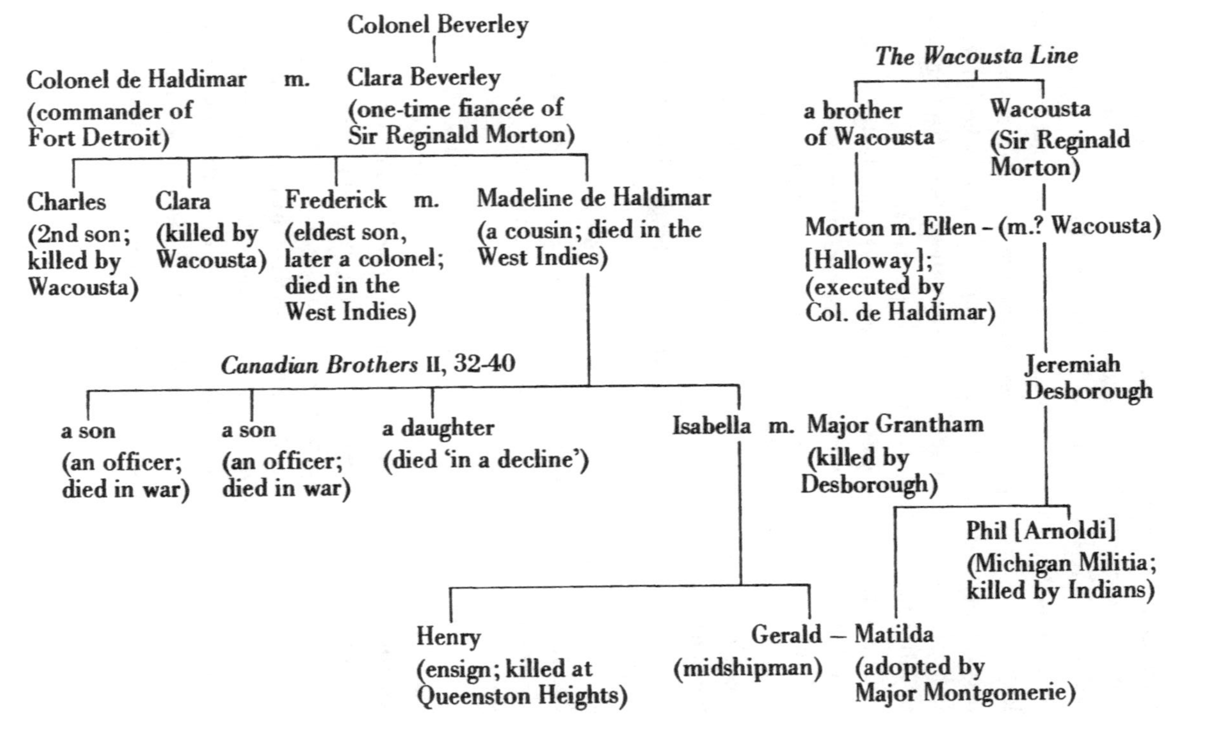

Colonel Beverley
Colonel de Haldimar (commander of Fort Detroit)
m.
Clara Beverley (one-time fiancée of Sir Reginald Morton)
The Wacousta Line
a brother of Wacousta
Wacousta (Sir Reginald Morton)
Charles (2nd son; killed by Wacousta)
Clara (killed by Wacousta)
Frederick (eldest son, later a colonel; died in the West Indies)
m.
Madeline de Haldimar (a cousin; died in the West Indies)
Morton m. Ellen – (m.? Wacousta)
[Halloway]; (executed by Col. de Haldimar)
Canadian Brothers II, 32-40
Jeremiah Desborough
a son (an officer; died in war)
a son (an officer; died in war)
a daughter (died 'in a decline')
Isabella
m.
Major Grantham (killed by Desborough)
Phil [Arnoldi] (Michigan Militia; killed by Indians)
Henry (ensign; killed at Queenston Heights)
Gerald (midshipman)
Gerald – Matilda
Matilda (adopted by Major Montgomerie)

they may be reserved for some death too horrible to be conceived!' Wacousta is the agent of death for two of the de Haldimar-Beverley children – Charles and Clara – young adults residing in the fort at Detroit. Ellen Halloway marries, or at least mates, with Wacousta, and bears him a villainous son, who becomes known as Jeremiah Desborough and who in turn fathers a daughter. In their own ways these two offspring help to fulfill the prophecy in *The Canadian Brothers.*

The retrospective passage in this novel (II, 32-40) records that Frederick de Haldimar, sole survivor of the family of the old colonel and Clara Beverley, lives long enough to have children. He and his wife Madeline die in the violence of a hurricane in the West Indies between the time of the American Revolution and 1812.

As *The Canadian Brothers* opens, Frederick's branch of the de Haldimars is also near extinction. Two sons have been killed in war, and a daughter, still young, has died after 'a decline.' The last one to die is Isabella, wife of Major Grantham (latterly of Amherstburg). Gerald and Henry are their sons, the only remaining targets of the curse.

It does not take one long to sense that Matilda, Gerald's beautiful captive, lacks the completeness of a father-daughter relationship with Major Montgomerie: she has put up all the defences of someone who must go her own way, self-centred, bitter, and alone. Predictably in a romance, Gerald falls passionately in love with this American girl. Her mysterious coldness and secret sorrow lure him on, although the reader does not forget that she can safely suck the venom of a rattlesnake from Gerald's arm. Under the spell of this fascinating creature, Gerald moves in, and often out of, the historical events, nursing his private dilemma, as Richardson himself recalled the sensations, cravings, dreams, resolves, obsessions, and passions of a sensitive young man denied normal responses under the stresses of war.

In the second volume of *The Canadian Brothers* Gerald is captured on his ship by the Americans at Buffalo, as he lingers after delivering the major and Matilda to their own country. He soon escapes and returns, oppressed by morbid thoughts, to the war near his home on the Detroit River. Here he takes part in the shelling at Frenchtown. At the siege of Sandusky, he is captured a second time by the enemy. Thus he misses Captain Barclay's battle against Commodore Perry's fleet at Put-in-Bay and the consequent collapse of Procter's position in the Malden area, capped by the destruction of the British Right Division at Moraviantown on the Thames in October 1813.

John Richardson had cause to know about this catastrophe, for he was one of the officers of the 41st taken there by Harrison's army and sent, with many hardships, to custody in Chillicothe, Ohio, and Frankfort, Kentucky. His account of the misery of these prisoners may be read in Chapter 12 of his *War of 1812.* In *The Canadian Brothers* Gerald suffers no less on his trip with Captain Jackson through the wilderness from Sandusky to Frankfort. On arrival, however, Gerald does not have to endure the year-long term which John Richardson himself found so galling – characterized at times by closest confinement, irons on his limbs, daily insults, threats of hanging, and other results of a breakdown in arrangements between the British and American authorities regarding rules and procedures for custody and exchange.

In Richardson's novel *Ecarté* (1829), there are hints of some courtesies extended to the British officers by the gentry of

Frankfort and by some of the Kentucky belles. One of the main characters, Frederick Dormer, tells his friend Clifford that, upon leaving school, he joined his regiment in Canada and was captured by the Americans (probably at Moraviantown). Like Richardson and Gerald Grantham, he was taken with his fellow officers across one of the lakes and conveyed through the wilderness to Frankfort. Dormer's story, designed to confess his addiction to gambling, stresses the cordiality of Kentucky gentlemen rather than the sorrows of a prisoner. One of his friends is a Mr Worthington.

Fact and fiction may be closely related here, for Richardson refers in *War of 1812*[4] to an early period of parole for himself and other officers in Frankfort, when they were befriended by certain gentlemen of the town – a Major Madison, who had himself been well treated as a prisoner of war in Lower Canada, and Mr Sproule, a banker who lent them money. It also appears that Major Madison had a daughter, as had Major Montgomerie in *The Canadian Brothers* and Mr Worthington had in *Ecarté.* Dormer wins the hand of Agatha Worthington, but loses her because of his degrading attachment to card playing. When he has endured a debtor's prison in Paris for a year, he rejoices in a reunion with Agatha and a happy wedding.

Not so in *The Canadian Brothers.* The 'daughter' of Major Montgomerie displays personal characteristics quite unlike those of the young, trusting, and endearing Agatha because Matilda came into Richardson's Canadian novel with a reputation and history ready-made in documentary sources. Proof of this is in the author's own introduction to an 1851 edition of *Wacousta,* where he makes this reference to *The Canadian Brothers:* 'The "Prophecy fulfilled." ... embraces and indeed is intimately connected with the Beauchamp tragedy, which took place at or near Weiseger's Hotel, in Frankfort, Kentucky, where I had been many years before confined as a prisoner of war...' He must have been informed through oral, journalistic, or 'literary' reports, for he had left Kentucky eleven years before the 'tragedy' occurred. A man named Beauchamp murdered Colonel Solomon B. Sharp on 5 November, 1825, and was hanged on 7 July, 1826. Beauchamp's wife and accomplice (Ann Cook) died in jail a few days before the execution. Ann's character was fully discussed since the details of the case were well publicized in the United States. Richardson, who began his novel in 1833, must have received his information about it while he was abroad.

Numerous reports appeared during the second quarter of the century. Some of the early accounts of the affair, in chronological order, are: *The Confession of Jereboam O. Beauchamp* [1826]; *Letters of Ann Cook* (1826); *Conrad and Eudora* (1834) by Thomas Holley Chivers; *A Winter in the West* (1835) by Charles Fenno Hoffman; 'Politian, An Unfinished Tragedy' by Edgar Allen Poe [mss 1835]; *Greyslaer: A Romance of the Mohawk* (1840) by Hoffman; *Beauchampe; or, The Kentucky Tragedy* (1842) by William Gilmore Simms.

It is not a safe bet that Richardson obtained copies of the *Confession* or the *Letters*. Nor is it likely that he saw Chivers's play or Poe's manuscript while he was involved with the British Legion in Spain (1835-7); he was not the kind of romancer to enjoy Chivers's or Poe's turning of Ann Cook into an Italian Eudora or Lalage. Simms's *Beauchampe*, a novel more in Richardson's own line, was published in 1842, too late to be a source. Hoffman's *Greyslaer*, a book whose setting and characters would have appealed to Richardson's interest in Indian history, was also too late since *The Canadian Brothers* was legally registered on 2 January 1840.

Richardson's acknowledgement of information about 'the existence of a work of the same character' by a 'fellow-laborer in the same field' – an 'American author' – was made, not in 1840, but rather in 1851 when he republished *Wacousta* and the Matilda story in New York. In the introduction on that occasion, he declared that he 'had not read or even heard of' an (unnamed) book 'of the same character,' which was evidently being mentioned by some persons as antedating and influencing his own. Indeed, he believed that his novel 'although not published until after a lapse of years, was the first written.' 'No similarity of treatment of the subject,' he said, 'exists between the two versions...'

Simms's *Beauchampe* looks similar enough if dates are disregarded, but it must be ruled out as a contemporary source. Speculation and further scholarly investigation, however, may profitably focus on Hoffman's travel book, *A Winter in the West* (1835)[5] under his heading of Appendix K. Hoffman's detailed account of the Beauchamp tragedy was then, and still is, a most enlightening document. Comparison of it with the Matilda story in *The Canadian Brothers* is certainly one of the best means of assessing critically the nature and extent of Richardson's invention and independence in constructing his novel.

The length of Hoffman's appendix forbids full quotation here, but the basic resemblance of the Ann Cook-Beauchamp tragedy to the Matilda-Gerald story in *The Canadian Brothers* is clear enough:

Beauchamp, while a student at law in a county town of Kentucky, became attached to Miss Cook, a young female who had been seduced by Colonel Sharp. The lady, in consequence of the stain upon her reputation, lived very much retired, and refused to receive the addresses of her new admirer until he had repeatedly tendered his hand in marriage. His solicitations at last prevailed with her; but she consented to become his wife solely upon the condition, that he would revenge her wrongs towards Colonel S. by taking his life before they were united at the altar. The infatuated student pledged himself to the bloody contract; and instantly challenged the seducer, who refused to meet him. Failing in the vengeance to which he had pledged himself in the hour of his wild betrothal, Beauchamp returned to his affianced wife; who from that moment, as Beauchamp expresses it, got the 'womanish whim' into her head to be herself the destroyer of her seducer. To this end she practised pistol-shooting for several months, until, as her lover avers, 'she could place a ball with perfect accuracy.' But their engagement having now subsisted for some time, and Beauchamp having completed his law studies, he prevailed upon the lady to give him the rights of a legal protector. 'I had now,' he says, 'married Miss C–, and felt that I had a sufficient apology before the world to revenge upon Colonel S– the injury he had done her. Neither could I any longer think of the wild idea of my wife's revenging her own wrongs.'

Colonel Sharp became a candidate for public office, and his seduction of Miss Cook was 'trumpeted to the world.' Beauchamp now decided to assassinate the villain secretly and in cold blood. On a dark night he knocked at Sharp's door, grabbed the colonel, choked and stabbed him. While Sharp's wife called the doctor and people of the town arrived, Beauchamp escaped, changed his clothes at the river bank, and then went home to his wife. There he was arrested and taken to Frankfort to await trial.

He was convicted of murder upon 'the most ample circumstantial evidence.' His wife was then allowed to remain with her husband in the prison:

> and the last moments of this infatuated and ill-fated pair were marked by the same strange intermixture of moral obliquity and religious fanaticism, blended with chivalric heroism and the most touching devotion to each other, by which their intercourse throughout appears to have been characterized. They passed their time together in composing prayers and verses. The first breathed all of Christian humility and contrition, mingled with a firm reliance upon heavenly mercy: the last are made up of the ravings of insane passion and gratified vengeance.

As the day of execution approached, they made a compact to share a vial of laudanum and die together: 'The laudanum failed in its effect. The day of execution arrived and the morning found them still both alive.' When Beauchamp was called to the gallows, they again tried suicide, this time with a dagger. The wife claimed that she had struck the fatal blow herself, and that she was dying for her dear husband. A group of doctors tried to save her life, but in a few hours she was dead. Beauchamp was carried to the place of public execution and was 'launched into eternity.' Husband and wife were buried in a single coffin.

In *Beauchampe* (1842), William Gilmore Simms made a sentimental romance by keeping fairly close to the action of the documentary record and by much expatiation upon 'vital truths' of motive and morality. Richardson's version emphasized pride and honour, and had a broader range of action, for he had planned a novel of real life – romanticized within the context of a very real war. Simms's setting was a community; Richardson's was a wild borderland.

Several chapters appeared in print before *The Canadian Brothers* was published. The March and April 1839 issues of *The Literary Garland* featured 'Jeremiah Desborough; or The Kentuckian' and 'The Settler, or The Prophecy Fulfilled.'[6] These were designed as teasers for the public: John Lovell was the printer of the Montreal *Garland* and also of Richardson's forthcoming novel. Armour and Ramsay published it after a campaign to enlist subscribers. 'I actually obtained,' the author confessed in his *Eight Years in Canada* (p 108), 'among a population little exceeding a million of persons, not less than two hundred and fifty subscribers – two thirds of whom even went so far as to take their books when published.'

After a number of other literary enterprises which brought in little money – the editing of a newspaper (the *New Era or Canadian Chronicle*, 1841-2) in Brockville; an ambitious project for a series of government-supported histories like *War of 1812* 'for the use of Schools in Canada'; and the autobiographical *Eight Years in Canada* (1847) – Richardson decided, as he said in the introduction to *Wacousta* (1851), that he might as well have published 'in Kamschatka.' *The Canadian Brothers* was, therefore, not republished in Canada, but merely offered for sale again in a different binding.[7] When Richardson moved to New York to lure American readers for his novels, *The Monk Knight of St John* [1850], *Ecarté* (1851), *Hardscrabble* (1850), *Wacousta*, and other books, he reissued *The Canadian Brothers* under the title of *Matilda Montgomerie.* The 'Kentucky' tragedy was featured. The front cover showed a picture of Matilda being accused by an old man. Below it were these words: 'The fearful Prophecy uttered in "Wacousta" is in this volume fulfilled to the very letter, in the complete destruction of the family who had incurred the terrible curse.'

The substance of the story was not altered, but the book was 'Americanized,' made more attractive to prospective buyers in the United States, by a reduction (although not a total surrender) of 'Canadian' characteristics. There were at least seventy omissions 'of more or less length and importance, ranging from three to four pages down to a single sentence' – as William Renwick Riddell pointed out in his *John Richardson.*[8] The author himself standardized the language or struck out the 'imperfect Scotch' of Captain Cranstoun, for which he had apologized in his 1840 'preface.'

So thorough was Judge Riddell's comparison of the two editions that the result of one's own examination must run parallel to his report. The 1851 edition of *Matilda Montgomerie* in my hands omits the dedication to Sir John Harvey and the preface, both of which are printed with our text of *The Canadian Brothers.* The letter from the King's secretary, approving the passage in Volume I, chapter 6, which 'treats of the policy of employing the Indians in any future war [the British] may have with the United States' was thus removed. Significant passages omitted from the text of this same chapter in *Matilda Montgomerie* were: 'But this we unequivocally deny ... which you, Major Montgomerie, appear to condemn.' (*Canadian Brothers*, I, p 73, l. 28 to p 75, l 8); 'They should rather censure ... the resisting and the helpless.' (*Canadian Brothers*, I, p 76, 1. 7 to p 77, 1 3). 'Whatever the abhorrence ... advocate the practice.' (*Canadian Brothers*, I, p 78, 1. 24 to p 79, I. 11). The 'Yankee' origin of Desborough is not rubbed in as it is in the original. From a Canadian point of view, the most lamentable excision is the vivid description of the Canadian victory at Queenston Heights (II, chapter 16). And the Canadian Lakes became 'the *American* Lakes'!

In both versions the Canadian reader still has loving descriptions of a historic border of his own country, an exhibition of the military glories of his people's past, and a strong sense of patriotism, along with the excitement of sentimental wilderness romance to be expected of a work by the author of *Wacousta* – sudden surprises, actions before explanations, mysterious happenings, terrors by night and day, deadly combats, pervading gloom, intriguing sexual encounters, haunted minds, and consuming passions.

NOTES

1 Toronto: Bibliographical Society of Canada 1973
2 *Westbrook, the Outlaw; or, The Avenging Wolf: An American Border Tale* (1851). See edition by Grant Woolmer Books, Montreal 1973.
3 C.W. Butterfield, *History of the Girtys* (Cincinnati 1890); reissued Columbus, Ohio 1950)
4 The original book is very rare. See the excellent edition of *Richardson's War of 1812*, with notes and a life of the author by Alexander Clark Casselman (Toronto 1902).
5 (New York 1835) II, 153, 332-43
6 *The Canadian Brothers*, I, chapter 7, and II, chapter 1, respectively
7 See Morley, *A Bibliographical Study of Major John Richardson* 51.
8 (Toronto: Ryerson Press [1923]) 58-62

TO

HIS EXCELLENCY

MAJOR GENERAL SIR JOHN HARVEY, K. C. B.: K. C. H.

LIEUTENANT GOVERNOR OF NEW BRUNSWICK,

WHO BORE A CONSPICUOUS PART IN THE WAR OF

1812,

AND WHO CONTRIBUTED SO ESSENTIALLY

TO THE SUCCESS OF THE BRITISH ARMS

DURING THE CAMPAIGNS OF

1813 AND 1814,

AND PARTICULARLY AT STONEY CREEK IN UPPER CANADA,

ON THE NIGHT OF THE

5TH JUNE 1813,

WHEN, ENTRUSTED WITH THE EXECUTION OF HIS OWN DARING PLAN,

HE, AT THE HEAD OF FIVE HUNDRED MEN

OF THE 8TH AND 49TH REGIMENTS,

(The former the Author's Corps,)

SURPRISED AND COMPLETELY ROUTED

AT THE POINT OF THE BAYONET,

A DIVISION OF THE AMERICAN ARMY,

(UNDER GENERALS WINDER AND CHANDLER,)

THREE THOUSAND FIVE HUNDRED STRONG,

CAPTURING THEIR LEADERS,

WITH MANY OTHER INFERIOR PRISONERS,

AND SEVERAL PIECES OF CANNON;

THE CANADIAN EDITION OF THIS HISTORICAL TALE

IS INSCRIBED, WITH SENTIMENTS

OF HIGH PUBLIC AND PERSONAL ESTEEM,

BY HIS FAITHFUL AND OBEDIENT SERVANT,

THE AUTHOR.

PREFACE.

WINDSOR CASTLE, *October* 29, 1832.

DEAR SIR,—I have received your letter of the 27th instant, and beg to reply that there cannot be the least objection to your sending a copy of your work, with the autograph addition; and that if you will send it to me, I will present it to His Majesty.

I do not presume you wish to apply for permission to dedicate the work to His Majesty, which is not usually given for works of fiction.

I remain, Dear Sir, your faithful Servant,

(Signed,) H. TAYLOR.

Lieut. RICHARDSON, &c. &c. &c.
H. P. 92nd Regt.

BRIGHTON, *December* 18, 1832.

DEAR SIR,—I beg to acknowledge the receipt of your letter of the 14th instant, and of the copy of your work, WACOUSTA, for the King, which I have had the honor of presenting to His Majesty, who received it very graciously.

I remain, Dear Sir, your faithful Servant,

(Signed,) H. TAYLOR.

Lieut. RICHARDSON, &c. &c. &c.
H. P. 92nd Regt.

WINDSOR CASTLE, *August* 7, 1833.

DEAR SIR,—I have to acknowledge your letter of the 1st instant, together with its enclosure, and beg to express the deep gratification I have felt in the perusal of that chapter of your new work which treats of the policy of employing the Indians in any future war we may have with the United States. Should you be desirous of dedicating it to His Majesty I can foresee no difficulty.

Permit me to avail myself of this opportunity of assuring you of the deep interest with which your WACOUSTA has been read by the whole Court.

I remain, Dear Sir, your faithful Servant,

(Signed,) H. TAYLOR.

Lieut. RICHARDSON, &c. &c. &c.
H. P. 92nd Regt.

WINDSOR CASTLE, *August* 12, 1833.

DEAR SIR,—I beg to acknowledge the receipt of your letter of the 9th, and to acquaint you that His Majesty acquiesces in your wish to be permitted to dedicate your new work to him.

I remain, Dear Sir, your faithful Servant,

(Signed,) H. TAYLOR.

Lieut. RICHARDSON, &c. &c. &c.
H. P. 92nd Regt.

By the above letters, two material points are established. The first is that, although works of fiction are not usually dedicated to the Sovereign, an exception was made in favour of the following tale, which is now for the first time submitted to the public, and which, from its historical character, was deemed of sufficient importance not to be confounded with mere works of fiction. The exception was grounded on a chapter of the book, which the seeker after incident alone will dismiss hastily, but over which the more serious reader may be induced to pause.

The second, and not least important, point disposed of, is one which the manner in which the principal American characters have been disposed of, renders in some degree imperative.

The Author has no hesitation in stating, that had it not been for the very strong interest taken in their appearance, by a portion of the American public in the first instance, these volumes never would have been submitted to the press of this country. Hence, to a corresponding feeling might, under other circumstances, have been ascribed the favorable light under which the American character has been portrayed. From the dates of the above letters from the principal Aid-de-Camp and Private Secretary to His late Majesty, it will, however, be seen, that the work was written in England, and therefore before there could have existed the slightest inducement to any undue partiality.

That this is the case, the Author has reason to rejoice; since in eschewing the ungenerous desire of most English writers on America, to convey a debasing impression of her people, and seeking, on the contrary, to do justice to their character, as far as the limited field afforded by a work, pre-eminently of fiction, will admit, no interested motive can be ascribed to him. Should these pages prove a means of dissipating the slightest portion of that irritation which has —and naturally—been engendered in every American heart, by the perverted and prejudiced statements of disappointed tourists, whose acerbity of stricture, not even a recollection of much hospitality could repress; and of renewing that healthy tone of feeling which it has been endeavoured to show had existed during the earlier years of the present century, the Author will indeed feel that he has not written in vain.

One observation in regard to the tale itself. There is a necessary anachronism in the book, of too palpable a nature not to be detected at a glance by the reader. It will, however, be perceived, that such anachronism does not in any way interfere with historical fact, while it has at the same time facilitated the introduction of events, which were necessary to the action of the story, and which have been brought on the scene before that which constitutes the anachronism, as indispensable precursors to it. We will not here mar the reader's interest in the story, by anticipating, but allow him to discover and judge of the propriety of the transposition himself.

Tecumseh, moreover, is introduced somewhat earlier than the strict record of facts will justify; but as his presence does not interfere with the general accuracy of the detail, we trust the matter of fact reader, who cannot, at least, be loth to make early acquaintance with this interesting Chieftain, will not refuse us the exercise of our privilege as a novelist, in disposing our characters, in the manner most pleasing to the eye.

We cannot conclude without apology for the imperfect Scotch, which we have (to use a homely phrase,) put into the mouth of one of our characters, our apology for which is that we were unaware of the error, until the work had been so far printed as not to admit of our remedying it. We are consoled, however, by the reflection that we have given the person in question so much of the national character that he can well afford to lose something in a minor particular.

THE AUTHOR.

THE CANADIAN BROTHERS;

OR,

THE PROPHECY FULFILLED.

CHAPTER I.

At the northern extremity of the small town which bears its name, situated at the head of Lake Erie, stands, or rather stood—for the fortifications then existing were subsequently destroyed—the small fortress of Amherstburg.

It was the summer of 1812. Intelligence had been some days received at that post, of the declaration of war by the United States, the great aim and object of which was the conquest, and incorporation with her own extensive territories, of provinces on which she had long cast an eye of political jealousy, and now assailed at a moment when England (fighting the battles of the, even to this moment, recreant and unredeemed Peninsula, could ill spare a solitary regiment to the rescue of her threatened, and but indifferently defended trans-atlantic possessions.

Few places in America, or in the world, could, at the period embraced by our narrative, have offered more delightful associations than that which we have selected for an opening scene. Amherstburg was at that time one of the loveliest spots that ever issued from the will of a beneficent and gorgeous nature, and were the world-disgusted wanderer to have selected a home in which to lose all memory of artificial and conventional forms, his choice would assuredly have fallen here. And insensible, indeed, to the beautiful realities of the sweet wild solitude that reigned around, must that man have been, who could have gazed unmoved, from the lofty banks of the Erie, on the placid lake beneath his feet, mirroring the bright starred heavens on its unbroken surface, or throwing into full and soft relief the snow white sail, and dark hull of some stately war-ship, becalmed in the offing, and only waiting the rising of the capricious breeze, to waft her onward on her *then* peaceful mission of dispatch. Lost indeed to all perception of the natural must he have been, who could have listened, without a feeling of voluptuous melancholy, to the plaintive notes of the whip-poor-will, breaking on the silence of night, and harmonising with the general stillness of the scene. How often have we ourselves, in joyous boyhood, lingered amid these beautiful haunts, drinking in the fascinating song of this strange night-bird, and revelling in a feeling we were too young to analyze, yet cherished deeply—yea, frequently, even to this hour, do we in our dreams revisit scenes no parallel to which has met our view, even in the course of a life passed in many climes; and on awaking, our first emotion is regret that the illusion is no more.

Such was Amherstburg, and its immediate vicinity, during the early years of the present century, and up to the period at which our story commences. Not, be it understood, that even *then* the scenery itself had lost one particle of its loveliness, or failed in aught to awaken and fix the same tender interest. The same placidity of earth, and sky, and lake remained, but the whip-poor-will, driven from his customary abode by the noisy hum of warlike preparation, was no longer heard, and the minds of the inhabitants, hitherto disposed, by the quiet pursuits of their uneventful lives, to feel pleasure in its song, had eye nor ear for aught beyond what tended to the preservation of their threatened homes.

Let us, however, introduce the reader more immediately to the scene. Close in his rear, as he stands on the elevated bank of the magnificent river of Detroit, and about a mile from its point of junction with Lake Erie, is the fort of Amherstburg, its defences consisting chiefly of stockade works, flanked, at its several angles, by strong bastions, and covered by a demi lune of five guns, so placed as to command every approach by water. Distant about three hundred yards on his right is a large, oblong square building, resembling in appearance the red low roofed blockhouses peering above the outward defences of the fort. Surrounding this, and extending to the skirt of the thinned forest, the original boundary of which is marked by an infinitude of dingy half blackened stumps, are to be seen numerous huts or wigwams of the Indians, from the fires before which arises a smoke that contributes, with the slight haze of the atmosphere, to envelope the tops of the tall trees in a veil of blue vapour, rendering them almost invisible. Between these wigwams and the extreme verge of the thickly wooded banks, which sweeping in bold curvature for an extent of many miles, brings into view the eastern extremity of Turkey Island, situated midway between Amherstburg and Detroit, are to be seen, containing the accumulated Indian dead of many years, tumuli, rudely executed it is true, but picturesquely decorated with such adornments as it is the custom of these simple mannered people to bestow on the last sanctuaries of their departed friends. Some three or four miles, and across the water, (for here it is that the river acquires her fullest majesty of expansion,) is to be seen the American Island of Gros Isle, which, at the period of which we write, bore few traces of cultivation—scarcely a habitation being visible throughout its extent—various necks of land, however, shoot out abruptly, and independently of the channel running between it and the American main shore, form small bays or harbours in which boats may always find shelter and concealment.

Thus far the view to the right of the spectator, whom we assume to be facing the river. Immediately opposite to the covering demi lune, and in front of the fort, appears, at a distance of less than half a mile, a blockhouse and battery, crowning the western extremity of the Island of Bois

Blanc, which, one mile in length and lashed at its opposite extremity by the waters of Lake Erie, at this precise point, receives into her capacious bosom the vast tribute of the noble river connecting her with the higher lakes. Between this island and the Canadian shore lies the only navigable channel for ships of heavy tonnage, for although the waters of the Detroit are of vast depth every where above the island, they are near their point of junction with the lake, and, in what is called the American channel, so interrupted by shallows and sandbars, that no craft larger than those of a description termed "Durham boats" can effect the passage—on the other hand the channel dividing the island from the Canadian shore is at once deep and rapid, and capable of receiving vessels of the largest size. The importance of such a passage is obvious; but although a state of war necessarily prevented aid from armed vessels to such forts of the Americans as lay to the westward of the lake, it by no means effectually cut off their supplies through the medium of the Durham boats already alluded to. In order to intercept those, a most vigilant watch was kept by the light gun boats despatched into the lesser channel for that purpose.

A blockhouse and battery crowned also the eastern extremity of the island, and both, provided with a flag staff for the purpose of communication by signal with the fort, were far from being wanting in picturesque effect. A subaltern's command of infantry, and a bombardiers of artillery, were the only troops stationed there, and these were there rather to look out for, and report the approach of whatever American boats might be seen stealing along their own channel, than with any view to the serious defence of a post already sufficiently commanded by the adjacent fortress. In every other direction the island was thickly wooded—not a house—not a hut arose to adversify the wild beauty of the scene. Frequently, it is true, along the margin of its sands might be seen a succession of Indian wigwams, and the dusky and sinewy forms of men gliding round their fires, as they danced to the monotonous sound of the war dance ; but these migratory people, seldom continuing long in the same spot, the island was again and again left to its solitude.

Strongly contrasted with this, would the spectator, whom we still suppose standing on the bank where we first placed him, find the view on his left. There would he behold a neat small town, composed entirely of wooden houses variously and not inelegantly painted; and receding gradually from the river's edge to the slowly disappearing forest, on which its latest rude edifice reposed. Between the town and the fort, was to be seen a dockyard of no despicable dimensions, in which the hum of human voices mingled with the sound of active labour—there too might be seen, in the deep harbour of the narrow channel that separated the town from the island we have just described, some half-dozen gallant vessels bearing the colours of England, breasting with their dark prows the rapid current that strained their creaking cables in every strand, and seemingly impatient of the curb that checked them from gliding impetuously into the broad lake, which some few hundred yards below, appeared to court them to her bosom. But although in these might be heard the bustle of warlike preparation, the chief attention would be observed to be directed towards a large half finished vessel, on which numerous workmen of all descriptions were busily employed, evidently with a view of preparing for immediate service.

Beyond the town again might be obtained a view of the high and cultivated banks, sweeping in gentle curve until they at length terminated in a low and sandy spot, called from the name of its proprietor, Elliott's Point. This stretched itself toward the eastern extremity of the island, so as to leave the outlet to the lake barely wide enough for a single vessel to pass at a time, and that not without skilful pilotage and much caution.

Assuming our reader to be now as fully familiar with the scene as ourselves, let him next, in imagination, people it, as on the occasion we have chosen for his introduction. It was a warm, sunny, day in the early part of July. The town itself was as quiet as if the glaive of war reposed in its sheath, and the inhabitants pursued their wonted avocations with the air of men who had nothing in common with the active interest which evidently dominated the more military portions of the scene. It was clear that among these latter some cause for excitement existed, for, independently of the unceasing bustle within the dock yard—a bustle which however had but one undivided object—the completion and equipment of the large vessel then on the stocks—the immediate neighbourhood of the fort presented evidence of some more than ordinary interest. The encampment of the Indians, on the verge of the forest, had given forth the great body of their warriors, and these clad in their gayest apparel, covered with feathers and leggings of bright colours, decorated with small tinkling bells that came not inharmoniously on the ear, as they kept tune to the measured walk of their proud wearers, were principally assembled around and in front of the large building we have described as being without, yet adjacent to, the fort. These warriors might have been about a thousand in number, and amused themselves variously—(the younger at least)—with leaping—wrestling—ball playing—and the foot race—in all which exercises they are unrivalled. The elders bore no part in these amusements, but stood, or sat cross legged, on the edge of the bank, smoking their pipes, and expressing their approbation of the prowess or dexterity of the victors in the games, by guttural, yet rapidly uttered exclamations. Mingled with these were some six or seven individuals, whose glittering costume of scarlet announced them for officers of the garrison, and elsewhere disposed, some along the banks and crowding the battery in front of the fort, or immediately round the building, yet quite apart from their officers, were a numerous body of the inferior soldiery.

But although these distinct parties were assembled, to all appearance, with a view, the one to perform in, the other to witness, the active sports we have enumerated, a close observer of the movements of all would have perceived there was something more important in contemplation, to the enactment of which these exercises were but a prelude. Both officers, and men, and even the participators in the sports, turned their gaze frequently up the Detroit, as if they expected some important approach. The broad reach of the wide river, affording an undisturbed view, as we have stated, for a distance of some nine or ten miles, where commenced the near extremity of Turkey Island, presented nothing, however, as yet, to their gaze, and repeatedly were the telescopes of the officers raised only to fall in dissappointment from the eye. At length a number of small dark specks were seen studding the tranquil bosom of the river, as they emerged rapidly, one after the other, from the cover of the island. The communication was made, by him who first discovered them, to his companions. The elder Indians who sat near the spot on which the officers stood, were made acquainted with what even their own sharp sight could not distinguish unaided by the glass. One sprang to his feet, raised the telescope to his eye, and with an exclamation of wonder at the strange properties of the instrument, confirmed to his followers the truth of the statement. The elders, principally chiefs, spoke in various tongues to their respective warriors. The sports were abandoned, and all crowded to the bank with anxiety and interest depicted in their attitudes and demeanor.

Meanwhile, the dark specks upon the water increased momentarily in size. Presently they could be distinguished for canoes, which, rapidly impelled, and aided in their course by the swift current, were not long in developing themselves to the naked eye. These canoes, about fifty in number, were of bark, and of so light a description, that a man of ordinary strength might, without undergoing serious fatigue, carry one for miles. The warriors who now propelled them, were naked in all save their leggings and waist cloths, their bodies and faces begrimed with paint: and as they drew nearer, fifteen was observed to be the complement of each. They sat by twos on the narrow thwarts ; and, with their faces to the prow, dipped their paddles simultaneously into the stream, with a regularity of movement not to be surpassed by the most experienced boat's crew of Europe. In the stern of each sat a chief guiding his bark, with the same unpretending but skilful and efficient paddle, and behind him, drooping in the breezeless air, and trailing in the silvery tide, was to be seen a long pendant, bearing the red cross of England.

It was a novel and beautiful sight to behold that imposing fleet of canoes, apparently so frail in texture that the dropping of a pebble between the skeleton ribs might be deemed sufficient to perforate and sink them, yet withal so ingeniously contrived as to bear safely not only the warriors who formed their crews, but also their arms of all descriptions, and such light equipment of raiment and necessaries as were indispensable to men who had to voyage long and far in pursuit of the goal they were now rapidly attaining. The Indians already encamped near the fort, were warriors of nations long rendered familiar by personal intercourse, not only with the inhabitants of the district, but with the troops themselves ; and these, from frequent association with the whites, had lost much of that fierceness which is so characteristic of the North American Indian in his ruder state. Among these, with the more intelligent Hurons, were the remnants of those very tribes of Shawanees and Delawares whom we have recorded to have borne, half a century ago, so prominent a share in the confederacy against England, but who, after the termination of that disastrous war, had so far abandoned their wild hostility, as to have settled in various points of contiguity to the forts to which they, periodically, repaired to receive those presents which a judicious policy so profusely bestowed.

The reinforcement just arriving was composed principally of warriors who had never yet pressed a soil wherein civilization had extended her influence—men who had never hitherto beheld the face of a white, unless it were that of the

Canadian trader, who, at stated periods, penetrated fearlessly into their wilds for purposes of traffic, and who to the bronzed cheek that exposure had rendered nearly as swarthy as their own, united not only the language but so wholly the dress—or rather the undress of those he visited, that he might easily have been confounded with one of their own dark blooded race. So remote, indeed, were the regions in which some of these warriors had been sought, that they were strangers to the existence of more than one of their tribes, and upon these they gazed with a surprise only inferior to what they manifested, when, for the first time, they marked the accoutrements of the British soldier, and turned with secret, but unacknowledged awe and admiration upon the frowning fort and stately shipping, bristling with cannon, and vomiting forth sheets of flame as they approached the shore. In these might have been studied the natural dignity of man. Firm of step—proud of mien—haughty yet penetrating of look, each leader offered in his own person a model to the sculptor, which he might vainly seek elsewhere. Free and unfettered in every limb, they moved in the majesty of nature, and with an air of dark reserve, passed, on landing, through the admiring crowd.

There was one of the number, however, and his canoe was decorated with a richer and a larger flag, whose costume was that of the more civilized Indians, and who in nobleness of deportment, even surpassed those we have last named. This was Tecumseh. He was not of the race of either of the parties who now accompanied him, but of one of the nations, many of whose warriors were assembled on the bank awaiting his arrival. As the head chief of the Indians, his authority was acknowledged by all, even to the remotest of these wild but interesting people, and the result of the exercise of his all-powerful influence had been the gathering together of those warriors, whom he had personally hastened to collect from the extreme west, passing in his course, and with impunity, the several American posts that lay in their way. In order more fully to comprehend the motives and character of this remarkable man, it may not be impertinent to recur summarily to events that took place prior to the declaration of war by the United States against England.

It being a well established—and even by themselves uncontradicted—fact, we can have no hesitation in stating (what we trust no American will conceive to be stated in illiberality of spirit, since such feeling we utterly disclaim) that the government of the United States, bent on the final acquisition of all the more proximate possessions of the Indians, had for many consecutive years, waged a war of extermination against these unfortunate people, and more especially those residing on the Wabash, to which the eye of interest or preference, or both, had directed a jealous attention. For a series of years the aggression had been prosecuted with fearful issue to the Indians, when, at length, one of those daring spirits, that appear like meteors, few and far between, in the horizon of glory and intelligence, suddenly started up in the person of Tecumseh, who, possessed of a genius, as splendid in conception, as it was bold in execution, long continued to baffle the plans and defeat the measures of his most experienced enemies. Whether the warrior owed his original influence, or rather the opportunity for development of his extraordinary talents, both diplomatic and warlike, to the fact of his being the brother of the Prophet—a similar, and rather mean looking person, whom a deep reading of the prejudices of his followers had bound to him in an enthusiasm of superstitious credence—whether, we repeat, Tecumseh owed his elevation to this circumstance in part, or wholly to his own merit, it is difficult to determine with certainty, but it is matter of history, that plausible and powerful as the Prophet had rendered himself, his more open and generous brother, while despising in his heart the mummeries practised by his wily relative, was not long in supplanting him in the affections, as he rapidly superseded him in authority and influence, over his people—All looked up to him as the defender and saviour of their race, and so well did he merit the confidence reposed in him, that it was not long after his first appearance as a leader in the war-path, that the Americans were made sensible, by repeated defeat, of the formidable character of the chief who had thrown himself into the breach of his nation's tottering fortunes, resolved rather to perish on the spot on which he stood, than to retire one foot from the home of their forefathers. What self-ennobling actions the warrior performed, and what talent he displayed during that warfare, the page of American history must tell. With the spirit to struggle against, and the subsequent good fortune to worst the Americans in many conflicts, these latter, although beaten, have not been wanting in generosity to admire their formidable enemy while living, neither have they failed to venerate his memory when dead. If they have helped to bind the laurel around his living brow, they have not been the less willing to weave the cypress that encircles his memory.

In almost every encounter with them, Tecumseh was more or less successful; but, like the conqueror of other days, he might have exclaimed, "another such victory and I am lost." Weakened in a constant succession of engagements, the Indians, and the Shawanees in particular, now presented but a skeleton of their former selves, while the Americans, on the contrary, with an indefatigability that would have done credit to a better cause, kept pouring in fresh forces to the frontier, until, in the end, opposition to their purpose seemed almost hopeless. It is doubtful, however, what would have been the final result of a contest against a warrior of such acknowledged ability and resource as Tecumseh, had it not unfortunately happened that the Americans, taking advantage of the performance of some of those mummeries by which the Prophet still sought to uphold his fast declining power, managed to surprise the Shawanee encampment in the dead of night, when, favoured by circumstances, they committed fearful havoc, nearly annihilating their enemies.

Finding every effort to preserve his situation on the Wabash unavailing, Tecumseh, accompanied by the remnant of his followers, fell back on the Ohio, Miami, and Detroit, where his first object was to enter into a treaty, offensive and defensive, with the formidable nations of the Delawares, Hurons, etc. An alliance with the English, then momentarily apprehending a rupture with the United States, was, moreover renewed, and then with the hope strong at his heart of combating his enemies once more, with success, he had with exulting spirit and bounding step, set out to win to the common interest, the more distant tribes of the Sioux, Minouminies, Winnebagoes, Kickapoos, etc., of whom he had secured the services of the warriors just arrived.

It was amidst the blaze of an united salvo from the demi lune crowning the bank, and from the shipping, that the noble chieftain, accompanied by the leaders of those wild tribes, leaped lightly, yet proudly to the beach ; and having ascended the steep bank by a flight of rude steps cut out of the earth, finally stood amid the party of officers waiting to receive them. It would not a little have surprised a Bond street exquisite of that day to have witnessed the cordiality with which the dark hand of the savage was successively pressed in the fairer palms of the English officers, neither would his astonishment have been abated, on remarking the proud dignity of carriage maintained by the former, in this exchange of courtesy, as though, while he joined heart to hand wherever the latter fell, he seemed rather to bestow than to receive a condescension.

Had none of those officers ever previously beheld him, the fame of his heroic deeds had gone sufficiently before the warrior to have insured him their warmest greeting and approbation, and none could mistake a form that, even amid those who were a password for native majesty, stood alone in its bearing : but Tecumseh was a stranger to few. Since his defeat on the Wabash he had been much at Amherstburg, where he had rendered himself conspicuous by one or two animated and highly eloquent speeches, having for their object the consolidation of a treaty, in which the Indian interests were subsequently bound in close union with those of England; and, up to the moment of his recent expedition, had cultivated the most perfect understanding with the English chiefs.

It might, however, be seen that even while pleasure and satisfaction at a reunion with those he in turn esteemed, flashed from his dark and eager eye, there was still lurking about his manner that secret jealousy of distinction, which is so characteristic of the haughty Indian. After the first warm salutations had passed, he became sensible of the absence of the English chief; but this was expressed rather by a certain outswelling of his chest, and the searching glance of his restless eye, than by any words that fell from his lips. Presently, he whom he sought, and whose person had hitherto been concealed by the battery on the bank, was seen advancing towards him, accompanied by his personal staff. In a moment the shade passed away from the brow of the warrior, and warmly grasping and pressing, for the second time, the hand of a youth—one of the group of junior officers among whom he yet stood, and who had manifested even more than his companions the unbounded pleasure he took in the chieftain's re-appearance—he moved forward, with an ardour of manner that was with difficulty restrained by his sense of dignity, to give them the meeting.

The first of the advancing party was a tall, martial looking man, wearing the dress and insignia of a general officer. His rather florid countenance was eminently fine, if not handsome, offering, in its more Roman than Grecian contour, a model of quiet, manly beauty; while the eye, beaming with intelligence and candour, gave, in the occasional flashes which it emitted, indication of a mind of no common order. There was, notwithstanding, a benevolence of expression about it that blended (in a manner to excite attention) with a dignity of deportment, as much the result of habitual self command, as of the proud eminence of distinction on which he stood. The sedative character of middle age, added to long acquired military habits, had given a certain rigidity to his fine form, that might have made him appear to a first observer even older than he was, but the placidity of a countenance beaming good will and affability, speedily removed the impression, and, if the portly figure added to his years, the unfurrowed countenance took from them in equal proportion.

At his side, hanging on his arm and habited in naval uniform, appeared one who, from his familiarity of address with the General, not less than by certain appropriate badges of distinction, might be known as the commander of the little fleet then lying in the harbour. Shorter in person than his companion, his frame made up in activity what it wanted in height, and there was that easy freedom in his movements which so usually distinguishes the carriage of the sailor, and which now offered a remarkable contrast to that rigidity we have stated to have attached (quite unaffectedly) to the military commander. His eyes, of a much darker hue, sparkled with a livelier intelligence, and although his complexion was also highly florid, it was softened down by the general vivacity of expression that pervaded his frank and smiling countenance. The features, regular and still youthful, wore a bland and pleasing character; while neither, in look, nor bearing, nor word could there be traced any of that haughty reserve usually ascribed to the "lords of the sea." There needed no other herald to proclaim him for one who had already seen honorable service, than the mutilated stump of what had once been an arm: yet in this there was no boastful display, as of one who deemed he had a right to tread more proudly because he had chanced to suffer, where all had been equally exposed, in the performance of a common duty. The empty sleeve, unostentatiously fastened by a loop from the wrist to a button of the lappel, was suffered to fall at his side, and by no one was the deficiency less remarked than by himself.

The greeting between Tecumseh and these officers, was such as might be expected from warriors bound to each other by mutual esteem. Each held the other in the highest honor, but it was particularly remarked that while the Indian Chieftain looked up to the General with the respect he felt to be due to him, not merely as the dignified representative of his "Great Father," but as one of a heart and actions claiming his highest personal admiration, his address to his companion, whom he now beheld for the first time, was warmer, and more energetic; and as he repeatedly glanced at the armless sleeve, he uttered one of those quick ejaculatory exclamations, peculiar to his race, and indicating, in this instance, the fullest extent of approbation. The secret bond of sympathy which chained his interest to the Commodore, might have owed its being to another cause. In the countenance of the latter there was much of that eagerness of expression, and in the eye that vivacious fire, that flashed, even in repose, from his own swarthier and more speaking features; and this assimilation of character might have been the means of producing that preference for, and devotedness to, the cause of the naval commander, that subsequently developed itself in the chieftain. In a word, the General seemed to claim the admiration and the respect of the Indian—the Commodore, his admiration and friendship.

The greeting between these generous leaders was brief. When the first salutations had been interchanged, it was intimated to Tecumseh, through the medium of an interpreter, then in attendance on the General, that a war-council had been ordered, for the purpose of taking into consideration the best means of defeating the designs of the Americans, who, with a view to offensive operations, had, in the interval of the warrior's absence, pushed on a considerable force to the frontier. The council, however, had been delayed, in order that it might have the benefit of his opinions, and of his experience in the peculiar warfare which was about to be commenced.

Tecumseh acknowledged his sense of the communication with the bold frankness of the inartificial son of nature, scorning to conceal his just self-estimate beneath a veil of affected modesty. He knew his own worth, and while he overvalued not one iota of that worth, so did he not affect to disclaim a consciousness of the fact—that within his swarthy chest and active brain there beat a heart and lived a judgment, as prompt to conceive and execute as those of the proudest *he* that ever swayed the destinies of a warlike people. Replying to the complimentary invitation of the General, he unhesitatingly said he had done well to await his (Tecumseh's) arrival, before he determined on his course of action, and that he should now have the full benefit of his opinions and advice.

If the chief had been forcibly prepossessed in favour of the naval commander, the latter had not been less interested. Since his recent arrival, to assume the direction of the fleet, Commodore Barclay had had opportunities of seeing such of the chiefs as were then assembled at Amherstburg; but great as had been his admiration of several of these, he had been given to understand they fell far short, in every moral and physical advantage, of what their renowned leader would be found to possess, when, on his return from the expedition in which he was engaged, fitting opportunity should be had of bringing them in personal proximity. This admission was now made in the fullest sense, and as the warrior moved away to give the greeting to the several chiefs, and conduct them to the council hall, the gallant sailor could not refrain from expressing, in the warmest terms to General Brock, as they moved slowly forward with the same intention, the enthusiastic admiration excited in him by the person, the manner, and the bearing, of the noble Tecumseh.

Again the cannon from the battery and the shipping pealed forth their thunder. It was the signal for the commencement of the council, and the scene at that moment was one of the most picturesque that can well be imagined. The sky was cloudless, and the river, no longer ruffled by the now motionless barks of the recently arrived Indians, yet obeying the action of the tide, offered, as it glided onward to the lake, the image of a flood of quick-silver; while, in the distance, that lake itself, smooth as a mirror, spread far and wide. Close under the bank yet lingered the canoes, emptied only of their helmsmen (the chiefs of the several tribes,) while, with strange tongues and wilder gestures, the warriors of these, as they rested on their paddles, greeted the loud report of the cannon—now watching with eager eye the flashes from the vessel's sides, and now upturning their gaze, and following with wild surprise, the deepening volumes of smoke that passed immediately over their heads, from the guns of the battery, hidden from their view by the elevated and overhanging bank. Blended with each discharge arose the wild yell, which they, in such a moment of novel excitement, felt it impossible to control, and this, answered from the Indians above and borne in echo almost to the American shore, had in it something indescribably startling. On the bank itself the effect was singularly picturesque. Here were to be seen the bright uniforms of the British officers, at the head of whom was the tall and martial figure of General Brock, furthermore conspicuous from the full and drooping feather that fell gracefully over his military hat, mingled with the wilder and more fanciful head dresses of the chiefs. Behind these again, and sauntering at a pace that showed them to have no share in the deliberative assembly, whither those we have just named were now proceeding amid the roar of artillery, yet mixed together in nearly as great dissimilarity of garb, were to be seen numbers of the inferior warriors and of the soldiery, while, in various directions, the games recently abandoned by the adult Indians, were now resumed by mere boys. The whole picture was one of strong animation, contrasting as it did with the quiet of the little post on the Island, where some twelve or fifteen men, composing the strength of the detachment, were now sitting or standing on the battery, crowned, as well as the fort and shipping, and in compliment to the newly arrived Indians, with the colours of England.

Such was the scene, varied only as the numerous actors in it varied their movements, when the event occurred, with which we commence our next chapter.

CHAPTER II.

Several hours had passed away in the interesting discussion of their war plans, and the council was nearly concluded, when suddenly the attention both of the officers and chiefs was arrested by the report of a single cannon. From the direction of the sound, it was evident the shot had been fired from the battery placed on the southern or lakeward extremity of the Island of Bois Blanc, and as the circumstance was unusual enough to indicate the existence of some approaching cause for excitement, several of the younger of both, who, from their youth, had been prevented from taking any active share in the deliberations of the day, stole, successively and unobservedly, through the large folding doors of the building, which, owing to the great heat of the weather, had been left open. After traversing about fifty yards of sward, intersecting the high road, which, running parallel with the river, separated the council hall from the elevated bank, the officers found, collected in groups on the extreme verge of this latter and anxiously watching certain movements in the battery opposite to them, most of the troops and inferior Indians they had left loitering there at the commencement of the council. Those movements were hasty, and as of men preparing to repeat the shot, the report of which had reached them from the opposite extremity of the Island. Presently the forms, hitherto intermingled, became separate and stationary—an arm of one was next extended—then was seen to rise a flash of light, and then a volume of dense smoke, amid which the loud report found its sullen way, bellowing like thunder through some blackening cloud, while, from the peculiar nature of the sound, it was recognized, by the experienced in those matters, to have proceeded from a shotted gun.

The war in Canada had its beginning in the manner thus described. They were the first shots fired in that struggle, and although at an object little calculated to inspire much alarm, still, as the first indications of an active hostility, they were proportionably exciting to those whose lot it was thus to "break ground," for operations on a larger scale.

Although many an eager chief had found it difficult to repress the strong feeling of mingled curiosity and excitement, that half raised him from the floor on which he sat, the first shot had been heard without the effect of actually disturbing the assembly from its fair propriety; but no sooner had the second report, accompanied as it was by the wild yell of their followers without, reached their ears, than, wholly losing sight of the dignity attached to their position as councillors, they sprang wildly up, and seizing the weapons that lay at their side, rushed confusedly forth, leaving Tecumseh, and two or three only of the more aged chiefs, behind them. The debate thus interrupted, the council was adjourned, and soon afterwards General Brock, accompanied by his staff, and conversing, through his interpreter, with the Shawanee chieftain as they walked, approached the groups still crowded along the bank of the river.

Meanwhile, after the discharge of the last gun, the battery on the Island had been quitted by the officer in command, who, descending to the beach, preceded by two of his men, stepped into a light skiff that lay chained to the gnarled root of a tree overhanging the current, and close under the battery. A few sturdy strokes of the oars soon brought the boat into the centre of the stream, when the stout, broad built, figure, and carbuncled face of an officer in the uniform of the ——— regiment, were successively recognised, as he stood upright in the stern.

"What the deuce brings Tom Raymond to us in such a hurry? I thought the order of the General was that he should on no account leave his post, unless summoned by signal," observed one of the group of younger officers who had first quitted the council hall, and who now waited with interest for the landing of their companion.

"What brings him here, can you ask?" replied one at the side of the questioner, and with a solemnity of tone and manner that caused the whole of the group to turn their eyes upon him, as he mournfully shook his head.

"Aye, *what* brings him here?" repeated more than one voice, while all closed inquiringly around for information.

"Why, the thing is as clear as the carbuncles on his own face—the boat to be sure." And the truism was perpetrated with the same provokingly ludicrous, yet evidently forced, gravity of tone and manner.

"Execrable, Middlemore—will you never give over that vile habit of punning?"

"Detestable," said another.

"Ridiculous," repeated a third.

"Pshaw, the worst you ever uttered," exclaimed a fourth, and each, as he thus expressed himself, turned away with a movement of impatience.

"That animal, Raymond, grows like a very porpoise," remarked a young captain, who prided himself much on the excessive smallness of his waist. "Methinks that, like the ground hogs that abound on his Island, he must fatten on hickory nuts. Only see how the man melts in the noon-day sun. But as you say, Villiers, what can bring him here without an order from the General? And then the gun last fired. Ha! I have it. He has discovered a Yankee boat stealing along through the other channel."

"No doubt there is *craft* of some description *in the wind*," pursued the incorrigible Middlemore, with the same affected unconsciousness; "and that may account for poor Raymond being *blown* here."

"Ha! severe, are you," returned Captain Molineux, the Officer who had commented so freely upon the appearance of the fat Lieutenant in the boat. "But your pun, infamous as it would be at the best, is utterly without point now, for there has not been a breath of wind stirring during the whole morning."

"Pun, did you say?" exclaimed Middlemore, with well affected surprise at the charge. "My dear fellow, I meant no pun."

Further remark was checked by an impatience to learn the cause of Lieutenant Raymond's abrupt appearance, and the officers approached the principal group. The former had now reached the shore, and, shuffling up the bank as fast as his own corpulency and the abruptness of the ascent would permit, hastened to the General, who stood at some little distance awaiting the expected communication of the messenger.

"Well, Mr. Raymond, what is it—what have you discovered from your post?" demanded the General, who, with those around him, found difficulty in repressing a smile at the heated appearance of the fat subaltern, the loud puffing of whose lungs had been audible before he himself drew near enough to address the chief—"something important, I should imagine, if we may judge from the haste with which you appear to have travelled over the short distance that separates us?"

"Something very important, indeed, General," answered the officer, touching his undress cap, and speaking huskily from exertion; "there is a large bark, sir, filled with men, stealing along shore in the American channel, and I can see nothing of the gun boat that should be stationed there. A shot was fired from the eastern battery, in the hope of bringing her to, but, as the guns mounted there are only carronades, the ball fell short, and the suspicious looking boat crept still closer to the shore—I ordered a shot from my battery to be tried, but without success, for, although within range, the boat hugs the land so closely that it is impossible to distinguish her hull with the naked eye."

"The gun boat not to be seen, Mr. Raymond?" exclaimed the General; "how is this, and who is the officer in command of her?"

"One," quickly rejoined the Commodore, to whom the last query was addressed; "whom I had selected for that duty for the very vigilance and desire for service attributed to him by my predecessor—of course I have not been long enough here, to have much personal knowledge of him myself."

"His name?" asked the General.

"Lieutenant Grantham."

"Grantham?" repeated the General, with a movement of surprise; "It is indeed strange that *he* should forego such an opportunity."

"Still more strange," remarked the Commodore, "that the boat he commands should have disappeared altogether. Can there be any question of his fidelity? the Granthams are Canadians, I understand."

The General smiled, while the young officer who had been noticed so particularly by Tecumseh on his landing, colored deeply.

"If," said the former, "the mere circumstance of their having received existence amid these wilds can make them Canadians, they certainly are Canadians; but if the blood of a proud race can make them Britons, such they are. Be they which they may however, I would stake my life on the fidelity of the Granthams—still, the cause of this young officer's absence must be inquired into, and no doubt it will be satisfactorily explained. Meanwhile, let a second gun-boat be detached in pursuit."

The Commodore having given the necessary instructions to a young midshipman, who attended him in the capacity of an aid-de-camp, and the general having dismissed Lieutenant Raymond back to his post on the island, these officers detached themselves from the crowd, and, while awaiting the execution of the order, engaged in earnest conversation.

"By Jove, the Commodore is quite right in his observation," remarked the young and affected looking officer, who had been so profuse in his witticisms on the corpulency of Lieutenant

Raymond; "the General may say what he will in their favour, but this is the result of entrusting so important a command to a Canadian."

"What do you mean, sir?" hastily demanded one even younger than himself—it was the youth already named, whose uniform attested him to be a brother officer of the speaker. He had been absent for a few minutes, and only now rejoined his companions, in time to hear the remark which had just been uttered.

"What do you mean, Captain Molineux?" he continued, his dark eye flashing indignation, and his downy cheek crimsoning with warmth. "Why this remark before me, sir, and wherefore this reflection on the Canadians?"

"Why really, Mr. Grantham," somewhat sententiously drawled the captain; "I do not altogether understand your right to question in this tone—nor am I accountable for any observations I may make. Let me tell you, moreover—" this was said with the advising air of a superior in rank—"that it will neither be wise nor prudent in you, having been received into a British regiment, to become the Don Quixotte of your countrymen."

"*Received* into a British regiment, sir! do you then imagine that I, more than yourself, should feel this to be a distinction," haughtily returned the indignant youth. "But, gentlemen, your pardon," checking himself and glancing at the rest of the group, who were silent witnesses of the scene; "I confess I do feel the distinction of being admitted into so gallant a corps—this in a way, however, that must be common to us all. Again I ask, Captain Molineux," turning to that officer, "the tendency of the observation you have publicly made in regard to my brother."

"Your question, Mr. Grantham, might, with as much propriety, be addressed to any other person in the full enjoyment of his senses, whom you see here, since it is the general topic of conversation; but, as you seem to require an answer from me particularly, you shall have it. My remark referred to the absence of the officer in charge of the gun boat, from the station allotted to him, at a moment when an *armed* vessel of the enemy is in sight. Is this the fact, or is it not?"

"By which remark," returned the other, "you would imply that officer is either guilty of gross neglect or—"

"I draw no inferences, Mr. Grantham, but, even if I did, I should be more borne out by circumstances than you imagine."

"It is plain you would insinuate that my brother shuns the enemy, Captain Molineux—You shall answer to me for this insult, sir."

"As you please, Mr. Grantham, but on one condition only."

"Name it, sir, name it," said the younger officer quickly.

"That it is satisfactorily proved your brother has *not* shunned the enemy."

Bitter feelings swelled the heart of the enthusiastic Grantham, as, unconsciously touching the hilt of his sword, he replied: "If your hope of avoidance rest on this, sir, it will be found to hang upon a very thread indeed."

The attention of the group where this unpleasant scene had occurred, and indeed of all parties, was now diverted by the sudden appearance of the American boat, as, shooting past the head of the Island, which had hitherto concealed her from the view of the assembled crowds, her spars and white sails became visible in the far distance. A slight and favorable breeze, blowing off the shore which she still closely hugged, had now apparently sprung up, and, spreading all her canvass, she was evidently making every effort to get beyond the reach of the battery,(whither Lieutenant Raymond had returned) under whose range she was unavoidably impelled by the very wind that favored her advance. Owing to some temporary difficulty, the gun boat, just ordered by the Commodore to follow in pursuit, was longer than suited the emergency in getting under way, and when she had succeeded in so doing, nearly half an hour elapsed, before, owing to the utter absence of wind (which was partial and wholly confined to the opposite shore) as well as the rapidity of the current, she could be brought by the aid of her long and cumbrous sweeps to clear the head of the Island. The American, now discovered to be full of troops, had by this time succeeded in getting out of the range of a fire,which although well directed had proved harmless, and, using every exertion of oar and sail, bade fair, favored as she was by the breeze which reached not the canvass of her enemy, to effect her escape.

Concern sat on every brow, and was variously expressed—loud yells marking the fierce disappointment of the Indians, and undisguised murmurs that of the more disciplined troops. Coupled with this feeling, among the officers at least, naturally arose the recollection of him to whose apparent neglect this escape of the enemy was to be attributed, until at length the conduct of Lieutenant Grantham was canvassed generally, and with a freedom little inferior to that which, falling from the lips of Captain Molineux, had so pained his sensitive brother; with this difference, however, that, in this instance they were the candidly expressed opinions of men arraigning the conduct of one of their fellows apparently guilty of a gross dereliction from duty, and not, as in the former they had seemed to be, with any ungenerous allusion to his fidelity.

Warmly, and therefore audibly, commented on as was the unaccountable absence of the officer, by individuals of almost every rank, it was impossible that many of those observations could escape the attention of the excited Henry Grantham. Mortified beyond measure at the fact, yet unable, as he had done before, to stand forth the champion of his brother's honor, where all (with a very few exceptions, among whom he had the consolation to find the General) were united in opinion against him, his situation was most painful. Not that he entertained the remotest doubt of his brother bearing himself harmlessly through the ordeal, but that his generous, yet haughty spirit, could ill endure the thought of any human being daring to cherish, much less to cast the slightest aspersion on his blood.

Finding it vain to oppose himself to the torrent of openly expressed opinion, the mortified youth withdrew to a distance, and, hastening among the rude tumuli we have described, as being scattered about the edge of the bank, stood watching, with folded arms and heaving chest, the gradually receding bark of the enemy. Alternately, as he thus gazed, his dark eye now flashed with the indignation of wounded pride, now dilated with the exulting consciousness of coming triumph. The assurance was strong within him, not only that his brother would soon make his appearance before the assembled groups who had had the cruelty to impugn his conduct, but that he would do so under circumstances calculated to change their warm censure into even more vehement applause. Fully impressed with the integrity of his absent relative, the impetuous and generous hearted youth paused not to reflect that circumstances were such as to justify the belief—or at least, the doubt—that had been expressed, even by the most impartial of those who had condemned him. It seemed to him that others ought to have known and judged him as he himself did, and he took a secret delight in dwelling on the self-reproach which (measuring the feelings of others by the standard of his own,) he conceived would attach to them, when it should be found how erroneous had been the estimate formed of his character.

While he thus gazed, with eyes intently bent upon the river, and manifesting even a deeper interest as the fleeing bark drew momentarily nearer to one particular point in the distance, the young officer heard footsteps approaching him. Hastily dashing away a tear which had been called up by a variety of emotions, he turned and beheld the Chieftain Tecumseh, and with him one, who, in the full uniform of the British Staff, united, in his tall and portly figure, the martial bearing of the soldier to the more polished graces of the habitual courtier.

"Henry, my noble boy," exclaimed the latter, as he pressed the hand of the youth, "you must not yield to these feelings. I have marked your impatience at the observations caused by Gerald's strange absence, but I have brought you one who is too partial to you both, to join in the condemnation. I have explained every thing to him, and he it was who, remarking you to be alone and suspecting the cause, first proposed coming to rouse you from your reverie."

Affectionately answering the grasp of his noble looking uncle, (such was the consanguinity of the parties,) Henry Grantham turned at the same time his eloquent eye upon that of the chieftain, and, in a few brief but expressive sentences, conveyed, in the language of the Warrior, (with which the brothers were partially conversant,) the gratification he experienced in his unchanged confidence in the absent officer.

As he concluded, with a warmth of manner that delighted him to whom he addressed himself, their hands met for the third time that day. Tecumseh at length replied, by pointing significantly to the canoes which still lay floating on the river, unemptied of their warriors, stating at the same time, that had not his confidence in his young friend been unbounded, he would long since have dispatched those canoes in pursuit; but he was unwilling the officer should lose any of the credit that must attach to the capture. "I know," he concluded, "where he is lying like the red skin in ambush for his enemy. Be patient, and we shall soon see him."

Before Henry Grantham could find time to inquire if the place of ambush was not the same to which his own hopes, induced by his perfect knowledge of localities, had, throughout, pointed as the spot most likely to conceal the hitherto invisible gun boat, his attention, and that of his immediate companion, was drawn to a scene that carried a glow of exultation to the bosoms of them all.

The American boat, long since out of range of the battery, and scudding with a speed that mocked the useless exertions of those on board of the second gun boat, who could with difficulty impel her through the powerful eddy, formed by the Island, had been gradually edging from her own shore into the centre of the stream. This movement, however, had the effect of rendering her more distinguishable to the eye, breasting, as she did, the rapid stream, than while hugging the land, even when much nearer, she had been confounded with the dark outline of brushwood which connected the forest with the shore. She had now arrived opposite a neck of land beyond which ran a narrow, deep creek, the existence of which was known only to few, and here it chanced that in the exultation of escape, (for they were not slow to perceive the difficulties opposed to the progress of their pursuer,) they gave a cheer that was echoed back from either shore, hoisting at the same moment the American colours. Scarcely, however, had this cheer been uttered, when a second and more animating, was heard from a different point, and presently, dashing into the river, and apparently issuing from the very heart of the wood, was to be seen the gun boat which had been the subject of so much conversation, every stitch of her white canvass bellying from the masts, and her dark prow buried in a wreath of foam created by her own speed. As she neared the American, a column of smoke, followed a second or two later, by a dull report, rose from her bows, enveloping her a moment from the view, and when next visible she was rapidly gaining on the chase. The yells of the Indians, and the hurrahs of the soldiers gave an indescribable animation to the scene.

This was, indeed, a moment of proud triumph to the heart of Henry Grantham. He saw his brother not only freed from every ungenerous imputation, but placed in a situation to win to himself the first laurels that were to be plucked in the approaching strife. The "Canadian" as he imagined he had been superciliously termed, would be the first to reap for Britain's sons the fruits of a war in which those latter were not only the most prominent actors, but also the most interested. Already in the enthusiasm of his imagination, he pictured to himself the honor and promotion, which bestowed upon his gallant brother, would be reflected upon himself, and, in the deep excitement of his feelings he could not avoid saying aloud, heedless of the presence of his uncle :

" Now, Captain Molineux, your own difficulty is removed —my brother has revenged himself. With me you will have an account to settle on my own score."

" What do you mean, Henry ?" seriously inquired Colonel D'Egville ; " surely you have not been imprudent enough to engage in a quarrel with one of your brother officers."

Henry briefly recounted the conversation which had taken place between Captain Molineux and himself.

" Far be it from my intention to check the nice sense of honor which should be inherent in the breast of every soldier," returned his uncle impressively, " but you are too sensitive, Henry ; Captain Molineux, who is, moreover, a very young man, may not have expressed himself in the most guarded manner, but he only repeated what I have been compelled to hear myself—and from persons not only older, but much higher in rank. Take my advice, therefore, and let the matter rest where it is ; Gerald, you see, has given the most practical denial to any observations which have been uttered of a nature derogatory to his honor."

" True," quickly returned the youth, with a flushing cheek, " Gerald is sufficiently avenged, but you forget the taunt he uttered against Canadians."

" And if he did utter such taunt, why acknowledge it as such," calmly rejoined Colonel D'Egville, " are you ashamed of the name ? I too am a Canadian, but so far from endeavoring to repudiate my country, I feel pride in having received my being in a land where every thing attests the sublimity and magnificence of nature. Look around you, my nephew, and ask yourself what there in the wild grandeur of these scenes to disown ? But ha !" as he cast his eyes upon the water ; " I fear Gerald will lose his prize after all—that cunning Yankee is giving him the Indian double.

During the foregoing short conversation, an important change had been effected in the position of the adverse boats. The shot fired, apparently with the view of bringing the enemy to, had produced no favorable result; but no sooner had the gun boat come abreast with the chase, than the latter, suddenly clewing up her sails, put her helm about, and plying every oar with an exertion proportioned to the emergency, made rapidly for the coast she had recently left. The intention of the crew was, evidently to abandon the unarmed boat, and to seek safety in the woods. Urged by the rapidity of her own course, the gun boat had shot considerably ahead, and when at length she also was put about, the breeze blew so immediately in her teeth that it was found impossible to regain the advantage which had been lost. Meanwhile, the American continued her flight, making directly for the land, with a rapidity that promised fair to baffle every exertion on the part of her pursuer. The moment was one of intense interest to the crowd of spectators who lined the bank. At each instant it was expected the fire of the gun boat would open upon the fugitives; but although this was obviously the course to be adopted, it being apparent a single shot was sufficient to sink her, not a flash was visible—not a report was heard. Presently, however, while the disappointment of the spectators from the bank was rising into murmurs, a skiff filled with men was seen to pull from the gun boat in the direction taken by the chase, which was speedily hidden from view by the point of land from which the latter had previously been observed to issue. Behind this, her pursuer, also disappeared, and after the lapse of a few minutes pistol and musket shots were distinguished, although they came but faintly on the ear. These gradually became more frequent and less distinct, until suddenly there was a profound pause—then three cheers were faintly heard—and all again was still.

CHAPTER III.

A full half hour had succeeded to these sounds of conflict, and yet nothing could be seen of the contending boats. Doubt and anxiety now took place of the confidence that had hitherto animated the bosoms of the spectators, and even Henry Grantham—his heart throbbing painfully with emotions induced by suspense—knew not what inference to draw from the fact of his brother's protracted absence. Could it be that the American, defended as she was by a force of armed men, had succeeded, not only in defeating the aim of her pursuer, but also in capturing her? Such a result was not impossible. The enemy against whom they had to contend yielded to none in bravery; and as the small bark which had quitted the gun boat was not one third of the size of that which they pursued, it followed of necessity, that the assailants must be infinitely weaker in numbers than the assailed. Still no signal of alarm was made by the gun boat, which continued to lie to, apparently in expectation of the return of the detached portion of her crew. Grantham knew enough of his brother's character to feel satisfied that he was in the absent boat, and yet it was impossible to suppose that one so imbued with the spirit of generous enterprise should have succumbed to his enemy, after a contest of so short duration, as, from the number of shots heard, this had appeared to be. That it was terminated, there could be no doubt. The cheers, which had been followed by an universal silence, had given evidence of this fact; yet why, in that case, if his brother had been victorious, was he not already on his return? Appearances, on the other hand, seemed to induce an impression of his defeat. The obvious course of the enemy, if successful, was to abandon their craft, cut off from escape by the gun boat without, and to make the best of their way through the woods, to their place of destination—the American fort of Detroit,—and, as neither party was visible, it was to be feared this object had been accomplished.

The minds of all were more or less influenced by these doubts, but that of Henry Grantham was especially disturbed. From the first appearance of the gun boat, his spirits had resumed their usual tone, for he had looked upon the fleeing bark as the certain prize of his brother, whose conquest was to afford the flattest denial to the insinuation that had been breathed against him. Moreover, his youthful pride had exulted in the reflection that the first halo of victory would play around the brow of one for whom he could have made every personal sacrifice ; and now, to have those fair anticipations clouded at the very moment when he was expecting their fullest accomplishment, was almost unendurable. He felt, also, that, although his resolution was thus made to stand prominently forth, the prudence of his brother would assuredly be called in question, for having given chase with so inferior a force, when a single gun fired into his enemy must have sunk her. In the impatience of his feelings, the excited young soldier could not refrain from adding his own censure of the imprudence, exclaiming as he played his foot nervously upon the ground: "Why the devil did he not fire and sink her, instead of following in that nutshell?"

While he was yet giving utterance to his disappointment, a hasty exclamation met his ear, from the chieftain at his side, who, placing one hand on the shoulder of the officer with a familiar and meaning grasp, pointed, with the forefinger of the other, in the direction in which the boats had disappeared. Before Grantham's eye could follow, an exulting yell from the distant masses of Indians announced an advantage that was soon made obvious to all. The small dark boat of the pursuing party was now seen issuing from behind the point, and pulling slowly towards the gun boat. In the course of a minute or two afterwards appeared the American, evidently following in the wake of the former, and attached by a tow line to her stern. The yell pealed forth by the Indians, when the second boat came in view, was deafening in the extreme; and every thing became commotion along the bank, while the little fleet of canoes, which still lay resting on the beach, put off one after the other to the scene of action.

Meanwhile, both objects had gained the side of the gun boat, which, favored by a partial shifting of the wind, now pursued her course down the river with expanded sails. Attached to her stern, and following at quarter cable distance, was to be seen her prize, from which the prisoners had been removed, while above the American flag was hoisted, in all the pride of a first conquest, the Union-Jack of England.

Informed of the success which had crowned the enterprise of their officer, the crews of the several vessels in the harbour swelled the crowd assembled on the bank near the fort, to which point curiosity and a feeling of interest had moreover brought many of the town's people, so that the scene finally became one of great animation.

The gun boat had now arrived opposite the fort, when the small bark, which had recently been used in pursuit, was again drawn up to the quarter. Into this, to the surprise of all, was first lowered a female, hitherto unobserved; next followed an officer in the blue uniform of the United States regular army; then another individual, whose garb announced him as being of the militia, and whose rank as an officer was only distinguishable from the cockade surmounting his round hat, and an ornamented dagger thrust into a red morocco belt encircling his waist. After these came the light and elegant form of one, habited in the undress of a British naval officer, who, with one arm supported by a black silk handkerchief, evidently taken from his throat, and suspended from his neck, and with the other grasping the tiller of the rudder, stood upright in the boat, which, urged by six stout rowers, now flew at his command towards the landing place, above which lingered, surrounded by several officers of either service, General Brock and Commodore Barclay.

"Well, Commodore, what think you of your Lieutenant now?" observed the former to his friend; "the young Canadian, you must admit, has nobly redeemed my pledge. On the score of his fidelity there could exist no doubt, and as for his courage, you see," pointing to the young man's arm, "his conquest has not been bloodless to himself, at least."

"With all my soul do I disclaim the wrong I have done him," was the emphatic and generous rejoinder. "He is, indeed, a spirited youth; and well worthy of the favorable report which led me to entrust him with the command—moreover he has an easy grace of carriage which pleased and interested me in his favor, when first I saw him. Even now, observe how courteously he bends himself to the ear of his female prisoner, as if to encourage her with words of assurance, that she may sustain the presence and yells of these clamorous beings."

The boat had now reached the beach, but the difficulty of effecting a passage, through the bands of wild Indians that crowded, yelling, in every direction, to take a nearer view of the prisoners, would, perhaps, have proved insurmountable, had it not been for the interference of one who alone possessed the secret of restraining their lawlessness. Tecumseh had descended to the beach, eager to be the first to congratulate his young friend. He pressed the hand promptly extended to receive his, and then, at a single word, made those give way whose presence impeded the landing of the party.

Pursuing their way up the rude steps by which Lieutenant Raymond had previously descended, the little band of prisoners soon stood in the presence of the group assembled to receive them. On alighting from the boat, the youthful captor had been seen to make the tender of his uninjured arm to the lady, who, however, had rejected it, with a movement, seemingly of indignant surprise, clinging in the same moment to her more elderly companion. A titter among the younger officers, at Gerald Grantham's expense, had followed this somewhat rude rejection of his proffered arm.

The young sailor was the first to gain the summit of the bank. Respectfully touching his hat, and pointing to the captives, who followed a few paces as in his rear:

"General--Commodore," he observed, his cheek flushing with a consciousness of the gratifying position in which he stood, "I have the honor to present to you the first fruits of our good fortune. We have taken thirty soldiers of the American regular regiment, now in garrison at Detroit, besides the boat's crew. This gentleman," pointing to the elder officer, "is the commander of the party, and the lady I believe is——"

"Certainly a non-combatant on this occasion," interrupted the General, raising his plumed hat, and bowing to the party alluded to; "Gentlemen," he pursued, addressing the two officers, "I am sorry we do not meet exactly on the terms to which we have so long been accustomed; but, although the fortune of war has made you rather unwilling guests in the present instance, the rites of hospitality shall not be the less observed. But, Mr. Grantham, you have forgotten to introduce these officers by name."

"I plead guilty, General, but the truth is I have neglected to make the inquiry myself."

"Major Montgomerie, sir, of the United States infantry," interposed the elderly officer, completely set at his ease by the affable and attentive manner of the British leader. "This young lady is my niece."

Again the general slightly, but courteously, bowed. "I will not, Major Montgomerie, pay you the ill timed compliment of expressing pleasure in seeing you on an occasion like the present, since we must unquestionably consider you a prisoner of war; but if the young lady your niece, has any desire to continue her journey to Detroit, I shall feel pleasure in forwarding her thither under a flag of truce."

"I thank you much, General, for this mark of your attention," returned the American; "but I think I may venture to answer for my niece, that she will prefer remaining with me."

"Not so, sir;" said a voice deep but femininely soft. "General," she continued, throwing aside her veil, which had hitherto concealed features pale even to wanness, "I have the strongest—the most urgent reasons—for the prosecution of my journey, and gladly do I accept your offer."

The earnest manner of her address struck every hearer with surprise, contrasting as it did, with the unchanging coldness of her look; but the matter was a source of serious concern to her uncle. He regarded her with an air of astonishment, not unmixed with displeasure.

"How is this, Matilda," he asked; "after having travelled thus far into the heart of this disturbed district would you now leave me?"

"Major Montgomerie," she pursued, somewhat impatiently, "we are in the presence of strangers, to whom this discussion must be uninteresting—My mind is fully made up, and I avail myself of the British General's offer."

"Certainly, certainly," observed that officer, somewhat disconcerted by the scene; "and I can do it the more readily, as it is my intention to send an instant summons to the garrison of Detroit. Miss Montgomerie will, however, do well to consider before she decides. If the summons be not obeyed, another week will see our columns marching to the assault, and she must be prepared for all the horrors of such an extremity, aided, as I am compelled to be, (and he glanced at the groups of Indians who were standing around, but at some distance, looking silently yet eagerly at the prisoners,) by these wild and ungovernable warriors. Should she, on the contrary, decide on remaining here with her uncle, she will be perfectly safe."

"General," emphatically returned Miss Montgomerie, "were I certain that the columns to which you allude would not be repulsed whenever they may venture upon that assault, and were I as certain of perishing beneath the tomahawk and scalping knife of these savages"—and she looked fearlessly towards them—"still would my determination remain the same."

As she concluded a hectic spot rose to either cheek, lingered there a moment, and then left it colorless as before.

"Be it so, Miss Montgomerie, my word is pledged, and you shall go—Grantham, I had intended sending one of my personal staff with the summons, but, on reflection, you shall be the bearer. As the captor of the lady, to you should be awarded the charge of delivering her over to her friends."

"Friends!" involuntarily repeated the fair American, her cheek becoming even paler than before, and her lips compressed in a way to indicate some deep and painful emotion. Again she dropped her veil.

No other notice was taken of the interruption than what the surprised manner of Major Montgomerie manifested, and the General proceeded:

"I would ask you, Major Montgomerie, to become my guest, while you remain with us, but fear that, as a bachelor, I have but indifferent accomodation to offer to your niece."

"If Miss Montgomerie will accept it," said Colonel D'Egville, interposing, "I shall be most happy to afford her the accomodation of a home until she finally departs for the opposite coast. If the attention of a family of daughters," he continued, more immediately addressing himself to the young lady, "can render your temporary sojourn among us less tedious, you have but to command them."

So friendly an offer could not well be refused. Miss Montgomerie inclined her head in acquiescence, and Colonel D'Egville drew her arm within his own.

"It were unkind," remarked the General good humouredly, "to separate Major Montgomerie altogether from his niece. Either the young lady must partake of our rude fare, or we shall consider ourselves included in your dinner party."

"You could not confer on me a greater pleasure, General—

and indeed I was about to solicit it. Commodore Barclay, may I hope that so short and unceremonious an invitation will be excused by the circumstances? Good—I shall expect you. But there is yet another to be included among our guests. Gerald, you will not fail to conduct this gentleman, whose name I have not yet had the pleasure of hearing"—and he looked at the latter, as if he expected him to announce himself.

"I fear sir," observed the young officer pointedly, "that your dinner party would be little honored by such an addition. Although he wears the uniform of an American officer, this person is wholly unworthy of a seat at your table."

" Every eye was turned with an expression of deep astonishment on the speaker, and thence upon the form of the hitherto scarcely noticed militia officer; who, with his head sunk sullenly upon his chest, and an eye now and then raised stealthily to surrounding objects, made no attempt to refute, or even to express surprise at, the singular accusation of his captor.

" This is strong language to apply to a captive enemy, and that enemy, apparently, an officer," gravely remarked the General: " yet I cannot believe Mr. Grantham to be wholly without grounds for his assertion."

Before Grantham could reply, a voice in the crowd exclaimed, as if the utterer had been thrown off his guard, " what, Phil!"

On the mention of this name, the American looked suddenly up from the earth on which his gaze had been rivetted, and cast a rapid glance around him.

" Nay, nay, my young friend, do not, as I see you are, feel hurt at my observation," resumed the General extending his hand to Gerald Grantham; " I confess I did at one moment imagine that you had been rash in your assertion, but from what has this instant occurred, it is evident your prisoner is known to others as well as to yourself—No doubt we shall have every thing explained in due season. By the bye, of what nature is your wound? Slight I should say, from the indifference with which you treat it.

"Slight, General—far slighter," he continued, coloring, "than the wound that was sought to be affixed to my fair name in absence."

All looked at the speaker, and at each other with surprise, for, as yet, there could have been no communication to him of the doubts which had been entertained.

"Who is it of you all, gentlemen," pursued the young man, with the same composedness of voice and manner, and turning particularly to the officers of the —— Regiment, who were grouped around their Chief; "Who is it, I ask, on whom has devolved the enviable duty of reporting me as capable of violating my faith as a subject, and my honor as an officer?"

There was no reply, although the same looks of surprise were interchanged; but, as he continued to glance his eye around the circle, it encountered, either by accident or design, that of Captain Molineux, on whose rather confused countenance the gaze of Henry Grantham was at that moment bent with an expression of much meaning.

"No one answers," continued the youth; "then the sting has been harmless. But I crave your pardon, General—I am claiming an exemption from censure which may not be conceded by all. Commodore, how shall I dispose of my prisoners?"

"Not so, Mr. Grantham; you have sufficiently established your right to repose, and I have already issued the necessary instructions. Yet, while you have nobly acquitted yourself of *your* duty, let me also perform *mine*. Gentlemen," he continued, addressing the large circle of officers, "I was the first to comment on Mr. Grantham's supposed neglect of duty, and to cast a doubt on his fidelity. That I was wrong I admit, but right I trust will be my reparation, and whatever momentary pain he may experience in knowing that he has been thus unjustly judged, it will I am sure be more than compensated for, when he hears that by General Brock himself his defence was undertaken, even to the pledging of his own honor—Mr. Grantham," concluded the gallant officer, "how you have obtained your knowledge of the conversation that passed here, during your absence, is a mystery I will not now pause to inquire into, but I would fain apologize for the wrong I have done. Have I your pardon?"

At the commencement of this address, the visible heaving of his full chest, the curling of his proud lip, and the burning flush of his dark cheek, betrayed the mortification Gerald felt, in having been placed in a position to be judged thus unjustly; but, as the Commodore proceeded, this feeling gradually passed away, and when the warm defence of his conduct, by the General, was alluded to, closed as the information was with a request for pardon, his temporary annoyance was banished, and he experienced only the generous triumph of one who is conscious of having won his way, through calumny and slander, to the well merited approbation of all right minded men.

"Come, come," interposed the General, more touched than he was willing to appear by the expressive manner in which the only hand of the Commodore now grasped that of his Lieutenant, and perceiving that the latter was about to reply; "We will defer all further explanation until a later period. But, before we depart, this person must be disposed of—Major Montgomerie, excuse my asking if you will be personally responsible for your fellow prisoner?"

"Certainly not," returned the Major quickly, and with something like alarm at the required responsibility; "that is to say, he does not belong to the United States regular service, and I know nothing of him. Indeed, I never saw him before last night, when he joined me with a verbal message from Detroit."

Hitherto the individual spoken of had preserved an unbroken silence, keeping, as we have already shown, his gaze rivetted on the ground, except at intervals when he seemed to look around, with an eye of suspicion, as if to measure the distance that separated him from the groups of Indians in the background. The disclaimer of the Major had, however, the effect of restoring to him the use of his tongue. Casting his uncertain eye on the gentlemanly person of the latter he exclaimed, in a tone of insufferable vulgarity;

"I'll tell you what it is, Mister Major—you may think yourself a devilish fine feller, but I guess as how an officer of the Michigan Militia is just as good and as spry as any blue coat in the United States rig'lars; so there's that (snapping his fingers) for pretendin' not to know me."

"An ill suppressed titter pervaded the group of British officers—the General alone preserving his *serieux*.

"May I ask your name?" he demanded.

"I guess, Giniril, it's Paul, Emilius, Theophilus, Arnoldi; Ensign in the United States Michigan Militia," was answered with a volubility strongly in contrast with the preceding silence of the speaker.

"Then, Mr. Arnoldi, as an officer in the American Militia, you shall enjoy your liberty on parole. I need not, I presume, sir, point out to you the breach of private honor and national faith consequent on any violation of that parole."

"I guess not, Giniril, for, I take it, the word of a Michigan Militia officer is as good as that of any United States rig'lar, as ever stepped in shoe leather."

Another very pardonable disposition, on the part of the younger officers to indulge in mirth, was interrupted by the General, desiring a young aid-de-camp to procure the necessary billet and accomodation for Ensign Arnoldi.

These two individuals having moved away in search of the required lodging, the General, with his staff and prisoner guests, withdrew towards the fort. Their departure was the signal for the breaking up of the groups; and all dispersed to their several homes, and in pursuit of their various duties. The recently arrived Indians were distributed throughuot the encampment, already occupied as we have described, and the prisoners taken in the morning were provided with suitable accommodation.

As Colonel D'Egville was about to enter the gate of the fort, with his fair charge leaning on his arm, Gerald Grantham approached the party, with the intention of addressing the General in regard to the prisoner Arnoldi; but finding him engaged in close conversation with Major Montgomerie, he lingered, as if awaiting a fitting opportuuity to open the subject.

While he yet loitered the eye of Miss Montgomerie met his. What it expressed we will not venture to describe, but its effect upon the young officer was profound. The moment before, discouraged by her apparent reserve, he had stood coldly by, but now startled into animation, he bent upon her an earnest and corresponding look; then with a wild tumult at his heart, which he neither sought to stifle nor to analyze, and wholly forgetting what had brought him to the spot, he turned and joined his brother, who, at a short distance, stood awaiting his return.

CHAPTER IV.

At the garrison mess table that evening the occurrences of the day naturally formed a chief topic of conversation; and a variety of conjectures, more or less probable, regarding the American lady, were hazarded by the officers, to some of whom she had become an object of curiosity, as she had to others of interest. This conversation, necessarily *parenthèsed* with much extraneous matter, in the nature of rapid demands for solids and liquids, during the interesting period devoted to the process of mastication, finally assumed a more regular character when the cloth had been removed, and the attendants retired.

"If a am at all a joodge of pheesogs, and a flatter meself a am," said a raw-boned Scotch Captain of Grenadiers, measuring six feet two in his stockings, "yon geerl has a bit of the deevil in her ee, therefor, me lads, tak heed that nane o' ye lose yer heerts to her."

"Why not, Cranstoun?" asked a young officer.

"Becoose, Veelliers, she seems to have art enoof, and, to gi' the witch her due, beauty enoof to mak' a mon play the fule, an' she tak it into her heed.

"By George, you are right, Cranstoun," said a remarkably bow-legged, shoulder-of-mutton-fisted, Ensign, whose sharp face, glowing as a harvest moon, made one feel absolutely hot in his presence—a sensation that was by no means diminished by his nasal tone and confident manner; "I have no fancy for your pale faced people who, even while their eyes are flashing anger upon all around, show you a cheek as cold and as pale as a turnip—they're alway so cursed deep. Don't you think so Granville, old fellow?

"Too deep for you I dare say, Mr. Langley," observed the officer last named, (a Captain of Light Infantry) with a slight degree of sarcasm, for he liked not the vulgar familiarity of the recently-joined Ensign's address; "however, be that as it may, I will wager a score of flour barrels, or even pork barrels, if you prefer them, that you cannot show me a finer girl. Were I a marrying man," he continued addressing his companions generally, "I do not know a woman I would sooner choose to share my barrack room with me."

"Bravo! bravo! propose to her Granville propose! propose!" shouted two or three young and joyous voices, amid the loud clapping of hands; "but what do you mean by offering Langley so singular a bet?"

"Ask himself," replied Captain Granville drily? "he knows the value of these things, if you do not. Besides we live in a country where most dealings are in produce. But," he continued, adverting to the first remark, and without seeming to notice the flush upon the red face of Ensign Langley, which momentarily increased until it finally assumed a purple hue—"What the devil should I do with a wife. Nay, even if I felt so inclined, I saw her give Gerald Grantham a look that would carry disappointment to the hopes of any other man—What say you, Henry," addressing his subaltern. "How would you like her for a sister-in-law?"

"Not at all," was the grave reply.

"Apropos," continued Captain Granville, who filled the president's chair—"we ought to have toasted your brother's gallant exploit—Gentlemen, fill your glasses—all full?—Then I will give you the health of Lieutenant Grantham of the squadron."

The toast was responded to by all but Captain Molineux—His glass had been filled and raised, but its contents remained untasted.

The omission was too marked not to be noticed by more than one of the party, Henry Grantham, whose eye had been fixed upon Captain Molineux at the time, of course detected the slight—He sat for some minutes conversing with an unusual and evidently forced animation, then, excusing his early departure under the plea of an engagement with his brother, rose and quitted the mess room.

"What ha' ye doon wi' the oogly loot ye took chairge of, De Courcy ?" inquired Captain Cranstoun, interrupting the short and meaning pause which had succeeded to Grantham's departure.

"Why, I calculate Captain," returned the lively aid-de-camp, imitating the nasal drawl and language which had called up so much mirth, even in presence of the General—"I calculate as how I have introduced Ensign Paul, Emilius, Theophilus, Arnoldi, of the United States Michigan Militia, into pretty considerable snug quarters—I have billeted him at the inn, in which he had scarcely set foot, when his first demand was for a glass of "gin sling," wherewith to moisten his partick'lar damn'd hot, baked clay."

"What a vulgar and uncouth animal," observed St. Clair, a Captain of Engineers—"I am not at all surprised at Major Montgomerie's disinclination to acknowledge him as a personal acquaintance."

"It is to be hoped," said De Courcy, "we shall not encounter many such during the approaching struggle, for, since we have been driven into this war, it will be a satisfaction to find ourselves opposed to an enemy rather more chivalrous than this specimen seems to promise."

"Nay, nay, De Courcy," remarked Captain Granville, "you must not judge of the American officers of the line by the standard of their backwoodsmen; as, for example, Major Montgomerie and the person just alluded to. Last winter," he continued, "there was a continued interchange of hospitality between the two posts, and, had you been here to participate in them, you would have admitted that, among the officers of Detroit, there were many very superior men indeed."

"Pleasant ball that last they gave," said Lieutenant Villiers with a malicious laugh, and fixing his eyes on the Captain of Grenadiers.

"The deevil tak' the ball," impatiently retorted Cranstoun, who did not seem to relish the allusion; "doont talk aboot it noo, mon."

"What was it, Villiers? do pray tell us. Something good, I am sure from Cranstoun's manner," eagerly asked the aid-de-camp, his curiosity excited by the general titter that followed the remark.

"Shall I tell him, Cranstoun?" asked Villiers in the same bantering tone.

"Hoot mon, doon't bother me," petulantly returned the other, as thrusting his long legs under the table, and turning his back upon the questioner he joined, or affected to join, in a conversation that was passing, in a low tone, at his end of the room.

"I must premise," began Villiers, addressing himself to the attentively listening De Courcy, "that such is the mania for dancing in this country, scarcely any obstacle is sufficient to deter a Canadian lady, particularly a French Canadian, from indulging in her favorite amusement. It is, therefore, by no means unusual to see women drawn in sleighs over drifting masses of ice, with chasms occasionally occurring of from fifteen to twenty feet; and that at a moment when, driven by wind and current, the huge fragments are impelled over each other with a roar that can only be likened to continuous thunder, forming, in various directions, lofty peaks from which the sun's rays are reflected in a thousand fantastic shades and shapes. On these occasions the sleighs, or carioles, are drawn, not as otherwise customary, by the fast trotting little horses of the country, but by expert natives whose mode of transport is as follows: A strong rope is fastened to the extremity of the shafts, and into this the French Canadian, buried to the chin in his blanket coat, and provided with a long pole terminating in an iron hook, harnesses himself, by first drawing the loop of the cord over the back of his neck, and then passing it under his arms—In this manner does he traverse the floating ice, stepping from mass to mass with a rapidity that affords no time for the detached fragment to sink under the weight with which it is temporarily laden— As the iron-shod runners obey the slightest impulsion, the draught is light; and the only fatigue encountered is in the act of bringing the detached bodies together. Wherever an opening intervenes, the Canadian throws forward his pole, and, securing the pointed hook in some projection of the floating ice, drags it towards that on the extreme verge of which he stands. In like manner he passes on to the next, when the same operation remains to be performed, until the passage is finally effected. Sometimes it happens that a chasm of more than ordinary extent occurs, in which case the pole is unavailable, and then his only alternative is to wait patiently until some distant mass, moving in a direction to fill up the interstice, arrives within his reach. In the meanwhile the ice on which he stands sinks slowly and gradually, until sometimes it quite disappears beneath the surface of the water."

"And the women, all this time?" demanded De Courcy, with something of the nervousness, which might be attributed to such a situation.

"Sit as quietly and as unconcernedly,wrapped in their furs, as if they were merely taking their customary drive on terra firma," continued Villiers, "nay, I am persuaded that if they ever entertain an anxiety on those occasions, it is either least the absence of one of these formidable masses should compel them to abandon an enterprize, the bare idea of entering upon which would give an European woman an attack of nerves, or that the delayed aid should be a means of depriving them of one half minute of their anticipated pleasure."

"Why," interrupted Middlemore, despite of a dozen ohs and ahs—"why, I say, is Villiers like a man of domestic habits? Do you give it up? Because he is fond of dwelling on his own premises."

"Middlemore, when will you renounce that vile habit of punning?" said De Courcy with an earnestness of adjuration that excited a general laugh at his end of the table—"Come, Villiers, never mind his nonsense, for your premises, although a little long, are not without deep interest—but what has all this to do with our good friend above ?"

"You shall hear. After a succession of balls last winter, to which the ladies on either shore were invariably invited, the concluding one was given by the officers in garrison at Detroit. This was at the very close of the season, and it chanced that, on the preceding night, the river had broken up, so that the roar and fracas of crashing ice, might have been likened, during forty eight hours afterwards, to some terrible disorganization of nature. Nothing daunted, however, by the circumstance, many of the Canadian ladies made the usual preparations, and amongst others the Miss D'Egvilles."

Here Villiers paused a moment, and with a significant "hem," sought to arouse the attention of the Grenadier; but Cranstoun, insensible to the appeal, and perhaps unwilling to listen to a story that occasioned so much mirth whenever it was repeated continued with his back immovably turned towards the speaker.

"All very well," pursued Villiers:—"but we know the adage—'none so deaf as those who will not hear'—I have said," again turning to De Courcy, while those who were near, listened not without interest to the story, familiar even as it was to them all, "that the Miss D'Egvilles were of the party—At that time our friend was doing the amiable to the lively Julia, although we never could persuade him to confess his penchant; and, on this occasion, he had attached himself to their immediate sleigh. Provided, like the Canadians, with poles terminated by an iron hook at one end and a spike at the other, we made our way after their fashion, but in quicker time than they possibly could, harnessed as they were in the sledges. With the aid of these poles, we cleared, with facility, chasms of from ten to twelve feet, and, alighting on our moccasined feet, seldom incurred much risk of losing our hold—Our ball dresses were taken in charge by the ladies, so that our chief care was the safe passage of our own persons. We all arrived without accident, and passed a delightful evening, the American officers exerting themselves to give the *coup d'éclat* to the last ball of the season."

"Yes," interrupted the incorrigible Middlemore, as he cracked a hickory nut, "and the balls reserved for us this season will also carry with them the *coup de grass*."

"The night," pursued Villiers, no one noticing the interruption save by an impatient 'pish,' "gave every indication of a speedy break up. The ice yet floated along in disjoined masses, but with even greater rapidity than on the preceding day. Two alternatives remained—either to attempt the crossing before further obstacle should be interposed, or to remain in Detroit until the river had been so far cleared of the ice as to admit of a passage in canoes. With our leaping poles, we were not so much at a loss, but the fear entertained was principally for the safety of the sleighs. Nothing dismayed, however, by the dangerous appearance of the river, the ladies, after due deliberation, courageously resolved on returning without delay, and we accordingly set out on our somewhat hazardous expedition.

"Notwithstanding it was, as I have already remarked, the close of winter, the cold was intense, and we were warmly clad. I do not know if you have ever seen Cranstoun's huge bear skin coat, (an affirmative nod was given by De Courcy,) well: in this formidable covering had he encased himself, so that when he quitted the town, surmounted as his head was moreover with a fur cap, he presented more of the appearance of a dancing bear than of a human creature. In this guise he attached himself to the sleigh of the D'Egvilles, which, in crossing, happened to be the farthest down the river, of the group."

"What a domn'd loong time ye are teelling that stoopid stoory Veelliers," at length noticed Cranstoun, wheeling round and regarding the narrator with a look of ill assumed indifference, "a coold a toold it mysel in half the time."

"I am afraid you would not tell it so faithfully" replied

Lieutenant Villiers, amid the loud laugh which was now raised at Cranstoun's expense. "You see it is so good a thing I like to make the most of it."

Here Cranstoun again turned his back upon the party, and Villiers pursued,

"The main body of the expedition had got nearly half way across the river, when suddenly our ears were assailed by moanings, resembling those of some wild beast, mingled with incessant and ungovernable laughter. Checking our course, and turning to behold the cause, we observed, about a hundred yards below us, the sledge of the D'Egvilles, from which the almost convulsive laughter proceeded, and at a considerable distance beyond this again, an object the true character of which we were some time in discovering.

"It appeared, on subsequent explanation, that Cranstoun, who had been whispering soft nothings in the ear of Julia D'Egville, (here the Captain was observed to prick his ear without materially altering his position) hem! Cranstoun, I say, it appeared had also taken it into his head to give her a specimen of his agility, by an attempt to clear a space between two masses of ice of somewhat too great a breadth for a heavy grenadier, buttoned up to the chin in a ponderous bear skin coat. He succeeded in gaining the opposite piece of ice, but had no sooner reached it, than he fell, entangled in such a manner in his covering that he found it impossible to extricate himself. To add to his disaster, the force of his fall broke off, from the main body, the section of ice on which he rested. Borne down by the current, in spite of his vain struggles to free himself, he was unable even to call for aid, his fingers moreover being so benumbed with cold that he found it impossible to unbutton the straps which confined his mouth. In this emergency he could only utter the strange and unintelligible moan which had reached our ears, and which, mingled with the bursts of laughter from Julia D'Egville, formed a most incongruous melange.

"The best of the adventure remains, however, to be told.

Numbers of the peasantry from either shore, provided with poles, guns, and ropes, were now to be seen rushing towards the half congealed Cranstoun, fully imagining—nay exclaiming—that it was a wild bear, which, in an attempt to cross the river, had had its retreat cut off, and was now, from insensibility, rendered harmless. Disputes even arose in the distance as to whom the prize should belong, each pursuer claiming to have seen it first. Nay, more than one gun had been levelled with a view of terminating all doubt by lodging a bullet in the carcase, when, fortunately for the subject in dispute, this proposal was overruled by the majority, who were more anxious to capture than to slay the supposed bear. Meanwhile the Canadian, harnessed to the sleigh of the D'Egvilles, roared out with all his lungs for the two parties to hasten to the assistance of the drowning British officer. In the confusion produced by their own voices, however, they did not appear to hear or understand him; yet all pursued the aim they had in view. Cranstoun's body was so doubled up that it was impossible for any one, who had not witnessed the accident, to imagine it any thing in nature but a bear; and this impression, the strange moaning he continued to make, tended to confirm.

"The party of Canadians, favored by the nature of their floating ice-bridges, were the first to come up to him. A desperate effort of his cramped muscles had enabled Cranstoun to extend one of his legs, at the moment when they were about to throw a noose round his neck, and this was the first intimation the astonished peasantry had of their supposed prize being a human being, instead of the fat bear they had expected. Poor Cranstoun was of course liberated from his 'durance vile,' but so chilled from long immersion, that he could not stand without assistance, and it was not until one of their companions had approached with a sleigh that he could be removed. He kept his bed three days, as much I believe from vexation as illness, and has never worn his unlucky bear skin since; neither has he forgiven Julia D'Egville the laugh she enjoyed at his expense. Cranstoun," he concluded, "you may turn now, the story is told."

But Cranstoun, apparently heedless of the laugh that followed this—as indeed it did every--narration of the anecdote, was not to be shaken from his equanimity. He continued silent and unmoved, as if he had not heard a word of the conclusion.

"Poor Cranstoun," exclaimed the joyous De Courcy, in a strain of provoking banter, "what an unfortunate leap that was of yours; and how delighted you must have felt when you again stepped on terra firma."

"I don't wonder at his leap being unfortunate," observed Middlemore, all eyes fixed upon him in expectation of what was to follow, "for Julia D'Egville can affirm that, while paying his court to her, he had not chosen a *leap year*."

While all were as usual abusing the far strained pun, a note was brought in by the head waiter and handed to the punster. The officer read it attentively, and then, with an air of seriousness which in him was remarkable, tossed it across the table to Captain Molineux, who, since the departure of Henry Grantham, had been sitting with his arms folded, apparently buried in profound thought, and taking no part either in the conversation or the laughter which accompanied it. A faint smile passed over his features, as, after having read, he returned, it with an assentient nod to Middlemore. Shortly afterwards, availing himself of the opportunity afforded by the introduction of some fresh topic of conversation, he quitted his seat, and whispering something in the ear of Villiers, left the mess room. Soon after, the latter officer disappeared from the table, and in a few moments his example was followed by Middlemore.

CHAPTER V.

The dinner party at Colonel D'Egville's was composed in a manner to inspire an English exclusive with irrepressible horror. At the suggestion of General Brock, Tecumseh had been invited, and, with him, three other celebrated Indian chiefs, whom we beg to introduce to our readers under their familiar names—Split-log—Round-head—and Walk-in-the-water—all of the formidable nation of the Hurons. In his capacity of superintendant of Indian affairs, Colonel D'Egville had been much in the habit of entertaining the superior chiefs, who, with a tact peculiar to men of their sedate and serious character, if they displayed few of the graces of European polish, at least gave no manifestation of an innate vulgarity. As it may not be uninteresting to the reader to have a slight sketch of the warriors, we will attempt the portraiture.

The chief Split-log, who indeed should rather have been named Split-ear, as we shall presently show, was afflicted with an aldermanic rotundity of person, by no means common among his race, and was one, who from his love of ease and naturally indolent disposition, seemed more fitted to take his seat in the council than to lead his warriors to battle. Yet was he not, in reality, the inactive character he appeared, and more than once, subsequently, he was engaged in expeditions of a predatory nature, carrying off the customary spoils. We cannot impart a better idea of the head of the warrior, than by stating, that we never recal that of the gigantic Memnon, in the British Museum, without being forcibly reminded of Split-log's. The Indian, however, was notorious for a peculiarity which the Egyptian had not. So enormous a head, seeming to require a corresponding portion of the several organs, nature had, in her great bounty, provided him with a nose, which, if it equalled not that of Smellfungus in length, might, in height and breadth, have laughed it utterly to scorn. Neither was it a single, but a double nose—two excrescences, equalling in bulk a moderate sized lemon, and of the spongy nature of a mushroom, bulging out, and lending an expression of owlish wisdom to his otherwise heavy features. As on that of the Memnon, not a vestige of a hair was to be seen on the head of Split-log. His lips were, moreover, of the same unsightly thickness, while the elephantine ear had been slit in such a manner, that the pliant cartilage, yielding to the weight of several ounces of lead which had for years adorned it, now lay stretched, and coquetting with the brawny shoulder on which it reposed. Such was the Huron, or Wyandot Chief, whose cognomen of Split-log had, in all probability, been derived from his facility in "suiting the action to the word;" for, in addition to his gigantic nose, he possessed a fist, which in size and strength might have disputed the palm with Maximilian himself: although his practice had chiefly been confined to knocking down his drunken wives, instead of oxen."

The second Chief, Round-head, who, by the way, was the principal in reputation after Tecumseh, we find the more difficulty in describing from the fact of his having had few or none of those peculiarities which we have, happily for our powers of description, been enabled to seize hold of in Split-log. His name we believe to have been derived from that indispensable portion of his frame. His eye was quick, even penetrating, and his stern brow denoted intelligence and decision of character. His straight, coal black, hair, cut square over the forehead, fell long and thickly over his face and shoulders. This, surmounted by a round slouched hat, ornamented with an eagle's feather, which he ordinarily wore and had not even now dispensed with, added to a blue capote or hunting frock, produced a *tout ensemble*, which cannot be more happily rendered than by a comparison with one of his puritanical sly-eyed namesakes of the English Revolution.

Whether our third hero, Walk-in-the-water, derived his name from any aquatic achievement which could possibly give a claim to its adoption, we have no means of ascertaining; but certain it is that in his features he bore a striking resemblance to the portraits of Oliver Cromwell. The same small, keen, searching eye—the same iron inflexibility of feature, together with the long black hair escaping from beneath the slouched hat, (for Walk-in-the-water, as well as Round-head, was characterized by an unconscious imitation of the Roundheads of the revolution)—all contributed to render the resemblance as perfect, as perfection of resemblance can be obtained where the physical, and not the moral, man, forms the ground of contrast.

Far above these in nobleness of person, as well as in brilliancy of intellect, was the graceful Tecumseh. Unlike his companions, whose dress was exceedingly plain, he wore his jerkin or hunting coat, of the most beautifully soft and pliant deer skin, on which were visible a variety of tasteful devices exquisitely embroidered with the stained quills of the porcupine. A shirt of dazzling whiteness was carefully drawn over his expansive chest, and in his equally white shawl-turban was placed an ostrich feather, the prized gift of the lady of the mansion. On all occasions of festivity, and latterly in the field, he was wont thus to decorate himself; and never did the noble warrior appear to greater advantage than when habited in this costume. The contrast it offered to his swarthy cheek and mobile features, animated as they were by the frequent flashing of his eagle eye, seldom failed to excite admiration in the bosoms of all who saw him.

The half hour that elapsed between the arrival of the several guests and the announcement of dinner, was passed under the influence of feelings almost as various in kind as the party itself. Messieurs Split-log, Round-head, and Walk-in-the-water, fascinated by the eagles on the buttons of Major Montgomerie's uniform, appeared to regard that officer, as if they saw no just cause or impediment why certain weapons dangling at their sides should not be made to perform, and that without delay, an incision in the cranium of their proprietor. True, there was a difficulty. The veteran Major was partially bald, and wanted the top knot or scalping tuft, which to a true warrior was indispensable ; not that we mean to insinuate that either of these chiefs would so far have forgotten the position in which that gentleman stood, as to have been tempted into any practical demonstration of their hostility : but there was a restlessness about the eye of each that, much like the instinct of the cat, which regards with natural avidity the bird that is suffered to go at large within his reach, without daring openly to attack it, betrayed the internal effort it cost them to lose sight of the enemy in the prisoner and friend of their superintendant. The Major, on the other hand, although satisfied he was under the roof of hospitality, did not at first appear altogether at his ease, but, while he conversed with the English officers, turned ever and anon an eye of distrust on the movements of his swarthy fellow guests. On the arrival of Tecumseh, who, detained until a late hour by the arrangements he had been making for the encampment and supplies of his new force, was the last to make his appearance, the Major's doubts passed entirely away. It was impossible to be in the presence of this chieftain, and fail, even without any other index to his soul than what the candour of his expression afforded, to entertain all the security that man may repose on man. He had in him, it is true, too much of the sincerity of nature to make any thing like a friendly advance to one of a people to whom he owed all the misfortunes of his race, and for whom he had avowed an inextinguishable hostility of heart and purpose; but, unless when this might with strict propriety be exercised, the spirit of his vengeance extended not; and not only would he have scorned to harm a fallen foe, but his arm would have been the first uplifted in his defence.

Notwithstanding the glance of intelligence which Captain Granville had remarked, and which we had previously stated to have been directed by Miss Montgomerie to her captor a few hours before, there was nothing in her manner during dinner to convey the semblance of a prepossession. True, that in the tumultuous glow of gratified vanity and dawning love, Gerald Grantham had executed a toilet into which, with a view to the improvement of the advantage he imagined himself to have gained, all the justifiable coquetry of personal embellishment had been thrown; but neither the handsome blue uniform with its glittering epaulette, nor the beautiful hair on which more than usual pains had been bestowed, nor the sparkling of his dark eye, nor the expression of a cheek, rendered doubly animated by excitement, nor the interestingly displayed arm *en écharpe*—none of these attractions, we repeat, seemed to claim even a partial notice from her they were intended to captivate. Cold, colourless, passionless, Miss Montgomerie met him with the calmness of an absolute stranger; and when, with the recollection of the indescribable look she had bestowed upon him glowing at his heart, Gerald again sought in her eyes some trace of the expression that had stirred every vein into transport, he found there indifference the most complete. How great his mortification was we will not venture to describe, but the arch and occasional raillery of his lively cousin, Julia D'Egville, seemed to denote most plainly that the conqueror and the conquered had exchanged positions.

Nor was this surprising; Miss Montgomerie's travelling habit had been discarded for the more decorative ornaments of a dinner toilet, in which, however, the most marked simplicity was preserved. A plain white muslin dress gave full developement to a person, which was of a perfection that no dress could have disguised. It was the bust of a Venus, united to a form, to create which would have taxed the imaginative powers of a Praxiteles—a form so faultlessly moulded that every movement presented some new and unpremeditated grace. What added to the surpassing richness of her beauty was her hair, which, black, glossy, and of eastern luxuriance, and seemingly disdaining the girlishness of curls, reposed in broad Grecian bands, across a brow, the intellectual expression of which they contributed to form. Yet, never did woman exhibit in her person and face, more opposite extremes of beauty. If the one was strikingly characteristic of warmth, the other was no less indicative of coldness. Fair, even to paleness, were her cheek and forehead, which wore an appearance of almost marble immobility, save when, in moments of oft recurring abstraction, a slight but marked contraction of the brow betrayed the existence of a feeling, indefinable indeed by the observer, but certainly unallied to softness. Still was she beautiful—coldly, classically, beautiful—eminently calculated to inspire passion, but seemingly incapable of feeling it.

The coldness of Miss Montgomerie's manner was no less remarkable. Her whole demeanour was one of abstraction. It seemed as if heedless, not only of ceremony, but of courtesy, her thoughts and feelings were far from the board of whose hospitality she was partaking. Indeed, the very few remarks she made during dinner referred to the period of departure of the boat, in which she was to be conveyed to Detroit, and on this subject she displayed an earnestness, which, even Grantham thought, might have been suppressed in the presence of his uncle's family. Perhaps he felt piqued at her readiness to leave him.

Under these circumstances, the dinner was not, as might be expected, particularly gay. There was an *embarras* among all, which even the circulating wine did not wholly remove. Major Montgomerie was nearly as silent as his niece. Mrs. D'Egville, although evincing all the kindness of her really benevolent nature—a task in which she was assisted by her amiable daughters, still felt that the reserve of her guest insensibly produced a corresponding effect upon herself, while Colonel D'Egville, gay, polished, and attentive, as he usually was, could not wholly overcome an apprehension that the introduction of the Indian Chiefs had given offence to both uncle and niece. Still, it was impossible to have acted otherwise. Independently of his strong personal attachment to Tecumseh, considerations involving the safety of the Province, threatened as it was, strongly demanded that the leading Chiefs should be treated with the respect due to their station; and moreover, while General Brock, and Commodore Barclay were present, there could be no ground for an impression that slight was intended. Both these officers saw the difficulty under which their host laboured, and sought by every gentlemanly attention, to remove whatever unpleasantness might lurk in the feelings of his American guests.

The dessert brought with it but little addition to the animation of the party, and it was a relief to all, when, after a toast proposed by the General, to the "Ladies of America," Mrs. D'Egville made the usual signal for withdrawing.

As soon as they had departed, followed a moment or two afterwards by Tecumseh and Gerald Grantham, Messieurs Split-log, Round-head, and Walk-in-the-Water, deliberately taking their pipe-bowl tomahawks from their belts, proceeded to fill them with kinni-kinnick, a mixture of Virginia tobacco, and odoriferous herbs, than which no perfume can be more fragrant. Amid the clouds of smoke puffed from these at the lower end of the table, where had been placed a supply of whiskey, their favorite liquor—did Colonel D'Egville and his more civilized guests quaff their claret; more gratified than annoyed by the savoury atmosphere wreathing around them, while, taking advantage of the early departure of the abstemious Tecumseh, they discussed the merits of that Chief, and the policy of employing the Indians as allies, as will be seen in the following chapter;—

CHAPTER VI.

"What a truly noble looking being," observed Major Montgomerie, as he followed with his eye the receding form of the athletic but graceful Tecumseh. "Do you know, Colonel D'Egville, I could almost forgive your nephew his success of this morning, in consideration of the pleasure he has procured me in this meeting."

Colonel D'Egville looked the gratification he felt at the avowal. "I am delighted, Major Montgomerie, to hear you say so. My only fear was that, in making those Chieftains my guests, at the same moment with yourself and niece, I might have unconsciously appeared to slight, where slight was certainly not intended. You must be aware, however, of the rank held by them among their respective nations, and of their consequent claim upon the attention of one to whom the Indian interests have been delegated."

"My dear sir," interrupted the Major, eager to disclaim, "I trust you have not mistaken me so far, as to have imputed a reserve of speech and manner during dinner, to which I cannot but plead guilty, to a fastidiousness which, situated as I am, (and he bowed to the General, and Commodore,) would have been wholly misplaced. My distraction, pardonable perhaps under all the circumstances, was produced entirely by a recurrence to certain inconveniences which I felt might arise to me from my imprisonment. The captive bird," he pursued, while a smile for the first time animated his very fine countenance, "will pine within its cage, however gilded the wires which compose it. In every sense, my experience of to-day only leads me to the expression of a hope, that all whom the chances of war may throw into a similar position, may meet with a similar reception."

"Since," observed the General, "your private affairs are of the importance you express, Major Montgomerie, you shall depart with your niece. Perhaps I am rather exceeding my powers in this respect, but, however this may be, I shall take the responsibility on myself. You will hold yourself pledged, of course, to take no part against us in the forthcoming struggle, until you have been regularly exchanged for whatever officer of your own rank, may happen to fall into the hands of your countrymen. I shall dispatch an express to the Commander-in-Chief, to intimate this fact, requesting at the same time, that your name may be put down in the first list for exchange."

Major Montgomerie warmly thanked the General for his kind offer, of which he said he should be glad to avail himself, as he did not like the idea of his niece proceeding without him to Detroit, where she was an entire stranger. This, he admitted, determined as she had appeared to be, was one of the unpleasant subjects of his reflection during dinner.

With a view of turning the conversation, and anxious moreover, to obtain every information on the subject, the General now inquired in what estimation Tecumseh was generally held in the United States.

"Among the more intelligent classes of our citizens, in the highest possible," was the reply; "but by those who are not so capable of judging, and who only see, in the indomitable courage and elevated talents of the patriot hero, the stubborn inflexibility of the mere savage, he is looked upon far less flatteringly. By all, however, is he admitted to be formidable without parallel, in the history of Indian warfare. His deeds are familiar to all, and his name is much such a bugbear to American childhood, as Marlborough's was in France, and Napoleon's is in England. It is a source of much regret to our Government never to have been enabled to conciliate this extraordinary man."

"What more feasible," remarked the General, but with a tone and manner that could not possibly give offence; "had not the difficulty been of its own creation? Treaty after treaty, you must admit, Major, had been made and violated under various pretexts, while the real motive—the aggrandizement of territories already embracing a vast portion of their early possessions—was carefully sought to be concealed from these unfortunate people. How was it to be expected then that a man, whom the necessities of his country had raised up to itself in the twofold character of statesman and warrior—one gifted with a power of analyzing motives which has never been surpassed in savage life—how, I ask, was it to be expected that he, with all these injuries of aggression staring him in the face, should have been won over by a show of conciliation, which long experience, independently of his matured judgment, must have assured him was only held forth to hoodwink, until fitting opportunity should be found for again throwing off the mask."

"To the charge of violating treaties," returned Major Montgomerie, who took the opposite argument in perfectly good part, "I fear, General, our Government must to a certain extent plead guilty—much, however, remains to be said in excuse. In the first place, it must be borne in mind that the territory of the United States, unlike the kingdoms of Europe, has no fixed or settled boundary whereby to determine its own relative bearing. True it is, that we have the Canadas on one portion of our frontier, but this being a fixed line of demarcation, there can exist no question as to a mutual knowledge of the territorial claims of both countries. Unlike that of the old world, however, our population is rapidly progressing, and where are we to find an outlet for the surplus of that population unless, unwilling as we are to come into collision with our more civilized neighbours, we can push them forward into the interior. In almost all the contracts entered into by our Government with the Indians, large sums have been given for the lands ceded by the latter. This was at once, of course, a tacit and mutual revocation of any antecedent arrangements, and if instances have occurred wherein the sacredness of treaty has been violated, it has only been where the Indians have refused to part with their lands for the proffered consideration and when those lands have been absolutely indispensable to our agricultural purposes. Then indeed has it been found necessary to resort to force. That this principle of "might being the better right," may be condemned *in limine* it is true, but how otherwise, with a superabundant population, can we possibly act?"

"A superabundance of territory, I grant you, but surely not of population," remarked the Commodore; "were the citizens of the United States condensed into the space allotted to Europeans, you might safely dispense with half the Union at this moment."

"And what advantages should we then derive from the possession of nearly a whole continent to ourselves?"

"Every advantage that may be reaped consistently with common justice. What would be thought in Europe, if, for instance to illustrate a point, and assuming these two countries to be in a state of profound peace, Spain, on the principle of might, should push her surplus population into Portugal, compelling the latter kingdom to retire back on herself, and crowd her own subjects into the few provinces that might yet be left to them."

"I cannot admit the justice of your remark, Commodore," returned Major Montgomerie, gradually warming into animation; "Both are civilized powers, holding the same rank and filling nearly the same scale among the nations of Europe. Moreover, there does not exist the same difference in the natural man. The uneducated negro is, from infancy and long custom, doomed to slavery, wherefore should the copper coloured Indian be more free? But my argument points not at their subjection. I would merely show that, incapable of benefitting by the advantages of the soil they inherit, they should learn to yield it with a good grace to those who can. Their wants are few, and interminable woods yet remain to them, in which their hunting pursuits may be indulged without a fear of interruption."

"That it will be long," observed the General, "before, in so vast a continent, they will be without a final resting place, I readily admit; but the hardship consists in this—that they are driven from particular positions to which their early associations lend a preference. What was it that stirred into a flame, the fierce hostility of Tecumseh but the determination evinced by your Government to wrest, from the hands of his tribe, their last remaining favorite haunts on the Wabash?"

"This cannot be denied, but it was utterly impossible we could forego the possession of countries bordering so immediately on our settlements. Had we pushed our colonization further, leaving the tribes of the Wabash in intermediate occupation, we ran the risk of having our settlers cut off in detail, at the slightest assumed provocation. Nay, pretexts would have been sought for the purpose, and the result of this would have been the very war into which we were unavoidably led. The only difference was, that, instead of taking up arms to avenge our slaughtered kinsmen, we anticipated the period that must sooner or later have arrived, by ridding ourselves of the presence of those from whose hostility we had every thing to apprehend."

"The expediency of these measures," said the General, "no one, Major, can of course doubt; the only question at issue is their justice, and in making this remark it must be obvious there is no particular allusion to the United States, further than that country serves to illustrate a general principle. I am merely arguing against the right of a strong power to wrest from a weaker what may be essential to its own interest, without reference to the comfort, or wishes, or convenience of the latter."

"In such light assuredly do I take it," observed Major Montgomerie, bowing his sense of the disclaimer. "But to prove to you, General, that we are only following in the course pursued by every other people of the world, let us, without going back to the days of barbarism, when the several kingdoms of Europe were overrun by the strongest, and when your own country in particular became in turn the prey of Saxons, Danes, Normans, &c. merely glance our eyes upon those provinces which have been subjugated by more civilized Europe. Look at South America for instance, and then say what we have done that has not been far exceeded by the Spaniards, in that portion of the hemisphere—and yet, with this vast difference in the balance, that there the European drove before him and mercilessly destroyed an unoffending race, while we, on the contrary, have had fierce hostility and treachery every where opposed to our progress. The Spaniards, moreover, offered no equivalent for the country subdued; now we have ever done so, and only where that equivalent has been rejected, have we found ourselves compelled to resort to force. Look again at the islands of the West Indies, the chief of which are conquests by England. Where are the people to whom Providence had originally assigned those countries, until the European, in his thirst for aggrandizement, on that very principle of might which you condemn, tore them violently away. Gone, extirpated, until scarce a vestige of their existence remains, even as it must be, in the course of time, with the Indians of these wilds—perhaps not in this century or the next, but soon or late assuredly. These two people—the South Americans and Caribs—I particularly instance, for the very reason that they offer the most striking parallel with the immediate subject under discussion. But shall I go further than this, gentlemen, and maintain that we, the United States, are only following in the course originally pointed out to us by England."

"I should be glad to hear your argument," said the Commodore, drawing his chair closer to the table.

"And I," added the General, "consider the position too

novel not to feel interested in the manner in which it will be maintained."

"I will not exactly say," observed Colonel D'Egville, smiling one of his blandest smiles, and few men understood the winning art better than himself, "that Major Montgomerie has the happy talent of making the worse appear the better cause; but, certainly I never remember to have heard that cause more ably advocated."

"More subtly perhaps you would say, Colonel; but seriously, I speak from conviction alone. It is true, as a citizen of the United States, and therefore one interested in the fair fame of its public acts, that conviction may partake in some degree of partial influences; still it is sincere. But to my argument. What I would maintain is, as I have before stated, that in all we have done, we have only followed the example of England. For instance, when the colonization of the Eastern and Southern States of the Union took place, that is to say when our common ancestors first settled in this country, how was their object effected? Why, by driving from their possessions near the sea, in order to make room for themselves, those very nations whom we are accused of a desire to exterminate, as if out of a mere spirit of wantonness. Did either Dutch or English then hesitate as to what course *they* should pursue, or suffer any qualms of conscience to interfere with their Colonial plans? No; as a measure of policy—as a means of security—they sought to conciliate the Indians, but not the less determined were they to attain their end. Who, then, among Englishmen, would have thought of blaming their fellow countrymen, when the object in view was the aggrandizement of the national power, and the furtherance of individual interests? While the Colonists continued tributary to England they could do no wrong; they incurred no censure. Each succeding year saw them, with a spirit of enterprize that was *then* deemed worthy of commendation, pushing their advantages, and extending their possessions to the utter exclusion, and at the expense of the original possessors of the soil. For this they incurred no blame: but mark the change. No sooner had the war of the revolution terminated in our emancipation from the leading strings of childhood; no sooner had we taken rank among the acknowledged nations of the world; no sooner had we, in a word, started into existence as an original people, than the course we had undeviatingly pursued in infancy, and from which we did not dream of swerving in manhood, became a subject for unqualified censure. What had been considered laudable enterprize in the English Colonist, became unpardonable ambition in the American Republican, and acts affecting the national prosperity, that carried with them the approbation of society and good government during our nonage, were stigmatized as odious and grasping, the moment we had attained our majority."

"Most ably and eloquently argued, Major," interrupted the General, "and I fear with rather more truth than we Englishmen are quite willing to acknowledge: still, it must be admitted, that what in the first instance was a necessity, partook no longer of that character at a later period. In order to colonize the country originally, it was necessary to select such portions as were, by their proximity to the sea, indispensable to the perfection of the plan. If the English Colonists drove the Indians into the interior, it was only for a period. They had still vast tracts to traverse, which have since, figuratively speaking, been reduced to a mere span: and their very sense of the difference of the motive—that is to say, of the difference between him who merely seeks whereon to erect his dwelling, and him who is anxious to usurp to himself the possession of almost illimitable territory—cannot be better expressed than by the different degrees of enmity manifested against the two several people. When did the fierceness of Indian hatred blaze forth against the English Colonists, who were limited in their views, as it has since against the subjects of the United States, who, since the revolution, have more than tripled their territorial acquisitions."

"Nay, General," replied the American, his lip partially curling with a smile, indicating consciousness of triumphant argument; "I shall defeat you on your own ground, and that by going back to a period anterior to the revolution—to the very period you describe as being characterized by less intense hostility to your own Government."

"What, for instance, have we seen in modern times to equal the famous Indian league which, under the direction of the celebrated Pontiac, a Chieftain only surpassed by Tecumseh, consigned so many of the European posts to destruction, along this very line of district, about the middle of the last century. It has been held up as a reproach to us, that we have principally subjected ourselves to the rancorous enmity of the Indians, in consequence of having wrested from them their favorite and beautiful hunting grounds, (Kentucky in particular,) to which their early associations had linked them. But to this I answer, that in Pontiac's time, this country was still their own, as well as Ohio, Louisiana, Indiana, &c. and yet the war of fierce extermination was not the less waged against the English; not because these latter had appropriated their principal haunts, but because they had driven them from their original possessions, near the sea. The hatred of the Indians has ever been the same towards those who first secured a footing on their continent, and, although we are a distinct people in the eyes of the civilized world, still we are the same in those of the natives, who see in us, not the emancipated American, but merely the descendant of the original Colonist. That their hostility has progressed in proportion with our extension of territory, I cannot altogether admit, for although our infant settlements have in a great degree suffered from occasional irruptions of the savages, when men, women and children, have alike been devoted to the murderous tomahawk, in no way have our fortresses been systematically assailed, as during the time of Pontiac."

"For this," interrupted the General, "there are two obvious reasons. In the first instance, your fortresses are less isolated than ours were at that period, and, secondly, no such intelligent being as the Chieftain you have named, had started up among the Indian nations until now. What Tecumseh may not effect in course of time, should he not perish in the struggle for his country's liberty, ought to be a matter of serious consideration with your Government."

"Of his great talent, and dauntless determination, they are fully aware," replied the Major, "but, as I have already said, nothing short, not merely of giving up all claim to future advantages, but of restoring the country wrested from him on the Wabash, can ever win him from his hostility; and this is a sacrifice the Government will never consent to make."

At this point of the argument, Messieurs Split-log, Roundhead, and Walk-in-the-Water, having finished their kinnikinnick, and imbibed a due quantum of whiskey: possibly, moreover, not much entertained by the conversation that was carried on in a language neither of them understood but imperfectly, rose to take their leave. They successively shook hands with the British leaders, then advancing last to Major Montgomerie, with a guttural "ugh," so accentuated as to express good will and satisfaction, tendered their dark palms to that officer also, muttering as they did so something about "good Chemocomon." They then with becoming dignity withdrew, followed by Colonel D'Egville, who had risen to conduct them to the door.

The conversation, thus temporarially interrupted, was resumed on that officer's return.

"Admitting the truth of your position, Major Montgomerie," remarked the Commodore, "that the Government of the United States is justified, both by expediency and example, in the course it has pursued, it will not at least be denied, that Tecumseh is, on the very same principle, borne out in the hatred and spirit of hostility, evinced by him towards the oppressors of his country."

"Granted," returned the Major, "but this point has no reference to my argument, which tends to maintain, that in all we have done, we have been justified by necessity and example."

"The fact is, however, that this condition of things is one unavoidably growing out of the clashing of adverse interests —the Indians being anxious to check, we to extend our dominion and power as a people; and the causes existing now, were in being nearly a century ago, and will, in all probability, continue until all vestige of Indian existence shall have passed utterly away. When the French were in the occupancy of the Canadas, having nothing to gain from them, they cultivated the alliance and friendship of the several nations, and by fostering, their fierce hostility against the English Colonists, rendered them subservient to their views. To-day the English stand precisely where the French did. Having little to expect from the Indians, but assistance in a case of need, they behold, and have for years beheld, with any thing but indifference, the struggle continued by the United States, which was commenced by themselves. I hope I shall not be understood as expressing my own opinion, when I add, that, in the United States, the same covert influence is attributed to the Commanders of the British fortresses that was imputed to the French. Indeed, it is a general belief, among the lower classes particularly, that, in all the wars undertaken against the American out-posts and settlements, the Indians have been instigated to the outrage by liberal distributions of money, and presents from the British Government."

"It will hardly be necessary to deny the justice of such an imputation to Major Montgomerie," remarked the General, with a smile; "especially after having disavowed the opinion as his own. The charge is too absurd for serious contradiction—yet, we are not altogether ignorant that such an impression has gone abroad."

"Few of the more enlightened of our citizens give into

the belief," said the Major; "still it will give me especial pleasure to have it in my power to contradict the assertion from the lips of General Brock himself."

"That we have entered into a treaty of alliance with the Indians," observed Colonel D'Egville, "is most certainly true; but it is an alliance wholly defensive. I must further observe that in whatever light the policy of the Government of the United States, in its relations with the Indians, may be privately viewed, we are, under all circumstances, the last people in the world who should condemn it as injurious to our public interests, since it has been productive of results affecting the very existence of these provinces. Had the American Government studied conciliation, rather than extension of territory, it is difficult to say to what side the great body of the Indians would, in the impending struggle, have leaned. The possibility of some such event as the present had not only been foreseen, but anticipated. It has long been obvious to us that the spirit of acquisition manifested by the United States, would not confine itself to its customary channels; but on the contrary, that, not contented with the appropriation of the hunting grounds of the Indians, it would finally extend its views to Canada. Such a crisis has long been provided against. Presents, to a large amount, have certainly been distributed among the Indians, and not only this, but every courtesy, consistent at once with our dignity and our interest, has been shown to them. You have seen, for instance," continued he with a smile, "my three friends, who have just left the room; they are not exactly the happiest specimens of Indian grace, but they have great weight in the council, and are the leading men in the alliance to which you have alluded, although not wholly for the same purpose. In the wars of Pontiac—and these are still fresh in the recollection of certain members of my own family—the English Commanders, with one or two exceptions, brought those disasters upon themselves. Forgetting that the Indians were a proud people, whom to neglect was to stir into hatred, they treated them, with indifference, if not with contempt; and dearly did they pay the penalty of their fault. As we all know, they, with one only exception, were destroyed. In their fall expired the hostility they themselves had provoked, and time had wholly obliterated the sense of injustice from the minds of the several nations. Were we then with these fearful examples, yet fresh in our recollection, to fall into a similar error? No; a course of conciliation was adopted, and has been pursued for years; and now do we reap the fruit of what, after all, is but an act of the most justifiable policy. In my capacity of superintendant of Indian affairs, Major Montgomerie, even more than as a Canadian brought up among them, I have had opportunities of studying the characters of the heads of the several nations. The most bitter enmity animates the bosoms of all against the Government and people of the United States, from whom, according to their own showing, they have to record injury upon injury; whereas from us they have received but benefits. I repeat, this is at once politic and just. What could Canada have hoped to accomplish in the approaching struggle, had the conduct of the American Government been such as to have neutralized the interest we had excited in, and for ourselves? She must have succumbed; and my firm impression is, that, at whatever epoch of her existence the United States may extend the hand of conquest over these provinces, with the Indian tribes that are now leagued with with us crowding to her own standard, not all the armies England may choose to send to their defence will be able to prevent it."

"Filling the situation you now occupy, Colonel, there can be no doubt you are in every way enabled to arrive at a full knowledge of Indian feelings and Indian interests; and we have but too much reason to fear that the strong hatred to the United States, you describe as existing on the part of their several leaders, has had a tendency to unite them more cordially to the British cause. But your course of observation suggests to another question. Why is it that, with the knowledge possessed by the British Government of the cruel nature of Indian warfare, it can consent to enlist them as allies? To prevent their taking up arms against the Canadas may be well, but in my opinion (and it is one very generally entertained through the United States,) the influence of the British authorities should have been confined to neutralizing their services."

"Nay, Major Montgomerie," observed the General, "it would indeed be exacting too much to require that we should offer ourselves unresisting victims to the ambitious designs (forgive the expression) of your Government; and what but self immolation would it be to abstain from the only means by which we can hope to save these threatened Provinces? Colonel D'Egville has just said that, with the Indians opposed to us, Canada would fall. I go farther, and aver that, without the aid of the Indians, circumstanced as England now is, Canada must be lost to us. It is a painful alternative I admit, for that a war, which is not carried on with the conventional courtesies of civilized belligerent nations, is little suited to our taste, you will do us the justice to believe; but by whom have we been forced into the dilemma? Had we been guilty of rousing the Indian spirit against you, with a view to selfish advantage; or had we in any may connived at the destruction of your settlements, from either dread or jealousy of your too close proximity, then should we have deserved all the odium of such conduct. But this we unequivocally deny. Had we even, presuming on the assistance to be derived from them, been the first to engage the Indians in this war, and sent them forth to lay waste your possessions, we might have submitted to well merited censure; but what is our real position? Without any fair pretext, and simply in furtherance of its ambitious views, the Government of the United States declares war against England, and, with an eagerness that sufficiently discloses its true object, marches its rapidly organized armies as rapidly to our weakly defended frontier. It is scarcely a week since an express reached this post bringing the announcement that hostilities had been declared and as a proof that these must have been long in contemplation, even the very day previous to its arrival, a numerous army marched past on their way to Detroit. The sound of their drums was the first intimation we had of their approach, and our surprise was only equalled by our utter ignorance of the motive, until the arrival of the express at once explained the enigma.* In such a case, I maintain, we stand justified before God and man in availing ourselves of every means of defence."

"I cannot acknowledge," replied the American, "that the war undertaken by our Government, is without sufficient pretext, or in a mere spirit of conquest. You forget that an insult was offered to our national flag."

"You of course allude," said the Commodore, "to the affair of the Little Belt, but I cannot help participating in the opinion expressed by General Brock. The right of search, on the part of our vessels, has been too universally admitted for the American Government to have resisted it to the extent they have, had they not in this circumstance found, or fancied they found, a pretext favorable to their ulterior and more important views. My own firm impression is, that had England not all her troops engaged at this moment in the Peninsula, this war never would have been declared. The opportunity, however, has been found too tempting, while there are only some half dozen regular Regiments distributed throughout both provinces; but the result will prove how far well or ill affected the Canadians are to the British Crown. Now is the season arrived to test their allegiance."

"I know not how far the United States Government may have taken in their calculation a chance of disaffection," remarked the General with a smile; "but I think I know the Canadians, and may venture to assert they will remain

* Fact.

staunch. Every where do they appear to manifest the utmost enthusiasm."*

"I am only delighted, General, that they have thus an opportunity of being put to the proof," remarked Colonel D'Egville. "If they should be found wanting, then do I much mistake my countrymen. To return, however, to the subject of the employment of the Indians, which you, Major Montgomerie, appear to condemn. I would ask you, if you are aware of the great exertions made by your Government, to induce them to take an active part in this very war. If not, I can acquaint you that several of the chiefs, now here, have been strongly urged to declare against us; and, not very long since, an important council was held among the several tribes, wherein some few, who had been won over by large bribes, had the temerity to discuss the propriety of deserting the British cause, in consideration of advantages which were promised them by the United States. These of course were overruled by the majority, who expressed the utmost indignation at the proposal, but the attempt to secure their active services was not the less made. We certainly have every reason to congratulate ourselves on its failure."

"This certainly partakes of the *argumentum ad hominem*," said the Major, good humouredly; "I do confess, I am aware, that since the idea of war against England was first entertained, great efforts have been made to attach the Indians to our interests; and in all probability had any other man than Tecumseh presided over their destinies, our Government would have been successful. I however, for one, am no abvocate for their employment on either side, for it must be admitted they are a terrible and a cruel enemy, sparing neither age nor sex."

"Again, Major," returned the General, "do we shield ourselves under our former plea—that, as an assailed party, we have a right to avail ourselves of whatever means of

*This certainly was the feeling in 1812.

defence are within our reach. One of two things—either we must retain the Indians, who are bound to us in one common interest, or we must, by discarding them, quietly surrender the Canadas to your armies. Few will be Quixotic enough to hesitate as to which of the alternatives we should adopt. If the people of the United States condemn us for employing the Indians, they are wrong. They should rather censure their own Government, either for declaring a war which subjects its inhabitants to these evils, or for having so long pursued a course of aggression towards the former, as to have precluded the means of securing their neutrality. But there is another powerful consideration which should have its due weight, I will not say in justifying our conduct, (that needs no justification,) but in quieting your apprehensions. As I have before remarked, had we been the first to enter on this war, sending forth into your settlements a ruthless enemy to lay waste and massacre wherever they passed, no time could have washed away the recollection of the atrocity; but we take our stand on high ground. We war not on your possessions; we merely await you on the defensive, and it must be borne in mind that, if those very people whose employment you deprecate are not let loose upon the Canadas in a career of unchecked spoliation, it is only because your Government has failed in the attempt to blind them to a sense of their numerous wrongs."

"No reasoning can be more candid, General," returned Major Montgomerie; "and far be it from me wholly to deny the justice of your observation. My own private impressions tend less to impugn your policy than to deplore the necessity for the services of such an ally: for, however, it may be sought on the part of the British Government, (and I certainly do differ from the majority of my countrymen in this instance, by believing it *will* impose every possible check to unnecessary cruelty,) however, I repeat, it may be sought to confine the Indians to defensive operations, their predatory habits will but too often lead them to the outskirts of our defenceless settlements, and then who shall restrain them from imbruing their hands in the blood of the young and the adult —the resisting and the helpless."

"If we should be accused of neglecting the means of preventing unnecessary cruelty," observed Colonel D'Egville, "the people of the United States will do us infinite wrong. This very circumstance has been foreseen and provided against. Without the power to prevent the Indians from entering upon these expeditions, we have at least done all that experience and a thorough knowledge of their character admits, to restrain their vengeance, by the promise of head money. It has been made generally known to them that every prisoner that is brought in and delivered up, shall entitle the captor to a certain sum. This promise, I have no doubt, will have the effect, not only of saving the lives of those who are attacked in their settlements, but also of checking any disposition to unnecessary outrage in the hour of conflict."

"The idea is one certainly reflecting credit on the humanity of the British authorities," returned Major Montgomerie; "but I confess I doubt its efficacy. We all know the nature of an Indian too well to hope that in the career of his vengeance, or the full flush of victory, he will waive his war trophy in consideration of a few dollars. The scalp he may bring, but seldom a living head with it."

"It is, I fear, the horrid estimation in which the scalp is held, that too frequently whets the blades of these people," observed the Commodore. "Were it not considered a trophy, more lives would be spared; but an Indian, from all I can understand, takes greater pride in exhibiting the scalp of a slain enemy, than a knight of ancient times did in displaying in his helmet, the glove that had been bestowed on him as a mark of favor by his lady-love."

"After all," said the General, necessary as it is to discourage it by every possible mark of our disapprobation, I do not (*entre nous*) see, in the mere act of scalping, half the horrors usually attached to the practice. The motive must be considered. It is not the mere desire to inflict wanton torture, that influences the warrior, but an anxiety to possess himself of that which gives undisputable evidence of his courage and success in war. The prejudice of Europeans is strong against the custom however, and we look upon it in a light very different, I am sure, from that in which is is viewed by the Indians themselves. The burnings of prisoners, which were practised many years ago, no longer continue; and the infliction of the torture has passed away, so that, after all, Indian cruelty does not exceed that which is practised even at this day in Europe, and by a nation bearing high rank among the Catholic powers of Europe. I have numerous letters, recently received from officers of my acquaintance now serving in Spain, all of which agree in stating that the mutilations perpetrated by the Guerilla bands, on the bodies of such of the unfortunate French detachments as they succeed in overpowering, far exceed any thing imputed to the Indians of America; and, as several of these letters are from individuals who joined the Peninsular Army from this country, in which they had passed many years, the statement may be relied on as coming from men who have had more than hearsay knowledge of both parties."

"Whatever the abhorrence in which scalping may be held by the people of the northern and eastern states," observed Colonel D'Egville, "it is notorious that the example of the Indians is followed by those of the western. The backwoodsman of the new States, and the Kentuckians particularly, almost invariably scalp the Indians they have slain in battle. Am I not right, Major Montgomerie?"

"Perfectly, Colonel—but then the Kentuckians," he added smiling, "are you know in some degree a separate race. They are scarcely looked upon as appertaining to the great American family. Half horse, half alligator, as they are pleased to term themselves, their roving mode of life and wild pursuits, are little removed from those of the native Indian, who scarcely inspires more curiosity among the civilized portion of the Union, than a genuine Keutuckian."

"Yet, if we may credit the accounts of our Indian spies," remarked the General, "the army to which I have alluded, as having marched forward to Detroit, is composed chiefly of those backwoodsmen."

"In which case," observed the Commodore, "it will only be savage pitted against savage after all, therefore, the exchange of a few scalps can prove but an indifferent source of national umbrage. Not, however, be it understood, that I advocate the practice."

Here a tall, fine looking black, wearing the livery of Colonel D'Egville, entering to announce that coffee was waiting for them in an adjoining room—the party rose and retired to the ladies.

CHAPTER VII.

Our readers doubtless bear in mind the spot called Elliott's Point, at the western extremity of Lake Erie, to which we have already introduced him. At a considerable distance beyond that again, (its intermediate shores washed by the silver waves of the Erie,) stretches a second, called also, from the name of its proprietor, Hartley's Point. Between these two necks, are three or four farms; one of which and adjoining Hartley's, was, at the period of which we treat, occupied by an individual of whom, unfortunately for the interests of Canada, too many of the species had been suffered to take root within her soil. For many years previous to the war, adventurers from the United States, chiefly men of desperate fortunes, and even more desperate characters, had, through a mistaken policy, been suffered to occupy the more valuable portion of the country. Upper Canada, in particular, was infested by these people, all of whom, even while taking the customary oath of allegiance to the crown, brought with them, and openly professed, all the partialities of American citizens. By the Canadians and their descendants, French and English, they were evidently looked upon with an eye of distrust, for, independently of the fact of their having been suffered to appropriate, during pleasure, many valuable tracts of land, they had experienced no inconsiderable partiality on the part of the Government. Those who believe in the possibility of attaching a renegade to the soil of his adoption and converting him into a serviceable defender of that soil in a moment of need, commit a great error in politics. The shrewd Canadians knew them better. They complained with bitterness, that at the first appearance of a war, they would hold their oaths of fealty as naught, or that if they did remain, it would only be with a view to embarrass the province with their presence, and secretly to serve the cause of their native country. The event proved that they knew their men. Scarcely had the American declaration of war gone forth, when numbers of these people, availing themselves of their near contiguity, abandoned their homes, and embarking in boats all their disposable property, easily succeeded, under cover of the night, in gaining the opposite coast. Not satisfied however with their double treason, they, in the true spirit of the dog-in the manger, seemed resolved others should not enjoy that which was no longer available to themselves, and the dawn that succeeded the night of their departure, more than once broke on scenes of spoliation of their several possessions, which it required one to know these desperate people well, to credit as being the work of their own hands. Melancholy as it was, however, to reflect that the spirit of conciliation had been thus repaid, the country had reason to rejoice in their flight; for, having thus declared themselves, there was nothing now, beyond their open hostility, to apprehend. Not so with the few who remained. Alike distrusted with those who had taken a more decided part, it was impossible to bring any charge home to them, on which to found a plea for compelling them to quit the country, in imitation of the example of their fellows. They had taken the oaths of allegiance to England—and, although ninety-nine had deliberately violated these, there was no legal cause for driving forth the hundredth, who still kept the "sound of promise to the ear," however he might break it to the hope. Not that, on this account, the hundredth was held to be one whit more honourable or loyal. It was felt and known, as though it had been written in characters of fire upon his brow, that if he did not follow in the steps of his predecessors, it was because his interests, not his inclination, induced his pursuing an apparently opposite course. It is true, those who remained were few in number; but scattered, as they were, over various isolated parts of the country, this only rendered them greater objects of suspicion. If the enemy became apprised of any of our movements, for the successful termination of which it was necessary they should be kept in ignorance, it was at once taken for granted their information had been derived from the traitors Canada had so long nourished in her bosom; and as several of them were in the pratice of absenting themselves for days in their boats, under the plea of duck-shooting, or some other equally plausible pretence, nothing was more easy of accomplishment. Under these circumstances of doubt, the general secession of the Yankees, as they were termed, which had first been regarded as a calamity, was now looked upon as a blessing; and if regret eventually lingered in the minds even of those who had been most forward to promote their introduction into the country, it arose, not because the many had departed, but because the few remained. That they were traitors, all believed; but, although narrowly watched, in no one instance could their treason be traced, much less established. In the course of time however they committed themselves in some one way or other, and then of necessity their only resource was to flee, as their companions had fled before them, until ultimately few of their number were left. If Canada has reason to feel happy in the late war, inasmuch as that war offered a means of proving her devoted attachment to the Mother Country, she has no less reason to rejoice in it, as having been the indirect means of purging her unrepublican soil of a set of hollow hearted persons, who occupied the place and enjoyed all the advantages of loyal men. Should she, failing to profit by the experience of the past, again tolerate the introduction of citizens of the United States into her flourishing provinces, when there are so many deserving families anxious to emigrate to her from the Mother Country; then will she merit all the evils which can attach, in a state of warfare, to a people diametrically opposed in their interests, their principles, their habits, and their attachments.

An individual of this description had his residence near Hartley's Point. Unlike those however whose dwellings rose at a distance, few and far between, hemmed in by the fruits of prosperous agriculture, he appeared to have paid but little attention to the cultivation of a soil, which in every part was of exceeding fertility. A rude log hut, situated in a clearing of the forest, the imperfect work of lazy labour, was his only habitation, and here he had for years resided without its being known how he contrived to procure the necessary means of subsistence; yet, in defiance of the apparent absence of all resources, it was subject of general remark, that he not only never wanted money, but had been enabled to bestow something like an education on a son, who had, at the epoch opened by our narrative, been absent from him upwards of five years. From his frequent voyages, and the direction his canoe was seen to take, it was inferred by his immediate neighbours, that he dealt in contraband, procuring various articles on the American coast, which he subsequently disposed of in the small town of Amherstburgh (one of the principal English posts) among certain subjects domiciliated there, who were suspected of no very scrupulous desire to benefit the revenue of the country they called their own. So well and so wisely, however, did he cover his operations, that he had always contrived to elude detection —and, although suspicion attached to his conduct, in no instance had he openly committed himself. The man himself, tall, stout and of a forbidding look, was of a fearless and resolute character, and if he resorted to cunning, it was because cunning alone could serve his purpose in a country, the laws of which were not openly to be defied.

For a series of years after his arrival, he had contrived to evade taking the customary oaths of allegiance; but this, eventually awakening the suspicions of the magistracy, brought him more immediately under their surveillance, when, year after year, he was compelled to a renewal of the oath, for the imposition of which, it was thought, he owed more than one of those magistrates a grudge. On the breaking out of the war, he still remained in undisturbed possession of his rude dwelling, watched as well as circumstances would permit, it is true, but not so narrowly as to be traced in his various nocturnal excursions by water. Nothing could be conceived more uncouth in manner and appearance than this man—nothing more villainous than the expression of his eye. No one knew from what particular point of the United States he had come, and whether Yankee or Kentuckian, it would have puzzled one of that race of beings, so proverbial for acumen—a Philadelphia lawyer—to have determined; for so completely did he unite the boasting language of the latter with the wary caution and sly cunning of the former, that he appeared a compound of both. The general opinion, however, seemed rather, to incline in favor of the presumption that he was less Kentuckian than Yankee.

The day following that of the capture of the American detachment was just beginning to dawn, as two individuals appeared on the skirt of the rude clearing in which the hut of the man we have just described, had been erected. The persons of both these, wrapt in blue military cloaks, reposed upon the dark foliage in a manner to enable them to observe, without being themselves seen, all that passed within the clearing, from the log hut to the sand of the lake shore. There had been an indication by one of these of a design to step forth from his concealment into the clearing, and advance boldly toward the house; but this had been checked by his companion, who, laying his hand upon his shoulder, arrested the movement, pointing out at the same time, the leisurely but cautious advance of two men from the hut towards the shore, on which lay a canoe half drawn up on the sands. Each, on issuing from the hut, had deposited a rifle against the rude exterior of the dwelling, the better to enable them to convey a light mast, sail, paddles, several blankets, and a common corn-bag, apparently containing provisions, with which they proceeded towards the canoe.

"So," said the taller of the first party, in a whisper, "there is that d——d rascal Desborough setting out on one of his contraband excursions. He seems to have a long absence in view, if we may judge from the contents of his provision sack."

"Hist," rejoined his companion, "there is more here than meets the eye. In the first instance, remove the pistols from the case, and be prepared to afford me assistance, should I require it."

"What the devil are you going to do, and what do you mean?" asked the first speaker, following however the hint that had been given him, and removing a pair of duelling pistols from their mahogany case.

While he was in the act of doing this, his companion had, without replying, quitted his side, and cautiously and noiselessly advanced to the hut. In the course of a few minutes he again appeared at the point whence he had started, grasping in either hand the rifles so recently deposited there.

"Well, what is the meaning of this feat? you do not intend, Yankee fashion, to exchange a long shot with poor Molineux, I hope—if so, my dear fellow, I cry off, for upon my honor, I cannot engage in any thing that is not strictly orthodox."

He, thus addressed, could scarcely restrain a laugh at the serious tone in which his companion expressed himself, as if he verily believed he had that object in view.

"Would you not like," he asked, "to be in some degree instrumental in banishing wholly from the country, a man whom we all suspect of treason, but are compelled to tolerate from inability to prove his guilt—this same notorious Desborough?"

"Now that you no longer speak and act in parables, I can understand you. Of course I should, but what proof of his treason are we to discover in the mere fact of his departing on what he may choose to call a hunting excursion? even admitting he is speculating in the contraband, *that* cannot banish him; and if it could, we could never descend to become informers."

"Nothing of the kind is required of us—his treason will soon unfold itself, and that in a manner to demand, as an imperative duty, that we secure the traitor. For this have I removed the rifles which may, in a moment of desperation, be turned at backwoodsman's odds against our pistols. Let us steal gently towards the beach, and then you shall satisfy yourself; but I had nearly forgotten—suppose the other party should arrive?"

"Then they must in their turn wait for us. They have already exceeded their time ten minutes."

"Look," exclaimed his companion, as he slightly grasped the shoulder on which his hand had rested, "he is returning for the rifles."

Only one of the two men now retrod his steps from the beach towards the hut, but with a more hurried action than before. As he passed where the friends still lingered, he gave a start of surprise, apparently produced by the absence of the rifles. A moment's reflection seeming to satisfy him it was possible his memory had failed him, and that they had been left within the building, he hurried forward to assure himself. After a few moments of apparently ineffectual search, he again made his appearance, making the circuit of the hut to discover his lost weapons, but in vain; when, in the fierceness of his anger, he cried aloud, with a bitterness that gave earnest of sincerity.

"By Gosh, I wish I had the curst British rascal who played me this trick, on t'other shore—if I wouldn't tuck my knife into his b——y gizzard, then is my name not Jeremiah Desborough. What the h—l's to be done now?"

Taking advantage of his entrance into the hut, the two individuals, first described, had stolen cautiously under cover of the forest, until they arrived at its termination, within about twenty yards of the shore, where however there was no outward or visible sign of the individual who had been Desborough's companion. In the bows of the canoe were piled the blankets, and in the centre was deposited the provision bag that had formed a portion of their mutual load. The mast had not been hoisted, but lay extended along the hull, its sail loosened and partially covering the before mentioned article of freightage. The bow half of the canoe pressed the beach, the other lay sunk in the water, apparently in the manner in which it had first approached the land.

Still uttering curses, but in a more subdued tone, against "the fellor who had stolen his small bores," the angry Desborough retraced his steps to the canoe. More than once he looked back to see if he could discover any traces of the purloiner, until at length his countenance seemed to assume an expression of deeper cause for concern, than even the loss of his weapons.

"Ha, I expect some d——d spy has been on the look out—if so, I must cut and run I calculate purty soon."

This apprehension was expressed as he arrived opposite the point where the forest terminated. A slight rustling among the underwood reduced that apprehension to certainty. He grasped the handle of his huge knife that was thrust into the girdle around his loins, and rivetting his gaze on the point whence the sound had proceeded, retreated in that attitude. Another and more distinct crush of underwood, and he stood still with surprise, on finding himself face to face with two officers of the garrison.

"We have alarmed you, Desborough," said the younger, as they both advanced leisurely to the beach. "Do you apprehend danger from our presence?"

A keen searching glance flashed from the ferocious eye of the Yankee. It was but momentary. Quitting his firm grasp of the knife, he suffered his limbs to relax their tension, and aiming at carelessness, observed, with a smile, that was tenfold more hideous from its being forced:

"Well now, I guess, who would have expected to see two officers so fur away from the fort at this early hour of the mornin'."

"Ah," said the taller of the two, availing himself of the first opening to a pun which had been afforded, "we are merely out on a *shooting* excursion."

Desborough gazed doubtingly on the speaker—"Strange sort of a dress that for shootin' I guess—them cloaks must be a great tanglement in the bushes."

"They serve to keep our *arms* warm," continued Middlemore, perpetrating another of his execrables.

"To keep your arms warm! well sure-*ly*, if that arn't droll. It may be some use to keep the primins dry, I reckon; but I can't see the good of keepin' the fowlin' pieces warm. Have you met any game yet, officers. I expect as how I can pint you out a purty spry place for pattridges and sich like."

"Thank you, my good fellow; but we have appointed to meet our *game* here."

The dry manner in which this was observed had a visible effect on the settler. He glanced an eye of suspicion around, to see if others than the two officers were in view, and it was not without effort that he assumed an air of unconcern, as he replied:

"Well I expect I have been many a long year a hunter, as well as other things, and yet, dang me if I ever calculated the game would come to me. It always costs me a purty good chase in the woods."

"How the fellow *beats* about the *bush*, to find what *game* we are driving at," observed Middlemore, in an under tone, to his companion.

"Let the Yankee alone for that," returned he, whom our readers have doubtless recognized for Henry Grantham; "I will match his cunning against your punning any day."

"The truth is, he is *fishing* to discover our motive for being here, and to find out if we are in any way connected with the disappearance of his rifles."

During this conversation *apart*, the Yankee had carelessly approached his canoe, and was affecting to make some alteration in the disposition of the sail. The officers, the younger especially, keeping a sharp look out upon his movements, followed at some little distance, until they, at length, stood on the extreme verge of the sands. Their near approach seemed to render Desborough impatient:

"I expect, officers," he said, with a hastiness that, at any other moment, would have called down immediate reproof, if not chastisement, "you will only be losin' time here for nothin'—About a mile beyond Hartley's there'll be plenty of pattridges at this hour, and I am jist goin' to start myself for a little shootin' in the Sandusky river."

"Then, I presume," said Grantham, with a smile, "you are well provided with silver bullets, Desborough—for, in the hurry of departure, you seem likely to forget the only medium through which leaden ones can be made available: not a rifle or a shot-gun do I see."

The Yankee fixed his eye for a moment, with a penetrating expression, on the youth, as if he would have sought a meaning deeper than the words implied. His reading seemed to satisfy him that all was right.

"What," he observed, with a leer, half cunning half insolent, "if I have hid my rifle near the Sandusky swamp, the last time I hunted there."

"In that case," observed the laughing Middlemore, to whom the opportunity was irresistible, "you are going out on a *wild goose chase*, indeed. Your prospects of a good hunt, as you call it, cannot be said to *be sure as a gun*, for in regard to the latter, you may depend some one has discovered and *rifled* it before this."

"You seem to have laid in a store of provisions for this trip, Desborough," remarked Henry Grantham; "how long do you purpose being absent?"

"I guess three or four days," was the sullen reply.

"Three or four days! why your bag contains," and the

officer partly raised a corner of the sail, "provisions for a week, or, at least, for *two* for half that period."

The manner in which the *two* was emphasised did not escape the attention of the settler. He was visibly disconcerted, nor was he at all reassured when the younger officer proceeded:

"By the bye, Desborough, we saw you leave the hut with a companion—what has become of him?"

The Yankee, who had now recovered his self-possession, met the question without the slightest show of hesitation:

"I expect you mean, young man," he said, with insufferable insolence, "a help as I had from Hartley's farm, to assist gittin' down the things. He took home along shore when I went back to the hut for the small bores."

"Oh ho, sir! the rifles are not then concealed near the Sandusky swamp, I find."

For once, the wily settler felt his cunning had over-reached itself. In the first fury of his subdued rage, he muttered something amounting to a desire that he could produce them at that moment, as he would well know where to lodge the bullets—but, recovering himself, he said aloud:

"The rale fact is, I've a long gun hid, as I said, near the swamp, but my small bore I always carry with me—only think, jist as I and Hartley's help left the hut, I pit my rifle against the outside wall, not being able to carry it down with the other things, and when I went back a minute or two ater, drot me if some tarnation rascal hadn't stole it."

"And if you had the British rascal on t'other shore, you wouldn't be long in tucking a knife into his gizzard, would you?" asked Middlemore, in a nearly verbatim repetition of the horrid oath originally uttered by Desborough, "I see nothing to warrant our interfering with him," he continued in an under tone to his companion.

Not a little surprised to hear his words repeated, the Yankee lost somewhat of his confidence as he replied, "well now sure-*ly*, you officers didn't think nothin' o' that—I expect I was in a mighty rage to find my small bore gone, and I did curse a little hearty, to be sure."

"The small bore multiplied in your absence," observed Grantham; "when I looked at the hut there were two."

"Then maybe you can tell who was the particular d——d rascal that stole them," said the settler eagerly.

Middlemore laughed heartily at his companion, who observed:

"The particular d——d rascal who removed, not stole them thence, stands before you."

Again the Yankee looked disconcerted. After a moment's hesitation, he continued, with a forced grin, that gave an atrocious expression to his whole countenance:

"Well now, you officers are playing a purty considerable spry trick--it's a good lark, I calculate—but you know, as the saying is, enough's as good as a feast. Do tell me, Mr. Grantham," and his discordant voice became more offensive in its effort at a tone of entreaty, "do tell me where you've hid my small bore—you little think," he concluded, with an emphasis then unnoticed by the officers, but subsequently remembered to have been perfectly ferocious, "what reason I have to vally it."

"We never descend to larks of the kind," coolly observed Grantham; "but as you say you value your rifle, it shall be restored to you on one condition."

"And what may that be?" asked the settler, somewhat startled at the serious manner of the officer.

"That you show us what your canoe is freighted with. Here in the bows I mean."

"Why," rejoined the Yankee quickly, but as if without design, intercepting the officers' nearer approach, "that bag, I calculate, contains my provisions, and these here blankets that you see, peepin' like from under the sail, are what I makes my bed of while out huntin'."

"And are you quite certain there is nothing under those blankets?—nay do not protest—you cannot answer for what may have occurred while your back was turned, on your way to the hut for the rifle."

"By hell," exclaimed the settler, blusteringly, "were any man to tell me, Jeremiah Desborough, there was any thin' beside them blankets in the canoe, I would lick him into a jelly, even though he could whip his own weight in wild cats."

"So is it? Now then, Jeremiah Desborough, although I have never yet tried to whip my own weight in wild cats, I tell you there is something more than those blankets; and what is more, I insist upon seeing what that something is."

The settler stood confounded. His eye rolled rapidly from one to the other of the officers at the boldness and determination of this language. Singly, he could have crushed Henry Grantham in his gripe, even as one of the bears of the forest, near the outskirt of which they stood; but there were two, and while attacking the one, he was sure of being assailed by the other; nay, what was worse, the neighborhood might be alarmed. Moreover, although they had kept their cloaks carefully wrapped around their persons, there could be little doubt that both officers were armed, not, as they had originally given him to understand, with fowling pieces, but with (at the present close quarters at least) far more efficient weapons—pistols. He was relieved from his embarrassment by Middlemore exclaiming:

"Nay, do not press the poor devil, Grantham; I dare say the story of his hunting is all a hum, and that the fact is, he is merely going to earn an honest penny in one of his free commercial speculations—a little contraband," pointing with his finger to the bows, "is it not Desborough?"

"Why now, officer," said the Yankee, rapidly assuming a dogged air, as if ashamed of the discovery that had been so acutely made, "I expect you won't hurt a poor fellor for doin' a little in this way. Drot me, these are hard times, and this here war jist beginnin', quite pits one to one's shifts."

"This might do, Desborough, were your present freight

an arrival instead of a departure, but we all know that contraband is imported, not exported."

"Mighty cute you are, I guess," replied the settler, warily, with something like the savage grin of the wild cat, to which he had so recently alluded; "but I expect it would be none so strange to have packed up a few dried hog skins to stow away the goods I am goin' for."

"I should like to try the effect of a bullet among the skins," said Grantham, leisurly drawing forth and cocking a pistol, after having whispered something in the ear of his companion.

"Nay, officer," said Desborough, now for the first time manifesting serious alarm—"you sure-*ly* dont mean to bore a hole through them innocent skins?"

"True," said Middlemore, imitating, "if he fires, the hole will be something more than *skin* deep I reckon—these pistols, to my knowledge, send a bullet through a two inch plank at twenty paces."

As Middlemore thus expressed himself, both he and Grantham saw, or fancied they saw, the blankets slightly agitated.

"Good place for *a hide* that," said the former, addressing his pun to the Yankee, on whom however it was totally lost, "show us those said skins, my good fellow, and if we find they are not filled with any thing it would be treason in a professed British subject to export thus clandestinely, we promise that you shall depart without further hindrance."

"Indeed, officer," muttered the settler, sullenly and doggedly, "I shan't do no sich thing. You don't belong to the custom-house I reckon, and so I wish you a good day, for I have a considerable long course to run, and must be movin'." Then, seizing the paddles that were lying on the sand, he prepared to shove the canoe from the beach.

"Not at least before I have sent a bullet, to ascertain the true quality of your skins," said Grantham, levelling his pistol.

"Sure-*ly*," said Desborough, as he turned and drew himself to the full height of his bony and muscular figure, while his eye measured the officer from head to foot, with a look of concentrated but suppressed fury, "you wouldn't *dare* to do this—you wouldn't dare to fire into my canoe—besides, consider," he said, in a tone somewhat deprecating, "your bullet may go through her, and you would hardly do a fellor the injury to make him lose the chance of a good cargo."

"Then why provoke such a disaster, by refusing to show us what is beneath those blankets?"

"Because it's my pleasure to do so," fiercely retorted the other, "and I won't show them to no man."

"Then is it my pleasure to fire," said Grantham. "The injury be on your own head, Desborough—one—two—."

At that moment the sail was violently agitated—something struggling for freedom, cast the blankets on one side, and presently the figure of a man stood upright in the bows of the canoe, and gazed around him with an air of stupid astonishment.

"What," exclaimed Middlemore, retreating back a pace or two, in unfeigned surprise; "has that pistol started up, like the ghost in Hamlet, Ensign Paul, Emilius, Theophilus, Arnoldi, of the United States Michigan Militia—a prisoner on his parole of honor? and yet attempting a clandestine departure from the country—how is this?"

"Not this merely," exclaimed Grantham, "but a traitor to his country, and a deserter from our service. This fellow," he pursued, in answer to an inquring look of his companion, "is a scoundrel, who deserted three years since from the regiment you relieved—I recognized him yesterday on his landing, as my brother Gerald, who proposed making his report to the General this morning, had done before. Let us secure both, Middlemore, for, thank Heaven we have been enabled to detect the traitor at last, in that which will excuse his final expulsion from the soil, even if no worse befall him. I have only tampered with him thus long to render his conviction more complete."

"Secure me! secure Jeremiah Desborough?" exclaimed the settler, with rage manifest in the clenching of his teeth and the tension of every muscle of his iron frame, "and that for jist tryin' to save a countryman—well, we'll see who'll have the best of it."

Before Grantham could anticipate the movement, the active and powerful Desborough had closed with him in a manner to prevent his making use of his pistol, had he even so desired. In the next instant it was wrested from him, and thrown far from the spot on which he struggled with his adversary, but at fearful odds, against himself. Henry Grantham, although well and actively made, was of slight proportion, and yet in boyhood. Desborough, on the contrary, was in the full force of a vigorous manhood. A struggle, hand to hand, between two combatants so disproportioned, could not, consequently, be long doubtful as to its issue. No sooner had the formidable Yankee closed with his enemy, than, pressing the knuckles of his iron hand which met round the body of the officer, with violence against his spine, he threw him backwards with force upon the sands. Grasping his victim with one hand as he lay upon him, he seemed, as Grantham afterwards declared, to be groping for his knife with the other. The settler was evidently anxious to despatch one enemy, in order that he might fly to the assistance of his son, for it was he whom Middlemore, with a powerful effort, had dragged from the canoe to the beach. While his right hand was still groping for the knife—an object which the powerful resistance of the yet unsubdued, though prostrate, officer rendered somewhat difficult of attainment—the report of a pistol was heard, fired evidently by one of the other combatants. Immediately the settler looked up to see who was the triumphant party. Neither had fallen, and Middlemore, if any thing, had the advantage of his enemy; but to his infinite dismay, Desborough beheld a horseman, evidently attracted by the report of the pistol, urging his course with the rapidity of lightning, along the firm sands, and advancing with cries and vehement gesticulations to the rescue.

Springing with the quickness of thought from his victim, the settler was in the next moment at the side of Middlemore. Seizing him from behind by the arm within his nervous grasp, he pressed the latter with such prodigious force as to cause him to relinquish, by a convulsive movement, the firm hold he had hitherto kept of his adversary.

"In, boy, to the canoe for your life," he exclaimed hurriedly, as following up his advantage, he spun the officer round, and sent him tottering to the spot were Grantham lay, still stupified and half throttled. The next instant saw him heaving the canoe from the shore, with all the exertion called for by his desperate situation. And all this was done so rapidly, in so much less time than it will take our readers to trace it, that before the horseman, so opportunely arriving, had reached the spot, the canoe, with its inmates, had pushed from the shore.

Without pausing to consider the rashness and apparent impracticability of his undertaking, the strange horseman, checking his rein, and burying the rowels of his spurs deep into the flanks of his steed, sent him bounding and plunging into the lake, in pursuit of the fugitives.

He himself evinced every symptom of one in a state of intoxication. Brandishing a stout cudgel over his head, and pealing forth shouts of defiance, he rolled from side to side on his spirited charger, like some labouring bark careening to the violence of the winds, but ever, like that bark, regaining an equilibrium that was never thoroughly lost. Shallow as the lake was at this point for a considerable distance, it was long before the noble animal lost its footing, and thus had its rider been enabled to arrive within a few paces of the canoe, at the very moment when the increasing depth of the water, in compelling the horse to the less expeditious process of swimming, gave a proportionate advantage to the pursued.

No sooner, however, did the Centaur-like rider find that he was losing ground, than, again darting his spurs into the flanks of his charger, he made every effort to reach the canoe, Maddened by the pain, the snorting beast half rose upon the calm element, like some monster of the deep, and, making two or three desperate plunges with his fore feet, succeeded in reaching the stern. Then commenced a short but extraordinary conflict. Bearing up his horse as he swam, with the bridle in his teeth, the bold rider threw his left hand upon the stern of the vessel, and brandishing his cudgel in the right, seemed to provoke both parties to the combat. Desborough, who had risen from the stern at his approach, stood upright in the centre, his companion still paddling at the bows; and between these two a singular contest now ensued. Armed with the formidable knife which he had about his person, the settler made the most desperate and infuriated efforts to reach his assailant; but in so masterly a manner did his adversary use his simple weapon, that every attempt was foiled, and more than once did the hard iron-wood descend upon his shoulders, in a manner to be heard from the shore. Once or twice the settler stooped to evade some falling blow, and, rushing forward, sought to sever the hand which still retained its hold of the stern; but, with an activity remarkable in so old a man as his assailant, for he was upwards of sixty years of age, the hand was removed—and the settler, defeated in his object, was amply repaid for his attempt, by a severe collision of his bones with the cudgel. At length, apparently enjoined by his companion, the younger removed his paddle, and, standing up also in the canoe, aimed a blow with its knobbed handle at the head of the horse, at a moment when his rider was fully engaged with Desborough. The quick-sighted old man saw the action, and, as the paddle descended, an upward stroke from his own heavy weapon sent it flying in fragments in the air, while a rapid and returning blow fell upon the head of the paddler, and prostrated him at length in the canoe. The opportunity afforded by this diversion, momentary as it was, was not lost upon Desborough. The horseman, who, in his impatience to avenge the injury offered to the animal, which seemed to form a part of himself, had utterly forgotten the peril of his hand ; and before he could return from the double blow that had been so skilfully wielded, to his first enemy, the knife of the latter had penetrated his hand, which, thus rendered powerless now relinquished its grasp. Desborough, whose object—desperate character as he usually was—seemed now rather to fly than to fight, availed himself of this advantage to hasten to the bows of the canoe, where, striding across the body of his insensible companion, he, with a few vigorous strokes of the remaining paddle, urged the lagging bark rapidly a-head. In no way intimidated by his disaster, the courageous old man, again brandishing his cudgel, and vociferating taunts of defiance, would have continued the pursuit, but panting as he was, not only with the exertion he had made, but under the weight of his impatient rider, in an element in which he was supported merely by his own buoyancy, the strength and spirit of the animal began now perceptibly to fail him, and he turned, despite of every effort to prevent him, towards the shore. It was fortunate for the former that there were no arms in the canoe, or neither he nor the horse would, in all probability, have returned alive ; such was the opinion, at least, pronounced by those who were witnesses of the strange scene, and who remarked the infuriated but impotent gestures of Desborough, as the old man, having once more gotten his steed into depth, slowly pursued his course towards the shore, but with the same wild brandishing of his enormous cudgel, and the same rocking from side to side, until his body was often at right angles with that of his jaded but sure-footed beast. As he is, however, a character meriting rather more than the casual notice we have bestowed, we shall take the opportunity while he is hastening to the discomfited officers on the beach, more particularly to describe him.

CHAPTER VIII.

NEARLY midway between Elliott's and Hartley's points, both of which are remarkable for the low and sandy nature of the soil, the land, rising gradually towards the centre, assumes a more healthy and arable aspect; and, on its highest elevation, stood a snug, well cultivated, property, called, at the period of which we write, Gattrie's farm. From this height, crowned on its extreme summit by a neat and commodious farm-house, the far reaching sands, forming the points above named, are distinctly visible. Immediately in the rear, and commencing beyond the orchard which surrounded the house, stretched forestward, and to a considerable distance, a tract of rich and cultivated soil, separated into strips by zig-zag enclosures, and offering to the eye of the traveller, in appropriate season, the several species of American produce, such as Indian corn, buck wheat, &c. with here and there a few patches of indifferent tobacco. Thus far of the property, a more minute description of which is unimportant. The proprietors of this neat little place were a father and son, to the latter of whom was consigned, for reasons which will appear presently, the sole management of the farm. Of him we will merely say, that, at the period of which we treat, he was a fine, strapping, dark curly-haired, white-teethed, red-lipped, broad-shouldered, and altogether comely and gentle tempered youth, of about twenty, who had, although unconsciously, monopolized the affections of almost every well favoured maiden of his class, for miles around him—advantages of nature, from which had resulted a union with one of the prettiest of the fair competitors for connubial happiness.

The father we may not dismiss so hastily. He was—but, before attempting the portraiture of his character, we will, to the best of our ability, sketch his person.

Let the reader fancy an old man of about sixty, possessed of that comfortable amplitude of person which is the result rather of a mind at peace with itself, and undisturbed by worldly care, than of any marked indulgence in indolent habits. Let him next invest this comfortable person in a sort of Oxford gray, coarse capote, or frock, of capacious size, tied closely round the waist with one of those parti-colored worsted sashes, we have, on a former occasion described as peculiar to the bourgeois settlers of the country. Next, suffering his eye to descend on and admire the rotund and fleshy thigh, let it drop gradually to the stout and muscular legs, which he must invest in a pair of closely fitting leathern trowsers, the wide-seamed edges of which are slit into innumerable small strips, much after the fashion of the American Indian. When he has completed the survey of the lower extremities, to which he must not fail to subjoin a foot of proportionate dimensions, tightly moccasined, and, moreover, furnished with a pair of old English hunting spurs, the reader must then examine the head with which this heavy piece of animated machinery is surmounted. From beneath a coarse felt hat, garnished with an inch-wide band or ribbon, let him imagine he sees the yet vigorous grey hair, descending over a forehead not altogether wanting in a certain dignity of expression, and terminating in a beetling brow, silvered also with the frost of years, and shadowing a sharp, grey, intelligent eye, the vivacity of whose expression denotes its possessor to be far in advance, in spirit, even of his still active and powerful frame. With these must be connected a snub nose—a double chin, adorned with grisly honors, which are borne, like the fleece of the lamb, only occasionally to the shears of the shearer—and a small, and not unhandsome, mouth, at certain periods pursed into an expression of irresistible humour, but more frequently expressing a sense of lofty independence. The grisly neck, little more or less bared, as the season may demand—a kerchief loosely tied around the collar of a checked shirt—and a knotted cudgel in his hand,—and we think our sketch of Sampson Gattrie is complete.

Nor must the reader picture to himself this combination of animal properties, either standing, or lying, or walking, or sitting; but in a measure glued, Centaur-like, to the back of a noble stallion, vigorous, active, and of a dark chesnut color, with silver mane and tail. In the course of many years that Sampson had resided in the neighbourhood, no one could remember to have seen him stand, or lie, or walk, or sit, while away from his home, unless absolutely compelled. Both horse and rider seemed as though they could not exist while separated, and yet Silvertail (thus was the stallion named) was not more remarkable in sleekness of coat, soundness of carcase, and fleetness of pace, than his rider was in the characteristics of corpulency and joviality.

Sampson Gattrie had passed the greater part of his younger days in America. He had borne arms in the revolution, and was one of those faithful loyalists, who, preferring rather to abandon a soil which, after all, was one of adoption, than the flag under which they had been nurtured, had, at the termination of that contest, passed over into Canada. Having served in one of those irregular corps, several of which had been employed with the Indians, during the revolutionary contest, he had acquired much of the language of these latter, and to this knowledge was indebted for the situation of interpreter which he had for years enjoyed. Unhappily for himself, however, the salary attached to the office was sufficient to keep him in independence, and, to the idleness consequent on this, (for the duties of an interpreter were only occasional,) might have been attributed the rapid growth of a vice—an addiction to liquor—which unchecked indulgence had now ripened into positive disease.

Great was the terror that Sampson was wont to excite in

the good people of Amherstburg. With Silvertail at his speed, he would gallop into the town, brandishing his cudgel, and reeling from side to side, exhibiting at one moment the joyous character of a Silenus, at another, as we have already shown—that of an inebriated Centaur. Occasionally he would make his appearance, holding his sides convulsed with laughter, as he reeled and tottered in every direction, but without ever losing his equilibrium. At other times he would utter a loud shout, and, brandishing his cudgel, dart at full speed along the streets, as if he purposed singly to carry the town by (what Middlemore often facetiously called) a *coup de main*. At these moments were to be seen mothers rushing into the street to look for, and hurry away, their loitering offspring, while even adults were glad to hasten their movements, in order to escape collision with the formidable Sampson; not that either apprehended the slightest act of personal violence from the old man, for he was harmless of evil as a child, but because they feared the polished hoofs of Silvertail, which shone amid the clouds of dust they raised as he passed, like rings of burnished silver. Even the very Indians, with whom the streets were at this period habitually crowded, were glad to hug the sides of the houses, while Sampson passed; and they who, on other occasions, would have deemed it in the highest degree derogatory to their dignity to have stepped aside at the approach of danger, or to have relaxed a muscle of their stern countenances, would then open a passage with a rapidity which in them was remarkable, and burst into loud laughter as they fled from side to side to make way for Sampson. Sometimes, on these occasions, the latter would suddenly check Silvertail, while in full career, and, in a voice that could be heard from almost every quarter of the little town, harangue them for half an hour together in their own language, and with an air of authority that was ludicrous to those who witnessed it—and must have been witnessed to be conceived. Occasionally a guttural "ugh" would be responded in mock approval of the speech, but more frequently a laugh, on the part of the more youthful of his red auditors, was the only notice taken. His lecture concluded, Sàmpson would again brandish his cudgel, and vociferate another shout; then betaking himself to the nearest store, he would urge Silvertail upon the footway, and with a tap of his rude cudgel against the door, summon whoever was within, to appear with a glass of his favorite beverage. And this would he repeat, until he had drained what he called his stirrup cup, at every shop in the place where the poisonous liquor was vended.

Were such a character to make his appearance in the Mother Country, endangering, to all perception, the lives of the Sovereign's liege subjects, he would, if in London, be hunted to death like a wild beast, by at least one half of the Metropolitan police; and, if in a provincial town, would be beset by a posse of constables. No one, however—not even the solitary constable of Amherstburg, ever ventured to interfere with Sampson Gattrie, who was in some degree a privileged character. Nay, strange as it may appear, notwithstanding his confirmed habit of inebriety, the old man stood high in the neighborhood, not only with simple but with gentle, for there were seasons when he evinced himself "a rational being," and there was a dignity of manner about him, which, added to his then quietude of demeanour, insensibly interested in his favor, those even who were most forward to condemn the vice to which he was invariably addicted. Not, be it understood, that in naming seasons of rationality, we mean seasons of positive abstemiousness; nor can this well be, seeing that Sampson never passed a day of strict sobriety during the last twenty years of his life. But, it might be said, that his three divisions of day—morning, noon and night—were characterized by three corresponding divisions of drunkenness—namely, drunk, drunker, and most drunk. It was, therefore, in the first stage of this graduated scale, that Sampson appeared in his most amiable and winning, because his least uproarious, mood. His libations commenced at early morn, and his inebriety became progressive to the close of the day. To one who could ride home at night, as he invariably did, after some twelve hours of hard and continued drinking, without rolling from his horse, it would not be difficult to enact the sober man in its earlier stages. As his intoxication was relative to himself, so was his sobriety in regard to others—and although, at mid-day, he might have swallowed sufficient to have caused another man to bite the dust, he looked and spoke, and acted, as if he had been a model of temperance. If he passed a lady in the street, or saw her at her window, Sampson Gattrie's hat was instantly removed from his venerable head, and his body inclined forward over his saddle-bow, with all the easy grace of a well-born gentleman, and one accustomed from infancy to pay deference to woman; nay, this at an hour when he had imbibed enough of his favorite liquor to have rendered most men insensible even to their presence. These habits of courtesy, extended moreover to the officers of the Garrison, and such others among the civilians as Sampson felt to be worthy of his notice. His tones of salutation, at these moments, were soft, his manner respectful, even graceful; and while there was nothing of the abashedness of the inferior, there was also no offensive familiarity, in the occasional conversations held by him with the different individuals, or groups, who surrounded and accosted him.

Such was Sampson Gattrie, in the first stage of his inebriety, no outward sign of which was visible. In the second, his perception became more obscured, his voice less distinct, his tones less gentle and insinuating, and occasionally the cudgel would rise in rapid flourish, while now and then a loud halloo would burst from lungs, which the oceans of whiskey they had imbibed had not yet, apparently, much affected. These were infallible indices of the more feverish stage, of which the gallopings of Silvertail—the vociferations of his master—the increased flourishing of the cudgel—the supposed danger of children—and the consequent alarm of mothers, together with the harangues to the Indian auditory, were the almost daily results.

There was one individual, however, in the town of Amherstburgh, of whom, despite his natural wilfulness of character, Sampson Gattrie stood much in awe, and that to such a degree, that if he chanced to encounter him in his mad progress, his presence had the effect of immediately quieting him. This gentleman was the father of the Granthams, who, although then filling a civil situation, had formerly been a field officer in the corps in which Sampson had served; and who had carried with him into private life, those qualities of stern excellence for which he had been remarkable as a soldier—qualities which had won to him the respect and affection, not only of the little community over which, in the capacity of its chief magistrate, he had presided, but also of the inhabitants of the country generally for many miles around. Temperate to an extreme himself, Major Grantham held the vice of drunkenness in deserved abhorrence, and so far from sharing the general toleration extended to the old man, whose originality (harmless as he ever was in his intoxication) often proved a motive for encouragement; he never failed, on encountering him, to bestow his censure in a manner that had an immediate and obvious effect on the culprit. If Sampson, from one end of the street, beheld Major Grantham approaching at the other, he was wont to turn abruptly away; but if perchance the magistrate came so unexpectedly upon him as to preclude the possibility of retreat, he appeared as one suddenly sobered, and would rein in his horse, fully prepared for the stern lecture which he was well aware would ensue.

It afforded no slight amusement to the townspeople, and particularly the young urchins, who usually looked up to Sampson with awe, to be witnesses of one of those rencontres. In a moment the shouting—galloping—rampaging cudgel-wielder was to be seen changed, as if by some magic power, into a being of almost child-like obedience, while he listened attentively and deferentially to the lecture of Major Grantham, whom he both feared and loved. On these occasions, he would hang his head upon his chest—confess his error—and promise solemnly to amend his course of life, although it must be needless to add that never was that promise heeded. Not unfrequently, after these lectures, when Major Grantham had left him, Sampson would turn his horse, and, with his arms still folded across his chest, suffer Silvertail to pursue his homeward course, while he himself, silent and thoughtful, and looking like a culprit taken in the fact, sat steadily in his saddle, without however venturing to turn his eye either to the right or to the left, as he passed through the crowd, who, with faces strongly expressive of mirth, marked their sense of the change which had been produced in the old interpreter. Those who had seen him thus, for the first time, might have supposed that a reformation in one so apparently touched would have ensued; but long experience had taught that, although a twinge of conscience, or more probably fear of, and respect for, the magistrate, might induce a momentary humiliation, all traces of cause and effect would have vanished with the coming dawn.

To the sterling public virtues he boasted, Sampson Gattrie united that of loyalty in no common degree. A more staunch adherent to the British Crown existed nowhere in the sovereign's dominions; and, such was his devotedness to "King George," that, albeit he could not in all probability have made the sacrifice of his love for whiskey, he would willingly have suffered his left arm to be severed from his body, had such proof of his attachment to the throne been required. Proportioned to his love for every thing British, arose, as a natural consequence, his dislike for every thing anti-British; and especially for those, who, under the guise of allegiance, had conducted themselves in a way to become objects of suspicion to the authorities. A near neighbour of Desborough, he had watched him as narrowly as his long indulged habits of intoxication would permit, and he had been the means of conveying to Major Grantham much of the information which had induced that uncompromising magistrate to seek the expulsion of the dangerous settler—an object which, however, had been defeated by the perjury of the unprincipled individual, in taking the customary oaths of allegiance. Since the death of Major Grantham, for whom, notwithstanding his numerous lectures, he had ever entertained that reverential esteem which is ever the result of the ascendancy of the powerful and virtuous mind over the weak, and not absolutely vicious; and for whose sons he felt almost a father's affection, old Gattrie had but indifferently troubled himself about Desborough, who was fully aware of what he had previously done to detect and expose him, and consequently repaid with usury—an hostility of feeling which, however, had never been brought to any practical issue.

As a matter of course, Sampson was of the number of anxious persons collected on the bank of the river, on the morning of the capture of the American gun boat; but, as he was only then emerging from his first stage of intoxication, (which we have already shown to be tantamount to perfect sobriety in any other person) there had been no time for a display of those uproarious qualities which characterized the last, and which, once let loose, scarcely even the presence of the General could have restrained. With an acuteness, however, which is often to be remarked in habitual drunkards at moments when their intellect is unclouded by the confusedness to which they are more commonly subject, the hawk's eye of the old man had detected several particulars which had escaped the general attention, and of which he had, at a later period of the day, retained sufficient recollection, to connect with an accidental yet important discovery.

At the moment when the prisoners were landed, he had remarked Desborough, who had uttered the hasty exclamation already recorded, stealing cautiously through the surrounding crowd, and apparently endeavouring to arrest the attention of the younger of the American officers. An occasional pressing of the spur into the flank of Silvertail, enabled him to turn as the settler turned, and thus to keep him constantly in view; until, at length, as the latter approached the group of which General Brock and Commodore Barclay formed the centre, he observed him distinctly to make a sign of intelligence to the Militia Officer, whose eye he at length attracted, and who now bestowed upon him a glance of hasty and furtive recognition. Curiosity induced Sampson to move Silvertail a little more in advance, in order to be enabled to obtain a better view of the prisoners; but the latter, turning away his head at the moment, although apparently without design, baffled his penetration. Still he had a confused and indistinct idea that the person was not wholly unknown to him.

When the prisoners had been disposed of, and the crowd dispersed, Sampson continued to linger near the council house, exchanging greetings with the newly arrived Chiefs, and drinking from whatever whiskey bottle was offered to him, until he at length gave rapid indication of arriving at his third or grand climacteric. Then were to be heard the loud shoutings of his voice, and the clattering of Silvertail's hoofs, as horse and rider flew like lightning past the fort into the town, where a more than usual quantity of the favorite liquid was quaffed at the several stores, in commemoration, as he said, of the victory of his noble boy, Gerald Grantham, and to the success of the British arms generally throughout the war.

Among the faults of Sampson Gattrie, was certainly not that of neglecting the noble animal to whom long habit had deeply attached him. Silvertail was equally a favorite with the son, who had more than once ridden him in the occasional races that took place upon the hard sands of the lake shore, and in which he had borne every thing away. As Sampson was ever conscious and collected about this hour, care was duly taken by him that his horse should be fed, without the trouble to himself of dismounting. Even as Gattrie sat in his saddle, Silvertail was in the daily practice of munching his corn out of a small trough that stood in the yard of the inn where he usually stopped, while his rider conversed with whoever chanced to be near him—the head of his cudgel resting on his ample thigh, and a glass of his favorite whiskey in his other and unoccupied hand.

Now it chanced, that on this particular day, Sampson had neglected to pay his customary visit to the inn, an omission which was owing rather to the hurry and excitement occasioned by the stirring events of the morning, than to any wilful neglect of his steed. Nor was it until some hours after dark that, seized with a sudden fit of caressing Silvertail, whose glossy neck he patted, until the tears of warm affection started to his eyes, he bethought him of the omission of which he had been guilty. Scarcely was the thought conceived, before Silvertail was again at full career, and on his way to the inn. The gate stood open, and, as Sampson entered, he saw two individuals retire, as if to escape observation, within a shed adjoining the stable. Drunk as he was, a vague consciousness of the truth, connected as it was with his earlier observation, flashed across the old man's mind, and when, in answer to his loud hallooing, a factotum, on whom devolved all the numerous offices of the inn, from waiter down to ostler, made his appearance, Sampson added to his loudly expressed demand for Silvertail's corn, a whispered injunction to return with a light. During the absence of the man he commenced trolling a verse of "Old King Cole," a favorite ballad with him, and with the indifference of one who believes himself to be alone. Presently the light appeared, and, as the bearer approached, its rays fell on the forms of two men, retired into the furthest extremity of the shed and crouching to the earth as if in concealment, whom Sampson recognized at a glance. He however took no notice of the circumstance to the ostler, or even gave the slightest indication, by look or movement, of what he had seen.

When the man had watered Silvertail, and put his corn in the trough, he returned to the house, and Sampson, with his arms folded across his chest, as his horse crunched his food, listened attentively to catch whatever conversation might ensue between the loiterers. Not a word however was uttered, and soon after he saw them emerge from their concealment—step cautiously behind him—cross the yard towards the gate by which he had entered—and then disappear altogether. During this movement the old man had kept himself perfectly still, so that there could be no suspicion that he had, in any way, observed them. Nay, he even spoke once or twice coaxingly to Silvertail, as if conscious only of the presence of that animal, and in short conducted himself in a manner well worthy of the cunning of a drunken man. The reflections to which this incident gave rise, had the effect of calling up a desperate fit of loyalty, which he only awaited the termination of Silvertail's hasty meal to put into immediate activity. Another shout to the ostler, a second glass swallowed, the reckoning paid, Silvertail bitted, and away went Sampson once more at his speed, through the now deserted town, the road out of which to his own place, skirted partly the banks of the river, and partly those of the lake.

After galloping about a mile, the old man found the feet of Silvertail burying themselves momentarily deeper in the sands which form the road near Elliot's Point. Unwilling to distress him more than was necessary, he pulled him up to a walk, and, throwing the reins upon his neck, folded his arms as usual, rolling from side to side at every moment, and audibly musing, in the thick husky voice that was common to him in inebriety.

"Yes, by Jove, I am as true and loyal a subject as any in the service of King George, God bless him, (here he bowed his head involuntarily and with respect) and though, as that poor dear old Grantham used to say, I do drink a little, (hiccup) still there's no great harm in that. It keeps a man alive. I am the boy, at all events, to scent a rogue. That was Desborough and his son I saw just now, and the rascals, he! he! he! the rascals thought, I suppose, I was too drunk, (hiccup) too drunk to twig them. We shall tell them another tale before the night is over. D—n such skulking scoundrels, I say. Whoa! Silvertail, whoa! what do you see there, my boy, eh?"

Silvertail only replied by the sharp pricking of his ears, and a side movement, which seemed to indicate a desire to keep as much aloof as possible from a cluster of walnut trees which, interspersed with wild grape-vines, may be seen to this hour, resting in gloomy relief on the white deep sands that extend considerably in that direction.

"Never mind, my boy, we shall be at home presently," pursued Sampson, patting the neck of his unquiet companion. "But no, I had forgotten; we must give chase to these (hiccup) to these rascals. Now there's that son Bill of mine fast asleep, I suppose, in the arms of his little wife. They do nothing but lie in bed, while their poor old father is obliged to be up at all hours, devising plans for the good of the King's service, God bless him! But I shall soon (hiccup)!—Whoa Silvertail! whoa I say. D—n you, you brute, do you mean to throw me?"

The restlessness of Silvertail, despite of his rider's caresses, had been visibly increasing as they approached the dark cluster of walnuts. Arrived opposite to this, his ears and tail erect, he had evinced even more than restlessness—alarm: and something, that did not meet the eye of his rider, caused him to take a sideward spring of several feet. It was this action that, nearly unseating Sampson, had drawn from him the impatient exclamation just recorded.

At length the thicket was passed, and Silvertail, recovered from his alarm, moved forward once more on the bound, in obedience to the well known whistle of his master.

"Good speed have they made," again mused Sampson, as he approached his home; "if indeed, as I suspect, it be them who are hiding in yonder thicket. Silvertail could not have been more than ten minutes finishing his (hiccup) his corn, and the sands had but little time to warm beneath his hoofs when he did start. These Yankees are swift footed fellows, as I have had good (hiccup) good experience, in the old war, when I could run a little myself after the best of them. But here we are at last. Whoa, Silvertail, whoa! and now to turn out Bill from his little wife. Bill, I say, hilloa! hilloa! Bill, hilloa!"

Long habit, which had taught the old man's truly excellent and exemplary son the utter hopelessness of his disease, had also familiarized him with these nightly interruptions to his slumbers. A light was speedily seen to flash across the chamber in which he slept, and presently the principal door of the lower building was unbarred, and unmurmuring, and uncomplaining, the half dressed young man stood in the presence of his father. Placing the light on the threshold, he prepared to assist him as usual to dismount, but Sampson, contrary to custom, rejected for a time every offer of the kind. His rapid gallop through the night air, added to the more than ordinary quantity of whiskey he had that day swallowed, was now producing its effect, and, while every feature of his countenance manifested the extreme of animal stupidity, his apprehension wandered and his voice became almost inarticulate. Without the power to acquaint his son with the purpose he had in view, and of which he himself now entertained but a very indistinct recollection, he yet strove, impelled as he was by his confusedness of intention to retain his seat, but was eventually unhorsed and handed over to the care of his pretty daughter in law, whose office it was to dispose of him for the night, while her husband rubbed down, fed, and otherwise attended to Silvertail.

A few hours of sound sleep restored Sampson to his voice and his recollection, when his desire to follow the two individuals he had seen in the yard of the inn the preceding night, and whom he felt persuaded he must have passed on the road, was more than ever powerfully revived. And yet, was it not highly probable that the favorable opportunity had been lost, and that, taking advantage of the night, they were already departed from the country, if such (and he doubted it not) was their intention. "What a cursed fool," he muttered to himself, "to let a thimbleful of liquor upset me on such an occasion; but, at all events, here goes for another trial. With the impatient, over-indulged Sampson, to determine on a course of action, was to carry it into effect."

"Hilloa! Bill, I say Bill my boy," he shouted from the chamber next to that in which his son slept. Hilloa! Bill, come here directly."

Bill answered not, but sounds were heard in his room as of one stepping out of bed, and presently the noise of flint and steel announced that a light was being struck. In a few minutes, the rather jaded-looking youth appeared at the bed-side of his parent.

"Bill, my dear boy," said Sampson, in a more subdued voice, "did you see any body pass last night after I came home? Try and recollect vourself; did you see two men on the road?

"I did, father; just as I had locked the stable door, and was coming in for the night, I saw two men passing down the road. But why do you ask!"

"Did you speak to them—could you recognize them," asked Sampson, without stating his motive for the question.

"I wished them good night, and one of them gruffly bade me good night too; but I could not make out who they were, though one did for a moment strike me to be Desborough, and both were tallish sort of men."

"You're a lad of penetration, Bill; now saddle me Silvertail as fast as you can."

"Saddle Silvertail! surely father, you are not going out yet: it's not day-light."

"Saddle me Silvertail, Bill," repeated the old man with

the air of one whose mandate was not to be questioned. "But where the devil are you going, sir," he added impatiently.

"Why to saddle Silvertail, to be sure," said the youth, who was just closing the door for that purpose.

"What, and leave me a miserable old man to get up without a light. Oh fie, Bill. I thought you loved your poor old father better than to neglect him so—there, that will do: now send in Lucy to dress me."

The light was kindled, Bill went in and spoke to his wife, then descended to the stable. A gentle tap at the door of the old interpreter, and Lucy entered in her pretty night dress, and, half asleep, half awake, but without a shadow of discontent in her look, proceeded to assist him in drawing on his stockings, &c. Sampson's toilet was soon completed, and Silvertail being announced as "all ready," he, without communicating a word of his purpose, issued forth from his home, just as the day was beginning to dawn.

Although the reflective powers of Gattrie had been in some measure restored by sleep, it is by no means to be assumed he was yet thoroughly sober. Uncertain in regard to the movements of those who had so strongly excited his loyal hostility, (and, mayhap, at the moment his curiosity,) it occurred to him that if Desborough had not already baffled his pursuit, a knowledge of the movements and intentions of that individual, might be better obtained from an observation of what was passing on the beach in front of his hut. The object of this reconnoissance was, therefore, only to see if the canoe of the settler was still on the shore, and with this object he suffered Silvertail to take the road along the sands, while he himself, with his arms folded and his head sunk on his chest, fell into a reverie with which was connected the manner and the means of securing the disloyal Desborough, should it happen that he had not yet departed. The accidental discharge of Middlemore's pistol, at the very moment when Silvertail had doubled a point that kept the scene of contention from his view, caused him to raise his eyes, and then the whole truth flashed suddenly upon him. We have already seen how gallantly he advanced to them, and how madly, and, in a manner peculiarly his own, he sought to arrest the traitor Desborough in his flight.

"Sorry I couldn't force the scoundrel back, gentlemen," said Sampson, as he now approached the discomfited officers. "Not much hurt, I hope," pointing with his own maimed and bleeding hand to the leg of Middlemore, which that officer, seated on the sand, was preparing to bind with a silk handkerchief. "Ah, a mere flesh wound, I see. Henry, Henry Grantham, my poor dear boy, what still alive after the desperate clutching of that fellow at your throat? But now that we have routed the enemy—must be off—drenched to the skin. No liquor on the stomach to keep out the cold, and if I once get an ague fit, its all over with poor old Sampson. Must gallop home, and, while his little wife wraps a bandage round my hand, shall send down Bill with a litter. Good morning, Mr. Middlemore, good bye Henry, my boy." And then, without giving time to either to reply, the old man applied his spurs once more to the flanks of Silvertail, who, with drooping mane and tail, resembled a half drowned rat; and again hallooing defiance to Desborough, who lay to at a distance, apparently watching the movements of his enemies, he retraced his way along the sands at full gallop, and was speedily out of sight.

Scarcely had Gattrie disappeared, when two other individuals, evidently officers, and cloaked precisely like the party he had just quitted, issued from the wood near the hut upon the clearing, and thence upon the sands—their countenances naturally expressing all the surprise that might he supposed to arise from the picture now offered to their view.

"What in the name of Heaven is the meaning of all this?" asked one of the new comers, as both now rapidly advanced to the spot where Middlemore was yet employed in coolly binding up his leg, while Henry Grantham, who had just risen, was gasping with almost ludicrous efforts to regain his respiration.

"You must ask the meaning of our friend here," answered Middlemore, with the low chuckling good-natured laugh that was habitual to him, while he proceeded with his bandaging. "All I know is, that I came out as a second, and here have I been made a first—a principal, which, by the way, is contrary to all my principle."

"Do be serious for once, Middlemore. How did you get wounded, and who are those scoundrels who have just quitted you? anxiously inquired Captain Molineux, for it was he, and Lieutenant Villiers, who, (the party already stated to have been expected,) had at length arrived.

"Two desperate fellows in their way, I can assure you," replied Middlemore, more amused than annoyed at the adventure. "Ensign Paul, Emilius, Theophilus, Arnoldi, is, I calculate, a pretty considerable strong ac*tyve* sort of fellow; and, to judge by Henry Grantham's half strangled look, his companion lacks not the same qualities. Why, in the name of all that is precious would you persist in poking your nose into the rascal's skins, Grantham? The ruffians had nearly made dried skins of ours."

"Ha! is that the scoundrel who calls himself Arnoldi," asked Captain Molineux? I have heard," and he glanced at Henry Grantham as he spoke, "a long story of his villainy from his captor within this very hour."

"Which is your apology, I suppose," said Middlemore, "for having so far exceeded your ap*point*ment, gentlemen."

"It certainly is," said Lieutenant Villiers, "but the fault was not ours. We chanced to fall in with Gerald Grantham, and on our way here, and that he detained us, should be a matter of congratulation to us all."

"Congratulation!" exclaimed Middlemore, dropping his bandage, and lifting his eyes with an expression of indescribable humour, "Am I then to think it matter of congratulation that, as an innocent second, I should have had a cursed piece of lead stuck in my flesh to spoil my next winter's dancing. And Grantham is to think it matter of congratulation that, instead of putting a bullet through you, Molineux, (as I intend he shall when I have finished dressing this confounded leg, if his nerves are not too much shaken,) he should have felt the gripe of that monster Desborough around his throat, until his eyes seem ready to start from their sockets, and all this because you did not choose to be in time. Upon my word, I do not know that it is quite meet that we should meet you. What say you, Grantham?"

"I hope," said Captain Molineux with a smile, "your principal will think as you do, for should he decline the meeting, nothing will afford more satisfaction to myself.

Both Grantham and Middlemore looked their utter surprise at the language thus used by Captain Molineux, but neither of them spoke.

"If an apology the most ample for my observation of yesterday," continued that officer, "an apology founded on my perfect conviction of error, (that conviction produced by certain recent explanations with your brother,) can satisfy you, Mr. Grantham, most sincerely do I make it. If, however, you hold me to my pledge, here am I of course to redeem it. I may as well observe to you in the presence of our friends, (and Villiers can corroborate my statement,) that my original intention on leaving your brother, was to receive your fire and then tender my apology, but, under the circumstances in which both you and Middlemore are placed at this moment, the idea would be altogether absurd. Again I tender my apology, which it will be a satisfaction to me to repeat this day at the mess table, where I yesterday refused to drink your brother's health. All I can add is that when you have heard the motives for my conduct, and learnt to what extent I have been deceived, you will readily admit that I acted not altogether from caprice."

"Your apology I accept, Captain Molineux," said Grantham, coming forward and unhesitatingly offering his hand. "If you have seen my brother, I am satisfied. Let there be no further question on the subject."

"So then I am to be the only bulleted man on this occasion," interrupted Middlemore, with ludicrous pathos—"the only poor devil who is to be made to remember Hartley's point for ever. But no matter. I am not the first instance of a second being shot, through the awkward bungling of his principal, and certainly Grantham you were in every sense the principal in this affair, for had you taken my advice you would have let the fellows go to the devil their own way."

"What! knowing, as I did, that the traitor Desborough had concealed in his canoe a prisoner on parole—nay, worse, a deserter from our service—with a view of conveying him out of the country?"

"How did you know it?"

"Because I at once recognized him, through the disguise in which he left the hut, for what he was. That discovery made, there remained but one course to pursue."

"Ah! and *course* work you made of it, with a vengeance," said Middlemore, "first started him up like a fox from his cover, got the mark of his teeth, and then suffered him to escape."

"Is there no chance of following—no means of overtaking them?" said Captain Molineux—"No, by Heaven, as he glanced his eye from right to left, not a single canoe to be seen any where along the shore."

"Following!" echoed Middlemore; "faith the scoundrels would desire nothing better: if two of us had such indifferent play with them on terra firma, you may rely upon it that double the number would have no better chance in one of these rickety canoes. See there how the rascals lie to within half musket shot, apparently hailing us."

Middlemore was right. Desborough had risen in the stern of the canoe, and now, stretched to his full height, called leisurely, through his closed hands, on the name of Henry Grantham. When he observed the attention of that officer had, in common with that of his companions, been arrested, he proceeded at the full extent of his lungs.

"I reckon, young man, as how I shall pay you out for

this, and drot my skin, if I once twists my fingers round your neck again, if any thing on this side hell shall make me quit it, afore you squeaks your last squeak. You've druv me from my home, and I'll have your curst blood for it yet. I'll sarve you, as I sarved your old father—You got my small bore, I expect, and if its any good to you to know that one of its nineties to the pound, sent the old rascal to the devil—why then you have it from Jeremiah Desborough's own lips, and be d—d to you."

And, with this horrible admission, the settler again seated himself in the stern of his canoe, and making good use of his paddle soon scudded away until his little vessel appeared but as a speck on the lake.

Henry Grantham was petrified with astonishment and dismay at a declaration, the full elucidation of which we must reserve for a future opportunity. The daring confession rang in his ears long after the voice had ceased, and it was not until a light vehicle had been brought for Middlemore from Sampson's farm, that he could be induced to quit the shore, where he still lingered, as if in expectation of the return of the avowed *murderer of his Father*.

CHAPTER IX.

At the especial invitation of Captain Molineux, Gerald Grantham dined at the garrison mess, on the evening of the day when the circumstances, detailed in our last chapter, took place. During dinner the extraordinary adventure of the morning formed the chief topic of conversation, for it had become one of general interest, not only throughout the military circles, but in the town of Amherstburg itself, in which the father of the Granthams had been held in an esteem amounting almost to veneration. Horrible as had been the announcement made by the detected and discomfited settler to him who now, for the first time, learnt that his parent had fallen a victim to ruffian vindictiveness, too many years had elapsed since that event, to produce more than the ordinary emotion which might be supposed to be awakened by a knowledge rather of the manner than the fact of his death. Whatever therefore might have been the pain inflicted on the hearts of the brothers, by this cruel re-opening of a partially closed wound, there was no other evidence of suffering than the suddenly compressed lip and glistening eye, whenever allusion was made to the villain with whom each felt he had a fearful account to settle. Much indeed of the interest of the hour was derived from the animated account, given by Gerald, of the circumstances which had led to his lying in ambuscade for the American on the preceding day; and as his narrative embraces not only the reasons for Captain Molineux's strange conduct, but other hitherto unexplained facts, we cannot do better than follow him in his detail.

"I think it must have been about half past eleven o'clock,

on the night preceding the capture," commenced Gerald, "that, as my gun boat was at anchor close under the American shore, at rather more than half a mile below the farther extremity of Bois Blanc, my faithful old Sambo silently approached me, while I lay wrapped in my watch cloak on deck, calculating the chances of falling in with some spirited bark of the enemy which would afford me an opportunity of proving the mettle of my crew.

"'Massa Geral,' he said in a mysterious whisper, for old age and long services in my family have given him privileges which I have neither the power nor the inclination to check—'Massa Geral,' pulling me by the collar—'I dam ib he no go sleep when him ought to hab all him eyes about him—him pretty fellow to keep watch when Yankee pass him in e channel.'

"'A Yankee pass me in the channel!'" I would have exclaimed aloud, starting to my feet with surprise, but Sambo, with ready thought, put his hand upon my mouth, in time to prevent more than the first word from being uttered.

"'Hush! dam him, Massa Geral, ib you make a noise you no catch him.'

"'What do you mean then—what have you seen?'" I asked in the same low whisper, the policy of which his action had enjoined on me.

"'Lookee dare, Massa Geral, lookee dare?'

"Following the direction in which he pointed, I now saw, but very indistinctly, a canoe in which was a solitary individual stealing across the lake to the impulsion of an apparently muffled paddle; for her course, notwithstanding the stillness of the night, was utterly noiseless. The moon, which is in her first quarter, had long since disappeared, yet the heavens, although not particularly bright, ware sufficiently dotted with stars to enable me, with the aid of a night telescope, to discover that the figure, which guided the cautiously moving bark, had nothing Indian in its outline. The crew of the gun boat (the watch only excepted) had long since turned in; and even the latter lay reposing on the forecastle, the sentinels only keeping the ordinary look out. So closely moreover did we lay in shore, that but for the caution of the paddler, it might have been assumed she was too nearly identified with the dark forest against which her hull and spars reposed, to be visible. Curious to ascertain her object, I watched the canoe in silence, as, whether accidentally or with design, I know not, she made the half circuit of the gun boat and then bore away in a direct line for the Canadian shore. A suspicion of the truth now flashed across my mind, and I resolved without delay to satisfy myself. My first care was to hasten to the forecastle, and enjoin on the sentinels, who I feared might see and hail the stranger, the strictest silence. Then desiring Sambo to prepare the light boat which, I dare say, most of you have remarked to form a part of my Lilliputian command, I proceeded to arm myself with cutlass and pistols. Thus equipped I sprang lightly in, and having again caught sight of the chase, on which I had moreover directed one of the sentinels to keep a steady eye as long as she was in sight, desired Sambo to steer as noiselessly as possible in pursuit. For some time we kept the stranger in view, but whether, owing to his superior paddling or lighter weight, we eventually lost sight of him. The suspicion which had at first induced my following, however, served also as a clue to the direction I should take. I was aware that the scoundred Desborough was an object of distrust—I knew that the strictness of my father, during his magistracy, in compelling him to choose between taking the oaths of allegiance, and quitting the country, had inspired him with deep hatred to himself and disaffection to the Government; and I felt that if the spirit of his vengeance had not earlier developed itself, it was solely because the opportunity and the power had hitherto been wanting; but that now, when hostilities between his natural and adopted countries had been declared, there would be ample room for the exercise of his treason. It was the strong assurance I felt that he was the solitary voyager on the face of the waters, which induced me to pursue him, for I had a presentiment that, could I but track him in his course, I should discover some proof of his guilt, which would suffice to rid us for ever of the presence of so dangerous a subject. The adventure was moreover one that pleased me, although perhaps I was not strictly justified in quitting my gun boat, especially as in the urgency of the moment, I had not even thought of leaving orders with my boatswain, in the event of any thing unexpected occurring during my absence. The sentinels alone were aware of my departure.

"The course we pursued was in the direction of Hartley's point, and so correct had been the steering and paddling of the keen-sighted negro, that when we made the beach, we found ourselves immediately opposite to Desborough's hut.

"'How is this, Sambo?' I asked in a low tone, as our canoe grated on the sand within a few paces of several others that lay where I expected to find but one--'are all these Desborough's?'

"'No, Massa Geral—'less him teal him toders, Desborough only got one—dis a public landin' place.'

"'Can you tell which is his?' I inquired.

"'To be sure—dis a one,' and he pointed to one nearly twice the dimensions of its fellows.

"'Has it been lately used, Sambo—can you tell?'

"'I soon find out, Massa Geral.'

"His device was the most simple and natural in the world, and yet I confess it was one which I never should have dreamt of. Stooping on the sands, he passed his hand under the bottom of the canoe, and then whispered.

"'Him not touch a water to night Massa Geral--him dry as a chip.'

"Here I was at fault. I began to apprehend that I had been baffled in my pursuit, and deceived in my supposition. I knew that Desborough had had for years, one large canoe only in his possession, and it was evident that this had not been used during the night. I was about to order Sambo to shove off again, when it suddenly occurred to me that, instead of returning from a visit, the suspected settler might have received a visiter, and I accordingly desired my *fides achates* to submit the remainder of the canoes to the same inspection.

"After having passed his hand ineffectually over several, he at length announced, as he stooped over one which I recognized, from a peculiar elevation of the bow and stern, to be the same we had passed.

"'Dis a one all drippin' wet, Massa Geral. May I nebber see a Hebben ib he not a same we follow.'

"A low tapping against the door of the hut, which although evidently intended to be subdued, was now, in the silence of night, distinctly audible; while our whispers, on the contrary, mingled as they were with the crisping sound of the waves rippling on the sands were, at that distance, undistinguishable. It was evident that I had erred in my original conjecture. Had it been Desborough himself, living alone as he did, he would not have knocked for admission where there was no one to afford it, but would have quietly let himself in. It could then be no other than a visiter—perhaps a spy from the enemy—and the same to whom we had given chase.

"From the moment that the tapping commenced, Sambo and I stood motionless on the shore, and without trusting our voices again, even to a whisper. In a little time we heard the door open, and the low voice of Desborough in conversation with another. Presently the door was shut, and soon afterwards, through an imperfectly closed shutter on the only floor of the hut, we could perceive a streak of light reflected on the clearing in front, as if from a candle or lamp, that was stationary.

"'I tink him dam rascal dat man, Massa Geral;' at length ventured my companion. "I 'member long time ago,' and he sighed, "'when Sambo no bigger nor dat paddle, one berry much like him. But, Massa Geral,' Missis always tell me nebber talk o' dat.'

"'A villain he is, I believe, Sambo, but let us advance cautiously and discover what he is about.'

"We now stole along the skirt of the forest, until we managed to approach the window, through which the light was still thrown in one long, fixed, but solitary ray. It was however impossible to see who were within, for although the voices of men were distinguishable, their forms were so placed as not to be visible through the partial opening.

"The conversation had evidently been some moments commenced. The first words I heard uttered, were by Desborough.

"'A Commissary boat, and filled with bags of goold eagles, and a fiftieth part oum, if we get her clean slick through to Detroit. Well, drot me, if that aint worth the trial. Why did'nt they try it by land, boy ?'

"'I reckon, father, that cock wouldn't fight. The Injuns are outlyin' every where to cut off our mails, and the ready is too much wanted to be thrown away. No, no : the river work's the safest I take it, for there they little expect it to come.'

"The voice of the last speaker, excited in me a strong desire to see the face of Desborough's visiter. Unable, where I stood, to catch the slightest view of either, I fancied that I might be more successful in rear of the hut. I therefore moved forward, followed by Sambo, but not so cautiously as to prevent my feet from crushing a fragment of decayed wood, that lay in my path.

"A bustle within, and the sudden opening of the door announced that the noise had been overheard. I held up my finger impressively to Sambo, and we both remained motionless.

"'Who the hell's there ?' shouted Desborough, and the

voice rang like the blast of a speaking trumpet along the skirt of the forest.

"'Some raccoon looking out for Hartley's chickens, I expect,' said his companion, after a short pause. 'There's nothin' human I reckon, to be seen movin' at this hour of the night.'

"'Who the hell's there ?' repeated Desborough—still no answer.

"Again the door was closed, and under cover of the slight noise made by the settler in doing this, and resuming his seat, Sambo and I accomplished the circuit of the hut. Here we had an unobstructed view of the persons of both. A small store room or pantry communicated with that in which they were sitting at a table, on which was a large flagon, we knew to contain whiskey, and a couple of japanned drinking cups, from which, ever and anon, they "wetted their whistles," as they termed it, and whetted their discourse. As they sat each with his back to the inner wall, or more correctly, the logs of the hut, and facing the door communicating with the store room left wide open, and in a direct line with the back window at which we had taken our stand, we could distinctly trace every movement of their features, while, thrown into the shade by the gloom with which we were enveloped we ran no risk of detection ourselves. It is almost unnecessary to observe, after what has occurred this morning, that the companion of Desborough was no other than the *soi-disant* Ensign Paul, Emelius, Theophilus, Arnoldi; or, more properly, the scoundrel son of a yet more scoundrel father. He wore the dress in which you yesterday beheld him, but beneath a Canadian blanket coat, which, when I first saw him in the hut, was buttoned up to the chin, so closely as to conceal every thing American about the dress.

"'Well now I reckon we must lay our heads to do this job;' said the son as he tossed off a portion of the liquid he had poured into his can. 'There's only that one gun boat I expect in t'other channel.'

"'Only one Phil, do you know who commands it?'

"'One of them curst Granthams, to be sure. I say, old boy,' and his eye lighted up significantly, as he pointed to the opposite wall, 'I see you've got the small bore still.'

"A knowing wink marked the father's sense of the allusion. 'The devil's in it,' he rejoined, 'if we can't come over that smooth faced chap, some how or other. Did you see any thin' of him as you come along?'

"'I reckon I did. Pretty chick he is to employ for a look out—why I paddled two or three times round his gun boat, as it lay 'gin the shore, without so much as a single livin' soul being on deck to see me.'

"It is proverbial," continued Grantham, "that listeners never hear any good of themselves. I paid the common penalty. But if I continued calm, my companion did not. Partly incensed at what had related to me—but more infuriated at the declaration made by the son, that he had paddled several times round the gun boat, without a soul being on deck to see him, he drew near to me, his white teeth displaying themselves in the gloom, as he whispered, but in a tone that betrayed extreme irritation.

"'What a dam Yankee liar rascal, Massa Geral. He nebber go round: I see him come a down a ribber long afore he see a boat at all.'

"'Hush Sambo—hush not a word,' I returned in the same low whisper. "The villians are at some treason, and if we stir, we shall lose all chance of discovering it."

"'Me no peak Massa Geral; but dam him lyin' teef,' he continued to mutter, 'I wish I had him board a gun boat.'

"'A dozen fellors well armed, might take the d—d British craft,' observed Desborough. 'How many men may there be aboard the Commissary.'

"'About forty, I reckon, under some d—d old rig'lar Major. I've got a letter for him here to desire him to come on, if so be as we gets the craft out of the way.'

"'Drot me if I know a better way than to jump slick aboard

her,' returned Desborough musingly; 'forty genuine Kaintucks ought to swallow her up, crew and all.'

"'I guess they would,' returned his companion, 'but they are not Kaintucks, but only rig'lars; and then agin if they are discovered one spry cannon shot might sink her; and if the eagles go to the bottom, we shall lose our fiftieth. You don't reckon that."

"'What the hell's to be done then,' exclaimed Desborough, resorting to his favorite oath when in doubt.

"'My plan's already cut and dried by a wiser head nor yours nor mine, as you shall larn; but first let a fellor wet his whistle.' Here they both drained off another portion of the poison that stood before them.

"Not to tire you," pursued Grantham, "with a repetition of the oaths and vulgar and interjectional chucklings that passed between the well assorted pair, during the disclosure of the younger, I will briefly state that it was one of the most stupid that could have been conceived, and reflected but little credit on the strategetic powers of whoever originated it.

"The younger scoundrel, who since his desertion from our service, claims to be a naturalized citizen of the United States (his name of Desborough being changed for that of Arnoldi, and his rank of full private for that of Ensign of Militia,) had been selected from his knowledge of the Canadian shore, and his connexion with the disaffected settler, as a proper person to entrust with a stratagem, having for its object the safe convoy of a boat, filled with specie, of which the American garrison it appears stands much in need. The renegade had been instructed to see his father, to whom he was to promise, a fiftieth of the value of the freight, provided he should by any means contrive to draw the gun boat from her station. The most plausible plan suggested, was that he should intimate to me, that a prize of value was lying between Turkey Island and our own shore, which it required but my sudden appearance to ensure, without even striking a blow. Here a number of armed boats were to be stationed in concealment, in order to take me at a disadvantage, and even if I avoided being captured, the great aim would be accomplished—namely, that of getting me out of the way, until the important boat should have cleared the channel, running between Bois Blanc and the American shore, and secreted herself in one of the several deep creeks which empty themselves into the river. Here she was to have remained until I had returned to my station, when her passage upward might be pursued, if not without observation, at least without risk. As Desborough was known to be suspected by us, it was further suggested that he should appear to have been influenced in the information conveyed to me, not by any motives of patriotism, which would have been in the highest degree misplaced, but by the mere principle of self interest. He was to require of me a pledge that, out of the proceeds of the proposed capture, a twentieth share should be his, or, if I would not undertake to guarantee this from the Government or my own authority, that I should promise my own eventual share should be divided with him. This stratagem successful, the younger Desborough was to repair to the boat which had been lying concealed for the last day or two, a few miles below me, with an order for her to make the best of her way during the night if possible. If failing on the other hand, she was to return to the port whence she had sailed, until a more fitting opportunity should present itself.

"This," continued Grantham, after a slight pause, during which the bottle was again circulated, "was delightful intelligence. Distrustful as I was of Desborough, I could not have been deceived by this device, even had I not thus fortunately become acquainted with the whole of the design: but now that I knew my man, and could see my way, I at once resolved to appear the dupe they purposed to make me. Specie too, for the payment of the garrison! This was no contemptible prize with which to commence my career.

Besides the boat was well manned, and although without cannon, still in point of military equipment quite able to cope with my crew, which did not exceed thirty men.

"With your knowledge of Desborough's character it will not surprise you to learn, although I confess I boiled with indignation at the moment to hear, that the object of the scoundrels was, with a view to the gratification of their own private vengeance, not merely to raise a doubt of my fidelity, but to prefer against me a direct charge of treason. Thus in their vulgar language they argued. If misled by their representations, I quitted my station on the channel, and fell into the ambuscade prepared for me near Turkey Island, I raised a suspicion of the cause of my absence, which might be confirmed by an anonymous communication; and if, on the other hand, I escaped that ambuscade, the suspicion would be even stronger, as care would be taken to announce to the English garrison, the fact of my having been bribed to leave the channel free for the passage of a boat, filled with money and necessaries for Detroit. My return to my post immediately afterwards, would confirm the assertion; and so perfectly had they, in their wise conceit, arranged their plans, that a paper was prepared by the son and handed to his father, for the purpose of being dropped in the way of one of the officers; the purport of which was an accusation against me, of holding a secret understanding with the enemy, in proof whereof it was stated that at an important moment, I should be found absent from my post—I think I am correct, Captain Molineux."

"'Perfectly,' returned that officer—'such indeed were the contents of the paper which I picked up in my rounds about day light yesterday morning, and which I have only again to express my regret that I should have allowed to make on me even a momentary impression. Indeed, Grantham, I am sure you will do me the justice to believe, that until we actually saw the American boat passing, while you were no where to be seen, I never for one moment doubted its being, what it has proved to be--the falsest and most atrocious of calumnies."

"Your after doubt was but natural," replied the sailor, "although I confess I could not help wincing under the thought of its being entertained. I knew that, on my return, I should be enabled to explain every thing, but yet felt nettled that even my short absence should, as I knew it must, give rise to any strictures on my conduct. It was that soreness of feeling which induced my impatient allusion to the subject, even after my good fortune of yesterday, for I at once detected that the slanderous paper had been received and commented on ; and from the peculiar glance, I saw Henry direct to you, I was at no loss to discover into whose hands it had fallen. But to resume.

"Their plan of action being finally settled, the traitors began to give indication of separating—the one to hasten and announce to the American boat the removal of all impediment to her passage upwards—the other to my gun boat, in order to play off the falsehood devised for the success of their stratagem.

"'Here's damnation to the curst race of Granthams,' said the son, as raising his tall and lanky body, he lifted the rude goblet to his lips.

"'Amen,' responded the father, rising also and drinking to the pledge, 'and what's more, here's to the goold eagles that'll repay us for our job. And now Phil, let's be movin'.'

"The heavy tread of their feet within the hut as they moved to and fro, to collect the several articles belonging to the equipment of Desborough's canoe, promising fair to cover the sound of our footsteps, I now whispered to Sambo, and we hastily made good our retreat to the point where we had left our skiff. In a few minutes, we were again on the lake, paddling swiftly but cautiously towards my gun boat. I had instructed the sentinels not to hail me on my retùrn, therefore when I gained the deck, it was without challenge or observation of any kind, which could denote to those from whom I had so recently parted, that any one had been absent,

"Again I had thrown myself upon the deck, and was ruminating on the singular events of the evening, associating the rich prize, which I now already looked upon as my own, with the rascality of those who, imagining me to be their dupe, were so soon to become mine; and moreover meditating such measures as I fancied most likely to secure a result so opposite to that which they anticipated, when the loud quick sharp hail of the sentinels announced that a craft of some kind was approaching.

"'Want to see the officer,' shouted a voice which I knew to be Desborough's. "Somethin' very partick'lar to tell him, I guess."

"Permission having been granted, the canoe came rapidly up to the side, and in the next minute, the tall heavy form of the settler stood distinctly defined against the lake, as he stepped on the gun-wale of the boat.

"It must be needless here to repeat the information of which he was the bearer," pursued Grantham. Its purport was, in every sense, what I had so recently overheard in the hut.

"'And how am I to know that this tale of yours is correct,' I demanded when he had concluded, yet in a tone that seemed to admit, I was as much his dupe as he could reasonably desire. 'You are aware Desborough, that your character for loyalty does not stand very high, and this may prove but a trick to get me out of the way. What good motive can you give for my believing you.'

"'The best I calculate as can be,' he unhesitatingly answered, 'and that is my own interest. I don't make no boast of my loyalty, as you say, to be sure, Mr. Grantham, but I've an eye like a hawk for the rhino, and I han't giv' you this piece of news without expectin' a promise that I shall git a purty considerable sum in eagles, if so be as you succeeds in wallopin' the prize.'

"'Walloping—what do you call walloping, man?'

"'What do I call wallopin'? why licking her slick and clean out, and gettin' hold of the dust to be sure.'

"I could have knocked the scoundrel to the deck, for the familiarity of the grin which accompanied this reply, and as for Sambo, I had more than once to look him peremptorily into patience.

"I knew from what had passed between father and son, that, until the former had communicated with, and impressed a conviction of the accuracy of his report, upon me, nothing was to be attempted by the boat, the capture of which was now, for a variety of reasons, an object of weighty consideration. Whatever violence I did to myself therefore, in abstaining from a castigation of the traitor, I felt that I could not hope for success, unless, by appearing implicitly to believe all he had stated, I thus set suspicion at rest.

"'A more satisfactory motive for your information you could not have given me Desborough,' I at length replied, with a sarcasm which was however lost upon him, 'and I certainly do you the justice to believe that to the self interest you have avowed, we shall be indebted for the capture of the prize in question. She lies, you say, between Turkey Island and our own shores.'

"'I guess as how she does,' replied the settler, with an eagerness that betrayed his conviction that the bait had taken; 'but Mr. Grantham,'—and I could detect a lurking sneer, 'I expect at least that when you have lick'd the prize you will make my loyalty stand a little higher than it seems to be at this moment, for I guess, puttin' the dollars out of the question, it's a right loyal act I am guilty of now.'

"'You may rely upon it, Desborough, you shall have all the credit you deserve for your conduct on the occasion—that it shall be faithfully reported on my return, you may take for granted.' Here I summoned all hands up to weigh anchor and make sail for Turkey Island. 'Now then, Desborough, unless you wish to be a sharer in our enterprize, the sooner you leave us the better, for we shall be off immediately.'

"'In obedience to my order, all hands were speedily upon deck, and busied in earnest preparation. In pleasing assurance that I was as completely his dupe as could be desired, the villain had now the audacity to demand from me a written promise that, in consideration of the information given, five hundred dollars should be paid to him on the disposal of the prize. This demand (aware as he was—or rather as he purposed—that I was to play the part of the captured instead of that of the captor), was intended to lull me into even greater reliance on his veracity. I had difficulty in restraining my indignation, for I felt that the fellow was laughing at me in his sleeve ; however the reflection that, in less than twenty-four hours, the tables would be turned upon him, operated as a check upon my feelings, and I said with a hurried voice and air :

"'Impossible, Desborough, I have no time now to give the paper, for as you perceive we are getting under way—I however, repeat to you my promise, that if your claims are not attended to elsewhere, you shall have my share of the profits, if I take this prize within the next eight and forty hours within the boundary of Turkey Island—Will that content you ?'

"'I expect as how it must,' returned the secretly delighted, yet seemingly disappointed settler, as he now prepared to recross the gun-wale into his canoe ; 'but I guess, Mr. Grantham, you might at least advance a fellor a little money out of hand, on the strength of the prize. Jist say twenty dollars.'

"'No, Desborough, not one. 'When the Turkey Island prize is mine, then if the Government refuse to confirm your claims, we will share equally ; but, as I said before, I must first capture her, before I consent to part with a shilling.'

"'Well then, I guess I must wait,' and the scoundrel confidently believing that he had gulled me to his heart's content, stepped heavily into his canoe, which he directed along the lake shore, while we with filling sails, glided up the channel and speedily lost him from our view.'

"A perfect adventure upon my word," interrupted De-Courcy."

"What a bold and deliberate scoundrel," added Captain Granville. "I confess, Grantham, I cannot but admire the coolness and self-possession you evinced on this occassion. Had I been there in your stead, I should have tied the rascal up, given him a dozen or two on the spot, and then tumbled him head foremost into the lake."

"Oh yes, but then you have such a short way of doing things, Captain Granville," remarked Ensign Langley, in a tone rather less marked by confidence than that of the preceding day, and, on this occasion, not omitting to prefix the rank of him whom he addressed, and his acquaintance with whom had been slight.

"I admit, Mr. Langley, I have a very short and unceremonious way of treating vulgar people, who are my antipathy," returned Captain Granville, in his usual dry manner.

"Had Geerald doon this he would ha' maired his feenal treomph over the veellain," observed Cranstoun. "Na, na, Granville, our friend here has acted like a prudent mon, as well as a gaillant officer. Geerald, the boottle stands with you."

"To say nothing of his desire to secure the prize money," gaily remarked the young sailor, as he helped himself to wine.

"Eh, true, the preeze mooney, and a very neecessary consederetion too, Geerald; and one that may weel joostify your prudence in the affair. I did na' theenk o' that at fairst."

"But come, Grantham," interrupted Captain Granville, you have not informed us of what happened after the departure of the settler."

"The remainder is soon told," continued Gerald. "On parting from Desborough I continued my course directly up the channel, with a view of gaining a point, where unseen myself, I could observe the movements of the American boat, which from all I had heard, I fully expected would attempt the passage in the course of the following day. My perfect knowledge of the country suggested to me, as the safest and most secure hiding place, the creek whence you saw me issue at a moment when it was supposed the American had altogether escaped. The chief object of the enemy was evidently to get me out of the channel. That free, it was of minor importance whether I fell into the ambuscade or not, so that the important boat could effect the passage unobserved, or at least in safety. If my gun boat should be seen returning unharmed from Turkey Island, the American was to run into the first creek along the shore, which she had orders to hug until I had passed and not until I had again resumed my station in the channel, was she to renew her course upwards to Detroit which post it was assumed she would then gain without difficulty."

"It was scarcely yet day," continued Grantham, "when I reached and ran into the creek of which I have just spoken, and which, owing to the narrowness of the stream and consequent difficulty of waring, I was obliged to enter stern foremost. That no time might be lost in getting her out at the proper moment, I, instead of dropping her anchor, made the gun boat fast to a tree ; and, desiring the men, with the exception of the watch, to take their rest as usual, lay quietly awaiting the advance of the enemy.

The gun fired from the lower battery on the island, was the first intimation we had of the approach of the prize which I had given my gallant fellows to understand was in reserve for us ; and presently afterwards Sambo, whom I had dispatched on the look out, appeared on the bank, stating that a large boat, which had been fired at ineffectually, was making the greatest exertions to clear the channel. A second shot discharged from a nearer point, soon after announced that the boat had gained the head of the Island, and might therefore be shortly expected. In the impatience of my curiosity I sprang to the shore, took the telescope out of the hands of Sambo, and hastened to climb the tree from which he had so recently descended. I now distinctly saw the boat, as, availing herself of the rising and partial breeze, she steered more into the centre of the stream; and I thought I could observe marks of confusion and impatience among the groups in front of the fort, whom I had justly imagined to have been assembled there to witness the arrival of the canoes, we had seen descending the river, long before the first gun was fired.

"The opportunity of achieving a daring enterprize, in the presence of those assembled groups," pursued Grantham with a slight blush, "was, I thought, one so little likely to occur again, that I felt I could not do better than turn it to the best account; and with this view my original intention had been to man my small boat with the picked men of my crew, and attempt the American by boarding. Two circumstances, however, induced me to change my plan. The first was that the enemy, no longer hugging the shore, had every chance of throwing me out by the sudden and unexpected use of her canvass, and the second (here Gerald slightly colored, while more than one emphatic hem! passed round the table,) that I had, with my telescope, discerned there was a lady in the boat. Under these circumstances, I repeat, I altered my mode of attack, and proposed rather to sink my laurels than to lose my prize. ("Hem! your prizes I suppose you mean," interrupted De Courcy,) "and adopted what I thought would be a surer expedient—that of firing over her. This demonstration, I imagined might have the effect of bringing her to, and causing her to surrender without effusion of blood. You were all witnesses however of the unexpected manner in which, owing to the sudden falling off of the wind, I was compelled to have recourse to the boat at last."

"But the chase, and the firing after you doubled the

point?" inquired Captain Granville. "We asw nothing of this."

"The American, plying his oars with vigour, gave us exercise enough," answered the young sailor, "and had made considerable way up the creek, before we came up with him. An attempt was then made to escape us by running ashore, and abandoning the boat, but it was too late. Our bow was almost touching his stern, and in the desperation of the moment, the American troops discharged their muskets, but with so uncertain an aim, in consequence of their being closely crowded upon each other, that only three of my men were wounded by their fire. Before they could load again we were enabled to grapple with them hand to hand. A few of my men had discharged their pistols, in answer to the American volley, before I had time to interfere to prevent them; but the majority, having reserved theirs, we had now unmeasurably the advantage. Removing the bayonets from their muskets, which at such close quarters were useless, they continued their contest a short time with these, but the cutlass soon overpowered them, and they surrendered."

"And the Major, Grantham; did he behave well on the occasion?"

"Gallantly. It was the Major that cut down the only man I had dangerously wounded in the affair, and he would have struck another fatally, had I not disarmed him. While in the act of doing so, I was treacherously shot (in the arm only, fortunately,) by the younger scoundrel Desborough, who in turn I saved from Sambo's vengeance, in order that he might receive a more fitting punishment. And now, gentlemen, you have the whole history."

"Yes, as far as regards the men portion," said De Courcy, with a malicious smile; "but what became of the lady all this time, my conquering hero? Did you find her playing a very active part in the skirmish?"

"Active, no;" replied Gerald, slightly coloring, as he

remarked all eyes directed to him at this demand, "but passively courageous she was to a degree I could not have supposed possible in woman. She sat calm and collected amid the din of conflict, as if she had been accustomed to the thing all her life, nor once moved from the seat which she occupied in the stern, except to make an effort to prevent me from disarming her uncle. I confess that her coolness astonished me, while it excited my warmest admiration.

"A hope it may be noothing beyoond admeeration," observed the Captain of Grenadiers, "a tell ye as a freend, Geerald, a do not like this accoont ye gi' of her coonduct. A wooman who could show no ageetation in sooch a scene, must have either a domn'd coold, or a domn'd block hairt, and there's but leetle claim to admeeration there."

"Upon my word, Captain Cranstoun," and the handsome features of Gerald crimsoned with a feeling not unmixed with serious displeasure, "I do not quite understand you—you appear to assume something between Miss Montgomerie and myself, that should not be imputed to either—and certainly, not thus publicly."

"Hoot toot mon, there's no use in making a secret of the maitter," returned the positive grenadier. "The soobject was discoosed after dinner yeesterday, and there was noobody preesent who didn't agree that if you had won her hairt you had geevin your own in exchange."

"God forbid," said Henry Grantham with unusual gravity of manner, while he looked affectionately on the changing and far from satisfied countenance of his conscious brother, "for I repeat, with Captain Cranstoun, I like her not. Why, I know not; still I like her not, and I shall be glad, Gerald, when you have consigned her to the place of her destination."

"Pooh! pooh! nonsense;" interrupted Captain Granville, "Never mind, Gerald," he pursued good humouredly "she is a splendid girl, and one that you need not be ashamed to own as a conquest. By heaven, she has a bust and hips to warm the bosom of an anchorite, and depend upon it, all that Cranstoun has said arises only from pique that he is not the object preferred. Those black eyes of hers have set his ice blood on the boil, and he would willingly exchange places with you, as I honestly confess I should.

Vexed as Gerald certainly felt at the familiar tone the conversation was now assuming in regard to Miss Montgomerie, and although satisfied that mere pleasantry was intended, it was not without a sensation of relief he found it interrupted by the entrance of the several non-commissioned officers with their order books. Soon after the party broke up.

CHAPTER X.

Before noon on the following day, the boat that was to convey Major Montgomerie and his niece to the American shore, pulled up to the landing place in front of the fort. The weather, as on the preceding day, was fine, and the river exhibited the same placidity of surface. Numerous bodies of Indians were collected on the banks, pointing to, and remarking on the singularity of the white flag which hung drooping at the stern of the boat. Presently the prisoners were seen advancing to the bank, accompanied by General Brock, Commodore Barclay, and the principal officers of the garrison. Major Montgomerie appeared pleased at the prospect of the liberty that awaited him, while the countenance of his niece, on the contrary, presented an expression of deep thought, although it was afterwards remarked by Granville and Villiers—both close observers of her demeanour that as her eye occasionally glanced in the direction of Detroit, it lighted up with an animation strongly in contrast with the general calm and abstractedness of her manner. All being now ready, Gerald Grantham, who had received his final instructions from the General, offered his arm to Miss Montgomerie, who, to all outward appearance, took it mechanically and unconsciously, although, in the animated look which the young sailor turned upon her in the next instant, there was evidence the contact had thrilled electrically to his heart. After exchanging a cordial pressure of the hand with his gallant entertainers, and reiterating to the General his thanks for the especial favor conferred upon him, the venerable Major followed them to the boat. His departure was the signal for much commotion among the Indians. Hitherto they had had no idea of what was in contemplation; but when they saw them enter and take their seats in the boat, they raised one of those terrific shouts which have so often struck terror and dismay, and brandishing their weapons seemed ready to testify their disapprobation by something more than words. It was however momentary—a commanding voice made itself heard, even amid the din of their loud yell, and, when silence had been obtained, a few animated sentences, uttered in a tone of deep authority, caused the tumult at once to subside. The voice was that of Tecumseh, and there were few among his race who, brave and indomitable as they were, could find courage to thwart his will. Meanwhile the boat, impelled by eight active seamen, urged its way through the silvery current, and in less than an hour from its departure had disappeared.

Two hours had elapsed—the General and superior officers had retired; and the Indians, few by few, had repaired to their several encampments, except a party of young warriors, who, wrapped in their blankets and mantles, lay indolently extended on the grass, smoking their pipes, or producing wild sounds from their melancholy flutes. Not far from these, sat, with their legs overhanging the edge of the steep bank, a group of the junior officers of the garrison, who, with that indifference which characterized their years, were occupied in casting pebbles into the river, and watching the bubbles that arose to the surface. Among the number was Henry Grantham, and, at a short distance from him, sat the old but athletic negro, Sambo, who, not having been required to accompany Gerald, to whom he was especially attached, had continued to linger on the bank long after his anxious eye had lost sight of the boat in which the latter had departed. While thus engaged, a new direction was given to the interest of all parties, by a peculiar cry, which reached them from a distance over the water, apparently from beyond the near extremity of the Island of Bois Blanc. To the officers the sound was unintelligible, for it was the first of the kind they had ever heard, but the young Indians appeared fully to understand its import. Starting from their lethargy, they sprang abruptly to their feet, and giving a sharp answering yell, stamped upon the green turf, and snuffed the hot air, with distended nostrils, like so many wild horses let loose upon the desert. Nor was the excitement confined to these, for, all along the line of encampment, the same wild notes were echoed, and forms came bounding again to the front, until the bank was once more peopled with savages.

" What was the meaning of that cry, Sambo, and whence came it ?" asked Henry Grantham, who, as well as his companions, had strained their eyes in every direction, but in vain, to discover its cause.

" Dat a calp cry, Massa Henry--see he dere a canoe not bigger nor a hick'ry nut," and he pointed with his finger to what in fact had the appearance of being little larger; " I wish," he pursued with bitterness, " dey bring him calp of dem billians Desborough—Dam him lying tief to hell."

" Bravo !" exclaimed De Courcy, who, in common with his companions, recollecting Gerald's story of the preceding day, was at no loss to understand why the latter epithet had been so emphatically bestowed ; " I see (winking to Henry Grantham) you have not yet forgiven his paddling round the gun boat the other night, while you and the rest of the crew were asleep, eh, Sambo ?

" So help me hebben, Obbicer, he no sail around a gun boat, he dam a Yankee. He come along a lake like a dam tief in e night and I tell a Massa Geral--and Massa Geral and me chase him all ober e water—I not a sleep Massa Courcy ;" pursued the old man with pique ; " I nebber sleep,—Massa Geral, nebber sleep."

" The devil ye don't" observed De Courcy quaintly, " then the Lord deliver *me* from gun boat service, I say."

" Amen " responded Villiers.

" Why," asked Middlemore, do Gerald Grantham and old

Frumpy here remind one of a certain Irish festival? Do you give it up? Because they are *awake*——"

The abuse heaped on the pre-eminently vile attempt was unmeasured—Sambo conceived it a personal affront to himself, and he said, with an air of mortification and wounded dignity, not unmixed with anger!

"Sambo poor black nigger—obbicer berry white man, but him heart all ob a color. He no Frumpy—Massa Geral no like an Irish bestibal. I wonder he no tick up for a broder, Massa Henry." His agitation here was extreme.

"Nonsense Sambo—don't you see we are only jesting with you, said the youth, in the kindest tone, for he perceived that the faithful creature was striving hard to check the rising tear—there is not an officer here who does not respect you for your long attachment to my family, and none would willingly give you pain—neither should you suppose they would say anything offensive in regard of my brother Gerald."

Pacified by this assurance, which was moreover, corroborated by several of his companions, really annoyed at having pained the old man, Sambo sank once more into respectful silence, still however continuing to occupy the same spot. During this colloquy the cry had been several times repeated, and as often replied to from the shore; and now a canoe was distinctly visible, urging its way to the beach. The warriors it contained were a scouting party, six in number—four paddling the light bark, and one at the helm, while the sixth who appeared, to be the leader, stood upright in the bow, waving from the long pole to which it was attached a human scalp. A few minutes and the whole had landed, and were encircled on the bank by their eager and inquiring comrades. Their story was soon told. They had encountered two Americans at some distance on the opposire shore, who were evidently making the best of their way through the forest to Detroit. They called upon them to deliver themselves up, but the only answer was an attempt at flight. The Indians fired, and one fell dead, pierced by many balls. The other, however, who happened to be considerably in advance, threw all his energy into his muscular frame, and being untouched by the discharge that had slain his companion, succeeded in gaining a dense underwood, through which he finally effected his escape. The scouts continued their pursuit for upwards of an hour, but finding it fruitless, returned to the place where they had left their canoe, having first secured the scalp and spoils of the fallen man."

"Dam him, debbel," exclaimed Sambo, who as well as the officers, had approached the party detailing their exploit, and had fixed his dark eye on the dangling trophy. "May I nebber see a hebben ib he not a calp of a younger Desborough. I know him lying tief by he hair—he all yaller like a sogers breast plate—curse him rascal (and his white and even teeth, were exbibited in the grin that accompanied the remark,) he nebber no more say he sail round Massa Geral gun boat, and Massa Geral and Sambo sleep."

"By Jove he is right," said De Courcy. "I recollect remarking the colour of the fellow's hair yesterday when on calling for a glass of "gin sling," at the inn to which I had conducted him, he threw his slouched hat unceremoniously on the table, and rubbed the fingers of both hands through his carrotty locks, until they actually appeared to stand like those of the Gorgon perfectly on end."

"And were there other proof wanting," said Villiers, "we have it here in the spoil his slayers are exhibiting to their companions. There is the identical powder horn, bullet pouch, and waist belt, which he wore when he landed on this very spot."

"And I," said Middlemore, "will swear by the crooked buck horn handle of that huge knife, or dagger; for in our struggle on the sands yesterday morning, his blanket coat came open, and discovered the weapon on which I kept a sharp eye, during the whole time. Had he but managed to plant that monster (and he affected to shudder,) under my middle ribs, then would it have been all over with poor Middlemore."

"There cannot be a doubt," remarked Henry Grantham. "With Sambo and De Courcy, I well recollect the hair, and I also particularly noticed the handle of his dagger, which, as you perceive, has a remarkable twist in it."

All doubt was put to rest by Sambo, who, having spoken with its possessor for a moment, now returned, bearing the knife, at the extremity of the handle of which, was engraved on a silver shield the letters P. E. T. A. Ens. M. M.

"Paul, Emilius, Theophilus, Arnoldi, Ensign Michigan Militia," pursued Grantham reading. "This then is conclusive, and we have to congratulate ourselves that one at least of two of the vilest scoundrels this country ever harboured, has at length met the fate he merited."

"Fate him merit, Massa Henry," muttered the aged and privileged negro, with something like anger in his tones, as he returned the knife to the Indian; "he dam 'serter from a king! No, no, he nebber deserb a die like dis. He ought to hab a rope roun him neck and die him lying teef like a dog."

"I guess however our friend Jeremiah has got clean slick off," said Villiers, imitating the tone and language of that individual, "and he, I take it, is by far the more formidable of the two. I expect that, before he dies, he will give one of us a long shot yet, in revenge for the fall of young hopeful."

"Traitorous and revengeful scoundrel," aspirated Henry Grantham, as the recollection of the manner of his father's death came over his mind. "It is, at least, some consolation to think his villainy has in part met its reward. I confess I exult in the death of young Desborough, less even because a dangerous enemy has been removed, than because in his fall the heart of the father will be racked in its only assailable point. I trust I am not naturally cruel, yet do I hope the image of his slain partner in infamy may ever after revisit his memory, and remind him of his crime."

An exclamation from the Indians now drew the attention of the officers to a boat that came in sight, in the direction in which that of Gerald Grantham had long since disappeared, and as she drew nearer, a white flag, floating in the stern became gradually distinguishable. Expressions of surprise passed among the officers, by whom various motives were assigned as the cause of the return of the flag of truce, for that it was their own boat no one doubted, especially, as, on approaching sufficiently near, the blue uniform of the officer who steered the boat was visible to the naked eye. On a yet nearer approach, however, it was perceived that the individual in question wore not the uniform of the British Navy, but that of an officer of the American line, the same precisely, indeed, as that of Major Montgomerie. It was further remarked that there was no lady in the boat, and that, independently of the crew, there was besides the officer already named, merely one individual, dressed in the non-commissioned uniform, who seemed to serve as his orderly. Full evidence being now had that this was a flag sent from the American Fort, which had, in all probability, missed Gerald by descending one channel of the river formed by Turkey Island, while the latter had ascended by the other, the aid-de-camp, De Courcy hastened to acquaint General Brock with the circumstance, and to receive his orders. By the time the American reached the landing place, the youth had returned, accompanying a superior officer of the staff. Both descended the flight of steps leading to the river, when, having saluted the officer, after a moment or two of conversation, they proceeded to blindfold him. This precaution having been taken, the American was then handed over the gun-wale of the boat, and assisted up the flight of steps by the two British officers on whose arms he leaned. As they passed through the crowd, on their way to the Fort, the ears of the stranger were assailed by loud yells from the bands of Indians, who, with looks of intense curiosity and interest, gazed on the passing, and to them in some degree inexplicable, scene.

Startling as was the fierce cry, the officer pursued his course without moving a muscle of his fine and manly form, beyond what was necessary to the action in which he was engaged. It was a position which demanded all his collectedness and courage, and he seemed as though he had previously made up his mind not to be deficient in either. Perhaps it was well that he had been temporarily deprived of sight, for could he have remarked the numerous tomahawks that were raised towards him, in pantomimic representation of what they would have done had they been permitted, the view would in no way have assisted his self-possession. The entrance to the fort once gained by the little party, the clamour began to subside, and the Indians, by whom they had been followed, returned to the bank of the river to satisfy their curiosity with a view of those who had been left in the boat, to which, as a security against all possible outrage, a sergeant's command had meanwhile been despatched.

It was in the drawing room of Colonel D'Egville, that the General, surrounded by his chief officers, awaited the arrival of the flag of truce. Into this the American Colonel, for such was his rank, after traversing the area of the fort that lay between, was now ushered, and, the bandage being removed, his eye encountered several to whom he was personally known, and with these such salutations as became the occasion were exchanged.

" The flag you bear, sir," commenced the General, after a few moments of pause succeeding these greetings, " relates I presume, to the prisoners so recently fallen into our hands."

" By no means, General," returned the American, " this is the first intimation I have had of such fact—my mission is of a wholly different nature. I am deputed by the officer commanding the forces of the United States, to summon the garrison of Amherstburg, with all its naval dependencies, to surrender within ten days from this period."

The General smiled. " A similar purpose seems to have actuated us both," he observed. " A shorter limit have I prescribed to the officer by whom I have, this very day, sent a flag to General Hull; I have caused it to be intimated, that, failing to comply with my summons, he may on the ensuing Sabbath expect to see the standard of England floating over the walls of his citadel. This, Colonel, you may moreover repeat as my answer to your mission."

The American bowed. "Such then, General, is your final determination?"

"Not more certain is it that the next Sabbath will dawn, than that the force I have the honor to command will attempt the assault upon that day."

"What, within three days? You would seem to hold us cheaply, General," said the American piquedly, "that you do not even leave us in doubt as to the moment of your intended attack."

"And if I would, it were useless," was the reply, "since what I do attempt shall be attempted openly. In the broad face of day will I lead my troops to the trenches. By this time, however, your chief must know my determination—where, may I ask, did you pass my flag?"

"I met with none, General," and yet my boat kept as nearly in the middle of the stream as possible."

"Then must ye have passed each other on the opposite sides of Turkey Island. The officer in charge was moreover accompanied by two of the prisoners to whom I have alluded —one a field officer in your own regiment."

"May I ask who?" interrupted the American quickly, and slightly coloring.

"Major Montgomerie."

"So I suspected. Was the other officer of my regiment?"

"The other," said the General, "bears no commission, and is simply a volunteer in the expedition—one in short, whose earnest wish to reach Detroit, was the principal motive for my offering the Major his liberty on parole."

"And may I ask the name of this individual, so unimimportant in rank, and yet so filled with ardor in the cause, as to be thus anxious to gain the theatre of war?"

"One probably not unknown to you, Colonel, as the niece of your brother officer—Miss Montgomerie."

"Miss Montgomerie here!" faltered the American, rising and paling as he spoke, while he mechanically placed on the table a glass of wine he had the instant before raised to his lips—"surely it connot be."

There was much to excite interest, not only in the changed tone but in the altered features of the American, as he thus involuntarily gave expression to his surprise. The younger officers winked at each other, and smiled their conviction of *une affaire de cœur*—while the seniors were no less ready to infer that they now had arrived at the true secret of the impatience of Miss Montgomerie to reach the place of her destination. To the penetrating eye of the General, however, there was an expression of pain on the countenance of the officer, which accorded ill with the feeling one might be supposed to entertain, who had been unexpectedly brought nearer to an object of attachment, and he kindly sought to relieve his evident embarrassment by remarking:

"I can readily comprehend your surprise, Colonel. One would scarcely have supposed that a female could have had courage to brave the dangers attendant on an expedition of this kind, in an open boat—but Miss Montgomerie, I confess, appears to me to be one whom no danger could daunt, and whose resoluteness of purpose, once directed, no secondary agency could divert from its original aim."

Before the officer, having partially regained his composure, could reply, Colonel D'Egville, who had absented himself during the latter part of the conversation, returned and addressing the former in terms that proved their acquaintance to have been of previous date, invited him to partake of some refreshment, which had been prepared for him in an adjoining apartment. This the American at first faintly declined, on the plea of delay having been prohibited by his chief; but, on the General jocosely remarking that, sharing their hospitality on the present occasion would be no barrier to breaking a lance a week hence, he assented; and, following Colonel D'Egville, passed through a short corridor into a smaller apartment where a copious but hurried refreshment had been prepared.

The entry of the officer was greeted by the presence of three ladies—Mrs. D'Egville and her daughters—all of whom received him with the frank cordiality that bespoke intimacy, while, on the countenance of one of the latter, might be detected evidences of an interest that had its foundation in something more than the mere esteem which dictated the conduct of her mother and sister. If Julia D'Egville was in reality the laughing, light hearted, creature represented in the mess room conversation of the officers of the garrison, it would have been difficult for a stranger to have recognized her in the somewhat serious girl who now added her greetings to theirs, but in a manner slightly tinctured with embarrassment.

The American, who seemed not to notice it, directed his conversation, as he partook of the refreshment, principally to Mrs. D'Egville, to whom he spoke of various ladies at Detroit, friends of both, who were deep deplorers of the war and the non-communication which it occasioned; alluded to the many delightful parties that had taken place, yet were now interrupted; and to the many warm friendships which had been formed, yet might by this event be severed for ever. He concluded by presenting a note from a very intimate friend of the family, to which, he said, he had been requested to take back a written answer.

A feeling of deep gratification pervaded the benevolent countenance of Mrs D'Egville, as, on perusal, she found that it contained the offer of an asylum for herself and daughters in case Amherstburg should be carried by storm, as, considering the American great superiority of force, was thought likely, in the event of the British General refusing to surrender.

"Excellent, kind hearted friend!" she exclaimed when she had finished—"this indeed does merit an answer. Need of assistance, however, there is none, since my noble friend, the General, has pledged himself to anticipate any attempt to make our soil the theatre of war—still, does it give me pleasure to be enabled to reciprocate her offer, by promising, in my turn, an asylum against all chances of outrage on the part of the wild Indians, attached to our cause"—and she left the room.

No sooner did the American find himself alone with the sisters, for Colonel D'Egville had previously retired to the General, than discarding all reserve, and throwing himself on his knees at the feet of her who sat next him, he exclaimed, in accents of the most touching pathos:

"Julia, dearest Julia! for this alone am I here. I volunteered to be the bearer of the summons to the British General, in the hope that some kind chance would give you to my view, and now that fortune, propitious beyond my utmost expectations, affords me the happiness of speaking to you whom I had feared never to behold more, oh, tell me that, whatever be the result of this unhappy war, you will not forget me. For me, I shall ever cherish you in my heart's core."

The glow which mantled over the cheek of the agitated girl, plainly told that this passionate appeal was made to no unwilling ear. Still she spoke not.

"Dearest Julia, answer me—the moments of my stay are few, and at each instant we are liable to interruption. In one word, therefore, may I hope? In less than a week, many who have long been friends will meet as enemies. Let me then at least have the consolation to know from your lips, that whatever be the event, that dearest of all gifts—your regard—is unchangeably mine."

"I do promise, Ernest," faltered the trembling girl. "My heart is yours and yours forever—but do not unnecessarily expose yourself," and her head sank confidingly on the shoulder of her lover.

"Thank you, dearest," and the encircling arm of the impassioned officer drew her form closer to his beating heart. Gertrude, you are witness of her vow, and before you, under more auspicious circumstances, will I claim its fulfilment. Oh Julia, Julia, this indeed does recompense me for many a long hour of anxiety and doubt."

"And hers too have been hours of anxiety and doubt," said the gentle Gertrude. "Ever since the war has been spoken of as certain, Julia has been no longer the gay girl she was. Her dejection has been subject of remark with all, and such is her dislike to any allusion to the past, that she never even rallies Captain Cranstoun on his bear-skin adventure of last winter on the ice."

"Ah," interrupted the American, "never shall I forget the evening that preceded that adventure. It was then, dearest Julia, that I ventured to express the feeling with which you had inspired me. It was then I had first the delight of hearing from your lips that I need not entirely despair. I often, often, think of that night."

"Of course you have not yet received my note, Ernest. Perhaps you will deem it inconsiderate in me to have written, but I could not resist the desire to afford you what I conceived would be a gratification, by communicating intelligence of ourselves."

"Note! what note! and by whom conveyed?"

"Have you not heard, enquired Gertrude, warming into animation, "that the General has sent a flag this morning to Detroit, and, under its protection, two prisoners captured by my gallant cousin, who is the officer that conducts them."

"And to that cousin you have confided the letter?" interrupted the Colonel, somewhat eagerly.

"No, not my cousin," said Julia, "but to one I conceived

better suited to the trust. You must know that my father, with his usual hospitality, insisted on Major Montgomerie and his niece, the parties in question, taking up their abode with us during the short time they remained."

"And to Miss Montgomerie you gave your letter," hurriedly exclaimed the Colonel, starting to his feet, and exhibiting a countenance of extreme paleness."

"Good heaven, Ernest! what is the matter? Surely you do not think me guilty of imprudence in this affair. I was anxious to write to you,—I imagined you would be glad to hear from me, and thought that the niece of one of your officers would be the most suitable medium of communication. I therefore confessed to her my secret, and requested her to take charge the letter."

"Oh, Julia, you have been indeed imprudent. But what said she—how looked she when you confided to her our secret?"

"She made no other remark than to ask how long our attachment had existed, adding that she had once known something of you herself; and her look and voice were calm, and her cheek underwent no variation from the settled paleness observable there since her arrival."

"And in what manner did she receive her trust?" again eagerly demanded the Colonel.

"With a solemn assurance that it should be delivered to you with her own hand—then, and then only, did a faint smile animate her still but beautiful features. Yet why all these questions, Ernest? Or can it really be? Tell me," and the voice of the young girl became imperative, "has Miss Montgomerie any claim upon your hand—she admitted to have known you?"

"On my honor, none;" impressively returned the Colonel.

"Oh, what a weight you have removed from my heart, Ernest, but wherefore your alarm, and wherein consists my imprudence?"

"In this only, dearest Julia, that I had much rather

another than she had been admitted into your confidence. But as you have acted for the best, I cannot blame you. Still I doubt not," and the tones of the American were low and desponding, "that, as she has promised, she will find means to deliver your note into my own hands—the seal is ——?"

"A fancy one—Andromache disarming Hector.

"Rise, for Heaven's sake rise," interrupted Gertrude; "here comes mamma."

One fond pressure of her graceful form, and the Colonel had resumed his seat. In the next moment Mrs. D'Egville entered, by one door, and immediately afterwards her husband by another. The former handed her note, and during the remarks which accompanied its delivery, gave the little party (for Gertrude was scarcely less agitated than her sister) time to recover from their embarassment. Some casual conversation then ensued, when the American, despite of Mrs. D'Egville's declaration that he could not have touched a single thing during her absence, expressed his anxiety to depart. The same testimonies of friendly greeting, which had marked his entrance, were exchanged, and preceded by his kind host. The Colonel once more gained the apartment where the General still lingered, awaiting his reappearance."

Nothing remaining to be added to the answer already given to the summons, the American, after exchanging salutations with such of the English Officers as were personally known to him, again submitted himself to the operation of blindfolding; after which he was reconducted to the beach, where his boat's crew, who had in their turn been supplied with refreshments, were ready to receive him. As on his arrival, the loud yellings of the Indians accompanied his departure but as these had been found to be harmless, they were even less heeded than before. Within two hours, despite of the strong current, the boat had disappeared altogether from the view.

Late in that day, the barge of Gerald Grantham returned from Detroit. Ushered into the presence of the General, the young sailor communicated the delivery of his charge into the hands of the American Chief, who had returned his personal acknowledgments for the courtesy. His answer to the summons, however, was that having a force fully adequate to the purpose, he was prepared to defend the fort to the last extremity, and waiving his own original plan of attack, would await the British General on the defensive, when to the God of Battles should be left the decision of the contest. To a question on the subject, the young officer added that he had seen nothing of the American flag of truce, either in going or returning.

That night orders were issued to the heads of the different departments, immediately to prepare *materiel* for a short siege; and, an assault at the termination of the third day. By both troops and Indians, this intelligence was received with pleasure; for all, sanguine as they were under such a leader, looked confidently to the speedy conquest of a post which was one of the highest importance on that frontier.

CHAPTER XI.

Conformably with the orders of the British General, the siege of the American fortress was commenced on the day following that of the mutual exchange of flags. The elevated ground above the village of Sandwich, immediately opposite to the enemy's fort, was chosen for the erection of three batteries, from which a well sustained and well directed fire was kept up for several successive days, yet without effecting any practicable breach in their defences. One of these batteries, manned principally by sailors, was under the direction of Gerald Grantham, whose look out duty had been in a great degree rendered unnecessary, by the advance of the English flotilla up the river, and who had consequently been appointed to this more active service.

During the whole of Saturday, the 15th of August, the British guns had continued to play upon the fort, vomiting shot and shell as from an exhaustless and angry volcano—and several of the latter falling short, the town which was of wood had been more than once set on fire. As, however, it was by no means the intention of the General to do injury to the inhabitants, no obstacle was opposed to the attempts of the enemy to get it under, and the flames were as often and as speedily extinguished. An advanced hour of night at length put an end to the firing, and the artillery men and seamen, extended on their great coats and pea jackets, in their several embrasures, snatched from fatigue that repose which their unceasing exertions of the many previous hours had rendered at once a luxury and a want.

The battery commanded by Gerald Grantham, was the central and most prominent of the three, and it had been remarked by all—and especially by the troops stationed in the rear in support of the guns—that his firing during the day, had been the most efficient, many of his shot going point blank into the hostile fortress, and (as could be distinctly seen with the telescope) occasioning evident confusion.

The several officers commanding batteries were now met in that of the young sailor, and habited in a garb befitting the rude duty at which they had presided, were earnestly engaged in discussing the contents of their haversacks, moistened by occasional drafts of rum and water from their wooden canteens, and seasoned with frequent reference to the events of the past day, and anticipations of what the morrow would bring forth. A lantern so closed as to prevent all possibility of contact with the powder that lay strewed about, was placed in the centre of the circle, and the dim reflexion from this upon the unwashed hands and faces of the party, begrimed as they were with powder and perspiration, contributed to give an air of wildness to the whole scene, that found its origin in the peculiar circumstances of the moment. Nor was the picture at all lessened in ferocity of effect, by the figure of Sambo in the back ground, who, dividing his time between the performances of such offices as his young master demanded, in the course of the frugal meal of the party, and a most assiduous application of his own white and shining teeth to a huge piece of venison ham, might, without effort, have called up the image of some lawless, yet obedient slave, attending on and sharing in the orgies of a company of buccaneers.

At length the meal was ended, and each was preparing to depart, with a view to snatch an hour or two of rest in his own battery, when the pricked ear and forward thrown head of the old negro, accompanied by a quick, "Husha, Massa Geral," stilled them all into attitudes of expectancy. Presently the sound of muffled oars was heard, and then the harsh grating as of a boat's keel upon the sands.

In the next minute the officers were at their posts; but

before they could succeed in awakening their jaded men, who seemed to sleep the sleep of death, the sentinel at the first battery had received, in answer to his hurried challenge, the proper countersign, and, as on closer inspection it was found that there was only one boat, he knew it must be their own, and the alarm which had seized them for the security of their trust passed away.

They were not long kept in suspense. One individual alone had ascended from the beach, and now stood among them, habited in a dread-nought jacket and trousers and round hat. His salutation to each was cordial, and he expressed in warm terms the appprobation he felt at the indefatigable and efficient manner in which the duty assigned to each had been conducted.

"Well, gentlemen," continued the Commodore, (for it was he), "you have done famously today—and in most masterly style did you silence those batteries, which the enemy, to divert your fire from the fort, had erected on the opposite bank. Much has been done, but more remains. Tomorrow you must work double tides. At daylight you must re-open with showers of shot and shell, for it is, during the confusion caused by your fire, that the General intends crossing his troops and advancing to the assault. But this is not all—we have some suspicion the enemy may attempt your batteries this very night, with a view of either spiking the guns, if they cannot maintain the position; or of turning them, if they can, on our advancing columns. Now all the troops destined for the assault, are assembled ready to effect their landing at daybreak, and none can be spared unless the emergency be palpable. What I seek is a volunteer to watch the movements of the enemy during the remainder of the night—one (and he looked at Grantham) whose knowledge of the country will enable him to approach the opposite coast unseen, and whose expedition will enable us to have due warning of any hostile attempt."

"I shall be most happy, sir, to undertake the task, if you consider me worthy of it," said Grantham, "but——"

"But what?" interrupted the Commodore hastily.

"My only difficulty, sir, is the means. Had I my light canoe here, with Sambo for my helmsman, I would seek their secret even on their own shores."

"Bravo, my gallant fellow," returned the Commodore, again cordially shaking the hand of his Lieutenant. "This I expected of you, and have come prepared. I have had the precaution to bring your canoe and paddles with me—you will find them below in my boat."

"Then is every difficulty at an end," exclaimed the young sailor joyously. "And our dress, sir?"

"No disguise whatever, in case of accidents—we must not have you run the risk of being hanged for a spy."

Gerald Grantham having secured his cutlass and pistols, now descended with the Commodore to the beach, whither Sambo (similarly armed) had already preceded him. Under the active and vigorous hands of the latter, the canoe had already been removed from the boat, and now rested on the sands ready to be shoved off. The final instructions of the Commodore to his officer, as to the manner of communicating intelligence of any movement on the part of the Americans, having been given, the latter glided noiselessly from the shore into the stream, while the boat, resuming the direction by which it had approached, was impelled down the river with as little noise as possible, and hugging the shore for greater secrecy, was soon lost both to the eye and to the ear.

It was with a caution rendered necessary by the presence of the vessels in the harbour, that Gerald Grantham and his faithful campanion, having gained the middle of the river, now sought to approach nearer to the shore. The night, although not absolutely gloomy, was yet sufficiently obscure to aid their enterprize; and notwithstanding they could dis-dinctly hear the tread of the American sentinels, as they paced the deck of their flotilla, such was the stillness of Sambo's practised paddle, that the little canoe glided past them unheard, and, stealing along the shore, was enabled to gain the farther extremity of the town, where however, despite of the most scrupulous inspection, not the slightest evidence of a collective movement was to be observed. Recollecting that most of the American boats used for the transport of their Army from the Canadian shore, (which they had occupied for some time,) were drawn up on the beach at the opposite end of the town, and deeming that if any attempt on the batteries was in contemplation, the troops ordered for that duty would naturally embark at a point whence, crossing the river considerably above the object of their expedition, they might drift down with the current, and effect a landing without noise, he determined to direct his course between the merchantmen and vessels of war, and pursue his way to the opposite end of the town. The enterprize, it ts true, was bold, and not by any means, without hazard; but Grantham's was a spirit that delighted in excitement, and moreover he trusted much to the skill of his pilot, the darkness of the night, and the seeming repose of the enemy. Even if seen, it was by no means certain he should be taken, for his light skiff could worm its way where another dared not follow, and as for any shot that might be sent in pursuit of them, its aim would, in the obscurity of the night, be extremely uncertain.

Devoted as the old negro was to Gerald's will, it was but to acquaint him with his intention to ensure a compliance; although, in this case, it must be admitted a reluctant one. Cautiously and silently, therefore, they moved between the line of vessels, keeping as close as they could to the merchantmen, in which there was apparently no guard, so that under the shadow of the hulls of these they might escape all observation from the more watchful vessels of war without. They had cleared all but one, when the head of the canoe suddenly came foul of the hawser of the latter, and was by the checked motion brought round, with her broadside completely under her stern, in the cabin windows oi which, much to the annoyance of our adventurer, a light was plainly visible. Rising as gently as he could to clear the bow of the light skiff, he found his head on a level with the windows, and as his eye naturally fell on all within, his attention was arrested sufficiently to cause a sign from him to Sambo to remain still. The cabin was spacious, and filled every where with female forms, who were lying in various attitudes of repose, while the whole character of the arrangements were such as to induce his belief, that the vessel had been appropriated to the reception of the families of the principal inhabitants of the place, and this with a view of their being more secure from outrage from the Indians on the ensuing day. In the midst of the profound repose in which, forgetful of the dangers of the morrow, all appeared to be wrapped, there was one striking exception. At a small table in the centre of the cabin, sat a figure enveloped in a long and ample dark cloak, and covered with a slouched hat. There was nothing to indicate sex in the figure, which might have been taken either for a woman, or for a youth. It was clear, however, that it wanted in its contour the proportions of manhood. At the moment when Gerald's attention was first arrested, the figure was occupied in reading a letter, which she afterwards sealed with black. The heart of the sailor beat violently, he knew not wherefore, but before he could explain his feelings even to himself, he saw the figure deposit the letter, and remove, apparently from the bosom of its dress, a miniature on which it gazed intently for upwards of a minute. The back being turned towards the windows he could trace no expression on the countenance, but in the manner there was none of that emotion, which usually accompanies the contemplation of the features of a beloved object. Depositing the picture in the folds of its cloak, the figure rose, and with a caution indicating desire not to disturb those who slumbered around, moved through the straggling forms that lay at its feet, and ascending the stairs, finally disappeared from the cabin.

Somewhat startled, the young officer hesitated as to what course he should pursue, for it was evident that if the figure, whoever it might prove, should come to the stern of the vessel, he and his companion must be discovered. For a moment he continued motionless, but with ear and eye keenly on the alert. At length he fancied he heard footsteps, as of one treading the loose plank that led from the vessel's side to the wharf. He pushed the canoe lightly along, so as to enable him to get clear of her stern, when glancing his eye in that direction, he saw the figure, still in the same dress, quit the plank it had been traversing, and move rapidly along the wharf towards the centre of the town.

Ruminating on the singularity of what he had observed, our adventurer now pursued his course up the river; but still without discovering any evidence of hostile preparation. On the contrary, a deep silence appeared to pervade every part of the town, the repose of which was the more remarkable, as it was generally known, that the attack on the fort was to be made on the following day. Arrived opposite the point where the town terminated, Grantham could distinctly count some twenty or thirty large boats drawn up on the beach, while in the fields beyond, the drowsy guard evidently stationed there for their protection, and visible by the dying embers of their watch-fire, denoted any thing but the activity which should have governed an enterprize of the nature apprehended. Satisfied that the information conveyed to his superiors was incorrect, the young officer dismissed from his mind all further anxiety on the subject; yet, impelled by recollections well befitting the hour and the circumstances, he could not avoid lingering near a spot, which, tradition had invested with much to excite the imagination and feeling. It was familiar to his memory, (for he had frequently heard it in boyhood,) that some dreadful tragedy had, in former days, been perpetrated near this bridge; and he had reason to believe that some of the actors in it, were those whose blood flowed in his own young veins. The extreme pain it seemed to give his parents, however, whenever allusion was made to the subject, had ever repressed inquiry, and all his knowledge of these events, was confined to what he had been enabled to glean from the aged Canadians. That Sambo, who was a very old servant of the family, had more than hear-say acquaintance with the circumstances, he was almost certain; for he had frequently remarked, when after having had his imagination excited by the oft told tale, he felt desirous of visiting the spot, the negro obedient in all things else, ever found some excuse to avoid accompanying him, nor, within his own recollection, had he once approached the scene. Certain vague allusions, of late date, by the old man, had moreover, confirmed him in his impression, and he now called forcibly to mind an observation made by his faithful attendant on the night of their pursuit of the younger Desborough, which, evidently referred to that period. Even on the present occasion, he had been struck by the urgency with which he contended for a return to their own shore, without pursuing their course to the extreme end of the town; nor was his unwillingness to approach the bridge overcome, until Gerald told him it was the positive order of the Commodore, that they should embrace the whole of the American lines in their inspection, and even *then*, it was with a relaxed vigour of arm, that he obeyed the instruction to proceed.

Determined to sound him, as to his knowledge of the fact, Grantham stole gently from the bow to the stern of the canoe, and he was about to question him, when the other, grasping his arm with an expressive touch, pointed to a dark object moving across the road. Gerald turned his head, and beheld the same figure that had so recently quitted the cabin of the merchantman. Following its movements, he saw it noiselessly enter into the grounds of a cottage, opposite an old tannery, where it totally disappeared.

A new direction was now given to the curiosity of the sailor. Expressing in a whisper to Sambo, his determination to follow, he desired him to make for the shore, near the tannery, beneath the shadow of which he might be secure, while he himself advanced, and traced the movements of the mysterious wanderer.

"Oh Massa Geral," urged the old man in the same whisper—his teeth chattering with fear—"for Hebben' sake e no go ashore. All dis a place berry bad, and dat no a livin' ting what e see yonder. Do Massa Geral take poor nigger word, and not go dere affer e ghost."

"Nay, Sambo, it is no ghost, but flesh and blood, for I saw it in the brig we were foul of just now; however be under no alarm. Armed as I am, I have nothing to fear from one individual, and if I am seen and pursued in my turn, it is but to spring in again, and before any one can put off in chase we shall have nearly reached the opposite shore—You shall remain in the canoe if you please, but I most certainly will see where that figure went."

"Berry well, Massa Geral," and the old man spoke piquedly, although partly re-assured by the assurance that it was no ghost. "If e no take e poor nigger wice e do as e like; but I no top in e canoe while e go and have him troat cut, or carry off by a debbil—I dam if e go—I go too."

This energetic rejoinder being conclusive, and in no wise opposed by his master, the old man made for the shore as desired. Both having disembarked, a cautious examination was first made of the premises, which tending to satisfy them that all within slumbered, the canoe was secreted under the shadow of the cottage, the adventurers crossed the road in the direction taken by the figure—Sambo following close in the rear of his master, and looking occasionally behind him, not with the air of one who fears a mortal enemy, but of one rather who shrinks from collision with a spirit of another world.

The front grounds of the cottage were separated from the high road by a fence of open pallisades, in the centre of which was a small gate of the same description. It was evidently through this latter that the figure had disappeared, and as its entrance had been effected without effort, Gerald came to the conclusion, on finding the latter yield to his touch, that this was the abode of the midnight wanderer. Perhaps some young American officer, whom intrigue or frolic had led forth in disguise on an excursion from which he was now returned. His curiosity was therefore on the point of yielding to the prudence which dictated an immediate relinquishment of the adventure, when he felt his right arm suddenly seized in the convulsed and trembling grasp of his attendant. Turning to ascertain the cause, he beheld as distinctly as the gloom of the night would permit, the features of the old man worked into an expression of horror, while trembling in every joint, he pointed to the mound of earth at the far extremity of the garden, which was known to contain the ashes of those from whom his imagination had been so suddenly diverted by the reappearance of the figure. This, owing to the position in which he stood, had hitherto escaped the notice of the officer, whose surprise may be imagined, when, looking in the direction pointed out to him, he beheld the same muffled figure, reposing its head apparently in an attitude of profound sorrow, against one of the white tomb stones that rose perpendicularly from the graves.

That Sambo feared nothing which emanated not from the world of spirits, Grantham well knew. It therefore became his first care to dismiss from the mind of the poor fellow the superstitious alarm that had taken possession of every faculty. From their proximity to the party, this could only be done by energetic signs, the progress of which was however interrupted by their mutual attention being diverted by a change in the position of the figure, which, throwing itself at its length upon the grave, for a moment or two sobbed andibly Presently afterwards it rose abruptly, and wraping its disguise more closely around it, quitted the mound and disappeared in the rear of the house.

The emotion of the figure, in giving evidence of its materiality, had, more than all the signs of his master, contributed to allay the agitation of the old negro. When therefore Gerald, urged by his irrepressible curiosity, in a whisper declared his intention to penetrate to the rear of the house, he was enabled to answer.

"For Gorramity's sake, Massa Geral, nebber go dare. Dis a place all berry bad for e family. Poor Sambo hair white now but when he black like a quirrel he see all a dis a people kill—" (and he pointed to the mound) "oh, berry much blood spill here, Massa Geral. It make a poor nigger heart sick to tink of it."

Gerald grasped the shoulder of the old man. "Sambo," he whispered, in the same low, but in a determined tone, "I have long thought you acquainted with the history of this place, although you have eluded my desire for information on the subject. After the admission you have now made, however, I expect you will tell me all and every thing connected with it. Not now—for I am resolved to see who that singular being is, who apparently, like myself, feels an interest in these mouldering bones. As you perceive it is no ghost, but flesh and blood like ourselves, stay here if you will, until I return; but something more must I see of this mystery before I quit the spot.

Without waiting for reply, he gently pushed the unlatched gate before him. It opened without noise, and quitting the pathway he moved along the green sward in the direction in which the figure had disappeared. Love for his master, even more than the superstitious awe he felt on being left alone, in that memorable spot, at so late an hour, put an end to the indecision of the old man. Entering and cautiously closing the gate, he followed in the footsteps of his master, and both in the next minute were opposite to the mound where the figure had first been observed.

As he was about to quit the grass, and enter upon the gravelled walk that led to the rear of the cottage, he fancied he distinguished a sound within, similar to that of a door cautiously opening. Pausing again to listen, he saw a light strongly reflected from an upper window, upon what had the appearance of a court yard in the rear, and in that light the dark shadow of a human form. This he at once recognized, from its peculiar costume to be the mysterious person who had so strongly excited his curiosity. For a moment or two all was obscurity, when again, but from a more distant window, the same light and figure were again reflected. Presently the figure disappeared, but the light still remained. Impelled by an uncontrollable desire to behold the features, and ascertain, if possible, the object of this strange wanderer, the young sailor cast his eye rapidly in search of the means of raising himself to a level with the window, when, much to his satisfaction, he remarked immediately beneath, a large water butt which was fully adequate to the purpose, and near this a rude wooden stool which would enable him to gain a footing on its edge, without exertion, or noise. It is true there was every reason to believe that what he had seen was, an officer belonging to the guard stationed in the adjoining field, who had his temporary residence in this building, and was now, after the prosecution of some love adventure returning home; but Gerald could not reconcile this with the strong emotion he had manifested near the tomb, and the startling secrecy with which, even when he had entered, he moved along his own apartments. These contradictions were stimulants to the gratification of his own curiosity, or interest, or whatever it might be; and although he could not conceal from himself that he incurred no inconsiderable risk from observation, by the party itself, the desire to see into the interior of the apartment and learn something further, rose paramount to all consideration for his personal safety. His first care now was to disencumber himself of his shoes and cutlass, which he gave in charge to Sambo, with directions to the latter to remain stationary on the sward, keeping a good look-out to guard against surprise. As by this arrangement his master would be kept in tolerable proximity, the old negro, whose repugnance to be left alone in that melancholy spot was invincible, offered no longer an objection, and Gerald, bracing more tightly round his loins, the belt which contained his pistols, proceeded cautiously to secure the stool, by the aid of which he speedily found his feet resting on the edge of the water butt, and his face level with the window. This, owing to the activity of his professional habits, he had been enabled to accomplish without perceptible noise.

The scene that met the fixed gaze of the adventurous officer, was one to startle and excite in no ordinary degree. The room into which he looked was square, with deep recesses on the side where he lingered, formed by the projection of a chimney in which, however, owing to the sultry season of the year, no traces of recent fire were visible. In the space between the chimney and wall, forming the innermost recess, was placed a rude uncurtained bed, and on this lay extended, and delineated beneath the covering, a human form, the upper extremities of which was hidden from view by the projecting chimney. The whole attitude of repose of this latter indicated the unconciousness of profound slumber. On a small table near the foot, were placed several books and papers, and an extinguished candle. Leaning over the bed and holding a small lamp which had evidently been brought and lighted since its entrance, stood the mysterious figure on whom the interest of Gerald had been so strongly excited. It seemed to be gazing intently on the features of the sleeper, and more than once, by the convulsed movements of its form, betrayed intense agitation. Once it made a motion as if to awaken the person on whom it gazed, but suddenly changing its purpose, drew from its dress a letter which Gerald recognized to be that so recently prepared in the cabin of the brig. Presently both letter and lamp were deposited on the bed, and in one upraised hand of the figure gleamed the blade of a knife or dagger, while the left grasped and shook, with an evident view to arouse, the sleeper. An exclamation of horror, accompanied by a violent struggle of its limbs, proclaimed reviving consciousness in the latter. A low wild laugh burst in scorn from the lips of the figure, and the strongly nerved arm was already descending to strike its assassin blow, when suddenly the pistol, which Gerald had almost unconsciously cocked and raised to the window, was discharged with a loud explosion. The awakened slumberer was now seen to spring from the bed to the floor, and in the action the lamp was overturned and extinguished; but all struggle appeared to have ceased.

Bewildered beyond measure in his reflection, yet secure in the conviction that he had by this desperate step saved the life of a human being from the dagger of the assassin, the only object of Gerald now was to secure himself from the consequences. Springing from his position he was soon at the side of the startled Sambo, who had witnessed his last act with inconceivable dismay. Already were the guard in the adjoining field, alarmed by the report of the pistol, hurrying toward the house, when they reached the little gate, and some even appeared to be making for their boats on the beach. With these motives to exertion, neither Gerald nor the old negro were likely to be deficient in activity. Bending low as they crossed the road, they managed unperceived to reach that part of the tannery where their canoe had been secreted, and Sambo having hastily launched it, they made directly for the opposite shore, unharmed by some fifteen or twenty shots that were fired at them by the guard, and drifting down with the current, reached, about an hour before dawn, the battery from which they had started.

CHAPTER XII.

At day-break on the morning of Sunday, the 16th of August, the fire from the batteries was resumed, and with a fury that must have satisfied the Americans, even had they been ignorant of the purpose, it was intended to cover some ulterior plan of operation on the part of the British General. Their own object appeared rather to make preparation of defence against the threatened assault, than to return a cannonade, which, having attained its true range, excessively annoyed and occasioned them much loss. Meanwhile every precaution had been taken to secure the safe transport of the army. The flotilla, considerably superior at the outset of the war, to that of the Americans, had worked up the river during the night, and anchored in the middle, lay with their broadsides ready to open upon any force that might appear to oppose the landing of the troops, while numerous scows, for the transport of a light brigade of horse artillery, and all the boats and batteaux that could be collected, added to those of the fleet, lay covering the sands, ready to receive their destined burdens. At length the embarkation was completed, and the signal having been given, the several divisions of boats moved off in the order prescribed to them. Never did a more picturesque scene present itself to the human eye, than during the half hour occupied in the transit of this little army. The sun was just rising gloriously and unclouded, as the first division of boats pushed from the shore, and every object within the British and American line of operation, tended to the production of an effect, that was little in unison with the anticipated issue of the whole. Not a breeze ruffled the fair face of the placid Detroit, through which the heavily laden boats now made their slow, but certain way, and a spectator who, in utter ignorance of events, might have been suddenly placed on the Canadian bank, would have been led to imagine, that a fête, not a battle, was intended. Immediately above the village of Sandwich, and in full view of the American Fort, lay the English flotilla at anchor, their white sails half clewed up, their masts decked with gay pendants, and their taffrails with ensigns that lay drooping over their sterns into the water, as if too indolent to bear up against the coming sultriness of the day. Below these, glittering in bright scarlet, that glowed not unpleasingly on the silvery stream, the sun's rays dancing on their polished muskets and accoutrements, glided like gay actors in an approaching pageant, the columns destined for the assault, while further down, and distributed far and wide over the expanse of water, were to be seen a multitude of canoes, filled with Indian warriors, whose war costume could not, in the distance, be distinguished from that of the dance; the whole contributing, with the air of quietude on both shores, and absence of all opposition on the American especially, to inspire feelings of joyousness and pleasure, rather than the melancholy consequent on a knowledge of the final destination of the whole. Nor would the incessant thunder of the cannon in the distance, have in any way diminished this impression; for as the volumes of smoke, vomited from the opposing batteries, met and wreathed themselves together in the centre of the stream, leaving at intervals the gay colours of England and America, brightly displayed to the view, the impression, to a spectator, would have been that of one who witnesses the exchange of military honors between two brave and friendly powers, preparing the one to confer, the other to receive all the becoming courtesies of a chivalrous hospitality. If any thing were wanting to complete the illusion, the sound of the early mass bell, summoning to the worship of that God whom no pageantry of man may dispossess of homage, would amply crown and heighten the effect of the whole, while the chaunting of the hymn of adoration, would appear a part of the worship of the Deity, and of the pageantry itself.

Vying, each with the other, who should first gain the land, the exertions of the several rowers increased, as the distance to be traversed diminished, so that many arrived simultaneously at the beach. Forming in close column of sections as they landed, the regular troops occupied the road, their right flank resting on the river, while a strong body of Indians under Round-head, Split-log, and Walk-in-the-Water, scouring the open country beyond, completely guarded their left from surprise. Among the first to reach the shore, was the gallant General, the planner of the enterprise, who, with his personal staff, crossed the river in the barge of the Commodore, steered by that officer himself. During the short period that the columns were delayed for the landing of the artillery, necessarily slower in their movements, a short conference among the leaders, to whom were added Tecumseh and Colonel D'Egville, as to their final operations, took place. Never did the noble Indian appear to greater advantage than on this occasion. A neat hunting dress, of smoked deer skin, handsomely ornamented, covered his fine and athletic person, while the swarthiness of his cheek and dazzling lustre of his eye, were admirably set off, not only by the snow white linen which hung loose and open about his throat, but by a full turban, in which waved a splendid white Ostrich feather, the much prized gift, as we have already observed, of Mrs. D'Egville. Firmly seated on his long tailed gray charger, which he managed with a dexterity uncommon to his race, his warrior and commanding air, might have called up the image of a Tamerlane, or a Genghis Khan, were it not known, that to the more savage qualities of these, he united others that would lend lustre to the most civilized Potentates. There was, however, that ardor of expression in his eye which rumor had ascribed to him, whenever an appeal to arms against the deadly foe of his country was about to be made, that could not fail to endear him to the soldier hearts of those who stood around, and to inspire them with a veneration and esteem, not even surpassed by what they entertained for their own immediate leader, who in his turn, animated by the inspiriting scene, and confident in his own powers, presented an appearance so anticipatory of coming success, that the least sanguine could not fail to be encouraged by it.

It had been arranged that on the landing of the troops, the flotilla should again weigh anchor, and approach as near as possible to the American Fort, with a view, in conjunction with the batteries, to a cross-fire that would cover the approach of the assaulting columns. The Indians, meanwhile, were to disperse themselves throughout the skirt of the forest, and, headed by the Chiefs already named, to advance under whatever they might find in the shape of hedges, clumps of trees, or fields, sufficiently near to maintain a heavy fire from their rifles on such force as might appear on the ramparts to oppose the assault—a task in which they were to be assisted by the brigade of light guns charged with shrapnell and grape. Tecumseh himself, accompanied hy Colonel D'Egville, was with the majority of his warriors, to gain the rear of the town, there to act as circumstances might require. To this, as an inferior post, the Chieftain had at first strongly objected, but when it was represented to him that the enemy, with a view to turn the English flank on the forest side, would probably detach in that direction a strong force, which he would have the exclusive merit of encountering, he finally assented; urged to it, as he was, moreover, by the consideration that his presence would be effectual in repressing any attempt at massacre, or outrage, of the helpless inhabitants, by his wild and excited bands.

The guns being at length disembarked and limbered, every thing was now in readiness for the advance. The horses of the General and his staff, had crossed in the scows appropriated to the artillery, and his favorite charger, being now brought up by his groom, the former mounted with an activity and vigour, not surpassed even by the youngest of his aides-de-camp, while his fine and martial form, towered above those around him, in a manner to excite admiration in all who beheld him. Giving his brief instructions to his second in command, he now grasped and shook the hand of his dark brother in arms, who, putting spurs to his horse, dashed off with Colonel D'Egville into the open country on the left, in the direction taken by his warriors, while the General and his staff, boldly, and without escort, pursued their way along the high road at a brisk trot. The Commodore in his turn, sprang once more into his barge, which, impelled by stout hearts, and willing hands, was soon seen to gain the side of the principal vessel of the little squadron, which, rapidly getting under weigh, had already loosened its sails to catch the light, yet favorable breeze, now beginniug to curl the surface of the river.

The little army composing this adventurous expedition, consisted of about five hundred men of the regular troops, forming the garrison of Amherstburgh, to which had been added about three hundred well organized militia, from the central district—volunteers on the occasion, and habited in a manner to give them the appearance of troops of the line —in all, however, there were not more than eight hundred men, exclusive of Indians; yet, these were advancing, confident of success, against a fortress defended with five and thirty pieces of cannon, and garrisoned by upwards of two thousand men. A stronger illustration of what the directing powers of a master mind may accomplish, over those under its control, was probably never afforded more than on this occasion. One would have imagined, from the reckless laugh and ready repartee, which marked the early part of the march, that they expected to possess themselves of the Fort merely by the will of their General, and without suffering any of those contingencies which are the unfailing results of such enterprizes. In short, it seemed as if they thought that whatever he directed, they could perform, no matter what the difficulty ; and such was their exuberance of spirits, that it was not without effort, that their officers, making all due allowance for the occasion, could keep them within those bounds required by discipline, and by the occasion.

During all this time, the cannon from our batteries, but faintly answered by the Americans, had continued to thunder without intermission, and as the columns drew nearer, each succeeding discharge came upon the ear with increased and more exciting loudness. Hitherto the view had been obstructed by the numerous farm houses and other buildings, that skirted the windings of the road, but when at length the column emerged into more open ground, the whole scene burst splendidly and imposingly upon the sight. Within half a mile, and to the left, rose the American ramparts, surmounted by the national flag, suspended from a staff planted on the idlentical spot which had been the scene of the fearful exploit of Wacousta in former days. Bristling with cannon, they seemed now to threaten with extermination those who should have the temerity to approach them, and the men,awed into silence, regarded them with a certain air of respect. Close under the town were anchored the American vessels of war, which, however, having taken no part in returning the bombardment, had been left unmolested across the river, and in full view of all, was to be seen the high ground where the batteries had been erected and, visible at such intervals as the continuous clouds of smoke and flashes of fire would permit, the Union Jack of England floating above the whole ; while in the river and immediately opposite to the point the columns had now reached, the English flotilla, which had kept pacewith their movements, were already taking up a position to commence their raking fire. What more than all, however, attracted the general attention, was the appearance of two or three heavy guns, crowning the ascent of the sloping road by which they had advanced, and now, at the distance of not quite half a mile, defending the entrance to the town. If the British force had felt surprise at the non-resistance to their landiug, that surprise was increased to astonishment on finding that not one of these guns, which might have raked the entire column, destroying numbers in the choked up road, opened upon them. Had the Americans done as they might, many a British soldier would have there found his grave; but Providence had decreed that a day so fair and beautiful, commencing in the homage of human hearts to the source of all good, should not be sullied by the further shedding of human blood.

It was on reaching this point of the road, that the little army, obedient to the command of the General, who from a farm house on the left, was then examining the American defences, filed off past the house into a large field, preparatory to forming into column to attack. Scarcely, however, had the General descended to the field to make his dispositions, when it was observed that the batteries had suddenly discontinued their fire, and on looking to ascertain the cause, a white flag was seen waving on the eminence where the heavy guns just alluded to had been placed. While all were yielding to their surprise at this unexpected circumstance, De Courcy, who by the direction of his General, had remained reconnoittring with his telescope, at the top of the house, announced that an officer, bearing a smaller white flag, was then descending the road, with an evident view to a parley.

"Ah! is it even so?" exclaimed the General, with vivacity, as if to himself. "Quick, my horse! I must go to meet him. He has seen that we have stout hearts—but he must not perceive the weakness of our numbers. Captain Stanley—De Courcy—mount—St. Julian (turning to his second in command) finish what I have begun—let the columns be got ready in the order I have directed. We may have need of them yet."

To saying he once more sprang into his saddle, and accompanied by his young aides-de-camp, galloped past the line of admiring troops, who involuntarily cheered him as he passed; and quitting the field hastened to reach the flag, before the bearer could approach sufficiently near to make any correct observation respecting his force.

Nearly twenty minutes of anxious suspense had succeeded the departure of the officer, when De Courcy again made his appearance at full speed.

"Hurrah! hurrah!" he shouted, as he approached a large group of his more immediate companions, who were canvassing the probable termination of this pacific demonstration on the part of the enemy—"the Fort is our own," (then turning to the second in command,) "Colonel St. Julian, it is the General's desire that the men pile their arms on the ground they occupy, and refresh themselves with whatever their haver sacks contain."

"How is this, De Courcy." "Surely the Americans do not capitulate"—"Is it to be child's play after all." "Dom it mon who would ha' thoat it poossible?" were among the various remarks made to the young aid-de-camp, on his return from the delivery of the last order.

"Heaven only knows how, Granville," said the vivacious officer, in reply to the first querist; "but certainly it is something very like it, for the General, accompanied by Stanley, has entered the town under the flag. However before we discuss the subject further, I vote that we enter the farm house and discuss wherewith to satisfy our own appetites—I saw a devilish pretty girl just now—one who seemed to have no sort of objection to a handsome scarlet uniform, whatever her predilection for a blue with red facings may formerly have been. She looked so good naturedly on Stanley and myself, that we should have ogled her into a breakfast ere this, had not the General sworn he would not break his fast until he had planted the colours of England on yon fortress, or failed in the attempt. Of course we, as young heroes, could not think of eating after that. But come along—Nay Cranstoun, do not look as if you were afraid to budge an inch without an order in writing—I have it in suggestion from Colonel St. Julian, that we go in and do the best we can.

"Hoot De Courcy, yer' speerits are so floostersome one would be inclined to theenk ye were not at all soorry to see the white cloot flying on yonder hill——"

"Bravo Cranstoun," said Villiers somewhat maliciously; "hard hit there De Courcy, eh!"

"Not so *hard hit* either as he might have been had he ventured into yonder trenches," said Middlemore.

"If Cranstoun means that I prefer entering the place with a whole head rather than a *bare* skin, I honestly confess that such is my peculiar taste," answered De Courcy, significantly smiling.

"Nay, nay De Courcy, you are too severe on poor Cranstoun," said Captain Granville with provoking sympathy—"that unfortunate bear skin affair should not be revived again, and so immedtately in the theatre near which it occurred.

"Particularly when we consider from what *difficult-tie* he was released" said Middlemore, who even under the cannon's mouth could not have forborne his inveterate habit.

"It is the sight of the old place that has stirred up his bile," remarked Captain Molineux. "Usually good tempered as he is, he would not have taken offence at De Courcy's unmeaning remark at any other moment."

"A very nice adventure that—I frequently think of it," said Villiers, adding his mite to the persiflage all appeared determined to bestow upon the touchy grenadier.

"Yes, quite *an ice* adventure," chimed in Middlemore, with the low chuckling laugh that betrayed his consciousness of having something not wholly intolerable.

But Cranstoun, now that his ludicrous disaster had been brought up, was not to be shaken from the imperturbility he ever adopted when it became a topic of conversation among his companions. Drawing his lengthy legs after him with slow and solemn precision, he continued to whistle a Scotch air, in utter seeming abstraction from all around, and in his attempt to appear independent and perfectly at his ease, nearly ran down the pretty girl alluded to by De Courcy, who stood in the door way curtseying graciously, and welcoming each of the British officers, as they passed into the house.

"Bread, eggs, milk, fruit, cider, and whatever the remains of yesterday's meal afforded, were successively brought forward by the dark eyed daughter of the farmer, who, as De Courcy had remarked, seemed by no means indisposed towards the gay looking invaders of her home. There was a recklessness about the carriage of most of these, and even a foppery about some, that was likely to be any thing but displeasing to a young girl, who, French Canadian by birth, although living under the Government of the United States, possessed all the natural vivacity of character peculiar to the original stock. Notwithstanding the pertinacity with which her aged father lingered in the room, the handsome and elegant De Courcy contrived more than once to address her in an under tone, and elicit a blush that greatly heightened the brilliant expression of her large black eyes, and Villiers subsequently declared that he had remarked the air of joyousness and triumph that pervaded her features on the young aid-de-camp promising to return to the farm as soon as the place had been entered, and leisure afforded him."

"But the particulars of the flag, De Courcy," said Captain Granville, as he devoured a hard boiled turkey egg, which in quantity fully made up for what it wanted in quality. "When you have finished flirting with that unfortunate girl, come and seat yourself quietly, and tell us what passed between the General and the officer who bore it. Why, I thought you had a devil of an appetite just now?"

"Ah, true," returned the young man, taking his seat at the rude naked table which bore their meal. "I had quite forgotten my appetite—mais çà viendra en mangent, n'est-ce pas?" and he looked at the young girl.

"Plait-il, monsieur?"

"Tais toi ma fille—ce n'est pas a toi qu'on parle," gruffly remarked her father.

"The old boy is becoming savage at your attentions," remarked Villiers, "you will get the girl into a scrape."

"Bah," ejaculated De Courcy, "Well but of the General. Who think you was the bearer of the flag. No other than that fine looking fellow, Colonel—what's his name, who came to us the other day."

"Indeed, singular enough—what said the General to him, on meeting?" asked Henry Grantham.

"'Well, Colonel,' said he smiling, 'you see I have kept my word. This is the day on which I promised that we should meet again.'

"What answer did he make?" demanded Villiers.

"'True, General, and most happily have you chosen. But one day sooner and we should have dared your utmost in our strong-hold. Today,' and he spoke in a tone of deep mortification, 'we have not resolution left to make a show even in vindication of our honor. In a word, I am here to conduct you to those who will offer terms derogatory at once to our national character, and insulting to our personal courage.'

"The General," pursued De Courcy, "respecting the humiliated manner of the American, again bowed, but said nothing—After a moment of pause, the latter stated that the Governor and Commander of the fortress were waiting to receive and confer with him as to the terms of capitulation. Whether the General had calculated upon this want of nerve in his antagonist, I know not, but on the communication of the intelligence I remarked a slight curl upon his lip, that seemed to express the triumph of one whose ruse had taken. This might or might not be, however, for as you are all aware, I pretend to very little observation except (and he turned his eye upon the daughter of their host,) where there is a pretty girl in the case. All I know is, that, attended by Stanley, he has accompanied the flag into the town, and that, having no immediate occasion for my valuable services, he sent me back to give to Colonel St. Julian the order you have heard.

"How vary extroordinary, to soorrender the ceetadel without firing a shoat," said Cranstoun, who ever ready to fight as to eat, seemed rather disappointed at the issue, if one might judge from the lengthened visage with which he listened to these tidings.

"Singular enough," added Captain Granville. "Did the Colonel hint at any cause for this sudden change of purpose, De Courcy."

"Oh, by the way, yes, I had forgotten. He stated with a sneer of contempt, that he believed the nerves of the Governor had been shaken by the reports conveyed to him of the destructive nature of the fire from the batteries, the centre of which especially had so completely got the range that every shot from it came into the fortress with fearful effect. One point blank in particular, had entered by the gate which was open, and killed and wounded four officers of rank, who were seated at breakfast in one of their barrack rooms, while a second had carried off no less than three surgeons."

"Well done, Gerald," exclaimed Captain Granville, delighted at the reflection, that he had been so mainly instrumental in determining the surrender of the Fort."

"Cleverly done, indeed," said Villiers, "that is pinking off the pill-boxes with a vengeance—an Indian rifle could not do better."

"It is by breeking the heeds of her coontrymen, A suppoose, he hopes to gain the feevor of his meestriss," drawled out Cranstoun. "A do na theenk she is joost the one to forgeeve that."

The deep roll of the drum summoning to fall in, drew them eagerly to their respective divisions. Captain Stanley, the senior aid-de-camp was just returned with an order for the several columns to advance and take up their ground close under the ramparts of the Fort.

It was an interesting and a novel sight, to see the comparatively insignificant British columns, flanked by the half dozen light guns which constituted their whole artillery, advance across the field, and occupy the plain or common surrounding the Fort, while the Americans on the ramparts appeared to regard with indignation and surprise, the mere handful of men to whom they were about to be surrendered. Such a phenomenon in modern warfare as that of a weak besieging force bearding a stronger in their hold, might well excite astonishment; and to an army, thrice as numerous as its captors, occupying a fortress well provided with cannon, as in this instance, must have been especially galling. More than one of the officers, as he looked down from his loftier and more advantageous position, showed by the scowl that lingered on his brow, how willingly he would have applied the match to the nearest gun whose proximity to his enemies promised annihiliation to their ranks. But the white flag still waved in the distance, affording perfect security to those who had confided in their honor, and although liberty and prosperity, and glory were the sacrifice, that honor might not be tarnished.

At length the terms of capitulation being finally adjusted, De Courcy, who, with his brother aid-de-camp, had long since rejoined the General, came up with instructions for a guard to enter and take possession preparatory to the Americans marching out. Detachments from the flank companies, under the command of Captain Granville, with whom were Middlemore and Henry Grantham, were selected for the duty, and these now moved forward, with drums beating and colours flying, towards the drawbridge then lowering to admit them.

The area of the fort in no way enlarged, and but slightly changed in appearance, since certain of our readers first made acquaintance with it, was filled with troops, and otherwise exhibited all the confusion incident to preparations for an immediate evacuation. These preparations, however were made with a savageness of mien by the irregulars, and a sullen silence by all, that attested how little their inclination had been consulted in the decision of their Chief. Many an oath was muttered, and many a fierce glance was cast by the half civilized back-woodsmen, upon the little detachment as it pursued its way, not without difficulty, through the dense masses that seemed rather to oppose than aid their advance to the occupancy of the several posts assigned them.

One voice, deepest and most bitter in its half suppressed execration, came familiarly on the ear of Henry Grantham, who brought up the rear of the detachment. He turned quickly in search of the speaker, but, although he felt persuaded it was Desborough who had spoken, coupling his own name even with his curses, the ruffian was no where to be seen. Satisfied that he must be within the Fort, and determined if possible, to secure the murderer who had, moreover, the double crime of treason and desertion, to be added to his list of offences, the young officer moved to the head of the detachment when halted, and communicated what he heard to Captain Granville. Entering at once into the views of his subaltern, and anxious to make an example of the traitor, yet unwilling to act wholly on his own responsibility, Captain Granville dispatched an orderly to Colonel St. Julian to receive his instructions. The man soon returned with a message to say that Desborough was by all means to be detained, and secured, until the General, who was still absent, should determine on his final disposal.

Meanwhile the sentinels at the several posts having been relieved, and every thing ready for their departure, the American army, leaving their arms piled in the area, commenced their evacuation of the Fort, the artillery and troops of the line taking the lead. Scarcely had these defiled across the draw-bridge into the road that conducted to a large esplanade in front, to which their baggage had previously been transported, when—amid a roar of artillery from the opposite batteries, the flotilla, and ramparts themselves—the flag of America was lowered, and that of England raised in its stead. In the enthusiasm of the moment, the men on the rampart employed on duty gave three cheers, which were answered by the columns without, who only waited until the last of the Garrison should have crossed the drawbridge, before they entered themselves. Watchfully alive to the order that had been received, Captain Granville and Henry Grantham lingered near the gate, regarding, yet with an air of carelessness, every countenance among the irregular troops as they issued forth. Hitherto their search had been ineffectual, and to their great surprise, although the last few files of the prisoners were now in the act of passing them, there was not the slightest trace of Desborough. It was well known that the fort had no other outlet, and any man attempting to escape over the ramparts, must have been seen and taken either by the troops or by the Indians, who in the far distance completely surrounded them. Captain Granville intimated the possibility of Henry Grantham having been deceived in the voice, but the latter as pertinaciously declared he could not be mistaken, for, independently of his former knowledge of the man, his tones had so peculiarly struck him on the day when he made boastful confession of his father's murder, that no time could efface them from his memory. This short discussion terminated just as the last few files were passing. Immediately in the rear of these were the litters, on which were borne such of the wounded as could be removed from the hospital without danger. These were some thirty in number, and it seemed to both officers as somewhat singular, that the faces of all were, in defiance of the heat of the day, covered with the sheets that had been spread over each litter. For a moment the suspicion occurred to Grantham, that Desborough might be of the number; but when he reflected on the impossibility that any of the wounded men could be the same whose voice had sounded so recently in the full vigour of health in his ear, he abandoned the idea. Most of the wounded, as they passed, indicated by low and feeble moaning, the inconvenience they experienced from the motion to which they were subjected, and more or less expressed by the contortions of their limbs, the extent of their sufferings. An exception to this very natural conduct was remarked by Grantham, in the person of one occupying nearly a central position in the line, who was carried with difficulty by the litter-men. He lay perfectly at his length, and without any exhibition whatever of that impatient movement which escaped his companions On the watchful eye of Grantham, this conduct was not lost. He had felt a strong inclination from the first, to uncover the faces of the wounded men in succession, and had only been restrained from so doing by the presence of the American medical officer who accompanied them, whom he feared to offend by an interference with his charge. Struck as he was however by the remarkable conduct of the individual alluded to, and the apparently much greater effort with which he was carried, he could not resist the temptation which urged him to know more.

"Stay," he exclaimed to the bearers of the litter, as they were in the act of passing. The men stopped. "This man, if not dead, is evidently either dying or fainting—give him air."

While speaking he had advanced a step or two, and now extending his right hand endeavoured gently to pull down the sheet from the head of the invalid, but the attempt was vain. Two strong and nervous arms were suddenly raised and entwined in the linen, in a manner to resist all his efforts.

Grantham glanced an expressive look at Captain Granville. The latter nodded his head in a manner to show he was understood, then desiring the litter-men to step out of the line and deposit their burden, he said to the medical officer with the sarcasm that so often tinged his address.

"I believe, sir, your charge embraces only the wounded of the garrison. This dead man can only be an incumbrance to you, and it shall be my care that his body is properly disposed of."

The officer coloured and looked confused. "Really, sir, you must be mistaken."

But Captain Granville cut short his remonstrance, by an order to the file of men in his rear, who each seizing on the covering of the litter, dragged it forcibly off, discovering in the act the robust and healthy form of Desborough.

"You may pass on, continued the officer to the remainder of the party. This fellow, at once a murderer and a traitor, is my prisoner."

"I know him only as an American, sir," was the reply. "He has taken the oaths of allegiance within the last week, and as such is an acknowledged subject of the American States."

"I have no time to enter into explanation, neither am I competent to discuss this question, sir. For what I have done, I have the instructions of my superior. If you have complaint to make it must be to your own Chief. To mine alone am I responsible. Let the scoundrel be well secured," he pursued, as the last of the litters at length defiled, and addressing the men to whom Desborough had been given in charge.

"Ha!" exclaimed Middlemore, who had all this time been absent on the duties connected with his guard, and now approached the scene of this little action for the first time; "what! do I see my friend Jeremiah Desborough—the prince of traitors, and the most vigorous of wrestlers—verily my poor bones ache at the sight of you. How came you to be caught in this trap, my old boy, better have been out duck-shooting with the small bores I reckon?"

But Desborough was in no humour to endure this mirth. Finding himself discovered, he had risen heavily from the litter to his feet, and now moved doggedly towards the guard house, where the men had orders to confine him. His look still wore the character of ferocity, which years had stamped there, but with this was mixed an expression that denoted more of the cowering villain, whom a sudden reverse of fortune may intimidate, than the dauntless adventurer to whom enterprizes of hazard are at once a stimulus and a necessity. In short, he was entirely crest fallen.

"Come and see the effect of Gerald's excellent fire," said Middlemore, when Desborough had disappeared within the guard room. No wonder the American General was frightened into *Sir-render*, hem! I will show you the room pointed out to me by the subaltern whom I relieved, as that in which the four field officers and three surgeons were killed."

Preceded by their companion, Captain Granville and Grantham entered the piazza, leading to the officers' rooms, several of which were completely pierced with twenty-four pound shot, known at once as coming from the centre battery, which alone mounted guns of that calibre. After surveying the interior a few moments, they passed into a small passage communicating with the room in question. On opening the door, all were painfully struck by the sight which presented itself. Numerous shot holes were visible every where throughout, while the walls at the inner extremity of the apartment, were completely bespotted with blood and brains, scarcely yet dry any where, and in several places dripping to the floor. At one corner of the rooom, and on a mattrass, lay the form of a wounded man, whom the blue uniform and silver epaulettes, that filled a chair near the head, attested for an American officer of rank. At the foot of the bed, dressed in black, her long hair floating wildly over her shoulders, and with a hand embracing one of those of the sufferer, sat a female, apparently wholly absorbed in the contemplation of the scene before her. The noise made by the officers on entering had not caused the slightest change in her position, nor was it until she heard the foot-fall of Captain Granville, as he advanced for the purpose of offering his services, that she turned to behold who were the intruders. The sight of the British uniform appeared to startle her, for she immediately sprang to her feet, as if alarmed at their presence. It was impossible they could mistake those features, and that face. It was Miss Montgomerie. He who lay at her feet, was her venerable uncle. He was one of the field officers who had fallen a victim to Gerald's fire, and the same ball which had destroyed his companions, had carried away his thigh, near the hip bone. The surgeons had given him over, and he had requested to be permitted to die where he lay. His wish had been attended to, but in the bustle of evacuation, it had been forgotten to acquaint the officers commanding the British guard that he was there. The last agonies of death had not yet passed away, but there seemed little probability that he could survive another hour.

Perceiving the desperate situation of the respectable officer, Captain Granville staid not to question on a subject that spoke so plainly for itself. Hastening back into the piazza with his subalterns, he reached the area just as the remaining troops, intended for the occupation of the Fort, were crossing the drawbridge, headed by Colonel St. Julian. To this officer he communicated the situation of the sufferer, when an order was given for the instant attendance of the head of the medical staff. After a careful examination, and dressing of the wound, the latter pronounced the case not altogether desperate. A great deal of blood had been lost, and extreme weakness had been the consequence, but still the Surgeon was not without hope that his life might yet be preserved, although, of course, he would be a cripple for the remainder of his days.

It might have been assumed, that the hope yet held out of preservation of life on any terms, would have been hailed with some manifestation of grateful emotion, on the part of Miss Montgomerie ; but it was remarked and commented on, by those who were present, that this unexpectedly favorable report, so far from being received with gratitude and delight, seemed to cast a deeper gloom over the spirit of this extraordinary girl. The contrast was inexplicable. She had tended him at the moment when he was supposed to be dying, with all the anxious solicitude of a fond child, and now that there was a prospect of his recovery, there was a sadness in her manner, that told too plainly the discomfort of her heart."

"In veerity an unaccoontable geerl," said Cranstoun, as he sipped his wine that day after dinner in the mess room at Detroit. "A always seed she was the cheeld of the deevil."

"Child of the devil in soul, if you will," observed Granville, "but a true woman—a beautiful, a superb woman in person at least, did she appear this morning, when we first entered that room—did she not Henry?"

"Beautiful indeed," was the reply—"yet, I confess, she more awed than pleased me. I could not avoid, even amid that melancholy scene, comparing her to a beautiful casket, which, on opening is found to contain not a gem of price, but a subtle poison, contact with which is fatal; or to a fair loooking fruit which, when divided, proves to be rotten at the core."

"Allegorical, by all that is good, bad, and indifferent," exclaimed Villiers. "How devilish severe you are Henry, upon the pale Venus. It is hardly fair in you thus to rate Gerald's intended."

"Gerald's intended! God forbid."

This was uttered with an energy that startled his companions. Perceiving that the subject gave him pain, they discontinued allusion to the lady in question, further than to inquire how she was to be disposed of, and whether she was to remain in attendance on her uncle.

In answer, they were informed, that as the Major could not be removed, orders had been given by the General, for every due care to be taken of him where he now lay, while Miss Montgomerie, yielding to solicitation, had been induced to retire into the family of the American General in the town, there to remain until it should be found convenient to have the whole party conveyed to the next American post on the frontier.

CHAPTER XIII.

It is impossible to review the whole tenor of General Brock's conduct, on the occasion more immediately before our notice, and fail to be struck by the energy and decision of character which must have prompted so bold an enterprise. To understand fully the importance of the operation it will be necessary to take a partial survey of the position of affairs anterior to this period. When the announcement of the American declaration of war first reached the Michigan frontier, the garrisons of Amherstburg and Detroit were nearly equal in strength, neither of them exceeding five húndred men; but the scale was soon made to preponderate immeasurably in favor of the latter, by the sudden arrival of a force of upwards of two thousand men. General Hull, who was in command of that army immediately crossed over into Canada, occupying the village of Sandwich as his head quarters, and pouring his wild Kentuckians over the face of the country which they speedily laid under contribution. Instead, however, of marching without delay upon Amherstburg, as ill defended as it was weakly garrisoned, he contented himself with pushing forward skirmishers, who amused themselves during the day, against an advanced post of regulars, militia and Indians, stationed for the defence of an important pass, and retired invariably on the approach of night. This pass, the Canard bridge—and the key to Amherstburg—was, at this period, the theatre of several hot and exciting affairs. In this manner passed the whole of the month of July.

Meanwhile, intelligence having been conveyed to General Brock, then in command of the centre division of the army, of the danger with which Amherstburg was threatened. He immediately embarked what remained of the Regiment occupying that post, with from one hundred and fifty to two hundred choice Militia, in boats he had caused to be collected for the purpose, and, coasting along the lake, made such despatch that he arrived at Amherstburg only a few days after General Hull, in his turn apprized of the advance of this reinforcement, had recrossed the river, and with the majority of his force, taken refuge within the fortifications of Detroit. Thus was that portion of Upper Canada, which by Proclamation of the American General, had already been incorporated with, and become a portion of the United States, restored to its original possessors.

Not a moment did the English Commander lose, in following up the advantage resulting from this mark of timidity in his opponent. As soon as he had arrived and ascertained the true state of affairs, he issued orders for the march of the whole force to Sandwich, and, having explained in a council with the Indian Chiefs, the main features of his plan of attack, proceeded to carry it into instant execution. His arrival at Amherstburg was about the 13th of August, so that until the morning of his meditated attack scarcely three days were occupied in preparations, including the march to Sandwich, a distance of eighteen miles.

It is difficult to imagine that the English General could, in any way have anticipated so easy a conquest. He had no reason to undervalue the resolution of the enemy, and yet he appears to have been fully sanguine of the success of his undertaking. Possibly he counted much on his own decision and judgment, which, added to the confidence reposed in him by all ranks and branches of the expedition, he might have felt fully adequate to the overthrow of the mere difficulty arising from superiority of numbers. Whatever his motive, or however founded his expectations of success, the service he performed was eminent, since he not merely relieved Amherstburgh, the key of Upper Canada, from all immediate danger, but at a single blow annihilated the American power throughout that extensive frontier. That this bold measure, powerfully contrasted as it was with his own previous vacillation of purpose, had greatly tended to intimidate the American General, and to render him distrustful of his own resources, there can be little doubt. The destructive fire from the well served breaching batteries, was moreover instanced as an influencing cause of the capitulation.

In justice to many American officers of rank, and to the Garrison generally, it must be admitted that the decision of their leader, if credence might be given to their looks and language, was any thing but satisfactory to them, and it must be confessed that it must have been mortifying in the extreme to have yielded without a blow a fortress so well provided with the means of defence. What the result would have been, had the British columns mounted to the assault, it is impossible to say. That they would have done their duty is beyond all question, but there is no reason to believe the Americans, under a suitable commander, would have failed in theirs. Superiority of numbers and position was on the one side : a daring Chief, an ardent desire of distinction, and the impossibility of retreat without humiliation, on the other.

In alluding thus to the capitulation of Detroit, we beg not to be understood as either reflecting on the American character, or unduly exalting our own. Question of personal bravery there was none, since no appeal was made to arms ; but the absence of sanguinary event left in high relief the daring of the British Commander, whose promptitude and genius alone secured to him so important yet bloodless a conquest. Had he evinced the slightest indecision, or lost a moment in preparing for action, the American General, already intimidated by the mere report of his approach (as was evinced by his hasty abandonment of the Canadian shore) would have had time to rally, and believing him to be not more enterprizing than his predecessors, would have recovered from his panic and assumed an attitude, at once, more worthy of his trust, commensurate with his means of defence, and in keeping with his former reputation. The quick apprehension of his opponent, immediately caught the weakness, while his ready action grappled intuitively with the advantage it presented. The batteries, as our narrative has shown, were opened without delay—the flotilla worked up the river within sight of the fortress—and the troops and Indians effected their landing in full view of the enemy. In fact, every thing was conducted in a manner to show a determination of the most active and undoubted description. With what result has been seen.

It was in the evening of the day of surrender, that the little English squadron, freighted with the prisoners taken in Detroit, dropped slowly past Amherstburg, into Lake Erie. By an article in the capitulation, it had been stipulated, that the irregular troops should be suffered to return to their homes, under the condition that they should not again serve during the war, while those of the line were to be conducted to the Lower Province, there to remain until duly exchanged. The appearance as captives of those who had, only a few days before, been comfortably established on the Sandwich shore, and had caused the country to feel already some of the horrors of invasion, naturally enough drew forth most of the inhabitants to witness the sight; and as the Sunday stroll of the little population of Amherstburg led in the direction of Elliot's point, where the lake began, the banks were soon alive with men, women and children, clad in holiday apparel, moving quickly, to keep up with the gliding vessels, and apparently, although not offensively, exulting in the triumph of that flag beneath which the dense masses of their enemies were now departing from their rescued territory.

Among those whom the passing barks had drawn in unusual numbers to the river's side, were the daughters of Colonel D'Egville, whose almost daily practice it was to take the air in that direction, where there was so much of the sublime beauty of American scenery to arrest the attention.

Something more however than that vague curiosity, which actuated the mass, seemed to have drawn the sisters to the bank, and one who had watched them narrowly, must have observed, that their interest was not divided among the many barks that glided onward to the lake, but was almost exclusively attracted by one, which now lay to, with her light bows breasting the current like a swan, and apparently waiting either for a boat which had been dispatched to the shore, or with an intention to send one. This vessel was filled in every part with troops, wearing the blue uniform of the American regular army, while those in advance were freighted with the irregulars and backwoodsmen.

"Is not this, Julia, the vessel to which the Commodore promised to promote Gerald, in reward of his gallant conduct last week?" asked the timid Gertrude, with a sigh, as they stood stationary for a few moments, watching the issue of the manœuvre just alluded to.

"It is, Gertrude," was the answer of one whose fixed eye and abstracted thought, betokened an interest in the same vessel, of a nature wholly different from that of her questioner.

"How very odd, then, he does not come on shore to us. I am sure he must see us, and it would not take him two minutes to let us know he is unhurt, and to shake hands with us. It is very unkind of him I think."

Struck by the peculiar tone in which the last sentence had been uttered, Julia D'Egville turned her eyes full upon those of her sister. The latter, could not stand the inquiring gaze, but sought the ground, while a conscious blush confirmed the suspicion.

"Dearest Gertrude," she said, as she drew the clasped arm of her sister more fondly within her own; "I see how it is; but does he love you in return. Has he ever told you so, or hinted it. Tell me my dear girl."

"Never," faltered the sensitive Gertrude, and she hung her head, to conceal the tear that trembled in her eye.

Her sister sighed deeply, and pressed the arm she held

more closely within her own. "My own own sister, for worlds I would not pain you; but if you would be happy, you must not yield to this preference for our cousin. Did you not remark how completely he seemed captivated by Miss Montgomerie? Depend upon it, his affections are centered in her."

Gertrude made no reply, but tears trickled down her cheeks, as they both slowly resumed their walk along the beach. Presently the splash of oars was heard, and turning quickly to discover the cause, Julia saw a boat leave the vessel, at which they had just been looking, and pull immediately towards them. In the stern stood an officer in American uniform, whom the eyes of Love were not slow to distinguish, even in the growing dusk of evening.

"It is Ernest," exclaimed the excited girl, forgetting for a moment her sister in herself. "I thought he would not have departed without seeking to see me."

A few strokes of the oars were sufficient to bring the boat to the shore. The American stepped out, and leaving the boat to follow the direction of the vessel, now drifting fast with the current towards the outlet, which the remainder of the flotilla had already passed, pursued his course along the sands in earnest conversation with the sisters, or rather with one of them, for poor Gertrude, after the first salutation, seemed to have lost all inclination to speak.

"Fate, dearest Julia," said the officer despondingly, "has decreed our interview earlier than I had expected. However, under all circumstances, I may esteem myself happy, to have seen you at all. I am indebted for this favor to the officer commanding yonder vessel, in which our regiment is embarked, for the satisfaction, melancholy as it is, of being enabled to bid you a temporary farewell."

"Then are we both indebted to one of my own family for the happiness; for that it is a happiness, Ernest, I can answer from the depression of my spirits just now, when I feared you were about to depart without seeing me at all. The officer in command of your vessel is, or ought to be, a cousin of our own."

"Indeed!—then is he doubly entitled to my regard. But, Julia, let the brief time that is given us, be devoted to the arrangement of plans for the future. I will not for a moment doubt your faith, after what occurred at our last interview; but shall I be certain of finding you here, when later we return to wash away the stain this day's proceedings have thrown upon our national honor. Forgive me, if I appear to mix up political feelings, with private grief, but it cannot be denied, (and he smiled faintly through the mortification evidently called up by the recollection,) that to have one's honor attainted, and to lose one's mistress in the same day, are heavier taxes on human patience, than it can be expected a soldier should quietly bear."

"And when I am yours at a later period, I suppose you will expect me to be as interested in the national honor, as you are," replied Julia, anxious to rally him on a subject she felt, could not but be painful to a man of high feelings, as she fully believed the Colonel to be. "How are we to reconcile such clashing interests? How am I so far to overcome my natural love for the country which gave me birth, as to rejoice in its subjugation by yours; and yet, that seems to be the eventual object at which you hint. Your plan, if I understand right, is to return here with an overwhelming army; overrun the province, and make me your property by right of conquest, while all connected with me, by blood, or friendship, are to be borne into captivity. If we marry, sir, we must draw lots which of us shall adopt a new country."

"Nay dearest Julia, this pleasantry is unseasonable. I certainly do intend, provided I am exchanged in time to return here with the army, which I doubt not will be instantly dispatched to restore our blighted fame, and then I shall claim you as my own. Will you then hesitate to become mine? Even as the daughter forsakes the home of her father without regret, to pass her days with him who is to her father, mother, all the charities of life, in short—so should she forsake her native land, adopting in preference that to which her husband is attached by every tie of honor, and of duty. However, let us hope that ere long, the folly of this war will be seen, and that the result of such perception, will be a peace founded on such permanent basis, that each shall be bound, by an equal tie of regard, to the home of the other."

"Let us hope so," eagerly replied Julia. "But what has become of our friend, Miss Montgomerie, in all the confusion of this day. Or am I right in supposing that she and her uncle, are of the number of those embarked in my cousin's vessel?"

The name of the interesting American, coupled as it was, with that of one infinitely more dear to her, caused Gertrude for the first time, to look up in the face of the officer, in expectation of his reply. She was struck by the sudden paleness that came over his features again, as on the former occasion, when allusion was made to her at his recent visit to Amherstburgh. He saw that his emotion was remarked, and sought to hide it under an appearance of unconcern, as he replied:

"Neither Miss Montgomerie nor her uncle are embarked. The latter, I regret to say, has been one of the few victims who have fallen."

"What! dead—that excellent kind old man—dead, demanded the sisters, nearly in the same breath?"

"No; not dead—but I fear with little hope of life. He was desperately wounded soon after day-break this morning, and when I saw him half an hour afterwards, he had been given over by the surgeons."

"Poor old Major," sighed Gertrude; "I felt when he was here the other day, that I could have loved him almost as my own father. How broken-hearted Miss Montgomerie must be at his loss."

A sneer of bitterness passed over the fine features of the American, as he replied with emphasis:

"Nay, dear Gertrude, your sympathies there are but ill bestowed. Miss Montgomerie's heart will scarcely sustain the injury you seem to apprehend."

"What mean you Ernest?" demanded Julia, with eagerness. "How is it that you judge thus harshly of her character. How, in short, do you pretend to enter into her most secret feelings, and yet deny all but a general knowledge of her? What can you possibly know of her heart?"

"I merely draw my inferences from surmise," replied the Colonel, after a few moments of pause. "The fact it, I have the vanity to imagine myself a correct reader of character, and my reading of Miss Montgomerie's has not been the happiest."

Julia's look betrayed incredulity. "There is evidently some mystery in all this," she rejoined; "but I will not seek to discover more than you choose at present to impart. Later I may hope to possess more of your confidence. One question more, however, and I have done. Have you seen her since your return to Detroit, and did she give you my letter?"

The Colonel made no answer, but produced from his pocket a note, which Julia at once recognized as her own.

"Then," said Gertrude, "there was not so much danger after all, in intrusting it. You seemed to be in a sad way, when you first heard that it had been given to her."

"I would have pledged myself on its safe deliverance," added her sister, "for the promise was too solemnly given, to be broken."

"And solemnly has it been kept," gravely returned the American. "But hark, already are they hailing the boat, and we must part."

The time occupied in conversation, had brought them down to the extreme point, where the river terminated, and the lake commenced. Beyond this lay a sand bar, which it was necessary to clear, before the increasing dusk of the evening rendered it hazardous. All the other vessels had already passed it, and were spreading their white sails before the breeze, which here, unbroken by the island, impelled them rapidly onward. A few strokes of the oar, and the boat once more touched the beach. Low and fervent adieus were exchanged, and the American, resuming his station in the stern, was soon seen to ascend the deck, he had so recently quitted. For a short time, the sisters continued to watch the movements of the vessel, as she in turn having passed, spread all her canvass to the wind, until the fast fading twilight warning them to depart, they retraced their steps along the sands to the town. Both were silent and pensive; and while all around them found subject for rejoicing in the public events of the day, they retired at an early hour to indulge at leisure in the several painful retrospections which related more particularly to themselves.

CHAPTER XIV.

If the few weeks preceding the fall of Detroit, had been characterized by much bustle and excitement, those which immediately succeeded, were no less remarkable for their utter inactivity and repose. With the surrender of the fortress vanished every vestige of hostility in that remote territory, enabling the sinews of watchfulness to undergo a relaxation, nor longer requiring the sacrifice of private interests to the public good. Scarcely had the American prisoners been despatched to their several destinations, when General Brock, whose activity and decision, were subject of universal remark, quitted his new conquest and again hastened to resume the command on the Niagara frontier, which he had only left to accomplish what had been so happily achieved. The Indians, too, finding their services no longer in immediate demand, dispersed over the country, or gave themselves up to the amusement of the chase, ready however to come forward whenever they should be re-summoned to the conflict; while the Canadians, who had cheerfully abandoned their homes to assist in the operations of the war, returned once more to the cultivation of that soil they had so recently looked upon as wrested from them for ever. Throughout the whole line of Detroit, on either shore, the utmost quietude prevailed; and although many of the inhabitants of the conquered town, looked with an eye of national jealousy on the English flag that waved in security above the Fort, they submitted uncomplainingly to the change, indulging only in secret, yet without bitterness, in the hope of a not far distant reaction of fortune, when their own National Stars should once more be in the ascendant.

The garrison left at Detroit consisted merely of two companies—those of Captains Granville and Molineux, which included among their officers, Middlemore, Villiers and Henry Grantham. After the first excitement produced in the minds of the townspeople, by their change of rulers, had passed away, these young men desirous of society, sought to renew their intimacy with such of the more respectable families as they had been in the habit of associating with prior to hostilities; but although in most instances they were successful, their reception was so different from what it had formerly been, (a change originating not so much in design perhaps as resulting from a certain irrepressible sense of humiliation, which gave an air of *gêne* to all their words and actions,) that they were glad to withdraw themselves altogether within the rude resources of their own walls. It happened however about this period that Colonel D'Egville had received a command to transfer the head of his department from Amherstburg to Detroit, and, with a view to his own residence on the spot, the large and commodious mansion of the late Governor was selected for the abode of his family. With the daughters of that officer, the D'Egvilles had long been intimate, and as the former were to continue under the same roof until their final departure from Detroit, it was with a mutual satisfaction the friends found themselves thus closely reunited—Added to this party were Major Montgomery, (already fast recovering from the effect of his wound,) and his niece, both of whom only awaited the entire restoration of the former, to embark immediately for the nearest American port.

At Colonel D'Egville's, it will therefore be supposed the officers passed nearly all their leisure hours; Molineux and Villiers flirting with the fair American sisters, until they had nearly been held fast by the chains with which they dallied, and Middlemore uttering his execrable puns with a coolness of premeditation that excited the laughter of the fair part of his auditors, while his companions, on the contrary, expressed their unmitigated abhorrence in a variety of ways.

As for the somewhat staid Captain Granville, he sought to carry his homage to the feet of Miss Montgomerie, but the severe and repellant manner in which she received all his advances, and the look which almost petrified where it fell, not only awed him effectually into distance, but drew down upon him the sarcastic felicitations of his watchful brother officers. There was one, however, on whose attentions her disapprobation fell not, and Henry Grantham, who played the part of an anxiou s observer, remarked with pain that *he* had been fascinated by her beauty, in a manner which showed her conquest to be complete.

The cousins of Gerald Grantham had been in error in supposing him to be the officer in command of the vessel on board which the lover of Julia had embarked. His transfer from the gun boat had taken place, but in consideration of the fatigue he had undergone during the three successive days in which he had been employed at the batteries, the Commodore had directed another officer to take command of the vessel in question, and charge himself with the custody of the prisoners on board. Finding himself at liberty, until the return of the flotilla from this duty, the first care of Gerald was to establish himself in lodgings at Detroit, whence he daily sallied forth to the apartments in the Governor's house, occupied by the unfortunate Major Montgomerie, in whose situation he felt an interest so much the more deep and lively as he knew his confinement to have been in some degree the work of his own hands. All that attention and kindness could effect was experienced by the respectable Major, who, in return found himself growing more and more attached to his youthful and generous captor. These constant visits to the uncle naturally brought our hero more immediately into the society of the niece, but although he had never been able to banish from his memory the recollection of one look which she had bestowed upon him on a former occasion, in almost every interview of the sort *now*, she preserved the same cold reserve and distance which was peculiar to her.

A week had elapsed in this manner, when it chanced that as they both sat one evening, about dusk, near the couch of the invalid, the latter, after complaining of extreme weakness and unusual suffering, expressed his anxiety at the possibility of his niece being left alone and unprotected in a strange country.

It was with a beating pulse and a glowing cheek that Gerald looked up to observe the effect of this observation on his companion. He was surprised, nay, hurt, to remark that an expression of almost contemptuous loathing sat upon her pale but beautiful countenance. He closed his eyes for a moment in bitterness of disappointment—and when they again opened and fell upon that countenance, he scarcely could believe the evidence of his senses. Every feature had undergone a change. With her face half turned away, as if to avoid the observation of her uncle, she now exhibited a cheek flushed with the expression of passionate excitement, while from her eye beamed that same unfathomable expression which had carried intoxication once before to the inmost soul of the youth. Almost wild with his feelings, it was with difficulty he restrained the impulse that would have urged him to her feet; but even while he hesitated, her countenance had again undergone a change, and she sat cold and reserved and colorless as before.

That look sealed, that night, the destiny of Gerald Grantham. The coldness of the general demeanour of Matilda, was forgotten in the ardor of character which had escaped from beneath the evident and habitual disguise; and the enthusiastic sailor could think of nothing but the witchery of that look. To his surprise and joy, the following day, and ever afterwards, he found that the manner of the American, although reserved as usual with others, had undergone a complete change towards himself. Whenever he appeared alone a smile was his welcome, and if others were present she always contrived to indemnifiy him for a coldness he now knew to be assumed, by conveying unobserved one of those seductive glances the power of which she seemed so fully to understand.

Such was the state of things when the D'Egvilles arrived. Exposed to the observations of more than one anxious friend, it was not likely that a youth of Gerald's open nature, could be long in concealing his prepossession ; and as Matilda, although usually guarded in her general manner, was observed sometimes to fix her eyes upon him with the expression of one immersed in deep and speculative thought, the suspicion acquired a character of greater certainty.

To Harry Grantham, who doated upon his brother, this attachment was a source of infinite disquiet, for, from the very commencement, Miss Montgomerie had unfavorably impressed him ; why he knew not, yet impelled by a feeling he was unable to analyze, he deeply lamented that they had ever become acquainted, infatuated as Gerald appeared by her attractions. There was another, too, who saw with regret the attachment of Gerald to his fair prisoner. It was Gertrude D'Egville, but her uncomplaining voice spoke not, even to her beloved sister, of the anguish she endured—she loved her cousin, but he knew it not—and although she felt that she was fast consuming with the disappointment that preyed upon her peace, she had obtained of her sister the promise that the secret should never reach the ear of its object.

In this manner passed the months of August and September. October had just commenced, and with it, that beautiful but brief season which is well known in Canada as the Indian summer. Anxious to set out on his return to that home to which his mutilation must confine him for the future, Major Montgomerie, now sufficiently recovered to admit of his travelling by water, expressed a desire to avail himself of the loveliness of the weather, and embark forthwith on his return.

By the officers whom the hospitality of Colonel D'Egville almost daily assembled beneath his roof, this announcement was received with dismay, and especially by Molineux, and Villiers who had so suffered themselves to be fascinated by the amiable daughters of General Hull, as to have found it necessary to hold a consultation (decided however in the negative,) whether they should, or should not tempt them to remain, by making an offer of their hands. It was also observed that these young ladies, who at first, had been all anxiety to rejoin their parent, evinced no particular satisfaction in the intimation of speedy departure thus given to them. Miss Montgomerie on the contrary, whose anxiety throughout, to quit Detroit, had been no less remarkable than her former impatience to reach it, manifested a pleasure that amounted almost to exultation; and yet it was observed that by a strange apparent contradiction, her preference for Gerald from that moment became more and more divested of disguise.

There are few spots in the world, perhaps, that unite so many inducements to the formation of those sociable little *réunions* which come under the denomination of pic-nics, as the small islands adorning most of the American rivers. Owing to the difficulty of procuring summer carriages, and in some degree to the rudeness of the soil, in the Upper Province especially, boats are in much more general use; and excursions on the water, are as common to that class "whose only toil is pleasure," as cockney trips to Richmond, or to any other of the thousand and one places of resort, which have sprung into existence, within twenty miles of the Metropolis of England. Not confined, however, to picking daisies for their doxies, as these said cockneys do, or carving their vulgar names on every magnificent tree, that spreads its gorgeous arms to afford them the temporary shelter of a home, the men generally devote themselves, for a period of the day, to manlier exercises. The woods, abounding with game, and the rivers with fish of the most delicate flavor—the address of the hunter and the fisher, is equally called into action; since upon their exertions, principally depend the party for the fish and fowl portion of their rural dinner. Guns and rods are, therefore, as indispensable part of the freightage, as the dried venison and bear hams, huge turkies, pasties, &c. which together with wines, spirits, and cider *ad libitum*, form the mass of alimentary matter; not to forget the some half dozen old novels, constituting the several libraries of the females of the party, and collected together for general amusement on these occasions. Bands, it is true, they possess not, but they have the music of their own, and boatmen's voices, and the rippling of the current over the pebbly shallow, or the impetuous dashing of some distant waterfall—while on every side the eye is arrested by images of grandeur, which dispose the heart to benevolence, towards man, and the soul to adoration towards the Creator. Here is to be heard, neither the impertinent coxcombry, of the European self styled exclusive, nor the unmeaning twaddle of the daughter of false fashion, spoiled by the example of the said exclusive, and almost become a dowager in silliness, before she has attained the first years of womanhood. No lack-a-daisical voice, the sex of which it is difficult to distinguish, is attempted to be raised in depreciation of the party to which it had been esteemed too great an happiness to be invited, the evening before; nor is the bride of last week heard boastingly to deplore, the enormous sums lost within the last week, at the private gaming table of her dear friend, the Duchess of this, or the Countess of that. One half of the party address not the other in doled accents of fashionable friendship, in one key, and abuse them piteously in another. No sarcastic allusion seeks to stamp with ridicule, the amusement in which the utterer is embarked, as if a sense of shame attached to the idea of being amused, by that which affords amusement to his associates; nor is the manner of the actors, that, of people suffering an infliction rather than participating in a pleasure. The sneer of contempt—the laugh of derision—is no where to be heard; neither is the pallid brow, and sunken cheek, the fruit of late hours and forced excitement to be seen. Content is in each heart, the glow of health upon each face. All appear eager to be happy, pleased with each other, and at ease with themselves. Not that theirs is the enjoyment of the mere holiday mind, which grasps with undiscerning avidity, at whatever offers to its gratification, but that of those, on whom education, acting on innate good breeding, has imposed a due sense of the courtesies of life, and on whom fashion has not superseded the kindlier emotions of nature. These at least *were* traits of simplicity, peculiar to Upper Canada, at an early period of its settlement. What they are now, we pretend not to determine.

Several of these pic-nics had taken place among the party at Detroit, confined, with one or two exceptions, to the officers of the garrison, and the family of Colonel D'Egville, with their American inmates; and it was proposed by the former, that a final one should be given a few days prior to the embarkation in Gerald Grantham's new command, which lay waiting in the river for the purpose. The Major remaining as hitherto at home, under the guardianship of the benevolent Mrs. D'Egville, whose habits of retirement disinclined her to out door amusement.

Hitherto their excursions had been principally directed to some of the smaller islands, which abound in the river nearer Amherstburgh, and where game being found in greater abundance, the skill of the officers had more immediate opportunity for display; but in this excursion, at the casual suggestion of Miss Montgomerie, Hog Island was selected, as the scene of their day's amusement. Thither, therefore the boat which contained the party now proceeded, the ladies costumed in a manner to thread the mazes of the wood, and the gentlemen in equally appropriate gear, as sportsmen, their guns and fishing rods, being by no means omitted in the catalogue of orders entrusted to their servants. In the stern of the boat, the trustworthy coxswain on this occasion—sat old Sambo, whose skill in the conduct of a helm, was acknowledged to be little inferior to his dexterity in the use of a paddle, and whose authoritative voice, as he issued his commands in broken English to the boatmen, added in no small degree, to the exhiliration of the party,

To reach Hog Island, it was necessary to pass by the tannery and cottage already described, which, latter, it will be remembered, had been the scene of a singular adventure to our hero, and his servant on the night of their reconnoitring the coast, in obedience to the order of the Commodore. By the extraordinary and almost romantic incidents of that night, the imagination of Gerald had been deeply impressed, and on retiring to his rude couch within the battery he had fully made up his mind to explore further into the mysterious affair, with as little delay as possible after the expected fall of the American fortress. In the hurry, confusion, and excitement, of that event however, his original intention was forgotten; or, rather so far delayed, that it was not until the third or fourth day of his establishment in the town, that it occurred to him to institute inquiry. He had accordingly repaired thither, but finding the house carefully shut up, and totally uninhabited, had contented himself with questioning the tanner and his family, in regard to its late inmates, reserving to a future opportunity the attempt to make himself personally acquainted with all that it contained. From this man he learnt, that, the house had once been the property of an aged Canadian, at whose death (supposed to have been occasioned by violence,) it had passed into the hands of an American, who led a roving and adventurous life, being frequently away for months together, and then returning with a canoe, but never continuing for more than a night or two. That latterly it had been wholly deserted by its owner, in consequence of which it had been taken possession of, and used as quarters by the officers of the American guard, stationed at this part of the town, for the protection of the boats, and as a check upon the incursions of the Indians. In all this statement, there was every appearance of truth, but in no part of it did Gerald find wherewith to elucidate what he himself had witnessed. He described the costume, and questioned of the mysterious figure, but the only reply he obtained from the independent tanner, when he admitted to him that he had been so near a visitor on that occasion, and had seen what he described, was an expressed regret that he had not been "wide awake when any Brittainer ventured to set foot upon his grounds, otherwise, tarnation seize him with all due respect, if he wouldn't a stuck an ounce o' lead in the region of his bread-basket, as quickly as he would tan a hide," a patriotic sentiment in which it may be supposed our hero in no way coincided. With the tanners assurance, however, that no living thing was there at this moment, Gerald was fain to content himself for the present, fully resolving to return at another time with Sambo, and effect a forcible entrance into a place, with which were connected such striking recollections. He had, however, been too much interested and occupied elsewhere, to find time to devote to the purpose.

CHAPTER. XV.

As the boat, which contained the party, pulled by six of the best oars-men among the soldiers of the Garrison, and steered, as we have shown, by the dexterous Sambo, now glided past the spot, the recollections of the tradition connected with the bridge drew from several of the party expressions of sympathy and feigned terror, as their several humours dictated. Remarking that Miss Montgomerie's attention appeared to be deeply excited by what she heard, while she gazed earnestly upon the dwelling in the back ground, Gerald Grantham thought to interest her yet more, and amuse and startle the rest of the party, by detailing his extraordinary, and hitherto unrevealed adventure, on a recent occasion. To this strange tale, as may naturally be supposed, some of his companions listened with an air of almost incredulity, nor indeed would they rest satisfied until Sambo, who kept his eyes turned steadily away from the shore, and to whom appeal was frequently made by his master, confirmed his statement in every particular; and with such marks of revived horror in his looks, as convinced them, Gerald was not playing upon their facility of belief. The more incredulous his brother officers, the more animated had become the sailor in his description, and, on arriving at that part ot his narrative which detailed the reappearance and reflection of the mysterious figure in the upper room, upon the court below, every one became insensibly fixed in mute attention. From the moment of his commencing, Miss Montgomerie had withdrawn her gaze from the land, and fixing it upon her lover, manifested all the interest he could desire. Her feelings were evidently touched by what she heard, for she grew paler as Gerald preceeded, while her breathing was suspended, as if fearful to lose a single syllable he uttered. At each more exciting crisis of the narrative, she betrayed a corresponding intensity of attention, until at length, when the officer described his mounting on the water butt, and obtaining a full view of all within the room, she looked as still and rigid as if she had been metamarphosed into a statue. This eagerness of attention, shared as it was, although not to the same extent perhaps, by the rest of Gerald's auditory, was only remarkable in Miss Montgomerie, in as much as she was one of too much mental preoccupation to feel or betray interest in any thing, and it might have been the risk encountered by her lover, and the share he had borne in the mysterious occurrence, that now caused her to lapse from her wonted innaccessibility to impressions of the sort. As the climax of the narrative approached, her interest became deeper, and her absorption more profound. An involuntary shudder passed over her form, and a slight contracttion of the nerves of her face was perceptible, when Gerald described to his attentive and shocked auditory, the raising of the arm of the assassin; and her emotion at length assumed such a character of nervousness, that when he exultingly told of the rapid discharge of his own pistol, as having been the only means of averting the fate of the doomed, she could not refrain from rising suddenly in the boat, and putting her hand to her side, with the shrinking movement of one who had been suddenly wounded.

While in the act of rising she had drawn the cloak with which, like the other ladies, she was provided more closely over her shoulders—Sambo seemed to have caught some new idea from this action, for furtively touching Henry Grantham, who sat immediately before him, and on the right of Miss Montgomerie, he leaned forward and whispered a few sentences in his ear.

Meanwhile Miss Montgomerie was not a little rallied on the extreme susceptibity which had led her as it were to identify herself with the scene. Gerald remarked that on recovering her presence of mind, she at first looked as if she fancied herself the subject of sarcasm, and would have resented the liberty; but finding there was nothing pointed in the manner of those who addressed her, finished by joining, yet with some appearance of constraint, in the laugh against herself.

"I confess," she said coloring, "that the strange incident which Mr. Grantham has related, and which he has so well described, has caused me to be guilty of a ridiculous emotion. I am not usually startled into the expression of strong feeling, but there was so much to excite and surprise in his catastrophe that I could not avoid in some measure identifying myself with the scene."

"Nay, Miss Montgomerie," remarked Julia D'Egville, "there can be no reason why such emotion should either be disavowed or termed ridiculous. For my part, I own that cannot sufficiently express my horror of the wretch who could thus deliberately attempt the life of another. How lucky was it Gerald that you arrived at that critical moment; but have you no idea—not the slightest—of the person of the assassin or of his intended victim?"

"Not the slightest—the disguise of the person was too effectual to be penetrated, and the face I had not once an opportunity of beholding."

"Yet," observed Miss Montgomerie, "from your previous description of the figure, it is by no means a matter of certainty that it was not a woman you pursued, instead of a man—or, was there any thing to betray the vacillation of purpose which would naturally attend one of our sex in an enterprize of the kind."

"What! a woman engage in so unnatural a deed," remarked Henry Grantham—"surely Miss Montgomerie," for he always spoke rather *at*, than *to* her "cannot seek to maintain a supposition so opposed to all probability—neither will she be so unjust towards herself as to admit the existence of such monstrous guilt in the heart of another of her sex."

"Impossible," said Gerald. "Whatever might have been my impression when I first saw the figure in the merchantman—that is to say, if I had then a doubt in regard to the sex, it was entirely removed, when later I beheld the unfaltering energy with which it entered upon its murderous purpose. The hand of woman never could have been armed with such fierce and unfliching determination as was that hand."

"The emergency of the occasion, it would seem, did not much interfere with your study of character," again observed Miss Montgomerie, with a faint smile—"but you say you fired—was it with intent to kill the killer?"

"I scarcely know with what intent myself; but if I can rightly understand my own impulse, it was more with a view to divert him from his deadly object, than to slay—and this impression acquires strengh from the fact of my having missed him—I am almost sorry now that I did."

"Perhaps," said Miss Montgomerie, "you might have slain one worthier than him you sought to save. As one of your oldest poets sings—'whatever it is right.——"

"What!" exclaimed the younger Grantham with emphasis "Can Miss Montgomerie then form any idea of the persons who figured in that scene?"

Most of the party looked at the questioner with surprise. Gerald frowned, and, for the first time in his life, entertained a feeling of anger against his brother. In no way moved or piqued by the demand, Miss Montgomerie calmly replied.

"I can see no just reason for such inference, Mr. Grantham; "I merely stated a case of possibility, without any thing which can refer to the merit of either of the parties."

Henry Grantham felt that he was rebuked—but although he could not avoid something like an apologetical explanation of his remark, he was not the more favorably disposed towards her who had forced it from him. In this feeling he was confirmed by the annoyance he felt at having been visited by the anger of the brother to whom he was so attached. Arrived at Hog Island, and equipped with their guns and fishing rods, the gentlemen dispersed in quest of game, some threading the mazes of the wood in pursuit of the various birds that frequent the vicinity, the others seeking these points of the island where the dense foliage affords a shade to the numerous delicately flavoured fish, which, luxuriating in the still deep water, seek relief from the heat of summer. To these latter sportsmen, the ladies of the party principally attached themselves, quitting them only at intervals to collect pebbles on the sands, or to saunter about the wood, in search of the wild flowers or fruits that abounded along its skirt, while the servants busied themselves in erecting the marquee and making preparation for dinner.

Among those who went in pursuit of game were the Granthams, who, like most Canadians, were not only excellent shots, but much given to a sport in which they had had considerable practice in early boyhood. For a short time they had continued with their companions, but as the wood became thicker, and their object consequently more attainable by dispersion, they took a course parallel with the point at which the fishers had assembled, while their companions continued to move in an opposite direction. There was an unusual reserve in the manner of the brothers as they now wound through the intricacies of the wood. Each appeared to feel that the other had given him cause for displeasure and each—unwilling to introduce the subject most at his heart—availed himself with avidity rather of the several opportunities which the starting of the game afforded for conversation of a general nature. They had gone on in this manner for some time, and having been tolerably successful in their sport were meditating their return to the party on the beach, when the ear of Gerald was arrested by the drumming of a partridge at a short distance. Glancing his quick eye in the direction whence the sound came, he beheld a remarkably fine bird, which while continuing to beat its wings violently against the fallen tree on which it was perched, had its neck outstretched and its gaze intently fixed on some object below. Tempted by the size and beauty of the bird Gerald fired and it fell to the earth. He advanced, stooped, and was in the act of picking it up, when a sharp and well known rattle was heard to issue from beneath the log. The warning was sufficient to save him had he consented even for an instant to forego his prize, but accustomed to meet with these reptiles on almost every excursion of the kind, and never having sustained any injury from them, he persevered in disengaging the partridge from some briers with which, in falling, it had got entangled. Before he could again raise himself an enormous rattlesnake had darted upon him, and stung with rage perhaps at being deprived of its victim, had severely bitten him above the left wrist. The instantaneous pang that darted throughout the whole limb caused Gerald to utter an exclamation, and dropping the bird, he sank almost fainting on the log whence his enemy had attacked him.

The cry of agony reached, Henry Grantham, as he was carelessly awaiting his brother's return, and at once forgetting their temporary extrangement, and full of eager love and apprehension--he flew to ascertain the nature of the injury. To his surprise and horror he remarked that, although not a minute had elapsed since the fangs of the reptile had penetrated into the flesh, the arm was already considerably inflamed and exhibiting then a dark and discolored hue. That a remedy was at hand he knew, but what it was, and how to be applied he was not aware, the Indians alone being in possession of the secret. Deeming that Sambo might have some knowledge of the kind, he now made the woods echo with the sound of his name, in a manner that could not fail to startle and alarm the whole of the scattered party. Soon afterwards the rustling of forms was heard in various directions, as they forced themselves through the underwood, and the first who came in sight was Miss Montgomerie, preceded by the old negro. The lamentation of the latter was intense and when on approaching his young master, he discovered the true nature of his accident and confessed his ignorance of all remedy, he burst into tears, and throwing himself upon the earth tore his gray woollen hair away, regardless of all entreaty on the part of Gerald to moderate his grief. Miss Montgomerie now came forward, and never did sounds of melody fall so harmoniously on the ear, as did her voice on that of the younger Grantham as she pledged herself to the cure, on their instant return to the spot where the marquee had been erected. With this promise she again disappeared, and several others of the party having now joined them, Gerald, duly supported, once more slowly retraced his way to the same point.

"Damn him pattridge" muttered Sambo, who lingered a moment or two in the rear to harness himself with the apparatus of which his master had disencumbered his person. "Damn him pattridge" and he kicked the lifeless bird indignantly with his foot "you all e cause e dis; what e hell e do here?"

This tirade however against the partridge did not by any means prevent the utterer from eventually consigning it to its proper destination in the game bag as the noblest specimen of the day's sport, and thus burthened he issued from the wood, nearly at the same moment with the wounded Gerald and his friends.

The consternation of all parties on witnessing the disaster of the sailor, whose arm had already been swollen to a fearful size, while the wound itself began to assume an appearance of mortification, was strongly contrasted with the calm silence of Miss Montgomerie, who was busily employed in stirring certain herbs which she was boiling over the fire that had been kindled in the distance for the preparation of the dinner. The sleeve of the sufferer's shooting jacket had been ripped to the shoulder by his brother and as he now sat on a pile of cloaks within the marquee, the rapid discoloration of the white skin, could be distinctly traced, marking as it did the progress of the deadly poison towards the vital portion of the system. In this trying emergency all eyes were turned with anxiety on the slightest movement of her who had undertaken the cure, and none more eagerly than those of Henry Grantham and Gertrude D'Egville, the latter of whom, gentle even as she was, could not but acknowledge a pang of regret that to another, and that other a favored rival—should be the task of alleviating the anguish and preserving the life of the only man she had ever loved.

At length Miss Montgomerie came forward; and never was beneficent angel more hailed than did Henry Grantham hail her, whom scarcely an hour since he had looked upon with aversion, when with a countenance of unwonted paleness but confident of success, she advanced towards the opening of the marquee, to which interest in the sufferer had drawn even the domestics. All made way for her approach. Kneeling at the side of Gerald, and depositing the vessel in which she had mixed her preparation, she took the wounded arm in her own fair hands with the view, it was supposed, of holding it while another applied the remedy. Scarcely however had she secured it in a firm grasp when, to the surprise and consternation of all around, she applied her own lips to the wound and continued them there in despite of the efforts of Gerald to withdraw his arm, nor was it until there was already a visible reduction in the size, and change in the color of the limb that she removed them. This done she arose and retired to the skirt of the wood whence she again returned in less than a minute. Even in the short time that had elapsed, the arm of the sufferer had experienced an almost miraculous change. The inflammation had greatly subsided, while the discoloration had retired to the immediate vicinity of the wound, which in its turn however had assumed a more virulent appearance. From this it was evident that the suction had been the means of recalling, to the neighbourhood of the injury, such portions of the poison as had expanded, concentrating all in one mass immediately beneath its surface, and thereby affording fuller exposure to the action of the final remedy. This—consisting of certain herbs of a dark colour, and spread at her direction by the trembling hands of Gertrude, on her white handkerchief—Miss Montgomerie now proceeded to apply, covering a considerable portion around the orifice of the two small wounds, inflicted by the fangs of the serpent, with the dense mass of the vegetable preparation. The relief produced by this was effectual, and in less than an hour, so completely had the poison been extracted, and the strength of the arm restored, that Gerald was enabled not merely to resume his shooting jacket, but to partake, although sparingly, of the meal which followed.

It may be presumed that the bold action of Miss Montgomerie passed not without the applause it so highly merited, yet even while applauding, there were some of the party, and particularly Henry Grantham, who regarded it with feelings not wholly untinctured with the unpleasant. Her countenance and figure, as she stood in the midst of the forest, preparing the embrocation, so well harmonizing with the scene and occupation; the avidity with which she sucked the open wound of the sufferer, and the fearless manner in which she imbibed that which was considered death to others; all this, combined with a general demeanour in which predominated a reserve deeply shaded with mystery, threw over the actor and the action, an air of the preternatural, occasioning more of surprise and awe than prepossession. Such, especially, as we have said, was the impression momentarily, produced on Henry Grantham; but when he beheld his brother's eye and cheek once more beaming with returning strength and health, he saw in her but the generous preserver of that brother's life to whom his own boundless debt of gratitude was due. It was at this moment that, in the course of conversation on the subject, Captain Molineux inquired of Miss Montgomerie, what antidote she possessed against the influence of the poison. Every eye was turned upon her as she vaguely answered, a smile of peculiar meaning playing over her lips, that "Captain Molineux must be satisfied with knowing she bore a charmed life." Then again it was that the young soldier's feelings underwent another reaction, and as he caught the words and look which accompanied them, he scarcely could persuade himself she was not the almost vampire and sorceress that his excited imagination had represented.

Not the least deeply interested in the events of the morning, was the old negro. During their meal, at the service of which he assisted, his eyes scarcely quitted her whom he appeared to regard with a mingled feeling of awe and adoration; nay, such was his abstraction that, in attempting to place a dish of game on the rude table at which the party sat, he lodged the whole of the contents in the lap of Middlemore, a *gaucherie* that drew from the latter an exclamation of horror, followed however the instant afterwards by Sambo's apology.

"I beg a pardon Massa Middlemore," he exclaimed, "I let him fall e gravey in e lap."

"Then will you by some means contrive to lap it up," returned the officer quaintly.

Sambo applied his napkin, and the dinner proceeded without other occurrence. Owing to an apprehension that the night air might tend to renew the inflammation of the wounded arm, the boat was early in readiness for the return of the party, whose day of pleasure had been in some manner turned into a day of mourning, so that long before sun set, they had again reached their respective homes at Detroit.

END OF VOLUME I.

THE CANADIAN BROTHERS;

OR,

THE PROPHECY FULFILLED.

CHAPTER I.

A FEW days after the adventure detailed in our last chapter, the American party, consisting of Major and Miss Montgomerie, and the daughters of the Governor, with their attendants, embarked in the schooner, to the command of which Gerald had been promoted. The destination of the whole was the American port of Buffalo, situate at the further extremity of the lake, nearly opposite to the fort of Erie; and thither our hero, perfectly recovered from the effect of his accident, received instructions to repair without loss of time, land his charge, and immediately rejoin the flotilla at Amherstburg.

However pleasing the first, the latter part of the order was by no means so strictly in consonance with the views and feelings of the new commander, as might have been expected from a young and enterprising spirit; but he justified his absence of zeal to himself, in the fact that there was no positive service to perform; no duty in which he could have an opportunity of signalizing himself, or rendering a benefit to his country.

If, however, the limited period allotted for the execution of his duty, was a source of much disappointment to Gerald, such was not the effect produced by it on his brother, to whom it gave promise of a speedy termination of an attachment, which he had all along regarded with disapprobation, and a concern amounting almost to dread. We have seen that Henry Grantham, on the occasion of his brother's disaster at the pic-nic, had been wound up into an enthusiasm of gratitude, which had nearly weaned him from his original aversion; but this feeling had not outlived the day on which the occurrence took place. Nay, on the very next morning, he had had a long private conversation with Gerald, in regard to Miss Montgomerie, which, ending as it did, in a partial coolness, had tended to make him dislike the person who had caused it still more. It was, therefore, not without secret delight that he overheard the order for the instant return of the schooner, which, although conveyed by the Commodore in the mildest manner, was yet so firm and decided as to admit neither of doubt nor dispute. While the dangerous American continued a resident at Detroit, there was every reason to fear that the attachment of his infatuated brother fed by opportunity, would lead him to the commission of some irrevocable act of imprudence; whereas, on the contrary, when she had departed, there was every probability that continued absence, added to the stirring incidents of war, which might be expected shortly to ensue, would prove effectual in restoring the tone of Gerald's mind. There was, consequently, much to please him in the order for departure. Miss Montgomerie once landed within the American lines, and his brother returned to his duty, the anxious soldier had no doubt that the feelings of the latter would resume their wonted channel, and that, in his desire to render himself worthy of glory, to whom he had been originally devoted, he would forget, at least after a season, all that was connected with love.

It was a beautiful autumnal morning, when the schooner weighed anchor from Detroit. Several of the officers of the garrison had accompanied the ladies on board, and having made fast their sailing boat to the stern, loitered on deck with the intention of descending the river a few miles, and then beating up against the current. The whole party were thus assembled, conversing together and watching the movements of the sailors, when a boat, in which were several armed men encircling a huge raw-boned individual, habited in the fashion of an American backwoodsman, approached the vessel. This was no other than the traitor Desborough, who, it will be recollected, was detained and confined in prison at the surrender of Detroit. He had been put upon his trial for the murder of Major Grantham, but had been acquitted through want of evidence to convict, his own original admission being negatived by a subsequent declaration that he had only made it through a spirit of bravado and revenge. Still, as the charges of desertion and treason had been substantiated against him, he was, by order of the Commandant of Amherstburg, destined for Fort Erie, in the schooner conveying the American party to Buffalo, with a view to his being sent on to the Lower Province, there to be disposed of as the General Commanding in Chief should deem fit.

The mien of the settler, as he now stepped over the vessel's side, partook of the mingled cunning and ferocity by which he had formerly been distinguished. While preparations were being made for his reception and security below deck, he bent his sinister, yet bold, glance on each of the little group in succession, as if he would have read in their countenances the probable fate that awaited himself. The last who fell under his scrutiny was Miss Montgomerie, on whom his eye had scarcely rested, when the insolent indifference of his manner seemed to give place at once to a new feeling. There was intelligence enough in the glance of both to show that an insensible interest had been created, and yet neither gave the slightest indication, by word, of what was passing in the mind.

"Well, Mister Jeremiah Desborough," said Middlemore, first breaking the silence, and, in the taunting mode of address he usually adopted towards the settler, "I reckon as how you'll shoot no wild ducks this season, on the Sandusky river—not likely to be much troubled with your small bores now."

The Yankee gazed at him a moment in silence, evidently ransacking his brain for something sufficiently insolent to offer in return. At length, he drew his hat slouchingly over one side of his head, folded his arms across his chest, and squirting a torrent of tobacco juice from his capacious jaws, exclaimed in his drawling voice:

"I guess, Mister Officer, as how you're mighty cute upon a fallen man—but tarnation seize me, if I don't expect you'll find some one cuter still afore long. The sogers all say," he continued with a low, cunning laugh, "as how you're a bit of a wit, and fond of a play upon words like. If so, I'll jist try you a little at your own game, and tell you that I had a thousand to one rather be troubled with my small bores than with such a confounded great bore as you are; and now, you may pit that down as something good, in your pun book when you please, and ax me no more questions."

Long and fitful was the laughter which burst from Villiers and Molineux, at this bitter retort upon their companion, which they vowed should be repeated at the mess table of either garrison, whenever he again attempted one of his execrables.

Desborough took courage at the license conveyed by this pleasantry, and pursued, winking familiarly to Captain Molineux, while he, at the same time, nodded to Middlemore,

"Mighty little time, I calculate, had he to think of aggravatin', when I gripped him down at Hartley's pint, that day. If it hadn't been for that old heathen scoundrel Gattrie, my poor boy Phil, as the Injuns killed, and me, I reckon, would have sent him and young Grantham to crack their puns upon the fishes of the lake. How scared they were, sure*ly*."

"Silence, fellow!" thundered Gerald Grantham, who now came up from the hold, whither he had been to examine the fastenings prepared for his prisoner. "How dare you open your lips here ?"—then pointing towards the steps he had just quitted—" descend, sir !"

Never did human countenance exhibit marks of greater rage than Desborough's at that moment. His eyes seemed about to start from their sockets--the large veins of his neck and brow swelled almost to bursting, and while his lips were compressed with violence, his nervous fingers played, as with convulsive anxiety to clutch themselves around the throat of the officer; every thing, in short, marked the effort it cost him to restrain himself within such bounds as his natural cunning and prudence dictated. Still, he neither spoke nor moved.

" Descend, sir, instantly !" repeated Gerald, " or, by Heaven, I will have you thrown in without further ceremony —descend this moment !"

The settler advanced, placed one foot upon the ladder, then turned his eye steadfastly upon the officer. Every one present shuddered to behold its expression—it was that of fierce, inextinguishable hatred.

" By hell, you will pay me one day or t'other for this, I reckon," he uttered, in a hoarse and fearful whisper— " every dog has his day—it will be Jeremiah Desborough's turn next."

" What ! do you presume to threaten, villain ?" vociferated Gerald, now excited beyond all bounds: " here men, gag me this fellow—tie him neck and heels, and throw him into the hold, as you would a bag of ballast."

Several men, with Sambo at their head, advanced for the purpose of executing the command of their officer, when the eldest daughter of the Governor, who had witnessed the whole scene, suddenly approached the latter, and interceded warmly for a repeal of the punishment. Miss Montgomerie, also, who had been a silent observer, glanced significantly towards the settler. What her look implied, no one was quick enough to detect; but its effect on the Yankee was evident—for, without uttering another syllable, or waiting to be again directed, he moved slowly and sullenly down the steps that led to his place of confinement.

Whatever the impressions produced upon the minds of the several spectators by this incident, they were not expressed. No comment was made, nor was further allusion had to the settler. Other topics of conversation were introduced, and it was not until the officers, having bid them a final and cordial adieu, had again taken to their boats, on their way back to Detroit, that the ladies quitted the deck for the cabin which had been prepared for them.

The short voyage down the lake was performed without incident. From the moment of the departure of the officers, an air of dulness and abstraction, originating, in a great degree, in the unpleasantness of separation—anticipated and past—pervaded the little party. Sensitive and amiable as were the daughters of the American Governor, it was not to be supposed that they parted without regret from men in whose society they had recently passed so many agreeable hours, and for two of whom they had insensibly formed preferences. Not, however, that that parting was to be considered final, for both Molineux and Villiers had promised to avail themselves of the first days of peace, to procure leave of absence, and revisit them in their native country. The feeling of disappointment acknowledged by the sisters, was much more perceptible in Gerald Grantham and Miss Montgomerie, both of whom became more thoughtful and abstracted, as the period of separation drew nearer.

It was about ten o'clock on the evening immediately preceding that on which they expected to gain their destination, that, as Gerald leaned ruminating over the side of the schooner, then going at the slow rate of two knots an hour, he fancied he heard voices, in a subdued tone, ascending apparently from the quarter of the vessel in which Desborough was confined. He listened attentively for a few moments, but even the slight gurgling of the water, as it was thrown from the prow, prevented further recognition. Deeming it possible that the sounds might not proceed from the place of confinement of the settler, but from the cabin which it adjoined, and with which it communicated, he was for a short time undecided whether or not he should disturb the party already retired to rest, by descending and passing into the room occupied by his prisoner. Anxiety to satisfy himself that the latter was secure determined him, and he had already planted a foot on the companion-ladder, when his further descent was arrested by Miss Montgomerie, who appeared emerging from the opening, bonneted and cloaked, as with a view of continuing on deck.

"What! you, dearest Matilda?" he asked, delightedly—"I thought you had long since retired to rest."

"To rest, Gerald!—can you, then, imagine mine is a soul to slumber, when I know that tomorrow we part--perhaps for ever?"

"No, by Heaven! not for ever," energetically returned the sailor, seizing and carrying the white hand that pressed his own, to his lips—"be but faithful to me, my own Matilda—love me but with one half the ardor with which my soul glows for you, and the moment duty can be sacrificed to affection, you may expect again to see me."

"Duty!" repeated the American, with something like reproach in her tone—"must the happiness of her you profess so ardently to love, be sacrificed to a mere cold sense of duty? But you are right—you have *your* duty to perform, and I have *mine*. Tomorrow we separate, and for ever."

"No, Matilda—not for ever, unless, indeed, such be your determination. *You* may find the task to forget an easy one—*I* never can. Hope—heart—life—happiness—all are centered in you. Were it not that honour demands my service to my country, I would fly with you tomorrow, delighted to encounter every dfficulty fortune might oppose, if, by successfully combating these, I should establish a deeper claim on your affection. Oh, Matilda!" continued the impassioned youth, "never did I feel more than at this moment, how devotedly I could be your slave for ever."

At the commencement of this conversation, Miss Montgomerie had gently led her lover towards the outer gangway of the vessel, over which they both now leaned. As Gerald made the last passionate avowal of his tenderness, a ray of triumphant expression, clearly visible in the light of the setting moon, passed over the features of the American.

"Gerald," she implored earnestly—"oh, repeat me that avowal. Again tell me that you will be the devoted of your Matilda, in *all* things--Gerald, swear most solemnly to me that you will--my every hope of happiness depends upon it."

How could he refuse, to such pleader, the repetition of his spontaneous vow? Already were his lips opened to swear, before high Heaven, that, in all things earthly, he would obey her will, when he was interrupted by a well known voice, hastily exclaiming:

"Who a debbel dat dare?"

Scarcely had these words been uttered, when they were followed apparently by a blow, then a bound, and then the falling of a human body upon the deck. Gently disengaging his companion, who had clung to him with an air of alarm, Gerald turned to discover the cause of the interruption. To his surprise, he beheld Sambo, whose post of duty was at the helm, lying extended on the deck, while, at the same moment, a sudden plunge was heard, as of a heavy body falling overboard. The first impulse of the officer was to seize the helm, with a view to right the vessel, already swerving from her course; the second, to awaken the crew, who were buried in sleep on the forecastle. These, with the habitual promptitude of their nature, speedily obeyed his call, and a light being brought, Gerald, confiding the helm to one of his best men, proceeded to examine the condition of Sambo.

It was evident that the aged negro had been stunned, but whether seriously injured, it was impossible to decide. No external wound was visible, and yet his breathing was that of one who had received some severe bodily harm. In a few minutes, however, he recovered his recollection, and the words he uttered, as he gazed wildly around, and addressed his master, were sufficient to explain the whole affair:

"Damn him debbel, Massa Geral, he get safe off, him billain."

"Ha, Desborough! it is then so? Quick, put the helm about —two of the lightest and most active into my canoe, and follow in pursuit. The fellow is making for the shore, no doubt. Now then, my lads," as two of the crew sprang into the canoe that had been instantly lowered, "fifty dollars between you, recollect, if you bring him back."

Although there needed no greater spur to exertion, than a desire both to please their officer, and to acquit themselves of a duty, the sum offered was not without its due weight. In an instant, the canoe was seen scuddling along the surface of the water, towards the shore, and, at intervals, as the anxious Gerald listened, he fancied he could distinguish the exertions of the fugitive swimmer from those made by the paddles of his pursuers. For a time all was silent, when, at length, a deriding laugh came over the surface of the lake, that too plainly told, the settler had reached the shore, and was beyond all chance of capture. In the bitterness of his disappointment, and heedless of the pleasure his change of purpose had procured him, Gerald could not help cursing his folly, in having suffered himself to be diverted from his original intention of descending to the prisoner's place of confinement. Had this been done, all might have been well. He had now no doubt that the voices had proceeded from thence, and he was resolved, as soon as the absent men came on board, to institute a strict inquiry into the affair.

No sooner, therefore, had the canoe returned, than all hands were summoned and questioned, under a threat of severe punishment, to whoever should be found prevaricating as to the manner of the prisoner's escape. Each positively denied having in any way violated the order which enjoined that no communication should take place between the prisoner and the crew, to whom indeed all access was denied, with the exception of Sambo, entrusted with the duty of carrying the former his meals. The denial of the men was so straight forward and clear, that Gerald knew not what to believe, and yet it was evident that the sounds he had heard, proceeded from human voices. Determined to satisfy himself, his first care was to descend between the decks, preceded by his boatswain, with a lantern. At the sternmost extremity of the little vessel there was a small room, used for stores, but which, empty on this trip, had been converted into a cell for Desborough. This was usually entered from the cabin ; but in order to avoid inconvenience to the ladies, a door had been effected in the bulk heads, the key of which was kept by Sambo. On inspection, this door was found hermetically closed, so that it became evident, if the key had not been purloined from its keeper, the escape of Desborough must have been accomplished through the cabin. Moreover, there was no opening of any description to be found, through which a knife might be passed to enable him to sever the bonds which confined his feet. Close to the partition, were swung the hammocks of two men, who had been somewhat dilatory in obeying the summons on deck, and between whom it was not impossible the conversation, which Gerald had detected, had been carried on. On re-ascending, he again questioned these men, but they most solemnly assured him they had not spoken either together or to others, within the last two hours, having fallen fast asleep on being relieved from their watch. Search was now made in the pockets of Sambo, whose injury had been found to be a violent blow given on the back of the head, and whose recovery from stupefaction was yet imperfect. The key being found, all suspicion of participation was removed from the crew, who could have only communicated from their own quarter of the vessel, and they were accordingly dismissed ; one half, comprising the first watch, to their hammocks, the remainder to their original station on the forecastle. The next care of the young Commander was to inspect the cabin, and institute a strict scrutiny as to the manner in which the escape had been effected. The door that opened into the prison, stood between the companion ladder and the recess occupied by the daughters of the Governor. To his surprise, Gerald found it locked, and the key that usually remained in a niche near the door, removed. On turning to search for it, he also noticed, for the first time, that the lamp, suspended from a beam in the centre of the cabin, had been extinguished. Struck by these remarkable circumstances, a suspicion, which he would have given much not to have entertained, forced itself upon his mind. As a first measure, and that there might be no doubt whatever on the subject, he broke open the door. Of course it was untenanted. Upon a small table lay the remains of the settler's last meal, but neither knife nor fork, both which articles had been interdicted, were to be found. At the foot of the chair on which he had evidently been seated for the purpose of freeing himself, lay the heavy cords that had bound his ancles. These had been severed in two places, and, as was discovered on close examination, by the application of some sharp and delicate cutting instrument. No where, however, was this visible. It was evident to Gerald that assistance had been afforded from some one within the cabin, and who that some one was, he scarcely doubted. With this impression fully formed, he re-entered from the prison, and standing near the curtained berth occupied by the daughters of the Governor, questioned as to whether they were aware that his prisoner Desborough had escaped. Both expressed surprise in so natural a manner, that Gerald knew not what to think; but when they added that they had not heard the slightest noise—nor had spoken themselves, nor heard others speak, professing moreover ignorance that the lamp even had been extinguished, he felt suspicion converted into certainty.

It was impossible, he conceived, that a door, which stood only two paces from the bed, could be locked and unlocked without their hearing it—neither was it probable that Desborough would have thought of thus needlessly securing the place of his late detention. Such an idea might occur to the aider, but not to the fugitive himself, to whom every moment must be of the highest importance. Who then could have assisted him? Not Major Montgomerie, for he slept in the after part of the cabin—not Miss Montgomerie, for she was upon deck—moreover, had not one of those, he had so much reason to suspect, interceded for the fellow only on the preceding day.

Such was the reasoning of Gerald, as he passed rapidly in review the several probabilities—but, although annoyed beyond measure at the escape of the villain, and incapable of believing other than that the daughters of the Governor had connived at it, his was too gallant a nature to make such a charge, even by implication, against them. He was aware of the strong spirit of nationality existing every where among citizens of the United States, and he had no doubt, that in liberating their countryman, they had acted under an erroneous impression of duty. Although extremely angry, he made no comment whatever on the subject, but contenting himself with wishing his charge a less than usually cordial good night, left them to their repose, and once more quitted the cabin.

During the whole of this examination, Miss Montgomerie had continued on deck. Gerald found her leaning over the gangway, at which he had left her, gazing intently on the water, through which the schooner was now gliding at an increased rate. From the moment of his being compelled to quit her side, to inquire into the cause of Sambo's exclamation and rapidly succeeding fall, he had not had an opportunity of again approaching her. Feeling that some apology was due, he hastened to make one; but, vexed and irritated as he was at the escape of the settler, his disappointment imparted to his manner a degree of restraint, and there was less of ardor in his address than he had latterly been in the habit of exhibiting. Miss Montgomerie remarked it, and sighed.

"I have been reflecting," she said, "on the little dependance that is to be placed upon the most flattering illusions of human existence—and here are you come to afford me a painful and veritable illustration of my theory."

"How, dearest Matilda! what mean you?" asked the officer, again warmed into tenderness by the presence of the fascinating being.

"Can you ask, Gerald?" and her voice assumed a tone of melancholy reproach—"recal but your manner—your language—your devotedness of soul, not an hour since—compare these with your present coldness, and then wonder that I should have reason for regret."

"Nay, Matilda, that coldness arose not from any change in my feelings towards yourself—I was piqued, disappointed, even angry, at the extraordinary escape of my prisoner, and could not sufficiently play the hypocrite to disguise my annoyance."

"Yet, what had I to do with the man's escape, that his offence should be visited upon me?" she demanded, quickly.

"Can you not find some excuse for my vexation, knowing, as you do that the wretch was a vile assassin—a man whose hands have been imbrued in the blood of my own father?"

"Was he not acquitted of the charge?"

"He was—but only from lack of evidence to convict; yet, although acquitted by the law, not surer is fate than that he is an assassin."

"You hold assassins in great horror," remarked the American, thoughtfully—"you are right—it is but natural."

"In horror, said you?—aye, in such loathing, that language can supply no term to express it."

"And yet, you once attempted an assassination yourself.

Nay, do not start, and look the image of astonishment. Have you not told me that you fired into the hut, on the night of your mysterious adventure? What right had you, if we argue the question on its real merit, to attempt the life of a being who had never injured you?"

"What right, Matilda?—every right, human and divine. I sought but to save a victim from the hands of a midnight murderer.

"And, to effect this, scrupled not to become a midnight murderer yourself!

"And is it thus you interpret my conduct, Matilda?"—the voice of Gerald spoke bitter reproach—"can you compare the act of that man with mine, and hold me no more blameless than him?"

"Nay, I did not say I blamed you," she returned, gaily—"but the fact is, you had left me so long to ruminate here alone, that I have fallen into a mood argumentative, or philosophical—whichsoever you may be pleased to term it—and I am willing to maintain my position, that you might, by possibility, have been more guilty than the culprit at whom you aimed, had your shot destroyed him.

The light tone in which Matilda spoke dispelled the seriousness which had begun to shadow the brow of the young Commander—"And pray how do you make this good?" he asked.

"Suppose for instance, the slumberer you preserved had been a being of crime, through whom the hopes, the happiness, the peace of mind, and above all, the fair fame of the other been cruelly and irrevocably blasted. Let us imagine that he had destroyed some dear friend or relative of him with whose vengeance you beheld him threatened."

"Could that be——."

"Or," interrupted the American, in the same careless tone "that he had betrayed a wife."

"Such a man——"

"Or, what is worse, infinitely worse, sought to put the finishing stroke to his villainy, by affixing to the name and conduct of his victim every ignominy and disgrace which can attach to insulted humanity."

"Matilda," eagerly exclaimed the youth, advancing close to her, and gazing into her dark eyes; "you are drawing a picture."

"No Gerald," she replied calmly, "I am merely supposing a case. Could you find no excuse for a man acting under a sense of so much injury?—would you still call him an assassin, if, with such provocation, he sought to destroy the hated life of one who had thus injured him?"

Gerald paused, apparently bewildered.

"Tell me, dearest Gerald," and her fair and beautiful hand caught and pressed his—"would you still bestow upon one so injured the degrading epithet of assassin?"

"Assassin!—most undoubtedly I would. But why this question, Matilda?"

The features of the American assumed a changed expression; she dropped the hand she had taken the instant before, and said, disappointedly:

"I find, then, my philosophy is totally at fault."

"Wherein, Matilda?" anxiously asked Gerald.

"In this, that I have not been able to make you a convert to my opinions."

"And these are—?" again questioned Gerald, his every pulse throbbing with intense emotion.

"Not to pronounce too harshly on the conduct of others, seeing that we ourselves may stand in much need of lenity of judgment. There might have existed motives for the action of him whom you designate as an assassin, quite as powerful as those which led to *your* interference, and quite as easily justified to himself."

"But, dearest Matilda——"

"Nay, I have done—I close at once my argument and my

philosophy. The humour is past, and I shall no longer attempt to make the worse appear the better cause. I dare say you thought me in earnest," she added, with slight sarcasm, "but a philosophical disquisition between two lovers on the eve of parting for ever, was too novel and piquant a seduction to be resisted."

That "parting for ever" was sufficient to drive all philosophy utterly away from our hero.

"For ever, did you say, Matilda?—no, not for ever; yet, how coldly do you allude to a separation, which, although I trust it will be only temporary, is to me a source of the deepest vexation. You did not manifest this indifference in the early part of our conversation this evening."

"And if there be a change," emphatically yet tenderly returned the beautiful American; "am *I* the only one changed. Is your manner *now* what it was *then*. Do you already forget at *what* a moment that conversation was interrupted?"

Gerald did not forget; and again, as they leaned over the vessel's side, his arm was passed around the waist of his companion.

The hour, the scene, the very rippling of the water—all contributed to lend a character of excitement to the feelings of the youth. Filled with tenderness and admiration for the facinating being who reposed thus confidingly on his shoulder, he scarcely dared to move, lest in so doing he should destroy the fabric of his happiness.

"First watch there, hilloa! rouse up, and be d—d to you, it's two o'clock."

Both Gerald and Matilda, although long and silently watching the progress of the vessel, had forgotten there was any such being as a steersman to direct her.

"Good Heaven, can it be so late?" whispered the American, gliding from her lover; "if my uncle be awake, he will certainly chide me for my imprudence. Good night, dear Gerald," and drawing her cloak more closely around her shoulders, she quickly crossed the deck, and descended to the cabin.

"What the devil's this?" said the relieving steersman, as, rubbing his heavy eyes with one hand, he stooped and raised with the other something from the deck against which he had kicked, in his advance to take the helm; "why, I'm blest if it arn't the apron off old Sally here. Have you been fingering Sall's apron, Bill?"

"Not I, faith," growled the party addressed, I've enough to do to steer the craft without thinking o' meddling with Sall's apron at this time o' night."

"I should like to know who it is that has hexposed the old gal to the night hair in this here manner," still muttered the other, holding up the object in question to his closer scrutiny; "it was only this morning I gave her a pair of bran new apron strings, and helped to dress her myself. If she doesn't hang fire after this, I'm a Dutchman that's all."

"What signifies jawing, Tom Fluke. I suppose she got unkivered in the scurry after the Yankee; but bear a hand, and kiver her, unless you wish a fellow to stay here all night."

Old Sal, our readers must know, was no other than the long twenty-four pounder, formerly belonging to Gerald's gun-boat, which, now removed to his new command, lay a mid ships, and mounted on a pivot, constituted the whole battery of the schooner. The apron was the leaden covering protecting the touch-hole, which, having unaccountably fallen off, had encountered the heavy foot of Tom Fluke, in his advance along the deck.

The apron was at length replaced. Tom Fluke took the helm, and his companion departed, as he said, to have a comfortable snooze.

Gerald, who had been an amused listener of the preceding dialogue, soon followed, first inquiring into the condition of his faithful Sambo, who, on examination, was found to have been stunned by the violence of the blow he had received. This, Gerald doubted not, had been given with the view of better facilitating Desborough's escape, by throwing the schooner out of her course, and occasioning a consequent confusion among the crew, which might have the effect of distracting their attention, for a time, from himself.

CHAPTER II.

THE following evening, an armed schooner was lying at anchor in the roadstead of Buffalo, at the southern extremity of Lake Erie, and within a mile of the American shore. It was past midnight—and although the lake was calm and unbroken as the face of a mirror, a dense fog had arisen which prevented objects at the head of the vessel from being seen from the stern. Two men only were visible upon the after deck; the one lay reclining upon an arm chest, muffled up in a dread-nought pea jacket, the other paced up and down hurriedly, and with an air of deep pre-occupation. At intervals he would stop and lean over the gang-way, apparently endeavouring to pierce through the fog and catch a glimpse of the adjacent shore, and, on these occasions, a profound sigh would burst from his chest. Then again he would resume his rapid walk, with the air of one who has resolved to conquer a weakness, and substitute determination in its stead. Altogether his manner was that of a man ill at ease from his own thoughts.

"Sambo," he at length exclaimed, addressing the man in the pea jacket for the first time, "I shall retire to my cabin, but fail not to call me an hour before day-break. Our friends being all landed, there can be nothing further to detain us here, we will therefore make the best of our way back to Amherstburg in the morning."

"Yes, Massa Geral," returned the negro, yawning and half raising his brawny form from his rude couch with one hand, while he rubbed his heavy eyes with the knuckles of the other.

"How is your head tonight?" inquired the officer in a kind tone.

"Berry well, Massa Geral—but berry sleepy."

"Then sleep, Sambo; but do not fail to awaken me in time: we shall weigh anchor the very first thing in the morning, provided the fog does not continue. By the bye, you superintended the landing of the baggage—was every thing sent ashore?"

"All, Massa Geral, I see him all pack in e wagon, for e Bubbalo town—all, except dis here I find in Miss Mungummery cabin under e pillow."

As he spoke, the negro quitted his half recumbent position, and drew from his breast a small clasped pocket book, on a steel entablature adorning the cover of which, were the initials of the young lady just named.

"How is it Sambo, that you had not sooner spoken of this? The pocket book contains papers that may be of importance; and yet there is now no means of forwarding it, unless I delay the schooner."

"I only find him hab an hour ago, Massa Geral, when I go to make e beds and put e cabin to rights," said the old man, in a tone that showed he felt, and was pained by the reproof of his young master. "Dis here too," producing a small ivory handled penknife, "I find same time in e Gubbanor's dater's bed."

Gerald extended his hand to receive it. "A penknife in the bed of the Governor's daughters!" he repeated with surprise. Ruminating a moment he added to himself, "By heaven, it must be so—it is then as I expected. Would that I had had this proof of their participation before they quitted the schooner. Very well, Sambo, no blame can attach to you—go to sleep, my good fellow, but not beyond the time I have given you."

"Tankee, Massa Geral," and drawing the collar of his pea jacket close under his ears, the negro again extended himself at his length upon the arm chest.

The first idea of the young Commander on descending to the cabin, was to examine the blade of the penknife. Passing it over his finger, he perceived that the edge had that particular bluntness which would have been produced by cutting through a rope, and on closer examination he found it full of numerous fine notches, apparently the result of the resistance it had met with. His next care was to examine the severed portions of the rope itself, and in these he could observe, by the reflection of the lamp, near which he held them minute particles of steel, which left no doubt in his mind that this had been the instrument by which the separation of Desborough's bonds had been effected. We will not venture to assert what were the actual feelings of the officer, on making this discovery ; but it may be supposed, that, added to the great annoyance he felt at the escape of the settler, his esteem for those who had so positively denied all knowledge of, or participation in, the evasion was sensibly diminished ; and yet it was not without pain that he came to a conclusion of the unworthiness of those whom he had known from boyhood, and loved no less than he had known.

In the fulness of his indignation at their duplicity, he now came to the resolution of staying the departure of the schooner, yet a few hours, that he might have an opportunity of going ashore himself, presenting this undoubted evidence of their guilt, and taxing them boldly with the purpose to which it had been appropriated. Perhaps there was another secret motive which induced this determination, and that was, the opportunity it would afford him of again seeing his beloved Matilda, and delivering her pocket book with his own hand.

This resolution taken, without deeming it necessary to countermand his order to Sambo, he placed the knife in a pocket in the breast of his uniform, where he had already deposited the souvenir ; and having retired to his own cabin, was about to undress himself, when he fancied he could distinguish, through one of the stern windows of the schooner, sounds similar to those of muffled oars. While he yet listened breathlessly to satisfy himself whether he had not been deceived, a dark form came hurriedly, yet noiselessly, down the steps of the cabin. Gerald turned, and discovered Sambo, who now perfectly awake, indicated by his manner, he was the bearer of some alarming intelligence. His report confirmed the suspicion already entertained by himself, and at that moment he fancied he heard the same subdued sounds but multiplied in several distinct points. A vague sense of danger came over the mind of the officer, and although his crew consisted of a mere handful of men, he at once resolved to defend himself to the last, against whatever force might be led to the attack. While Sambo hastened to arouse the men, he girded his cutlass and pistols around his loins, and taking down two huge blunderbusses from a beam in the ceiling of the cabin, loaded them heavily with musket balls. Thus armed he sprang once more upon deck.

The alarm was soon given, and the preparation became general, but neither among the watch, who slumbered in the forecastle, nor those who had turned into their hammocks, was there the slightest indication of confusion. These latter "tumbled up," with no other addition to the shirts in which they had left their cots, then their trousers, a light state of costume to which those who were "boxed up" in their pea jackets and great coats on the forecastle, soon reduced themselves also—not but that the fog admitted of much warmer raiment, but that their activity might be unimpeded—handkerchiefed heads and tucked up sleeves, with the habiliments which we have named, being the most approved fighting dress in the navy.

Meanwhile, although nothing could be distinguished through the fog, the sounds which had originally attracted the notice of the officer and his trusty servant, increased, despite of the caution evidently used, to such a degree as to be now audible to all on board. What most excited the astonishment of the crew, and the suspicion of Gerald, was the exactness of the course taken by the advancing boats, in which not the slightest deviation was perceptible. It was evident that they were guided by some one who had well studied the distance and bearing of the schooner from the shore, and as it was impossible to hope that even the fog would afford them concealment from the approaching enemy, all that was left them was to make the best defence they could. One other alternative remained, it is true, and this was to cut their cable and allow themselves to drop down silently out of the course by which the boats were advancing, but as this step involved the possibility of running ashore on the American coast, when the same danger of captivity would await them, Gerald, after an instant's consideration, rejected the idea, prefering the worthier and more chivalrous dependence on his own and crew's exertions.

From the moment of the general arming, the long gun, which we have already shown to constitute the sole defence of the schooner, was brought nearer to the inshore gang-way, and mounted on its elevated pivot, with its formidable muzzle overtopping and projecting above the low bulwarks, could in an instant be brought to bear on whatever point it might be found advisable to vomit forth its mass of wrath, consisting of grape, cannister, and chain shot. On this gun indeed, the general expectation much depended, for the crew, composed of sixteen men only, exclusive of petty officers, could hope to make but a poor resistance, despite of all the resolution they might bring into the contest, against a squadron of well armed boats, unless some very considerable diminution in the numbers and efforts of these latter should be made by "old Sally," before they actually came to close quarters. The weakness of the crew was in a great degree attributable to the schooner having been employed as a cartel; a fact which must moreover explain the want of caution, on this occasion, on the part of Gerald, whose reputation for vigilance, in all matters of duty, was universally acknowledged. It had not occurred to him that the instant he landed his prisoners his vessel ceased to be a cartel, and therefore a fit subject for the enterprize of his enemies, or the probability is, that in the hour in which he had landed them he would again have weighed anchor, and made the best of his way back to Amherstburg.

"Stand by your gun, men—steady," whispered the officer, as the noise of many oars immediately abreast, and at a distance of not more than twenty yards, announced that the main effort of their enemies was about to be made in that quarter. "Depress a little—there you have her—now into them—fire."

Fiz-z-z-z, and a small pyramid of light rose from the breech of the gun, which sufficed, during the moment it lasted, to discover three boats filled with armed men, advancing immediately opposite, while two others could be seen diverging, apparently one towards the quarter, the other towards the bows of the devoted little vessel. The crew bent their gaze eagerly over her side, to witness the havoc they expected to ensue among their enemies. To their surprise and mortification there was no report. The advancing boats gave three deriding cheers.

"D—n my eyes, if I didn't say she would miss fire, from having her breech unkivered last night," shouted the man who held the match, and who was no other than Tom Fluke. "Quick, here, give us a picker."

A picker was handed to him by one, who also held the powder horn for priming.

"Its no use," he pursued, throwing away the wire, and springing to the deck. "She 's a spike in the touch-hole, and the devil himself wouldn't get it out now."

"A spike!—what mean you?" eagerly demanded Gerald.

"It's too true, Mr. Grantham," said the boatswain, who had flown to examine the touch-hole, "there is a great piece of steel in it, and for all the world like a woman's bodkin, or some such sort of thing."

"Ah! it all comes o' that wench that was here on deck last night," muttered the helmsman, who had succeeded Sambo on duty the preceding night. "I thought I see her fiddlin' about the gun, when the chase was made after the Yankee, although I didn't think to say nothing about it, when you axed Tom Fluke about Sal's apron."

Whatever conjecture might have arisen with others, there was no time to think of, much less to discuss it—the boats were already within a few yards of the vessel.

"Steady, men—silence," commanded Gerald in a low tone: "Since Sal has failed us, we must depend upon ourselves. Down beneath the bulwarks, and move not one of you until they begin to board—then let each man single his enemy and fire; the cutlass must do the rest."

The order was obeyed. Each moment brought the crisis of action nearer: the rowers had discontinued their oars, but the bows of the several boats could be heard obeying the impetus already given them, and dividing the water close to the vessel.

"Now then, Sambo," whispered the officer. At that moment a torch was raised high over the head of the negro and his master. Its rays fell upon the first of the three boats, the crews of which were seen standing up with arms outstretched to grapple with the schooner. Another instant and they would have touched. The negro dropped his light.

Gerald pulled the trigger of his blunderbuss, aimed into the very centre of the boat. Shrieks, curses and plashings, as of bodies falling in the water succeeded; and in the confusion occasioned by the murderous fire, the first boat evidently fell off.

"Again, Sambo," whispered the officer. A second time the torch streamed suddenly in air, and the contents of the yet undischarged blunderbuss spread confusion, dismay and death, into the second boat.

"Old Sal herself couldn't have done better: pity he hadn't a hundred of them," growled Tom Fluke, who although concealed behind the bulwarks, had availed himself of a crevice near him, to watch the effect produced by the formidable weapons.

There was a momentary indecision among the enemy, after the second destructive fire; it was but momentary. Again they advanced, and closing with the vessel, evinced a determination of purpose, that left little doubt as to the result. A few sprang into the chains and rigging, while others sought to enter by her bows, but the main effort seemed to be made at her gangway, at which Gerald had stationed himself with ten of his best men, the rest being detached to make the best defence they could, against those who sought to enter in the manner above described.

Notwithstanding the great disparity of numbers, the little crew of the schooner had for some time a considerable advantage over their enemies. At the first onset of these latter, their pistols had been discharged, but in so random a manner as to have done no injury—whereas the assailed, scrupulously obeying the order of their Commander, fired not a shot until they found themselves face to face with an enemy; the consequence of which was, that every pistol ball killed an American, or otherwise placed him *hors de combat*. Still, in despite of their loss, the latter were more than adequate to the capture, unless a miracle should interpose to prevent it, and exasperated as they were by the fall of their comrades, their efforts became at each moment more resolute and successful. A deadly contest had been maintained in the gangway, from which, however, Gerald was compelled to retire, although bravely supported by his handful of followers. Step by step he had retreated, until at length he found his back against the main-mast, and his enemies pressing him on every side. Five of his men lay dead in the space between the gangway and the position he now occupied, and Sambo, who had not quitted his side for an instant, was also senseless at his feet, felled by a tremendous blow from a cutlass upon the head. His force now consisted merely of the five men remaining of his own party, and three of those who had been detached, who, all that were left alive, had been compelled to fall back upon their commander. How long he would have continued the hopeless and desperate struggle, in this manner is doubtful, had not a fresh enemy appeared in his rear. These were the crews of two other boats, who, having boarded without difficulty, now came up to the assistance of their comrades. So completely taken by surprise was Gerald in this quarter, that the first intimation he had of his danger was, in the violent seizure of his sword arm from behind, and a general rush upon, and disarming of the remainder of his followers. On turning to behold his enemy, he saw with concern the triumphant face of Desborough.

"Every dog has his day, I guess," huskily chuckled the settler, as by the glare of several torches which had been suddenly lighted, he was now seen casting looks of savage vengeance, and holding his formidable knife threateningly over the head of the officer whom he had grappled. "I reckon as how I told you it would be Jeremiah Desborough's turn next."

"Silence fellow, loose your hold," shouted one whose authoritative voice and manner, announced him for an officer, apparently the leader of the boarding party.

Awed by the tone in which he was addressed, the settler quitted his grasp, and retired muttering into the crowd behind him.

"I regret much, sir," pursued the American Commander seriously, and turning to Gerald, "that your obstinate defence should have been carried to the length it has. We were given to understand, that ours would not be an easy conquest—yet, little deemed it would have been purchased with the lives of nearly half our force. Still, even while we deplore our loss, have we hearts to estimate the valour of our foe. I cannot give you freedom, since the gift is not at my disposal; but at least I may spare you the pain of surrendering a blade you have so nobly wielded. Retain your sword, sir."

Gerald's was not a nature to remain untouched by such an act of chivalrous courtesy, and he expressed in brief, but pointed terms, his sense of the compliment.

A dozen of the boarders, under the command of a midshipman, now received orders to remain, and bring the prize into Buffalo as soon as day light would permit, and with these were left the killed and wounded of both parties, the latter receiving such attention as the rude experience of their comrades enabled them to afford. Five minutes afterwards Gerald, who had exchanged his trusty cutlass, for the sword he had been so flatteringly permitted to retain, found himself in the leading boat of the little return squadron, and seated at the side of his generous captor. It may be easily imagined what his mortification was at this unexpected reverse, and how bitterly he regretted not having weighed anchor the moment his prisoners had been landed. Regret however, was now unavailing, and dismissing this consideration for a while, he reverted to the strange circumstance of the spiking of his gun, and the mocking cheers, which had burst from the lips of his enemies, on the attempt to discharge it. This reflection drew from him a remark to his companion.

"I think you said," he observed, "that you had been informed, the conquest of the schooner would not be an easy one. Would it be seeking too much to know who was your informant?"

The American officer shook his head. I fear I am not at liberty exactly to name—but thus much I may venture to state, that the person who has so rightly estimated your gallantry, is one not wholly unknown to you.

"This is ambiguous. One question more, were you prepared to expect the failure of the schooner's principal means of defence—her long gun?"

If you recollect the cheer that burst from my fellows, at the moment when the harmless flash was seen ascending, you will require no further elucidation on that head," replied the American evasively.

This was sufficient for Gerald. He folded his arms, sank his head upon his chest, and continued to muse deeply. Soon afterwards the boat touched the beach, where many of the citizens were assembled to hear tidings of the enterprize, and congratulate the captors. Thence he was conducted to the neat little inn, which was the only place of public accommodation the small town, or rather village of Buffalo, at that period afforded.

CHAPTER III.

At the termination of the memorable war of the revolution—that war which, on the one hand, severed, and for ever, the ties that bound the Colonies in interest and affection with the parent land, and, on the other, seemed as by way of indemnification, to have rivetted the Canadas in closer love to their adopted Mother—hundreds of families who had remained staunch in their allegiance, quitted the republican soil, to which they had been unwillingly transferred, and hastened to close on one side of the vast chain of waters, that separated the descendants of France from the descendants of England, the evening of an existence, whose morning and noon had been passed on the other. Among the number of these was Major Grantham, who, at the close of the revolution, had espoused a daughter, (the only remaining child,) of Frederick and Madeline De Haldimar, whose many vicissitudes of suffering, prior to their marriage, have been fully detailed in Wacousta. When, at that period, the different garrisons on the frontier were given up to the American troops, the several British regiments crossed over into Canada, and, after a short term of service in that country, were successively relieved by fresh corps from England. One of the earliest recalled of these, was the regiment of Colonel Frederick De Haldimar. Local interests, however, attaching his son-in-law to Upper Canada, the latter had, on the reduction of his corps, (a provincial regiment, well known throughout the war of the revolution, for its strength, activity, and good service,) finally fixed himself at Amherstburgh. In the neighbourhood of this post he had acquired extensive possessions, and, almost from the first formation of the settlement, exchanged the duties of a military, for those of a scarcely less active magisterial, life. Austere in manner, severe in his administration of justice, Major Grantham might have been considered a harsh man, had not these qualities been tempered by his well known benevolence to the poor, and his staunch, yet, unostentatious, support of the deserving and the well intentioned. And, as his life was a continuous illustration of the principles he inculcated, no one could be unjust enough to ascribe to intolerance or oppression, the rigour with which he exacted obedience, to those laws which he so well obeyed himself. It was remarked, moreover, that, while his general bearing to those who sought to place themselves in the scale of arrogant superiority, was proud and unconciliating, his demeanour to his inferiors, was ever that of one sensible that condescension may soothe and gratify the humble spirit, without its exercise at all detracting from the independence of him who offers it. But we cannot better sum up his general excellence, and the high estimation in which he was held in the town of his adoption, than by stating that, at the period of his demise, there was not to be seen one tearless eye among the congregated poor, who with religious respect, flocked to tender the last duties of humanity to the remains of their benefactor and friend.

In the domestic relations of life, Major Grantham was no less exemplary, although perhaps his rigid notions of right, had obtained for him more of the respect than of the love of those who came within their influence, and yet no mean portion of both. Tenderly attached to his wife, whom he had lost when Gerald was yet in his twelfth year, he had not ceased to deplore her loss; and this perhaps had contributed to nourish a reservedness of disposition, which, without at all aiming at, or purposing, such effect, insensibly tended to the production of a corresponding reserve on the part of his children, that increased with their years. Indeed, on their mother, all the tenderness of their young hearts had been lavished, and, when they suddenly saw themselves deprived of her who loved, and had been loved by them, with doting fondness, they felt as if a void had been left in their affections, which, the less tender evidences of paternal love, were but insufficient wholly to supply. Still, (although not to the same extent,) did they love their father also; and what was wanted in intensity of feeling, was more than made up by the deep, the exalted respect, they entertained for his principles and conduct. It was with pride they beheld him, not merely the deservedly idolized of the low, but the respected of the high —the example of one class, and the revered of another; one whose high position in the social scale, had been attained, less by his striking exterior advantages, than the inward worth that governed every action of his life, and whose moral character, as completely *sans tâche* as his fulfilment of the social duties was proverbially *sans reproche*, could not fail, in a certain degree, to reflect the respect it commanded upon themselves.

As we have before observed, however, all the fervor of their affection had been centered in their mother, and that was indeed a melancholy night in which the youths had been summoned to watch the passing away of her gentle spirit for ever from their love. Isabella De Haldimar had, from her earliest infancy, been remarkable for her quiet and contemplative character; and, bred amid scenes that brought at every retrospect, recollections of some acted horror, it is not surprising that the bias given by nature, should have been developed and strengthened by the events that had surrounded her. Not dissimilar in disposition, as she was not unlike in form, to her mother, she was by that mother carefully endowed with those gentler attributes of goodness, which, taking root within a soil so eminently disposed to their reception, could not fail to render her in after life a model of excellence, both as a mother and a wife. Notwithstanding, however, this moulding of her pliant, and well directed mind, there was about her a melancholy, which while it gave promise of the devoted affection of the mother, offered but little prospect of cheerfulness, in an union with one, who, reserved himself, could not be expected to temper that melancholy, by the introduction of a gaiety that was not natural to him. And yet it was for this very melancholy, tender and fascinating in her, that Major Grantham had sought the hand of Isabella De Haldimar; and it was for the very austerity and reserve of his general manner, more than from the manly beauty of his tall dark person, that he too, had become the object of her secret choice, long before he had proposed for her. Keenly alive to the happiness of her daughter, Mrs. De Haldimar had feared that such union was ill assorted, for, as she called to mind the manner and character of her unfortunate uncle, it seemed to her there were points ot resemblance between him and the proposed husband of her child, which augured ill for the future quiet of Isabella; but, when she consulted her on the subject, and found that every feeling of her heart, that was not claimed by her fond and indulgent parents, was given to Major Grantham, she no longer hesitated, and the marriage took place. Contrary to the expectation, and much to the delight of Mrs. De Haldimar, the first year of the union proved one of complete and unalloyed happiness, and she saw with pleasure, that if Major Grantham did not descend to those little *empressemens* which mark the doting lover, he was never deficient in those manlier, and more respectful attentions, that by a woman of the mild and reflecting disposition of Isabella, were so likely to be appreciated. More than the first year, however, it was not permitted Mrs. De Haldimar to witness her daughter's happiness. Her husband's regiment having been ordered home; but, in the past, she had a sufficient guarantee for the future, and, when she parted from Isabella, it was under the full conviction, that she had confided her to a man in every way sensible of her worth, and desirous of making her happy.

So far the event justified her expectation. The austerity which Major Grantham carried with him into public life, was, if not wholly laid aside, at least considerably softened, in the presence of his wife, and when, later, the births of two sons crowned their union, there was nothing left her to desire, which it was in the power of circumstances to bestow. But Mrs. De Haldimar had not taken into account the effect likely to be produced by a separation from herself—the final severing, as it were, of every tie of blood. Of the four children who had composed the family of Colonel Frederick De Haldimar, the two oldest, (officers in his own corps,) had perished in the war; the fourth, a daughter, had died young, of a decline; and the loss of the former especially, who had grown up with her from childhood to youth, was deeply felt by the sensitive Isabella. With the dreadful scenes perpetrated at Detroit—scenes in which their family had been the principal sufferers—the boys had been familiarized by the old soldiers of their father's regiment, who often took them to the several points most worthy of remark, from the incidents connected with them; and, pointing out the spots on which their uncle Charles and their aunt Clara had fallen victims to the terrible hatred of Wacousta, for their grandfather, detailed the horrors of those days with a rude fidelity of coloring, that brought dismay and indignation to the hearts of their wondering and youthful auditors. On these occasions, Isabella became the depository of all that they had gleaned. To her they confided, under the same pledge of secrecy which had been exacted from themselves, every circumstance of horror connected with those days; nor were they satisfied until they had shewn her those scenes with which so many dreadful recollections were associated. On one naturally of a melancholy temperament, these oft recurring visits could not fail to produce a deep effect; and insensibly that gloom of disposition, which might have yielded to the influence of years and circumstances, was more and more confirmed by the darkness of the imagery on which it reposed. Had she been permitted to disclose to her kind mother all that she had heard and known on the subject, the reciprocation of their sympathies might have relieved her heart, and partially dissipated the phantasms that her knowledge of those events had conjured up; but this her brothers had positively prohibited, alleging, as powerful reasons, not merely that the men who had confided in their promise, would be severely taken to task by their father, but also that it could only tend to grieve their mother unnecessarily, and to re-open wounds that were nearly closed.

Thus was the melancholy of Isabella fed by the very silence in which she was compelled to indulge. Often was her pillow wetted with tears, as she passed in review the several fearful incidents connected with the tale in which her brothers had so deeply interested her, and she would have given worlds at those moments, had they been hers to bestow, to recal to life and animation, the beloved but unfortunate uncle and aunt, to whose fate, her brothers assured her, even their veteran friends never alluded without sorrow. Often, too, did she dwell on the share her own fond mother had borne in those transactions, and the anguish which must have pierced her heart, when first apprized of the loss of her, whom, she had even *then* loved with all a mother's love. Nay, more than once, while gazing on the face of the former, her inmost soul given up to the recollection of all she had endured, first at Michillimackinac, and afterwards at Detroit, had she unconsciously suffered the tears to course down her cheeks without an effort to restrain them. Ignorant of the cause, Mrs. De Haldimar only ascribed this emotion to the natural melancholy of her daughter's character, and then she would gently chide her, and seek, by a variety of means, to divert her thoughts into some lively channel; but she had little success in the attempt to eradicate reflections already rooted in so congenial a soil.

Her sister died very young, and she scarcely felt her loss; but, when, subsequently, the vicissitudes of a military life had deprived her for ever of her beloved brothers, her melancholy increased. It was, however, the silent, tearless melancholy, that knows not the paroxysm of outrageous grief. The quiet resignation of her character formed an obstacle to the inroads of all vivacious sorrow; yet was her health not the less effectually undermined by the slow action of her innate feeling, unfortunately too much fostered by outward influences. By her marriage and the birth of her sons, whom she loved with all a mother's fondness, her mental malady had been materially diminished, and indeed, in a great degree superseded, but, unhappily previous to these events, it had seriously affected her constitution, and produced a morbid susceptibility of mind and person, that exposed her to be overwhelmed by the occurrence of any of those afflictions which, otherwise, she might, with ordinary fortitude, have endured. When, therefore, intelligence from England announced that her parents had both perished in a hurricane on their route to the West Indies, whither the regiment of Colonel De Haldimar had been ordered, the shock was too great for her, mentally and personally enfeebled as she had been, to sustain, and she sank gradually under this final infliction of Providence.

Major Grantham beheld with dismay the effect of this blow upon his beloved wife. Fell consumption had now marked her for his own, and so rapid was the progress of the disease acting on a temperament already too much pre-disposed to its influence, that, in despite of all human preventives, the sensitive Isabella, before six months had elapsed, was summoned to a better world.

And never did human being meet the summons with more perfect resignation to the Divine will. The death-bed scene between that tender mother and her sorrowing family, was one which might have edified even the most pious. Gerald, as we have already said, was in his twelfth year at the period of this afflicting event--his brother Henry, one year younger; both were summoned from school on the morning of her death--both knew that their fond mother was ill—but so far were they from imagining the scene about to be offered to their young observation, that when they reached home it was with the joyous feeling of boys, exulting in a momentary liberation from scholastic restraint, and eagerly turning into holiday, that which they little deemed would so soon become a day of mourning. How rapidly was the deceitful illusion dispelled, when, on entering the sick chamber of their adored parent, they beheld what every surrounding circumstance told them was not the mere bed of sickness, but the bed of death. Propped on pillows that supported her feeble head—her beautiful black hair streaming across her pallid, placid brow, and her countenance wearing a holy and religious calm, Mrs. Grantham presented an image of resignation, so perfect, so superhuman, that the disposition to a violent ebullition of grief, which at first manifested itself in the youths, gave place to a certain mysterious awe, that chained them almost spell-bound at the foot of her bed. A strict observer of the ordinances of her religion, she had had every preparation made for her reception of the sacrament, the administering of which was only deferred until the arrival of her children. This duty being now performed, with the imposing solemnity befitting the occasion, the venerable clergyman, who had known and loved her from her infancy, imprinted a last kiss upon her brow, and left the apartment deeply affected. Then, indeed, for the first time, was a loose given to the grief that pervaded every bosom, even to the lowest of the domestics, who had been summoned to receive her parting blessing. Close to the bed-side, each pressing one of her emaciated hands to his lips, knelt her heart-broken sons, weeping bitterly, while, from the chest of a tall negro, apparently an old and attached servant, burst forth at intervals convulsive sobs. Even the austere Major Grantham, seated at some little distance from the bed, contemplating the serene features of his dying wife, could not restrain the tears that forced themselves forth, and trickled through his fingers, as he half sought to conceal his emotion from his servants. In the midst of the profound sorrow which environed her, Mrs. Grantham alone was unappalled by her approaching end: she spoke calmly and collectedly, gently chiding some and encouraging others; giving advice, and conveying orders, as if she was merely about to undertake a short customary journey instead of that long, and untravelled one, whence there is neither communication nor return. To her unhappy sons she gave it in tender injunction to recompense their father by their love for the loss he was about to sustain in herself; and to her servants she enjoined to be at once dutiful to their master and affectionate to her children. Having made her peace with God, and disposed, of herself, her consideration, was now exclusively for others—and, during the hour which intervened between the departure of the clergyman and her death, the whole tenor of her thoughts was directed to the alleviation of the sorrow which she felt would succeed the flight of her spirit from earth. As she grew fainter, she motioned to her husband to come near her—He did so, and, with a smile of rapt serenity that bespoke the conviction strong at her heart, she said in a low tone, as she clasped his warm hand within her own, already stiffening with the chill of death: "Grieve not, I entreat you, for recollect that, although we part, it is not for ever. Oh, no! my father, my mother, my brothers, and you my husband, and beloved children, we shall all meet again." Exhausted with the energy she had thrown into these last words, she sank back upon the pillow, from which she had partially raised her head. After a short pause, she glanced her eye on a portrait that hung on the opposite wall. It represented an officer habited in the full uniform of her father's regiment. She next looked at the negro, who, amid his unchecked sorrow, had been an attentive observer of her every action, and pointed expressively first to her kneeling children, and then to the portrait. The black seemed to understand her meaning; for he made a sign of acquiescence. She then extended her hand to him, which he kissed, and bedewed with his tears, and retreated sobbing to his position near the foot of the bed. Two minutes afterwards, Mrs. Grantham had breathed her last, but so insensibly that, although every eye was fixed upon her, no one could tell the precise moment at which she had ceased to exist.

We will pass over the deep grief which preyed upon the hearts of the unfortunate brothers, for weeks after they had been compelled to acknowledge the stern truth that they were indeed motherless. Those who have, at that tender age, known what it is to lose an affectionate mother, and under circumstances at all similar to those just described, will be at no loss to comprehend the utter desolation of their bruised spirits: to those who have not sustained this most grievous of human afflictions, it would be a waste of time to detail what cannot possibly be understood, save through the soul-withering ordeal of a like experience.

If, in early youth, however, the impressions of sorrow are more lively, so is the return to hope more rapid. Time, and the elasticity of spirit common to their years, gradually dissipated the cloud of melancholy that had rested on the hearts of the Canadian Brothers; and, although they never ceased to lament their mother with that tenderness and respect which her many virtues, and love for them especially, demanded, still did their thoughts gradually take the bias to which a variety of outward and important circumstances afterwards directed them. It was soon after this event, that the first seeds of disunion began to spring up between England and the United States, the inevitable results of which, it was anticipated, would be the involving of Canada in the struggle; and, notwithstanding the explosion did not take place for several years afterwards, preparations were made on either shore, to an extent that kept the spirit of enterprise constantly on the alert,

Inheriting the martial spirit of their family, the inclinations of the young Granthams led them to the service; and, as their father could have no reasonable objection to oppose to a choice which promised not merely to secure his sons in an eligible profession, but to render them in some degree of benefit to their country, he consented to their views. Gerald's preference leading him to the navy, he was placed on that establishment as a midshipman; while Henry, several years later, obtained, through the influence of their father's old friend General Brock, an Ensigncy in the —— Regiment then quartered at Amherstburg.

Meanwhile, Major Grantham, whose reserve appeared to have increased since the death of his wife, seemed to seek, in the active discharge of his magisterial duties, a relief from the recollection of the loss he had sustained; and it was about this period that, in consequence of many of the American settlers in Canada, having, in anticipation of a rupture between the two countries, secretly withdrawn themselves to the opposite shore, his exaction of the duties of British subjects from those who remained, became more vigorous than ever.

We have already shewn Desborough to have been the most unruly and disorderly of the worthless set; and as no opportunity was omitted of compelling him to renew his oath of allegiance, (while his general conduct was strictly watched,) the hatred of the man for the stern magistrate was daily matured, until at length it grew into an inextinguishable desire for revenge.

The chief, and almost only recreation, in which Major Grantham indulged, was that of fowling. An excellent shot himself, he had been in some degree the instructor of his sons; and, although, owing to the wooded nature of the country, the facilities afforded to the enjoyment of his favorite pursuit in the orthodox manner of a true English sportsman, were few, still, as game was every where abundant, he had continued to turn to account the advantages that were actually offered. Both Gerald and Henry had been his earlier companions in the sport, but, of late years and especially since the death of their mother, he had been in the habit of going out alone.

It was one morning in that season of the year when the migratory pigeons pursue their course towards what are termed the "burnt woods," on which they feed, and in such numbers as to cover the surface of the heavens, as with a dense and darkening cloud, that Major Grantham sallied forth at early dawn, with his favorite dog and gun, and, as was his custom, towards Hartley's point. Disdaining, as unworthy of his skill, the myriads of pigeons that every where presented themselves, he passed from the skirt of the forest towards an extensive swamp, in the rear of Hartley's, which, abounding in golden plover and snipe, usually afforded him a plentiful supply. On this occasion he was singularly successful, and, having bagged as many birds as he could conveniently carry, was in the act of ramming down his last charge, when the report of a shot came unexpectedly from the forest. In the next instant he was sensible he was wounded, and, placing his hand to his back, felt it wet with blood. As there was at the moment several large wild ducks within a few yards of the spot where he stood, and between himself and the person who had fired, he at once concluded that he had been the victim of an accident, and, feeling the necessity of assistance, he called loudly on the unseen sportsman, to come forward to his aid; but, although his demand was several times repeated, no answer was returned, and no one appeared. With some difficulty he contrived, after disembarrassing himself of his game-bag, to reach the farm at Hartley's, where every assistance was afforded him, and, a waggon having been procured, he was conducted to his home, when, on examination, the wound was pronounced to be mortal.

On the third day from this event, Major Grantham breathed his last, bequeathing the guardianship of his sons to Colonel D'Egville, who had married his sister. At this epoch, Gerald was absent with his vessel on a cruise, but Henry received his parting blessing upon both, accompanied by a solemn injunction, that they should never be guilty of any act which could sully the memory, either of their mother or himself. This Henry promised, in the name of both, most religiously to observe; and, when Gerald returned, and to his utter dismay beheld the lifeless form of the parent, whom he had quitted only a few days before in all the vigour of health, he not only renewed the pledge given by his brother, but with the vivacity of character habitual to him, called down the vengeane of Heaven upon his head, should he ever be found to swerve from those principles of virtue and honor, which had been so sedulously inculcated on him.

Meanwhile, there was nothing to throw even the faintest light on the actual cause of Major Grantham's death. On the first probing and dressing of the wound, the murderous lead had been extracted, and, as it was discovered to be a rifle ball it was taken for granted that some Indian, engaged in the chase, had, in the eagerness of pursuit, missed an intermediate object at which he had taken aim, and lodged the ball accidentally in the body of the unfortunate gentleman; and that, terrified at the discovery of the mischief he had done, and perhaps apprehending punishment, he had hastily fled from the spot, to avoid detection. This opinion, unanimously entertained by the townspeople, was shared by the brothers, who knowing the unbounded love and respect of all for their parent, dreamt not for one moment that his death could have been the result of premeditation. It was left for Desborough to avow, at a later period, that he had been the murderer; and with what startling effect on him, to whom the admission was exultingly made, we have already seen.

When Desborough was subsequently tried, there was no other evidence by which to establish his guilt, than the admission alluded to, and this he declared, in his defence, he had only made with a view to annoy Mr. Grantham, to whom he owed a grudge for persecuting him so closely on the occasion of his flight with his son; and, although, on reference to the period, it was found that Major Grantham had received the wound which occasioned his death two days after Desborough had been ordered, on pain of instant expulsion from the country, to renew his oaths, and perform service with the militia of the district, still, as this fact admitted only of a presumptive interpretation the charge could not be sufficiently brought home to him, and he was, however reluctantly, acquitted. The rifles which, it will be remembered, were seized by Henry Grantham on the occasion of his detection of the settler in an act of treason, were still in his possession, and, as they were of a remarkably small calibre, the conviction would have taken place, had the ball which killed Major Grantham been forthcoming, and found to fit either of the bores. Unfortunately, however, it so happened that it had not been preserved, so that an essential link in the chain of circumstances had been irrecoverably lost. When the question was mooted by the court, before whom he was tried, the countenance of the settler was discovered to fall, and there was a restlessness about him, totally at variance with the almost insolent calm he had preserved throughout; but when it appeared that, from the impression previously entertained of the manner of the death, it had not been thought necessary to preserve the ball, he again resumed his confidence, and listened to the remainder of the proceedings unmoved.

We have seen him subsequently escaping from the confinement to which he had been subjected, with a view to trial for another offence, and, later still, unshackled and exultingly brandishing his knife over the head of one of the objects of his bitterest hatred, on the deck of the very vessel in which he had so recently been a prisoner.

CHAPTER IV.

AUTUMN had passed away, and winter, the stern invigorating winter of Canada, had already covered the earth with enduring snows, and the waters with bridges of seemingly eternal ice, and yet no effort had been made by the Americans to repossess themselves of the country they had so recently lost. The several garrisons of Detroit and Amherstburgh, reposing under the laurels they had so easily won, made holiday of their conquest; and, secure in the distance that separated them from the more populous districts of the Union, seemed to have taken it for granted that they had played their final part in the active operations of the war, and would be suffered to remain in undisturbed possession. But the storm was already brewing in the far distance which, advancing progressively like the waves of the coming tempest, was destined first to shake them in their security, and finally to overwhelm them in its vortex. With the natural enterprize of their character, the Americans had no sooner ascertained the fall of Detroit, than means, slow but certain, were taken for the recovery of a post, with which, their national glory was in no slight degree identified. The country whence they drew their resources for the occasion, were the new states of Ohio and Kentucky, and one who had previously travelled through those immense tracts of forests, where the dwelling of the backwoodsman is met with at long intervals, would have marvelled at the zeal and promptitude with which these adventurous people, abandoning their homes, and disregarding their personal interests, flocked to the several rallying points. Armed and accoutred at their own expence, with the unerring rifle that provided them with game, and the faithful hatchet that had brought down the dark forest into ready subjection, their claim upon the public was for the mere sustenance they required on service. It is true that this partial independence of the Government whom they served rather in the character of volunteers, than of conscripts, was in a great measure fatal to their discipline; but in the peculiar warfare of the country, absence of discipline was rather an advantage than a demerit, since when checked, or thrown into confusion, they looked not for a remedy in the resumption of order, but in the exercise each of his own individual exertions, facilitated as he was by his general knowledge of localities, and his confidence in his own personal resources.

But, although new armies were speedily organized—if organized, may be termed those who brought with them into the contest much courage and devotedness, yet, little discipline, the Americans, in this instance, proceeded with a caution that proved their respect for the British garrison, strongly supported as it was by a numerous force of Indians. Within two months after the capitulation of Detroit, a considerable army, Ohioans and Kentuckians, with some regular Infantry, had been pushed forward as with a view to feel their way; but these having been checked by the sudden appearance of a detachment from Amherstburgh, had limited their advance to the Miami River, on the banks of which, and on the ruins of one of the old English forts of Pontiac's days, they had constructed new fortifications, and otherwise strongly entrenched themselves. It was a mistake, however, to imagine that the enemy would be content with establishing himself here. The new fort merely served as a nucleus for the concentration of such resources of men and warlike equipment, as were necessary to the subjection, firstly of Detroit, and afterwards of Amherstburgh. Deprived of the means of transport, the shallow bed of the Miami aiding them but little, it was a matter of no mean difficulty with the Americans to convey through several hundred miles of forest, the heavy guns they required for battering, and as it was only at intervals this could be effected; the most patient endurance and unrelaxing perseverance being necessary to the end. From the inactivity of this force, or rather the confinement of its operations to objects of defence, the English garrison had calculated on undisturbed security, at least throughout the winter, if not for a longer period; but although it was not until this latter season was far advanced, that the enemy broke up from his entrenchments on the Miami, and pushed himself forward for the attainment of his final view, the error of imputing inactivity to him was discovered at a moment when it was least expected.

It was during a public ball given at Amherstburgh on the 18th of January 1813, that the first intelligence was brought of the advance of a strong American force, whose object it was supposed was to push rapidly on to Detroit, leaving Amherstburgh behind to be disposed of later. The officer who brought this intelligence was the fat Lieutenant Raymond, who commanding an outpost at the distance of some leagues had been surprised, and after a resistance very creditable under the circumstances, driven in by the American advanced guard with a loss of nearly half his command.

Thus, "parva componere magnis," was the same consternation produced in the ball-room at Amherstburg, that, at a later period, occurred in a similar place of amusement at Brussels, and although not followed by the same momentous public results, producing the same host of fluttering fears and anxieties in the bosoms of the female votaries of Terpsichore. We believe, however, that there existed some dissimilarity in the several modes of communication—the Duke of Wellington receiving his with some appearance of regard, on the part of the communicator, for the nerves of the ladies, while to Colonel St. Julian, commanding at Amherstberg, and engaged at the moment at the whist table, the news was imparted in stentorian tones, which were audible to every one in the adjoining ball-room.

But even if his voice had not been heard, the appearance of Lieutenant Raymond would have justified the apprehension of any reasonable person, for, in the importance of the moment, he had not deemed it necessary to make any change in the dress in which he had been surprised and driven back. Let the reader figure to himself a remarkably fat, ruddy faced man, of middle age, dressed in a pair of tightly fitting dread-nought trowsers, and a shell jacket, that had once been scarlet, but now, from use and exposure, rather resembled the colour of brickdust; boots from which all polish had been taken by the grease employed to render them snow-proof; a brace of pistols thrust into the black waist belt that encircled his huge circumference, and from which depended a sword, whose steel scabbard shewed the rust of the rudest bivouac. Let him, moreover, figure to himself that ruddy carbuncled face, and nearly as ruddy brow, suffused with perspiration, although in a desperately cold winter's night, and the unwashed hands, and mouth, and lips black from the frequent biting of the ends of cartridges, while ever and anon the puffed cheeks, in the effort to procure air and relieve the panting chest, recal the idea of a Bacchus, after one of his most lengthened orgies—let him figure all this, and if he will add short, curling, wiry, damp hair, surmounting a head as round as a turnip, a snubby, red, *retroussé* nose, and light gray eyes; he will have a tolerable idea of the startling figure that thus abruptly made its appearance in the person of Lieutenant Raymond, first among the dancers, and bustlingly thence into the adjoining card room.

At the moment of his entrance, every eye had been turned upon this strange apparition, while an almost instinctive sense of the cause of his presence pervaded every breast. Indeed it was impossible to behold him arrayed in the bivouac garb in which we have described him, contrasted as it was with the elegant ball dresses of his brother officers, and not attribute his presence to some extraordinary motive; and as almost every one in the room was aware of his having been absent on detachment, his mission had been half divined even before he had opened his lips to Colonel St. Julian, for whom, on entering, he had hurriedly inquired.

But when the latter officer was seen soon afterwards to rise from and leave the card table, and, after communicating hurriedly with the several heads of Departments, quit altogether the scene of festivity, there could be no longer a doubt; and, as in all cases of the sort, the danger was magnified, as it flew from lip to lip, even as the tiny snow ball becometh a mountain by the accession it receives in its rolling course. Suddenly the dance was discontinued, and indeed in time, for the fingers of the non-combatant musicians, sharing in the general nervousness, had already given notice, by numerous falsettos, of their inability to proceed much longer. Bonnets, cloaks, muffs, tippets, shawls, snow shoes, and all the paraphernalia of female winter equipment peculiar to the country, were brought unceremoniously in, and thrown *en masse* upon the deserted benches of the ball room. Then was there a scramble among the fair dancers, who, having secured their respective property, quitted the house, not however, without a secret fear on the part of many, that the first object they should encounter, on sallying forth, would be a corps of American sharp-shooters. To the confusion within was added the clamour without, arising from swearing drivers, neighing horses, jingling bells, and jostling sledges. Finally the only remaining ladies of the party were the D'Egvilles, whose sledge had not yet arrived, and with these lingered Captain Molineux, Middlemore, and Henry Grantham, all of whom, having obtained leave of absence for the occasion, had accompanied them from Detroit. The two former, who had just terminated one of the old fashioned cotillons, then peculiar to the Canadas, stood leaning over the chairs of their partners, indulging in no very charitable comments on the unfortunate Raymond, to whose "ugly" presence at that unseasonable hour they ascribed a host of most important momentary evils; as, for example, the early breaking up of the pleasantest ball of the season, the loss of an excellent anticipated supper that had been prepared for a later hour, and, although last not least, the necessity it imposed upon them of an immediate return, that bitter cold night, to Detroit. Near the blazing wood fire, at their side, stood Henry Grantham, and Captain St. Clair of the Engineers. The former with his thoughts evidently far away from the passing scene, the latter joining in the criticisms on Raymond.

"I always said," observed Molineux, shrugging his shoulders, "that he resembled one of the ground hogs of his old command of Bois Blanc, more than any thing human; and hang me if he does not tonight look like a hog in armour."

"There certainly is something of the *arma*dilla about him," said Middlemore; "if we may judge from the formidable weapons he brought into the room."

"And, notwithstanding his alert retreat, few officers can have made such *head* against, and shewn such *face* to the enemy," added St. Clair.

"True," retorted Middlemore, "there were certainly some extraordinary *features* in the affair."

"If," remarked Molineux, "he faced the enemy, I am certain he must have kept the boldest at bay; but if he shewed them his back, as from his heated appearance I strongly suspect that he did, he must have afforded the Yankee riflemen as much fun as if they had been in pursuit of a fat old raccoon."

"Shall I ask him that he may answer for himself?" inquired Henry Grantham, whose attention had been aroused by the ironical remarks of his companions.

"By no means," replied Middlemore, "we have *anser* enough in his mere look."

"Ha! ha! ha!" roared Molineux and St. Clair in concert.

"Nay, nay," interposed Julia D'Egville, who had listened

impatiently to the comments passed upon the unfortunate and unconscious officer, "this keen exercise of your powers on poor Mr. Raymond is hardly fair. Recollect (turning to Middlemore,) it is not given to all to possess the refinement of wit, nor, (addressing St. Clair) the advantages of personal attraction, therefore is it more incumbent on those, to whom such gifts are given, to be merciful unto the wanting in both." This was uttered with marked expression.

"Brava, my most excellent and spirited partner," whispered Molineux, secretly delighted that the lash of the reprover had not immediately embraced him in its circuit.

"Thank you, my good, kind hearted, considerate cousin," looked Henry Grantham.

"Oh, the devil," muttered Middlemore to St. Clair, we shall have her next exclaiming, in the words of Monk Lewis' Bleeding Nun,

'Raymond, Raymond, I am thine
'Raymond, Raymond, thou art mine.'"

St. Clair shrugged his shoulders, bit his lip, threw up his large blue eyes, shewed his white teeth, slightly reddened, and looked altogether exceedingly at a loss whether to feel complimented or reproved.

"But here comes Mr. Raymond, to fight his own battles," continued Miss D'Egville with vivacity.

"Hush," whispered Molineux.

"Honor among thieves," added Middlemore, in the same low tone.

"Egad," said Raymond, wiping the yet lingering dews from his red forehead, as he advanced from the card room where he had been detained, talking over his adventure with one or two of the anxious townspeople; "I have, within the last twenty four hours, had so much running and fighting for my country, that strength is scarcely left me to fight my own battles. But what is it, Miss d'Egville?" as he saluted Julia and her sister, "what battle am I to fight now—some fresh quizzing of these wags, I suppose—ah, Middlemore, how do you do; Molineux, St. Clair, Henry Grantham, how do you all do?"

"Ah, Raymond, my dear fellow, how do you do?" greeted Captain Molineux, with the air of one who really rejoices in the reappearance of a long absent friend.

"Raymond, I am delighted to see you," exclaimed St. Clair.

"Your bivouac has done you good," joined Middlemore, following the example of the others, and extending his hand, "I never saw you looking to greater advantage."

"Pretty well, pretty well thank you," returned the good humoured, but not too acute subaltern, as he passed his hand over his Falstaffian stomach; "only a little fatigued with the last six hours, retreating. Egad! I began to think I never should get away, the fellows pursued us so hotly."

"And hotly you fled, it would appear," returned Middlemore.

"I dare be sworn, there was not a six foot Kentuckian of the whole American army active enough to come within a mile of him," added Molineux.

"And yet, considering the speed he made, he seems to have lost but little of his flesh," said St. Clair.

"Of course," chuckled Middlemore, "these long fellows come from Troy county in Ohio."

"Egad, I don't know; why do you ask?"

"Because you know it is not for the men of *Troy* to reduce the men of *Grease*—hence your escape."

"Are the enemy then so near, Mr. Raymond?" inquired Julia D'Egville, anxious to turn the conversation.

"I should think not very far, Miss D'Egville, since, as you see, they have not given me time to change my dress."

At that moment the noise of horses' bells were heard without; and they were soon distinguished to be those of Colonel D'Egville's berlin.

A few moments afterwards, that officer entered the room

now wholly deserted save by the little coterie near the fire place. Like Lieutenant Raymond's, his dress was more suited to the bivouac than the ball room, and his countenance otherwise bore traces of fatigue.

His daughters flew to meet him. The officers also grouped around, desirous to hear what tidings he brought of the enemy, to corroborate the statement of Raymond. To the great mortification of the latter, it was now found that he and his little detachment had had all the running to themselves, and that while they fancied the whole of the American army to be close at their heels, the latter had been so kept in check by the force of Indians, under Colonel D'Egville in person, as to be compelled to retire upon the point whence the original attack had been made. They had not followed the broken English outpost more than a mile, and yet, so convinced of close pursuit had been the latter, that for the space of six leagues they had scarce relaxed in their retreat. The information now brought by Colonel D'Egville, was that the Americans had not advanced a single foot beyond the outpost in question, but on the contrary had commenced constructing a stockade, and throwing up entrenchments. He added, moreover, that he had just dispatched an express to Sandwich, to General Proctor, (who had, since the departure of General Brock, succeeded to the command of the district,) communicating the intelligence, and suggesting the propriety of an attack before they could advance farther, and favor any movement on the part of the inhabitants of Detroit. As this counter-movement on our part would require every man that could be spared from the latter fortress, Colonel D'Egville seemed to think that before the officers could reach it, its garrison would be already on the way to join the expedition, which would doubtless be ordered to move from Amherstburg; and as the same impression appeared to exist in the mind of Colonel St. Julian, whom he had only just parted from to proceed in search of his daughters, the latter had taken it upon himself to determine that they should remain where they were until the answer, communicating the final decision of General Proctor, should arrive.

If the young officers were delighted at the idea of escaping the horror of an eighteen miles drive, on one of the bitterest nights of the season, supperless, and at the moment of issuing from a comfortable ball room, their annoyance at (what they termed) the pusillanimity of Raymond, who had come thus unnecessarily in, to the utter annihilation of their evening's amusement, was in equal proportion. For this, on their way home, they revenged themselves by every sort of persiflage their humour could adapt to the occasion, until in the end, they completely succeeded in destroying the good humor of Raymond, who eventually quitted them under feelings of mortified pride, which excited all the generous sympathy of the younger Grantham, while it created in his breast a sentiment of almost wrath against his inconsiderate companions. Even these latter were at length sensible that they had gone too far, and, as their better feelings returned, they sought to assure the offended object of their pleasantry that what they had uttered was merely in jest; but finding he received these disclaimers in moody silence, they renewed their attack, nor discontinued it until they separated for their mutual quarters for the night.

Poor Raymond was, it will be perceived, one of those unfortunates termed "butts," which are to be met with in almost all societies, and but too often in a regiment. Conscious of his great corpulence, and its disadvantages to him as a soldier, he not only made every allowance for the sallies of his lively and more favored brother officers, but often good-naturedly joined in the laugh against himself—all the badinage uttered against his personal appearance, he had, on this occasion, borne with the most perfect temper; but when, presuming on his forbearance, they proceeded to reflect on the hurried, and, under all circumstances, justifiable manner of his retreat, after having sustained an unequal conflict against an overpowering enemy for upwards of two hours, his honest heart was wounded to the core; and, although he uttered not one word, the unkindness sank deeply into his memory.

The following dawn broke in, decked with all the sad and sober gray, peculiar to a Canadian sky in the depth of winter, and, with the first rising of the almost rayless sun, commenced numerous warlike preparations that gave promise to the inhabitants of some approaching crisis. The event justified their expectation, the suggestion of Colonel D'Egville had been adopted, and the same express, which carried to General Proctor the information of the advance of the enemy, and the expulsion of Lieutenant Raymond from his post, was pushed on to Detroit, with an order for every man who could be spared from that fortress, to be marched, without a moment's delay, to Amherstburg. At noon the detachment had arrived, and, the General making his appearance soon after, the expedition, composed of the strength of the two garrisons, with a few light guns, and a considerable body of Indians, under the Chief Roundhead, were pushed rapidly across the lake, and the same night occupied the only road by which the enemy could advance.

It was a picturesque sight, to those who lingered on the banks of the Detroit, to watch the movement of that mass of guns, ammunition cars, sledges, &c. preceding the regular march of the troops, as the whole crossed the firm yet rumbling ice, at the head of the now deserted Island of Bois-Blanc. Nor was this at all lessened in effect by the wild and irregular movements of the Indians, who advancing by twos and threes, but more often singly, and bounding nimbly, yet tortuously, along the vast white field with which the outline of their swarthy forms contrasted, called up, at the outset, the idea of a legion of devils.

But there was more than the mere indulgence of curiosity in the contemplation of this scene, so highly characteristic of the country. On the result of the efforts of those now scarcely discernable atoms, depended the fate, not merely of the town and garrison of Amherstburgh, but of the whole adjoining country. If successful, then would the repose of the anxious inhabitants once more be secured, and the horrors of invasion again averted from their soil; but if on the contrary, they should be defeated, then must every hope be extinguished, and the so recently conquered completely change sides with their conquerors. Such were the thoughts that filled the breasts of many of the townspeople of Amherstburg, and considering that in the present instance they had much to lose, nothing to gain, they may fairly enough be pardoned for having entertained some litte nervousness as to the result.

It was during one of the coldest mornings of January, that this little army bivouaced on the banks of a small rivulet, distant, little more than a league from the position which had been taken up by the Americans. So unexpected and rapid had been the advance of the expedition, that not the slightest suspicion appeared to have been entertained by the Americans even of its departure; and from information, brought at a late hour by the Indian scouts, who had been dispatched at nightfall to observe their motions, it was gathered that, so far from apprehending or being prepared for an attack, all was quiet in their camp, in which the customary night fires were then burning. Thus favored by the false security of their enemies, the British force, after partaking of their rude, but substantial meal, and preparing their arms, laid themselves down to rest in their accoutrements and great coats; their heads reclining on whatever elevation, however small, presented itself, and their feet half buried in the embers of the fires they had with difficulty kindled on the frozen ground, from which the snow had been removed—all, sanguine of success, and all, more or less endeavouring to snatch, even amid the nipping frost to which their upper persons were exposed, a few hours of sleep prior to the final advance, which was to take place an hour before dawn.

In the midst of the general desolateness of aspect which encompassed all, there were few privations, endured by the men, that were not equally shared by their officers. A solitary and deserted log hut, was the only thing in the shape of a human habitation to be seen within the bivouac, and this had been secured as the head quarters of the General and his staff—all besides had no other canopy than the clear starry heavens, or, here and there, the leafless and unsheltering branches of some forest tree, and yet, around one large and blazing fire, which continued to be fed at intervals by masses of half decayed wood, that, divested of their snow, lay simmering and dying before it, was frequently to be heard the joyous yet suppressed laugh, and piquant sally, as of men whose spirits no temporary hardship or concern for the eventful future could effectually depress. These issued from the immediate bivouac of the officers, who, seated squatted around their fire after the manner of the Indians, instead of courting a sleep which the intense cold rendered as difficult of attainment, as unrefreshing when attained, rather sought solace in humourous conversation, while the animal warmth was kept alive by frequent puffings from that campaigners' first resource the cigar, seasoned by short and occasional libations from the well filled canteen. Most of them wore over their regimentals, the grey great coat then peculiar to the service, and had made these in the highest posssible degree available by fur trimmings on the cuffs and collar, which latter was tightly buttoned round the chin, while their heads were protected by furred caps, made like those of the men, of the raccoon skin. To this uniformity of costume, there was, as far as regarded the outward clothing, one exception in the person of Captain Cranstoun, who had wisely inducted himself in the bear skin coat so frequently quizzed by his companions, and in which he now sat as undisturbed by the cold, so sensibly felt by his associates, as unmoved by the criticisms they passed on its grotesque appearance, and unprovoked by the recurrence to the history of his former ludicrous adventure. Finding that Cranstoun was inaccessible, they again, with the waywardness of their years and humour, adverted to the retreat of Raymond, to whom Molineux, Middlemore, and St. Clair—the latter a volunteer in the expedition—attributed the unpardonable fact of the breaking up of a most delightful party, and the deprivation of a capital supper. Such was the conversation—such were the serious complaints of men, who, before another sun should rise, might see cause to upbraid themselves, and bitterly, for the levity in which they were so inconsiderately indulging.

During the whole of the march, Raymond had evinced a seriousness of demeanor by no means common to him, and, although he had made one of the party in the general bivouac, he had scarcely opened his lips, except to reply to the most direct questions. The renewed attack, at first, drew from him no comment, although it was evident he felt greatly pained; but when he had finished smoking his cigar, he raised himself, not without difficulty, from the ground, (a circumstance, which, by the way, provoked a fresh burst of humour from the young men,) and began, with a seriousness of manner, that, being unusual, not a little surprised them: "Gentlemen, you have long been pleased to select me as your butt."

"Of course," hastily interrupted Molineux, hazarding his pun, "we naturally select you for what you most resemble."

"Captain Molineux—gentlemen!" resumed Raymond with greater emphasis.

"He is getting warm on the subject," observed Middlemore. "Have a care Molineux, that the butt does not *churn* until in the end it becomes the *butter*."

"Ha! ha! ha!" vociferated St. Clair, "good, excellent, the best you ever made, Middlemore."

"Gentlemen," persevered Raymond, in a tone, and with a gesture, of impatience, "this trifling will be deeply regretted by you all tomorrow; I repeat," he pursued, when he found he had at length secceeded in procuring silence, "you have long been pleased to select me as your butt, and while this was confined to my personal appearance, painful as I have sometimes found your humour, I could still endure it; but when I perceive those whom I have looked upon as friends and brothers, casting imputations upon my courage, I may be excused for feeling offended. You have succeeded in wounding my heart, and some of you will regret the hour when you did so. Another perhaps, would adopt a different course, but I am not disposed to return evil for evil. I wish to believe, that in all your taunts upon this subject, you have merely indulged your bantering humour—but not the less have you pained an honest heart. Tomorrow will prove that you have grievously wronged me, and I am mistaken, if you will not deeply regret it."

"Noonsense, noonsense, Raymoond, ma deer fallow; do na' heed the queeps of the hair-breened deevils. Ye see a neever tak any nootice o' them, but joost leet them ha' their way."

But Raymond stayed not—he hurried away across the snow towards a distant fire, which lighted the ruder bivouac of the adjutant and quarter master, and was there seen to seat himself, with the air of one who has composed himself for the night.

"What a silly fellow, to take the thing so seriously," said Molineux, half vexed at himself, half moved by the reproachful tone of Raymond's address.

"For God's sake, Grantham, call him back. Tell him we are ready to make any—every atonement for our offence," urged St. Clair.

"And I will promise never to utter another pun at his expense as long as I live," added Middlemore.

But before Henry Grantham, who had been a pained and silent witness of the scene, and who had already risen with a view to follow the wounded Raymond, could take a single step on his mission of peace, the low roll of the drum, summoning to fall in, warned them that the hour of action had already arrived, and each, quitting his fire, hastened to the more immediate and pressing duties of assembling his men, and carefully examining into the state of their appointments.

In ten minutes from the beating of the *reveillé*—considerably shorn of its wonted proportions, as the occasion demanded—the bivouac had been abandoned, and the little army again upon their march. What remained to be traversed of the space that separated them from the enemy, was an alternation of plain and open forest, but so completely in juxtaposition, that the head of the column had time to clear one wood and enter a second before its rear could disengage itself from the first. The effect of this, by the dim and peculiar light reflected from the snow across which they moved, was picturesque in the extreme, nor was the interest diminished by the utter silence that had pervaded every part of the little army, the measured tramp of whose march, mingled with the hollow and unavoidable rumbling of the light guns, being the only sounds to be heard amid that mass of living matter. The Indians, with the exception of a party of scouts, had been the last to quit their rude encampment, and as they now, in their eagerness to get to the front, glided stealthily by in the deep snows on either side of the more beaten track by which the troops advanced, and so utterly without sound in their foot-fall, that they might rather have been compared to spirits of the wilds, than to human beings.

The regiment having been told off into divisions, it so happened that Raymond and Henry Grantham, although belonging to different companies, now found themselves near each other. The latter had been most anxious to approach his really good hearted companion, with a view to soothe his wounded feelings, and to convey, in the fullest and most convincing terms, the utter disclaimer of his inconsiderate brother officers, to reflect seriously on his conduct in the recent retreat—or, indeed, to intend their observations for any thing beyond a mere pleasantry. As, however, the strictest order had been commanded to be observed in the march, and Raymond and he happened to be at opposite extremities of the division, this had been for some time impracticable. A temporary halt having occurred, just as the head of the column came within sight of the enemy's fires, Grantham quitted his station on the flank, and hastened to the head of his division, where he found Raymond with his arms folded across his chest, and apparently absorbed in deep thought. He tapped him lightly on the shoulder, and inquired in a tone of much kindness the subject of his musing.

Touched by the manner in which he was addressed, Raymand dropped his arms, and grasping the hand of the youth, observed in his usual voice; "Ah, is it you Henry—Egad, my dear boy, I was just thinking of you--and how very kind you have always been; never quizzing me as those thoughtless fellows have done—and certainly never insinuating any thing against my courage—that was too bad Henry, too bad, I could have forgiven anything but that."

"Nay, nay, Raymond," answered his companion, soothingly; "believe me, neither Molineux, nor Middlemore, nor St. Clair, meant anything beyond a jest. I can assure you they did not, for when you quitted us they asked me to go in search of you, but the assembly then commencing to beat, I was compelled to hasten to my company, nor have I had an opportunity of seeing you until now."

"Very well, Henry, I forgive them, for it is not in my nature to keep anger long; but tell them that they should not wantonly wound the feelings of an unoffending comrade. As I told them, they may regret their unkindness to me before another sun has set. If so, I wish them no other punishment."

"What mean you, my dear Raymond?"

"Egad! I scarcely know myself, but something tells me very forcibly my hour is come."

"Nonsense, this is but the effect of the depression, produced by fatigue and over excitement, added to the recent annoyance of your feelings."

"Whatever it proceed from, I had made up my mind

to it before we set out. Henry, my kind good Henry, I have neither friend nor relative on earth—no one to inherit the little property I possess. In the event of my falling, you will find the key of my desk in the breast pocket of my coat. A paper in that desk appoints you my executor. Will you accept the trust?"

"Most sacredly, Raymond, will I fulfil every instruction it contains, should I myself survive; but I cannot, will not, bring myself to anticipate your fall."

"Move on, move on," passed quickly in a whisper from front to rear of the column.

"God bless you, Henry" exclaimed Raymond, again pressing the hand of the youth—"remember the key."

"We shall talk of that to night," was the light reply. "Meanwhile, dear Raymond, God bless you," and again Grantham fell back to his place in the rear of the division.

Five minutes later, and the troops were silently drawn up in front of the enemy. A long line of fires marked the extent of the encampment, from which, even then, the "all's well" of the sentinels could be occasionally heard. Except these, all profoundly slept, nor was there anything to indicate they had the slightest suspicion of an enemy being within twenty miles of them—not a picket had been thrown out, not an outpost established. It was evident the Americans were yet young in the art of self defence.

"What glorious bayonet work we shall have presently," whispered Villiers to Cranstoun, as they were brought together by their stations at the adjacent extremities of their respective division. "Only mark how the fellows sleep."

"The deevil a beet," responded Cranstoun, "a joost noo heerd Coolonel St Julian propoose and even enseest upoon it. But the Geeneral seems to theenk that coold steel and a coold froosty morning do not asseemelate togeether.

"What! does he not mean to attack them with the bayonet, when two minutes would suffice to bring us into the very heart of the encampment, and that before they could well have time to arm themselves ?

"Hoot mon" coolly pursued the Grenadier, with something very like satire in his expression. "Would ye ha' the Geeneral so uncheevalrous as to pooncе upoon a set of poor unarmed and unprepared creeturs. Depeend upoon it he would na sleep coomfortably on his peelow, after having put coold steel into the geezzard of each of yon sleeping loons"

"The devil take his consideration," muttered Villiers; "but you are right, for see, there go the guns to the front—hark there is a shot; the sentinels have discovered us at last; and now the sluggards are starting from before their fires, and hastening to snatch their arms.

"True enoof, Veelliers, and pleenty o' brooken heeds they will gi' us soon, in retoorn for sparing their goots. There oopen too those stooped leetle three poonders. Tha might joost as weel be used for brass warming pons, to tak the cheel off the damp beeds some of us will be pressing preesently."

Whist, whist, whist, flew three balls successively between their heads. "Ha, here they begin to talk to us in earnest, and now to our duty."

The next moment all was roar, and bustle, and confusion, and death.

We will not stop to inquire why the British General, Proctor, lost an advantage which had made itself apparent to the meanest soldier of his army, by opening a desultory and aimless fire of his light guns upon an enemy to whom he thus afforded every possible opportunity for preparation and defence; when, like Colonel, (now Sir John) Harvey, not long subsequently at Stoney Creek, he might have annihilated that enemy with the bayonet, and with little comparative loss to himself. We will merely observe that having failed to do so, nothing but the determination and courage of his troops brought him through the difficulties he himself had created, and to the final attainment of the general order, complimenting him on the highly judicious arrangements he had made on the occasion; although, (as Cranstoun had predicted) not before a damp bed had been pressed for the last time by more than one of those who had so gallantly followed—or, more strictly, preceded him.

The sun was in the meridian; all sounds of combat had ceased, and such of the American Army as had survived the total defeat, were to be seen disarmed and guarded, wending their way sullenly in the direction by which the victors had advanced in the morning. From the field, in which the troops had commenced the action, numerous sledges were seen departing, laden with the dead—the wounded having previously been sent off. One of these sledges remained stationary at some distance within the line, where the ravages of death were marked by pools of blood upon the snow, and at this point were grouped several individuals, assembled round a body which was about to be conveyed away.

"By Heavens, I would give the world never to have said an unkind word to him," observed one, whose arm, suspended from a sling, attested he had not come scatheless out of the action. It was St. Clair, whose great ambition it had always been to have his name borne among the list of wounded—provided there were no broken bones in the question.

"As brave as he was honest hearted," added a second, "you say Grantham, that he forgave us all our nonsense."

"He did, Molineux. He declared he could not bear resentment against you long. But still, I fear, he could not so easily forget. He observed to me, jestingly, just before deploying into line, that he felt his time was come, but there can be no doubt, from what we all witnessed, that he was determined from the outset to court his death."

Captain Molineux turned away, apparently much affected—Middlemore spoke not, but it was evident he also was deeply pained. Each seemed to feel that he had been in some degree accessory to the catastrophe, but the past could not be recalled. The body, covered with blood, exuding from several wounds, was now placed with that of Ensign Langley, (who had also fallen, and lay at a little distance beyond), on the sledge which was drawn off to join several others just departed, and the lingering officers hastened to overtake their several companies.

When the action was at the hottest, one of the small guns in front (all of which had been fearfully exposed), was left without a single artilleryman. Availing themselves of this circumstance, the enemy, who were unprovided with artillery of any description, made a movement as if to possess themselves of, and turn it against the attacking force, then closing rapidly to dispute the possession of the breast work which covered their riflemen. Colonel St. Julian, who had continued to ride along the line with as much coolness as if he had been assisting at a field day, and who was literally covered with wounds, having received no less than five balls, in various parts of his body, seeing this movement, called out for volunteers to recue the gun from its perilous situation. Scarcely had the words passed his lips when an individual moved forward from the line, in the direction indicated.—It was Lieutenant Raymond—Exposed to the fire, both of friends and foes, the unfortunate officer advanced calmly and unconcernedly, in the presence of the whole line, and before the Americans, (kept in check by a hot and incessant musketry), could succeed in even crossing their defences, had seized the gun by the drag rope, and withdrawn it under cover of the English fire. But this gallant act of self-devotedness was not without its terrible price. Pierced by many balls, which the American rifleman had immediately directed at him, he fell dying within ten feet of the British line, brandishing his sword and faintly shouting a "huzza," that was answered by his companions with the fierce spirit of men stung to new exertion, and determined to avenge his fall.

Thus perished the fat, the plain, the carbuncled, but really gallant-hearted Raymond—whose intrinsic worth was never estimated until he had ceased to exist. His fall, and all connected therewith, forms a sort of episode in our story, yet is it one not altogether without its moral. A private monument, on which was inscribed all that may soothe and flatter after death, was erected to his memory by those very officers whose persiflage, attacking in this instance even his honor as a soldier, had driven him to seek the fate he found. Of this there could be no question—for, brave as he unquestionably was, Raymond would not have acted as if courting death throughout, had he not fully made up his mind either to gain great distinction or to die under the eyes of those who had, he conceived, so greatly injured him. It is but justice to add that, for three days from his death—Middlemore did not utter a single pun—neither did St. Clair, or Molineux, indulge in a satirical observation.

CHAPTER V.

The spring of 1813 had passed nearly away, yet without producing any renewed effort on the part of the Americans. From information obtained from the Indian scouts, it however appeared that, far from being discouraged by their recent disaster, they had moved forward a third Army to the Miami, where they had strongly entrenched themselves, until fitting opportunity should be found to renew their attempt to recover the lost district. It was also ascertained that, with a perseverance and industry peculiar to themselves, they had been occupied throughout the rigorous winter, in preparing a fleet of sufficient force to compete with that of the British; and that, abandoning the plan hitherto pursued by his predecessors, the American leader of this third army of invasion, purposed transporting his troops across the lake, instead of running the risk of being harrassed and cut up in an advance by land. To effect this, it was of course necessary to have the command of the lake, and there were all the sinews of exertion called into full exercise, to obtain the desired ascendancy.

To defeat this intention, became now the chief object of the British General. With the close of winter had ceased the hunting pursuits of the warriors, so that each day brought with it a considerable accession to the strength of this wild people, vast numbers of whom had betaken themselves to their hunting grounds, shortly after the capture of Detroit. The chiefs of these several nations were now summoned to a Council, in the course of which it was decided that a formidable expedition, accompanied by a heavy train of battering artillery, should embark in batteaux, with a view to the reduction of the American post established on the Miami; —a nucleus, around which was fast gathering a spirit of activity that threatened danger, if not annihilation, to the English influence in the North Western districts. In the event of the accomplishment of this design, Detroit and Amherstburg would necessarily be released from all apprehension, since, even admitting the Americans could acquire a superiority of naval force on the lake, such superiority could only be essentially injurious to us, as a means of affording transport to, and covering the operations of an invading army. If, however, that already on the Miami could be defeated, and their fortress razed, it was not probable that a fourth could be equipped and pushed forward, with a view to offensive operations, in sufficient time to accomplish any thing decisive before the winter should set in. Tecumseh, who had just returned from collecting new bodies of warriors, warmly approved the project, and undertook to bring two thousand men into the field, as his quota of the expedition, the departure of which was decided for the seventh day from the Council.

Meanwhile, no exertions were wanting to place the little fleet in a state of efficiency. During the winter, the vessel described in our opening chapter of this tale, as that on the completion of which numerous workmen were intently engaged, had, after the fall of Detroit, and the consequent capture of whatever barks the Americans possessed, been utterly neglected; but now that it was known the enemy were secretly and rapidly preparing an overpowering force at the opposite extremity of the lake, the toils of the preceding summer were renewed, and every where, throughout the dock-yard, the same stirring industry was perceptible. By all were these movements regarded with an interest proportioned to the important consequences at stake, but by none more than by Commodore Barclay himself, whose watchful eye marked the progress, and whose experience and judgment directed the organization of the whole. The difficulties he had to contend with were great, for not only were the artificers, employed in the construction of the ship, men of limited knowledge in their art, but even those who manned her, when completed, were without the nautical experience and practice indispensable to success ; yet these disadvantages was he prepared to overlook in the cheerfulness and ardor with which each lent himself to exertion, and sought to supply deficiency with zeal. The feelings of the gallant officer in this position—on the one hand, sensible that to him was confided the task of upholding the supremacy of his country's flag, and on the other, compelled to confess the inadequacy of the means placed at his disposal for this object—may be easily understood. That his men were brave he knew, but mere bravery would not suffice in a contest where the skill of the seamen, not less than brute courage, must be called into requisition. He had reason to know that his enemy would not merely bring stout hearts into the conflict, but active hands—men whose lives had been passed on the restless waters of ocean, and whose training had been perfected in the battle and the tempest, while nine tenths of his own crews had never planted foot beyond the limit of the lake on which the merits and rescources of both would be so shortly tested. But "*aut agere aut mori*," was his motto, and of the appropriateness of this his actions have formed the most striking illustration.

The day on which the Council relative to the proposed expedition to the Miami was held, was characterized by one of those sudden outbursts of elemental war, so common to the Canadas in early summer—and, which, in awful grandeur of desolation, are frequently sarcely inferior to the hurricanes of the tropics. The morning had been oppressively sultry, and there was that general and heavy lethargy of nature that usually precedes a violent reaction. About noon, a small dark speck was visible in the hitherto cloudless horizon, and this presently grew in size until the whole western sky was one dense mass of threatening black, which eventually spread itself over the entire surface of the heavens, leaving not a hand's breadth any where visible. Presently, amid the sultry stillness that prevailed, there came a slight breeze over the face of the waters, and then, as if some vast battering train had suddenly opened its hundred mouths of terror, vomiting forth showers of grape and other missiles, came astounding thunder-claps, and forked lightnings, and rain, and hail, and whistling wind—all in such terrible union, yet such fearful disorder, that man, the last to take warning, or feel awed by the anger of the common parent, Nature, bent his head in lowliness and silence to her voice, and awaited tremblingly the passing away of her wrath.

Henry Grantham, whose turn of duty had again brought him to Amherstburg, was in the mess-room of the garrison when the storm was at the fiercest. Notwithstanding the excitement of the Council scene, at which he had been present, he had experienced an unusual depression throughout the day, originating partly in the languid state of the atmosphere, but infinitely more in the anxiety under which he labored in regard to his brother, of whom no other intelligence had been received, since his departure with his prisoners for Buffalo, than what vague rumour, coupled with the fact of the continued absence of the schooner, afforded. That the vessel had been captured by the enemy there could be no doubt; but, knowing as he did, the gallant spirit of Gerald, there was reason to imagine that he had not yielded to his enemies, before every means of resistance had been exhausted: and, if so, what might not have been the effect of his obstinacy (if such a term could be applied to unshaken intrepidity,) on men exasperated by opposition, and eager for revenge. In the outset he had admitted his gentle cousin Gertrude to his confidence, as one most suited, by her docility, to soothe without appearing to remark on his alarm, but when, little suspecting the true motive of her agitation, he saw her evince an emotion surpassing his own, and admitting and giving way to fears beyond any he would openly avow, he grew impatient and disappointed, and preferring rather to hear the tocsin of alarm sounded from his own heart than from the lips of another, he suddenly, and much to the surprise of the affectionate girl, discontinued all allusion to the subject. But Henry's anxiety was not the less poignant from being confined within his own breast, and although it gratified him to find that flattering mention was frequently made of his brother at the mess-table, coupled with regret for his absence, it was reserved for his hours of privacy and abstraction to dwell upon the fears which daily became more harrassing and perplexing.

On the present occasion, even while his brother officers had thought nor ear but for the terrible tempest that raged without, and at one moment threatened to bury them beneath the trembling roof, the mind of Henry was full of his absent brother, whom, more than ever, he now seemed to regret, from the association of the howling tempest with the wild element on which he had last beheld him; and so complete at length had become the ascendancy of his melancholy, that when the storm had been in some degree stilled, and the rain abated, he took an early leave of his companions, with a view to indulge in privacy the gloomy feelings by which he felt himself oppressed.

In passing through the gate of the Fort, on his way into the town, his attention was arrested by several groups of persons, consisting of soldiers, Indians, and inhabitants, who, notwithstanding the inclemency of the hour, were gathered on the high bank in front of the *demi-lune* battery, eagerly bending their gaze upon the river. Half curious to know what could have attracted them in such weather from shelter, Henry advanced and mingled in the crowd, which gave way at his approach. Although the fury of the tempest had spent itself, there was still wind enough to render it a matter of necessary precaution that the bystanders should secure a firm footing on the bank, while the water, violently agitated and covered with foam, resembled rather a pigmy sea than an inland river—so unusual and so vast were its waves. The current, moreover, increased in strength by the sudden swelling of the waters, dashed furiously down, giving its direction to the leaping billows that rode impatiently upon its surface; and at the point of intersection by the island of Bois Blanc, formed so violent an eddy within twenty feet of the land, as to produce the effect of a whirlpool, while again, between the island and the Canadian shore, the current, always rapid and of great force, flew boiling down its channel, and with a violence almost quadrupled.

Amid this uproar of the usually placid river, there was but one bark found bold enough to venture upon her angered bosom, and this, although but an epitome of those that have subdued the world of waters, and chained them in subservience to the will of man, now danced gallantly, almost terrifically, from billow to billow, and, with the feathery lightness of her peculiar class, seemed borne onward, less by the leaping waves themselves than by the white and driving spray that fringed their summits. This bark—a canoe evidently of the smallest description—had been watched in its progress, from afar, by the groups assembled on the bank, who had gathered at each other's call, to witness and marvel at the gallant daring of those who had committed it to the boiling element. Two persons composed her crew—the one, seated in the stern, and carefully guiding the bark so as to enable her to breast the threatening waves, which, in quick succession, rose as if to accomplish her overthrow—the other, standing at her bows, the outline of his upper figure designed against the snow-white sail, and, with his arms folded across his chest, apparently gazing without fear on the danger which surrounded him. It was evident, from their manner of conducting the bark, that the adventurers were not Indians, and yet there was nothing to indicate to what class of the white family they belonged. Both were closely wrapped in short, dark coloured pea coats, and their heads were surmounted with glazed hats—a species of costume that more than any thing else, proved their familiarity with the element whose brawling they appeared to brave with an indifference bordering on madness.

Such was the position of the parties, at the moment when Henry Grantham gained the bank. Hitherto the canoe, in the broad reach that divided the island from the American mainland, had had merely the turbulence of the short heavy waves, and a comparatively modified current, to contend against. Overwhelming even as these difficulties would have proved to men less gifted with the power of opposing and vanquishing them, they were but light in comparison with what remained to be overcome. The canoe was now fast gaining the head of the island, and pursuing a direct course for the whirlpool already described. The only means of avoiding this was by closely hugging the shore, between which and the violent eddy without, the water, broken in its impetuosity by the covering head land, presented a more even and less agitated surface. This head land once doubled, the safety of the adventurers was ensured, since, although the tremendous current which swept through the inner channel must have borne them considerably downwards, still the canoe would have accomplished the transit below the town in perfect safety. The fact of this opportunity being neglected, led at once to the inference that the adventurers were total strangers, and distinct voices were now raised by those on the bank, to warn them of their danger—but whether it was that they heard not, or understood not, the warning was unnoticed. Once indeed it seemed as if he who so ably conducted the course of the bark, had comprehended and would have followed the suggestion so earnestly given, for his tiny sail was seen to flutter for the first time in the wind, as with the intention to alter his course. But an impatient gesture from his companion in the bow, who was seen to turn suddenly round, and utter something, (which was however inaudible to those on shore,) again brought the head of the fragile vessel to her original course, and onward she went leaping and bounding, apparently with the design to clear the whirlpool at a higher point of the river. Nothing short of a miracle could now possibly enable them to escape being drawn into the boiling vortex, and, during the moments that succeeded, every heart beat high with fearful expectation as to the result. At length the canoe came with a sudden plunge into the very centre of the current, which, all the skill of the steersman was insufficient to enable him to clear. Her bow yawed, her little sail fluttered—and away she flew, broadside foremost, down the stream with as little power of resistance as a feather or a straw. Scarcely had the eye time to follow her in this peculiar descent, when she was in the very heart of the raging eddy. For a moment she reeled like a top, then rolled two or three times over, and finally disappeared altogether. Various expressions of horror broke from the several groups of whites and Indians, all of whom had anticipated the catastrophe without the power of actively interposing. Beyond the advice that was given, not a word was uttered, but every eye continued fixed on the whirlpool, as though momentarily expecting to see something issue from its bosom. After the lapse of a minute, a dark object suddenly presented itself some twenty yards below, between the island and the town. It was the canoe which, bottom upwards, and deprived of its little mast and sail, had again risen to the surface, and was floating rapidly down with the current. Presently afterwards two heads were seen nearly at the point where the canoe had again emerged. They were the unfortunate adventurers, one of whom appeared to be supporting his companion with one arm, whilst with the other he dashed away the waters that bore them impetuously along. The hats of both had fallen off, and as he who exerted himself so strenuously, rose once or twice in the vigour of his efforts above the element with which he contended, he seemed to present the grisly, woolly hair, and the sable countenance of an aged negro. A vague surmise of the truth now flashed upon the mind, of the excited officer, but when, presently afterwards, he saw the powerful form once more raised, and in a voice that made itself distinctly heard above the howling of the wind, exclaim : "Help a dare," there was no longer a doubt, and he rushed towards the dock yard, to gain which the exertions of the negro were now directed.

On reaching it, he found both Gerald and his faithful attendant just touching the shore. Aroused by the cry for help which Sambo had pealed forth, several of the workmen had quitted the shelter of the block houses in which they were lodged, and hastened to the rescue of him whom they immediately afterwards saw struggling furiously to free himself and companion from the violent current. Stepping to the extremity on some loose timber which lay secured to the shore, yet floating in the river—they threw out poles, one of which Sambo seized like an enraged mastiff in his teeth, and still supporting the body, and repelling the water with his disengaged arm, in this manner succeeded in gaining the land. The crews of the little fleet, which lay armed a hundred yards lower down, had also witnessed the rapid descent of two apparently drowning men, and ropes had every where been thrown out from the vessels. As for lowering a boat it was out of the question, for no boat could have resisted the violence of the current, even for some hours after the storm had wholly ceased.

It may be easily conceived with what mingled emotions the generous Henry, whose anxiety had been so long excited in regard to his brother's fate, now beheld that brother suddenly restored to him. Filled with an affection, that was rendered the more intense by the very fact of the danger from which he had just seen him rescued, he, regardless of those around, and in defiance of his wet and dripping clothes, sprang eagerly to his embrace, but Gerald received him with a cold—almost averted air. Suffering, rather than sharing, this mark of his fraternal love, he turned the instant afterwards to his servant, and in a tone of querulousness, said—"Sambo, give me more wine."

Inexpressibly shocked, and not knowing what to make of this conduct, Henry bent his glance upon the negro. The old man shook his head mournfully, and even with the dripping spray that continued to fall from his woollen locks upon his cheeks, tears might be seen to mingle. A dreadful misgiving came over the mind of the youth, and he felt his very hair rise thrillingly, as he for a moment admitted the horrible possibility, that the shock produced by his recent accident had affected his brother's intellect. Sambo replied to his master's demand, by saying "there was no wine—the canoe and its contents had been utterly lost."

All this passed during the first few moments of their landing. The necessity for an immediate change of apparel was obvious, and Gerald and his servant were led into the nearest block house, where each of the honest fellows occupying it was eager in producing whatever his rude wardrobe afforded. The brothers then made the best of their way, followed by the negro, to their own abode in the town.

The evening being damp and chilly, a fire was kindled in the apartment in which Gerald dined—the same in which both had witnessed the dying moments of their mother, and Henry those of their father. It had been chosen by the former, in the height of her malady, for its cheerfulness, and she had continued in it until the hour of her decease; while Major Grantham had selected it for his chamber of death, for the very reason, that it had been that of his regretted wife. Henry, having already dined, sat at the opposite extremity of the table, watching his brother whose features he had so longed to behold once more; yet, not without a deep and bitter feeling of grief that those features should have undergone so complete a change in their expression towards himself. Gerald had thrown off the temporary and ill fitting vestments exchanged for his own wet clothing, and now that he appeared once more in his customary garb, an extraordinary alteration was perceptible in his whole appearance. Instead of the blooming cheek, and rounded and elegant form, for which he had always been remarkable, he now offered to the eye of his anxious brother an emaciated figure, and a countenance pale even unto wanness—while evidence of much care, and inward suffering, might be traced in the stern contraction of his hitherto open brow. There was also a dryness in his speech that startled and perplexed even more than the change in his person. The latter might be the effect of imprisonment, and its anxiety and privation, coupled with the exhaustion arising from his recent accident, but how was the first to be accounted for, and wherefore was he, after so long a separation, and under such circumstances, thus uncommunicative and unaffectionate? All these reflections occurred to the mind of the sensitive Henry, as he sat watching, and occasionally addressing a remark to, his taciturn brother, until he became fairly bewildered in his efforts to find a clue to his conduct. The horrible dread which had first suggested itself, of the partial overthrow of intellect, had passed away, but to this had succeeded a discovery, attended by quite as much concern—although creating less positive alarm. He had seen, with inexpressible pain, that Gerald ate but little, seeming rather to loathe his food, while on the other hand, he had recourse more frequently to wine, drinking off bumpers with greedy avidity, until, yielding at length to the excess of his potations, he fell fast asleep in the arm chair he had drawn to the fire, overcome by the mingled influence of wine, fatigue, and drowsiness.

Bitter were the feelings of Henry Grantham, as thus he gazed upon his sleeping brother. Fain would he have persuaded himself, that the effect he now witnessed was an isolated instance, and occurring only under the peculiar circumstances of the moment. It was impossible to recal the manner in which he had demanded "wine," from their faithful old servant and friend, and not feel satisfied, that the tone proclaimed him one who had been in the frequent habit of repeating that demand, as the prepared, yet painful manner of the black, indicated a sense of having been too frequently called upon to administer to it. Alas, thought the heart-stricken Henry, can it really be, that he whom I have cherished in my heart of hearts, with more than brother's love has thus fallen? Has Gerald, formerly as remarkable for sobriety, as for every honorable principle, acquired even during the months I have so wretchedly mourned his absence, the fearful propensities of the drunkard. The bare idea overpowered him, and with difficulty restraining his tears, he rose from his seat, and paced the room for some time, in a state of indescribable agitation. Then again he stopped, and when he looked in the sleeping face of his unconscious brother, he was more than ever struck by the strange change which had been wrought in his appearance. Finding that Gerald still slept profoundly, he took the resolution of instantly questioning Sambo, as to all that had befallen them during their absence, and ascertaining, if possible, to what circumstance the mystery which perplexed him was attributable. Opening and reclosing the door with caution, he hastened to the room, which, owing to his years and long and faithful services, had been set apart for the accommodation of the old man when on shore. Here he found Sambo, who had dispatched his substantial meal, busily occupied in drying his master's wet dress, before a large blazing wood fire—and laying out, with the same view, certain papers, the contents of a pocket book, which had been completely saturated with water. A ray of satisfaction lighted the dark, but intelligent face of the negro, which the instant before, had worn an expression of suffering, as the young officer, pressing his hand with warmth, thanked him deeply and fervently, for the noble, almost superhuman exertions he had made that day, to preserve his brother's life.

"Oh Massa Henry," was all the poor creature could say in reply, as he returned the pressure with an emphasis that spoke his profound attachment to both. Then leaning his white head upon his hand against the chimney, and bursting into tears; "berry much change, he poor broder Geral, he not a same at all."

Here was a sad opening indeed to the subject. The heart of the youth sank within him, yet feeling the necessity of knowing all connected with his brother's unhappiness, he succeeded in drawing the old man into conversation, and finally into a narration of all their adventures, as far, at least, as he had personal knowledge, from the moment of their leaving Detroit in the preceding autumn.

When, after the expiration of an hour, he returned to the drawing room, Gerald was awake, and so far restored by the effect of his sound sleep, as to be, not only more communicative, but more cordial towards his brother. He even reverted to past scenes, and spoke of the mutual frolics of their youth, with a cheerfulness bordering on levity; but this pained Henry the more, for he saw in it but the fruit of a forced excitement—as melancholy in adoption as pernicious in effect—and his own heart repugned all participation in so unnatural a gaiety, although, he enforced himself to share it to the outward eye. Fatigue at length compelled Gerald to court the quiet of his pillow, and, overcome as his senses were with wine, he slept profoundly until morning.

CHAPTER VI.

When they met at breakfast, Henry was more than ever struck and afflicted by the alteration in his brother's person and manner. All traces of the last night's excitement had disappeared with its cause, and pale, haggard, and embarrassed, he seemed but the shadow of his former self, while the melancholy of his countenance had in it something wild and even fierce. As at their first meeting, his language was dry and reserved, and he seemed rather impatient of conversation, as though it interfered with the indulgence of some secret and all absorbing reflection, while, to Henry's affectionate questioning of his adventures since they first parted, he replied in the vague unsatisfactory manner of one who seeks to shun the subject altogether. At another moment, this apparent prostration of the physical man might have been ascribed to his long immersion of the preceding day, and the efforts that were necessary to rescue him from a watery grave; but, from the account Sambo had given him, Henry had but too much reason to fear that the disease of body and mind which had so completely encompassed his unfortunate brother, not only had its being in a different cause, but might be dated from an earlier period. Although burning with desire to share that confidence which it grieved him to the soul to find thus unkindly withheld, he made no effort to remove the cloak of reserve in which his brother had invested himself. That day they both dined at the garrison mess, and Henry saw, with additional pain, that the warm felicitation of his brother officers on his return, were received by Gerald with the same reserve and indifference which had characterized his meeting with him, while he evinced the same disinclination to enter upon the solicited history of his captivity, as well as the causes which led to his bold venture, and consequent narrow escape, of the preceding day. Finding him thus uncommunicative, and not comprehending the change in his manner, they rallied him; and, as the bottle circulated, he seemed more and more disposed to meet their raillery with a cheerfulness and good humour that brought even the color into his sunken cheeks; but when, finally, some of them proceeded to ask him, in their taunting manner, what he had done with his old flame and fascinating prisoner, Miss Montgomerie, a deadly paleness overspread his countenance, and he lost in the moment, all power of disguising his feelings. His emotion was too sudden, and too palpable not to be observed by those who had unwillingly called it forth, and they at once, with considerate tact, changed the conversation. Hereupon Gerald again made an effort to rally, but no one returned to the subject. Piqued at this conduct, he had more frequent recourse to the bottle, and laughed and talked in a manner that proved him to be laboring under the influence of extraordinary excitement. When he took leave of his brother to retire to rest, he was silent, peevish, dissatisfied—almost angry.

Henry passed a night of extreme disquiet. It was evident from what had occurred at the mess-table, in relation to the beautiful American, that to her was to be ascribed the wretchedness to which Gerald had become a victim, and he resolved, on the following morning, to waive all false delicacy, and, throwing himself upon his affection, to solicit his confidence, and offer whatever counsel he conceived would best tend to promote his peace of mind.

At breakfast the conversation turned on the intended movement, which was to take place within three days, and, on this subject, Gerald evinced a vivacity that warmed into eagerness. He had risen early that morning, with a view to obtain the permission of the Commodore to make one of the detachment of sailors who were to accompany the expedition, and, having succeeded in obtaining the command of one of the two gun-boats which were destined to ascend the Miami, and form part of the battering force, seemed highly pleased. This apparant return to himself might have led his brother into the belief that his feelings had indeed undergone a re-action, had he not, unfortunately, but too much reason to know that the momentary gaiety was the result of the very melancholy which consumed him. However, it gave him a more favorable opportunity to open the subject next his heart, and, as a preparatory step, he dexterously contrived to turn the conversation into the channel most suited to his purpose.

The only ill effect arising from Gerald's recent immersion was a sense of pain in that part of his arm which had been bitten by the rattle snake, on the day of the pic-nic to Hog Island, and it chanced that this morning especially it had a good deal annoyed him, evincing some slight predisposition to inflammation. To subdue this, Henry applied, with his own hand, a liniment which had been recommended, and took occasion, when he had finished, to remark on the devotedness and fearlessness Miss Montgomerie had manifested in coming so opportunely to his rescue—in all probability, thereby preserving his life.

At the sound of this name Gerald started, and evinced the same impatience of the subject he had manifested on the preceding day. Henry keenly remarked his emotion, and Gerald was sensible that he did.

Both sat for some minutes gazing at each other in expressive silence, the one as if waiting to hear, the other as if conscious that he was expected to afford some explanation of the cause of so marked an emotion. At length Gerald said, and in a tone of deep and touching despondency, "Henry, I fear you find me very unamiable and much altered; but indeed I am very unhappy."

Here was touched the first chord of their sympathies. Henry's already on the *élan*, flew to meet this demonstration of returning confidence, and he replied in a voice broken by the overflowing of his full heart.

"Oh, my beloved brother, changed must you indeed be, when even the admission that you are unhappy, inspires me with a thankfulness such as I now feel. Gerald, I entreat, I implore, you by the love we have borne each other from infancy to disguise nothing from me. Tell me what it is that weighs so heavily at your heart. Repose implicit confidence in me, your brother, and let me assist and advise you in your extremity, as my poor ability will permit. Tell me Gerald, wherefore are you thus altered—what dreadful disappointment has thus turned the milk of your nature into gall?"

Gerald gazed at him a moment intently. He was much affected, and a sudden and unbidden tear stole down his pallid cheek. "If *you* have found the milk of my nature turned into gall, then indeed am I even more wretched than I thought myself. But, Henry, you ask me what I cannot yield—my confidence—and, even were it so, the yielding would advantage neither. I am unhappy, as I have said, but the cause of that unhappiness must ever remain buried here," and he pointed to his chest. This was said kindly, yet determinedly.

"Enough, Gerald," and his brother spoke in tones of deep reproach, "since you persist in withholding your confidence, I will no longer urge it; but you cannot wonder that I who love but you alone on earth, should sorrow as one without hope, at beholding you subject to a grief so overwhelming as to have driven you to seek refuge from it, in an unhallowed grave."

"I do not understand you—what mean you?" quickly interrupted Gerald, raising his head from the hand which supported it upon the breakfast table, while he colored faintly.

"You cannot well be ignorant of my meaning," pursued Henry in the same tone, "if you but recur to the circumstances attending your arrival here."

"I am still in the dark," continued Gerald, with some degree of impatience.

"Because you know not that I am acquainted with all that took place on the melancholy occasion. Gerald," he pursued, "forgive the apparent harshness of what I am about to observe--but was it generous—was it kind in you to incur the risk you did, when you must have known that your death would have entailed upon me an eternal grief? Was it worthy of yourself, moreover, to make the devoted follower of your fortunes, a sharer in the danger you so eagerly and wantonly courted!"

"Nay, my good brother," and Gerald made an attempt at levity, "you are indeed an unsparing monitor; but suppose I should offer in reply, that a spirit of enterprize was upon me on the occasion to which you allude, and that, fired by a desire to astonish you all with a bold feat, I had had resolved to do what no other had done before me, yet without apprehending the serious consequences which ensued—or even assuming the danger to have been so great."

"All this, Gerald, you might, yet would not say; because, in saying it, would have to charge yourself with a gross insincerity, and although you do not deem me worthy to share your confidence, I still have pleasure in knowing that my affection will not be repaid with deceit—however plausible the motives for its adoption may appear—by the substitution in short, of that which is not for that which is."

"A gross insincerity?" repeated Gerald, again slightly coloring.

"Yes, my brother—I say it not in anger, nor in reproach—but a gross insincerity it would certainly be. Alas, Gerald, your motives are but too well known to me. The danger you incurred was incurred wilfully, wantonly, and with a view to your own destruction."

Gerald started. The color had again fled from his sunken cheek, and he was ashy pale; "And *how* knew you this," he asked with a trembling voice.

"Even, Gerald, as I know that you have been driven to seek in wine that upbearing against the secret grief which consumes you, which should be found alone in the fortitude of a strong mind, and the consciousness of an untainted honor. Oh, Gerald, had these been your supporters, you never would have steeped your reason so far in forgetfulness, as to have dared what you did on that eventful day. Good Heaven! how little did I ever expect to see the brother of my love degenerated so far as to border on the character of the drunkard and the suicide."

The quick, but sunken eyes of the sailor flashed fire; and he pressed his lips, and clenched his teeth together as one strongly attempting to restrain his indignation. It was but a momentary flashing of the chafed and bruised spirit.

"You probe me deeply, Henry," he said calmly, and in a voice of much melancholy. "These are severe expressions for a brother to use—but you are right—I did seek oblivion of my wretchedness in that whirlpool, as the only means of destroying the worm that feeds incessantly upon my heart; but Providence has willed it otherwise—and, moreover, I had not taken the danger of my faithful servant into the account. Had Sambo not saved me, I must have perished, for I made not the slightest effort to preserve myself. However it matters but little, the mere manner of one's death," he pursued with increased despondency. "It is easy for you, Henry, whose mind is at peace with itself and the world, to preach fortitude and resignation, but, felt you the burning flame which scorches my vitals, you would acknowledge the wide, wide difference between theory and practice."

Henry rose deeply agitated—he went to the door and secured the bolt, then returning, knelt at his brother's feet. Gerald had one hand covering his eyes from which, however, the tears forced themselves through his closed fingers. The other was seized and warmly pressed in his brother's grasp.

"Gerald," he said in the most emphatic manner, "by the love you ever bore to our sainted parents, in whose chamber of death I now appeal to your better feelings—by the friendship that has united our hearts from youth to manhood —by all and every tie of affection, let me implore you once more to confide this dreadful grief to me, that I may share it with you, and counsel you for your good. Oh, my brother, on my bended knees, do I solicit your confidence. Believe me no mean curiosity prompts my prayer. I would soothe, console, assist you--aye, even to the very sacrifice of life."

The feelings of the sailor were evidently touched, yet he uttered not a word. His hand still covered his face, and the tears seemed to flow even faster than before.

"Gerald," pursued his brother with bitterness; "I see with pain, that I have not your confidence, and I desist—yet answer me one question. From the faithful Sambo, as you must perceive, I have learnt all connected with your absence, and from him I have gained that, during your captivity, you were much with Miss Montgomerie, (he pronounced the name with an involuntary shuddering), all I ask, therefore, is whether your wretchedness proceeds from the rejection of your suit, or from any levity or inconstancy you may have found in her?"

Gerald raised his head from his supporting hand, and turned upon his brother a look, in which mortified pride predominated over an infinitude of conflicting emotions.

"Rejected, Henry, *my* suit rejected—oh, no! In supposing my grief to originate with her, you are correct, but imagine not it is because my suit is rejected—certainly not."

"Then," exclaimed Henry with generous emphasis, while he pressed the thin hand which he held more closely between his own, "Why not marry her?"

Gerald started.

"Yes, marry her," continued Henry; "marry her and be at peace. Oh! Gerald, you know not what sad agency I attached to that insidious American from the first moment of her landing on this shore—you know not how much I have disliked, and still dislike her—but what are these considerations when my brother's happiness is at stake—Gerald, marry her—and be happy."

"Impossible," returned the sailor in a feeble voice, and again his head sank upon the open palm of his hand.

"Do you no longer love her then?" eagerly questioned the astonished youth.

Once more Gerald raised his head, and fixed his large, dim, eyes full upon those of his brother. "To madness!" he said, in a voice, and with a look that made Henry shudder. There was a moment of painful pause. The latter at length ventured to observe.

"You speak in riddles, Gerald. If you love this Miss Montgomerie to madness, and are, as you seem to intimate loved by her in return, why not, as I have urged, marry her?"

"Because," replied the sailor, turning paler than before, and almost gasping for breath," there is a condition attached to the possession of her hand."

"And that is?" pursued Henry inquiringly, after another long and painful pause.

"My secret," and Gerald pointed significantly to his breast.

"True," returned Henry, slightly coloring; "I had forgotten—but what condition, Gerald, (and here he spoke as if piqued at the abrupt manner in which his brother had concluded his half confidence), what condition, I ask, may a woman entitled to our respect, as well as to our love, propose, which should be held of more account than that severest of offences againt the Divine will—self murder—nay, look not thus surprised, for have you not admitted that you had guiltily attempted to throw away your life—to commit suicide in short—rather than comply with an earthly condition?"

"What if in this," returned Gerald, with a smile of bitterness, "I have preferred the lesser guilt to the greater?"

"I can understand no condition, my brother, a woman worthy of your esteem could impose, which should one moment weigh in the same scale against the inexpiable crime of self destruction. But, really, all this mystery so startles and confounds me, that I know not what to think—what inference to draw."

"Henry," observed the sailor, with some show of impatience —"considering your promise not to urge it further, it seems to me you push the matter to an extremity."

The youth made no reply, but, raising himself from his knees, moved towards the door, which he again unbolted. He then walked to the window at the further end of the apartment.

Gerald saw that he was deeply pained; and impatient, and angry with himself, he also rose and paced the room with hurried steps. At length he stopped, and putting one hand upon the shoulder of his brother, who stood gazing vacantly from the window, pointed with the other towards that part of the apartment in which both their parents had breathed their last.

"Henry, my kind, good, Henry," he said, with a voice faltering with emotion, "do you recollect the morning, when, on our return from school, we found our young holiday joy changed into heart-breaking and mourning by the sight of our dying mother?"

"Remember it, Gerald! aye, even as though it had been yesterday. Oh, my brother, little did I think at the moment, when, with hands closely clasped together, we sank, overcome with grief, upon our bended knees, to receive that mother's blessing, a day would ever arrive when the joy or sorrow of the one, should form no portion of the joy or sorrow of the other."

"It was there," pursued Gerald, and without noticing the interruption, "that we solemnly pledged ourselves to do the will and bidding of our father in all things."

"Even so, Gerald, I remember it well."

"And it was there," continued the sailor, with the emphasis of strong emotion, "that, during my unfortunate absence from the death bed of our yet surviving parent, you gave a pledge for *both*, that no action of our lives should reflect dishonor on his unsullied name."

"I did. Both in your name and in my own, I gave the pledge, well knowing that, in that, I merely anticipated your desire."

"Most assuredly—what then would be your sensations were you to know that I had violated that sacred obligation?"

"Deep, poignant, ceaseless, regret, that my once noble and high spirited brother, should have been so lost to respect for his father's memory, and to himself." This was uttered, not without deep agitation.

"You are right, Henry," added Gerald mournfully; "better—far better—is it to die, than live on in the consciousness of having forfeited all claim to esteem.

The young soldier started as if a viper had stung him. "Gerald," he said eagerly, "you have not dishonored yourself. Oh no—tell me, my brother, that you have not."

"No," was the cold, repulsive answer, "although my peace of mind is fled," he pursued, rather more mildly, "my honor, thank heaven, remains as pure as when you first pledged yourself for its preservation."

"Thanks, my brother, for that. But can it really be possible, that the mysterious condition attached to Miss Montgomerie's love, involves the loss of honor?"

Gerald made no answer.

"And can *you* really be weak enough to entertain a passion for a woman, who would make the dishonoring of the fair fame of him she professes to love, the fearful price at which her affection is to be purchased?"

Gerald seemed to wince at the word "weak," which was rather emphatically pronounced, and looked displeased at the concluding part of the sentence.

"I said not that the condition attached to her *love*," he remarked, with the piqued expression of a wounded vanity;

"her affection is mine, I know, beyond her own power of control—the condition, relates not to her heart, but to her hand."

"Alas, my poor infatuated brother. Blinding indeed must be the delusions of passion, when a nature so sensitive and so honorable shrinks not from such a connexion. My only surprise is, that, with such a perversion of judgment, you have returned at all."

"No more of this Henry. It is not in man to control his destiny, and mine appears to be to love with a fervor that must bear me, ere long, to my grave. Of this, however, be assured—that, whatever my weakness, or infatuation, as you may be pleased to call it, *that* passion shall never be gratified at the expense of my honor. Deeply—madly as I doat upon her image, Miss Montgomerie and I have met for the last time."

Overcome by the emotion with which he had thus expressed himself, Gerald could not restrain a few burning tears that forced their way down his hollow cheeks. Henry caught eagerly at this indication of returning softness, and again essayed, in reference to the concluding declaration of his brother, to urge upon him the unworthiness of her who had thus cast her deadly spell upon his happiness. But Gerald could ill endure the slightest allusion to the subject.

"Henry," he said, "I have already told you that Miss Montgomerie and I have parted for ever; but not the less devotedly do I love her. If, therefore, you would not further wring a heart already half broken with affliction, oblige me by never making the slightest mention of her name in my presence—or ever adverting again to our conversation of this morning. I am sure Henry, you will not deny me this."

Henry offered no other reply than by throwing himself into the arms that were extended to receive him. The embrace of the brothers was long and fervent, and, although there was perhaps more of pain than pleasure, in their mutual sense of the causes which had led to it in the present instance—

still was it productive of a luxury the most heartfelt. It seemed to both as if the spirits of their departed parents hovered over, and blessed them in this indication of their returning affection, hallowing, with their invisible presence, a scene connected with the last admonitions from their dying lips. When they had thus given vent to their feelings, although the sense of unhappiness continued undiminished, their hearts experienced a sensible relief; and when they separated for the morning, in pursuit of their respective avocations, it was with a subdued manner on the part of Gerald, and a vague hope with Henry, that his brother's disease would eventually yield to various influences, and that other and happier days were yet in store for both.

CHAPTER VII.

Meanwhile the preparations for the departure of the expedition for the Miami were rapidly completing. To the majority of the regular force of the two garrisons were added several companies of militia, and a considerable body of Indians, under Tecumseh—the two former portions of the force being destined to advance by water, the latter by land. The spring had been unusually early, and the whole of April remarkably warm; on some occasions sultry to oppressiveness --as for instance on the morning of the tempest. They were now in the first days of the last week of that month, and every where a quick and luxuriant vegetation had succeeded to the stubborn barrenness and monotony of winter. Not a vestige of that dense mass of ice which, three months previously, had borne them over lake and river, was now to be seen. The sun danced joyously and sportively on the golden wave, and where recently towered the rugged surface of the tiny iceberg, the still, calm, unbroken level of the mirroring lake was only visible. On the beach, just below the town, and on a line with the little fleet, that lay at anchor between the island and the main, were drawn up numerous batteaux, ready for the reception of the troops, while on the decks of two gun boats, that were moored a few yards without them, were to be seen the battering train and entrenching tools intended to accompany the expedition. Opposite to each batteau was kindled a fire, around which were grouped the *voyageurs* composing the crew, some dividing their salt pork or salt fish upon their bread, with a greasy clasped knife, and quenching the thirst excited by this with occasional libations from tin cans, containing a mixture of water and the poisonous distillation of the country, miscalled whiskey. In other directions, those who had dined sat puffing the smoke from their dingy pipes, while again, they who had sufficiently luxuriated on the weed, might be seen sleeping, after the manner of the Indians, with their heads resting on the first rude pillow that offered itself, and their feet close upon the embers of the fire on which they had prepared their meal. The indolence of inactivity was more or less upon all, but it was the indolence consequent on previous exertion, and a want of further employment. The whole scene was characteristic of the peculiar manners of the French Canadian boatmen.

Since the morning of the long and partial explanation between the brothers, no further allusion had been made to the forbidden subject. Henry saw, with unfeigned satisfaction, that Gerald not only abstained from the false excitement to which he had hitherto had recourse, but that he apparently sought to rally against his dejection. It is true that whenever he chanced to surprise him alone, he observed him pale, thoughtful, and full of care, but, as he invariably endeavored to hide the feeling at his approach, he argued favorably even from the effort. Early on the day previous to that of the sailing of the expedition, Gerald asked leave for a visit of a few hours to Detroit, urging a desire to see the family of his uncle, who still remained quartered at that post, and whom he had not met since his return from captivity. This had been readily granted by the Commodore, in whom the change in the health and spirits of his young favorite had excited both surprise and concern, and who, anxious for his restoration, was ready to promote whatever might conduce to his comfort. He had even gone so far as to hint the propriety of his relinquishing his intention of accompanying the expedition, (which was likely to be attended with much privation and exposure to those engaged in it,) and suffering another officer to be substituted to his command, while he remained at home to recruit his health. But Gerald heard the well meant proposal with ill disguised impatience, and he replied, with a burning cheek, that if his absence for a day could not be allowed without inconvenience to the service, he was ready to submit; but, as far as regarded his making one of the expedition, nothing short of a positive command should compel him to remain behind. Finding him thus obstinate, the Commodore good humouredly called him a silly, wilful, fellow, and bade him have his own way; however he felt confident that, if he accompanied the Miami expedition in his then state of health, he never would rerturn from it.

Gerald admitted it was probable enough he should not, but, although he deeply felt the kindness of his Commander's motive in wishing him to remain, he was not the less determined, since the matter was left to his own choice, to go where his duty led him. Then, promising to be back long before the hour fixed for sailing the ensuing day, he warmly pressed the cordially extended hand, and soon afterwards, accompanied by Sambo, whose skill as a rider was in no way inferior to his dexterity as a steersman, mounted a favorite horse, and was soon far on his road to Detroit.

Towards midnight of that day, two men were observed by the American tanner, to enter by the gate that led into the grounds of the cottage, and, after lingering for a few moments, near the graves to which tradition had attached so much of the marvellous, to disappear round the angle of the building into the court behind. Curiosity induced him to follow and watch their movements, and, although he could not refrain from turning his head at least a dozen times, as if expecting at each moment to encounter some dread inhabitant of the tomb, he at length contrived to place himself in the very position in which Gerald had formerly been a witness of the attempt at assassination. From the same window now flashed a strong light upon the court below, and by this the features of the officer and his servant were distinctly revealed to the astonished tanner, who, ignorant of their return, and scarcely knowing whether he gazed upon the living or the dead, would have fled, had he not, as he afterwards confessed, been rooted by fear, and a species of fascination, to the spot. The appearance and actions of the parties indeed seemed to justify, not only the delusion, but the alarm of the worthy citizen. Both Gerald and Sambo were disguised in large dark cloaks, and as the light fell upon the thin person and pale, attenuated, sunken countenance of the former, he could scarcely persuade himself this was the living man, who a few months before, rich in beauty and in health, had questioned him of the very spot in which he now, under such strange circumstances, beheld him. Nor was the appearance of the negro more assuring. Filled with the terror that ever inspired him on approaching this scene of past horrors, his usually dark cheek wore the dingy paleness characteristic of death in one of his colour, while every muscle, stiff, set, contracted by superstitious fear, seemed to have lost all power of relaxation. The solemnity moreover of the manner of both, was in strict keeping with their personal appearance, so that it can scarcely be wondered that in a mind not the strongest nor the most free from a belief in the supernatural, a due quantum of awe and alarm should have been instilled. Fear, however, had not wholly subdued curiosity, and even while trembling to such a degree that he could scarcely keep his teeth from chattering, the tanner followed with eager eye the movements of those he knew not whether to look upon as ghosts or living beings. The room was exactly in the state in which we last described it, with this difference merely, that the table, on which the lamp and books had been placed now lay overturned, as if in the course of some violent scuffle, and its contents distributed over the floor. The bed still remained, in the same corner, unmade, and its covering tossed. It was evident no one had entered the apartment since the night of the attempted assassination.

The first act of Gerald, who bore the light, followed closely by Sambo, was to motion the latter to raise the fallen table. When this was done he placed his lamp upon it, and sinking upon the foot of the bed, and covering his eyes with his hands, seemed for some moments utterly absorbed in bitter recollections. The negro, meanwhile, an apparent stranger to the scene, cast his eyes around him with the shrinking caution of one who finds himself in a position of danger, and fears to encounter some terrific sight, then, as if the effort was beyond his power, he drew the collar of his cloak over his face, and shuffling to get as near as possible to the bed as though in the act he came more immediately under the protection of him who sat upon it, awaited, in an attitude of statue-like immobility, the awakening of his master from his reverie.

Gerald at length withdrew his hands from his pallid face, on which the glare of the lamp rested forcibly, and, with a wild look and low, but imperative, voice, bade the old negro seat himself beside him still lower on the bed.

"Sambo," he inquired abruptly—"how old were you when the Indian massacre took place near this spot. You were then, I think I have heard it stated, the servant of Sir Everard Valletort?"

The old negro looked aghast. It was long since direct allusion had been made to his unfortunate master or the events of that period. Questioned in such a spot, and at such an hour, he could not repress the feeling of terror conjured up by the allusion. Scarcely daring to exceed a whisper, he answered.

"Oh Massa Geral, for Hebben's sake no talkee dat. It berry long time ago, and break poor nigger heart to tink ob it——"

"But I insist on knowing," returned Gerald loudly and peremptorily; "were you old enough to recollect the curse that poor heart-broken woman, Ellen Halloway, uttered on all our race, and if so what was it?"

"No, Massa Geral, I no sabby dat. Sambo den only piccaninny and Sir Ebbered make him top in e fort—oh berry bad times dat, Massa Geral. Poor Frank Hallabay e shot fust, because e let he grand fadder out ob e fort, and den ebery ting go bad—berry bad indeed."

"But the curse of Ellen Halloway, Sambo—you must have heard of it surely—even if you were not present at the utterance. Did she not," he continued, finding that the other replied not: "Did she not pray that the blood of my great grand father's children might be spilt on the very spot that had been moistened with that of her ill fated husband—and, that if any of the race should survive, it might be only with a view to their perishing in some unnatural and horrible manner. Was not this the case?"

"Oh yes, Massa Geral, berry bad tongue Ellen, affir he lose he husband—but, poor ting, he half mad and no sabby what he say. He time to start for he gun boat, Massa Geral."

The part Sambo had sustained in this short dialogue was a forced one. He had answered almost mechanically, and not altogether without embarrassment, the few queries that were put to him. Nay, so far was he governed by surrounding local influences, that the anguish he would, under other circumstances, have experienced, at this raking up of recollections he so sedulously avoided, was lost in terror, produced by his near and midnight propinquity to the fatal theatre of death. His only idea now was to leave the spot as quickly as he could.

Gerald had again covered his face with his hands, and appeared to be laboring under strong agitation of mind. At length he started abruptly up, and seizing the light, held it forward, stooping over the bed, as if gazing fixedly on some object within.

"No," he said with vehemence, "it shall never be. That part of the malediction, at least, shall *not* be accomplished. For once shall the curse of the innocent be unheeded."

The strange action and words of the excited officer, by no means contributed to allay the nervousness of the brave but superstitious negro. He had approached as near as he could to Gerald, without actually touching him; but when he remarked his abrupt movement, and heard the sudden outburst of feeling which accompanied it, he half fancied he was apostrophizing some spirit visible only to himself, and shocked and terrified at this idea, he turned away his head.

Sambo's alarm was not to terminate here. Scarcely had he bent his glance upon the window when he beheld two glaring eyes, magnified by his fear into thrice their natural size, fixed intently on that part of the room in which they stood. He attempted to cry out, but the sound was stifled in his throat, and he sank upon his knees, holding up his hands in an attitude of prayer—his teeth chattering, and his eyes fascinated by those which had produced in him this paroxysm of terror. Presently he thought he saw a mouth open, and a row of large and ragged teeth display themselves in a grin of derision. With a desperate effort he broke the spell that seemed to enchain every faculty, and called piteously and imploringly on the name of Gerald. The officer, who had continued gazing on the untenanted bed in deep abstraction, and seeming forgetfulness of all surrounding objects, turned hastily round, and was much concerned to observe the terrified expression of the old man's countenance.—Following the direction of his fixed gaze, he looked towards the window for a solution of the cause. At that moment a noise was heard without, as of a falling body. Gerald sprang towards the window, and hastily lifting it, thrust the lamp through; but nothing was visible, neither was there sound of footsteps to be heard.

Before daybreak on the following morning, the poor old negro, whom no living danger could daunt, had given but too alarming evidence that his reason was utterly alienated. His ravings were wild and fearful, and nothing could remove from his mind that the face he had beheld was that of the once terrible Wacousta—the same face which had presented itself, under such extraordinary circumstances, at the window of the Canadian's hut, on the night of the departure of his master, Sir Everard Valletort, and Captain De Haldimar, for Michillimackinac in 1763. Nay, so rooted was this belief, that, with the fervor of that zeal which had governed his whole life and conduct towards each succeeding generation of the family, he prayed and obtained, during a momentary gleam of reason, the promise of the much shocked Gerald, that he would never again set foot within the precincts of those fatal grounds.

Inexpressibly grieved as Gerald was at this sad and unexpected termination to his adventure, he had no time to linger near his unfortunate servant. The expedition was to set out in a few hours, and he had too completely bent his mind upon accompanying it to incur the slightest chance of a disappointment. Leaving the faithful and unfortunate creature to the care of his uncle's family, by every member of whom he was scarcely less loved than by himself, he took the ferry to the opposite shore within an hour after day break, and made such speed that, when Henry came down to breakfast he found, to his surprise, his brother already there.

During his ride, Gerald had had leisure to reflect on the events of the preceding night, and bitterly did he regret having yielded to a curiosity which had cost the unfortunate Sambo so much. He judged correctly that they had been followed in their nocturnal excursion, and that it was the face of some prying visitant which Sambo's superstitious dread had transformed into a hideous vision of the past. He recalled the insuperable aversion the old man had ever entertained to approach or even make mention of the spot, and greatly did he blame himself for having persisted in offering a violence to his nature, the extent of which had been made so fearfully obvious. It brought no consolation to him to reflect that the spot itself contained nought that should have produced so alarming an effect on a mind properly constituted. He felt that, knowing his weakness as he did, he ought not to have trifled with it, and could not deny to himself, that in enforcing his attendance,(with a view to obtain information on several points connected with the past), he had been indirectly the destroyer of his reason. There had been a season when the unhappy sailor would have felt a sorrow even deeper than he did, but Gerald was indeed an altered being—too much rapt in himself to give heed to others.

The painful nature of his reflections, added to the fatigue he had undergone, had given to his coumenance a more than usually haggard expression. Henry remarked it and inquired the cause, when his brother, in a few brief sentences, explained all that had occurred during his absence. Full of affection as he was for the old man, and utterly unprepared for such a communication, Henry could not avoid expressing deep vexation that his brother, aware as he was of the peculiar weakness of their aged friend, should have been inconsiderate enough to have drawn him thither. Gerald felt the reproof to be just, and for that very reason grew piqued under it. Shocked as he was at the condition of Sambo, Henry was even more distressed at witnessing the apparent apathy of his brother for the fate of one, who had not merely saved his life on a recent occasion, but had evinced a devotedness—a love for him—in every circumstance of life which seldom had had their parallel in the annals of human servitude. It was in vain that he endeavored to follow the example of Gerald, who, having seated himself at the breakfast table, was silently appeasing an appetite such as he had not exhibited since his return. Incapable of swallowing his food, Henry paced up and down the room, violently agitated and sick at heart. It seemed to him as if Sambo had been a sort of connecting link between themselves and the departed parents; and now that he was suddenly and fearfully afflicted, he thought he could see in the vista of futurity a long train of evils that threw their shadows before, and portended the consummation of some unknown, unseen affliction; having its origin in the incomprehensible alienation of his brother's heart from the things of his early love.

While he was yet indulging in these painful thoughts, the firing of a gun from the harbour—the signal for the embarkation of the troops—brought both Gerald and himself to a sense of other considerations. The latter was the first to quit the house. "Henry," he said with much emotion, "God bless you. It is possible that, as our service lies in different lines, we shall see but little of each other during this expedition—Of one thing however be assured—that although I am an unhappy man I am any thing but dead to feeling—Henry," he continued pressing his hand with warmth, "think not unkindly hereafter of your poor brother Gerald." A long embrace, in which each, although in silence, seemed to blend heart with heart, ensued, and both greatly relieved, as they always were after this generous expansion of their feelings, separated forthwith whither their respective duties summoned them.

CHAPTER VIII.

Seldom has there been witnessed a more romantic or picturesque sight than that presented by an expedition of batteaux moving across one of the Canadian lakes, during a season of profound calm. The uniform and steady pull of the crew, directed in their time by the wild chaunt of the steersman, with whom they ever and anon join in full chorus—the measured plash of the oars into the calm surface of the water—the joyous laugh and rude, but witty, jest of the more youthful and buoyant of the soldiery, from whom, at such moments, although in presence of their officers, the trammels of restraint are partially removed—all these, added to the inspiriting sight of their gay scarlet uniforms, and the dancing of the sunbeams upon their polished arms, have a tendency to call up impressions of a wild interest, tempered only by the recollection that many of those who move gaily on, as if to a festival—bright in hope as though the season of existence were to last for ever, may never more set eye upon the scenes they are fast quitting, with the joyousness produced by the natural thirst of the human heart for adventure, and a love of change.

On the second day of its departure from Amhertsburg, the expedition, preceded by the gun boats, entered the narrow river of the Miami, and, the woods on either shore being scoured by the Indians, gained without opposition the point of debarkation. Batteries having, under great difficulties, been erected on the right bank, immediately opposite to, and about six hundred yards from the American fort, which had been recently and hurriedly constructed, a heavy and destructive fire was, on the morning of the third day, opened from them, supported by the gun boats, one of which, commanded by Gerald Grantham, had advanced so close to the enemy's position as to have diverted upon herself the fire which would else have been directed to the demolition of a British battery, hastily thrown up on the left bank. The daring manifested by the gallant sailor was subject of surprise and admiration at once to friends and foes, and yet, although his boat lay moored within musket shot of the defences, he sustained but trifling loss. The very recklessness and boldness of his advance had been the means of his preservation, for, as almost all the shots from the battery flew over him, it was evident he owed his safety to the difficulty the Americans found in depressing their guns sufficiently to bear advantageously upon the boat, which, if anchored fifty yards beyond, they might have blown out of the water.

The limits of our story will not admit of a further detail of the operations of this siege. Suffice it that, notwithstanding the entire defeat and capture of a strong corps of the enemy, who were advancing to relieve the place, in the course of which a handful of British troops rendered themselves as conspicuous for valour, as the noble Tecumseh did for valour and clemency united, the siege, (a second time attempted,) was, after a final but fruitless attempt to decoy the enemy from his defences, abandoned as hopeless, and the expedition re-embarked and directed against Fort Sandusky, a post of the Americans, situate on the river of that name, and running also into Lake Erie.

Here, once more, was the British Artillery landed, while, under a heavy fire from the fort, the troops advanced within range, to take possession of an eminence whereon it was intended to erect the batteries. Two days were passed in incessant cannnonading, but, as at the Miami, without making the slightest impression on the green wood, that opened to receive each ball and closed unshaken the moment afterwards. Finding all idea of a practicable breach hopeless, it was at length resolved that an attempt at assault should be made, and, with this view, the troops were, on the afternoon of the second day, ordered to hold themselves in immediate readiness.

In consequence of the shallowness of the river, it had been found necessary to moor the gun boats at a point considerably below, and out of sight of the fort. Gerald Grantham had obtained permission to leave his command, and take charge of one of the batteries, which, however, he relinquished on the day of the assault, having successfully petitioned to be suffered to join the attack as a volunteer. In the dress of a grenadier soldier, disabled during the siege, he now joined the party of animated officers, who, delighted at the prospect of being brought once more in close contact with their enemies, after so many wearying days of inaction, were seated at a rude but plentiful repast in Captain Cranstoun's tent, and indulging in remarks which, although often uttered without aim or ill-nature, are as often but too bitter subject of after self-reproach to those who have uttered them. Of those who had originally set out on the expedition, the only officer of the —— Regiment absent was Henry Grantham, who, having been slightly wounded at the Miami, had, much against his inclination, been ordered back to Amhertsburgh, in charge of the sick and wounded of the detachment, and this so suddenly, that he had not had an opportunity of taking leave of his brother.

"Ha! Gerald, my fine fellow," exclaimed Captain Molineux, as the youth now joined their circle, so you have clapped on the true harness at last. I always said that your figure became a red jacket a devilish deal better than a blue. But what new freak is this? Had you not a close enough berth to Jonathan in the Miami, without running the risk of a broken head with us today in his trenches?"

"No such luck is there in store for my juniors, I fancy," replied Grantham, swallowing off a goblet of wine, which had been presented to him—"but if I do fall, it will be in good company. Although the American seems to lie quietly enough within his defences, there is that about him which promises us rather a hot reception."

"So much the better," said Villiers; "there will be broken heads for some of us--who do you think we have booked for a place to the other world?"

Gerald made no answer, but his look and manner implied that he understood himself to be the party thus favored.

"Not so," returned Villiers, "we can't afford to spare you yet besides the death of a blue jacket can in no way benefit us. What's the use of 'a bloody war and a sickly season,' that standard toast at every West India mess, if the juniors are to go off and not the seniors—Cranstoun's the man we've booked."

"Captain Cranstoun, I have the honor of wishing you a safe passage, and speedy promotion in Heaven," said Middlemore, draining off his glass. "Devilish good port this of yours. By the bye, as you have a better port in view, you cannot do better than assign over what is left of this to me."

"Thonk ye, Mr. Meeddlemore," retorted Cranstoun drily, yet good humouredly; "yeet as ye're to be attoched to my deveesion y'ell perhops roon jeest the same reesk, and as it may be that y'ell not want more wine than we've taken the day, any moore than mysel', a pleedge ye, in retoorn, a safe possage to Heeven, when a troost ye will be joodged for better qualities than ye poossess as a poonster."

"What," asked Gerald, with an unfeigned surprise, when the laugh against Middlemore had subsided; "and is it really in his own wine that you have all thus been courteously pledging Captain Cranstoun's death?"

"Even so," said Middlemore, rallying and returning to the attack, "he invited us all to lunch in his tent, and how could we better repay him for opening his hampers, than by returning his *spirit scot-free* and *unhampered* to Heaven."

"Oh, oh, oh," ejaculated St. Clair, stopping his ears and throwing up his eyes; "surely, Middlemore, if you are not shot this day, it must be that you were born to be hanged—

no man can perpetrate so horrible a pun, and expect to live."

"I'm hanged if I am then," returned the other; "but, talking of being shot—is a there another shot in the locker, Cranstoun—another bottle of port?"

"The shot that is reserved for you, will bring you acquainted with another locker than Cranstoun's I suspect," said Villiers; "one Mr. David Jones' locker—hit there eh?"

The low roll of a muffled drum, suddenly recalled the party from their trifling to considerations of a graver interest. It was the signal for forming the columns of attack. In a moment the tone—the air of ribaldry was exchanged for a seriousness that befitted the occasion, and it seemed as if a momentary reproach passed over the minds of those who had most amused themselves at the expense of Cranstoun, for each, as he quitted the tent, gave his extended hand to his host, who pressed it in a manner to show all was forgiven.

The English batteries had been constructed on the skirt of the wood surrounding the fort, from which latter they were separated by a meadow covered with long grass, about six hundred yards across at the narrowest point. Behind these the columns of attack, three in number, were now rapidly and silently formed. To that commanded by Captain Cranstoun, on the extreme left, and intended to assault the fort at the strongest point, Gerald Grantham had attached himself, in the simple dress, as we have observed, of a private soldier, and armed with a common musket. In passing, with the former officer, to take his position in front of the column, he was struck by the utter want of means for executing, with success, the duty assigned to the several divisions. Each column was provided with a certain number of axemen, selected to act as pioneers; but not one of the necessary implements was in a condition to be used; neither had a single fascine or ladder been provided, although it was well known a deep ditch remained to be passed before the axes, inefficient as they were, could be brought into use.

" Sooch," said Captain Cranstoun, with a sneer of much bitterness, and pointing to the blunted and useless implements, " are the peetiful theengs on which hong the lives of our brave fallows. Nae doot the next dispotches will say a great deal aboot the eexcellent arrangements for attock; but if ye do not fall, Geerald, a hope ye'll make a proper repreesentation of the affair. As ye belong to the other seervice, there's leetle fear the Geeneral can hurt your promotion for jeest speaking the truth. A Geeneral indeed! who'll say Fortune is not bleind to make a Geeneral of sooch as he?

It was not an usual thing for Cranstoun to express himself thus in regard to his superiors; but he was really vexed at the idea of the sacrifice of human life that must attend this wantonness of neglect, and imbecility of arrangement. He had, moreover, taken wine enough, not in any way to intoxicate, but sufficient to thaw his habitual caution and reserve. Fearless as his sword, he cared not for his own life; but, although a strict officer, he was ever attentive to the interests of his men, who, in their turn, admired him for his cool, unflinching courage, and would have dared any thing, under the direction of their Captain.

It was evident that the contempt of the sailor for the capacity of the leader, to whom it was well known all the minute arrangements were submitted, was not one whit inferior to what was entertained by the brave and honest Cranstoun. He, however, merely answered, as they both assumed their places in front, and with the air of one utterly indifferent to these disadvantages.

" No matter, Cranstoun, the greater the obstacles we have to contend against, the more glorious will be our victory. Where you lead, however, we shall not be long in following."

" Hem! since it is to be a game of follow-my-leader," said Middlemore, who now joined them, " I must not be far behind. A month's pay with either of you I reach the stockade first."

"Doone, Meeddlemore, doone," eagerly replied Cranstoun, and they joined hands in confirmation of the bet.

This conversation had taken place during the intervals occupied by the movements of the right and centre columns along the skirt of the wood, to equidistant points in the half circle embraced in the plan of attack. A single blast of the bugle now announced that the furthermost had reached its place of destination, when suddenly a gun—the first fired since noon from the English batteries—gave the signal for which all were now prepared.

In the next minute the heads of the several columns debouched from the wood, and, the whole advancing in double quick time, with their arms at the trail, moved across the meadow in the several directions assigned them. The space to be traversed by Captain Cranstoun's division was considerably the shortest of the three; but, on the other hand, he was opposed to that part of the enemy's defences where there was the least cover afforded to an assailing force. Meanwhile there was an utter repose in the fort, which for some moments induced the belief that the Americans were preparing to surrender their trust without a struggle, and loud yells from the Indians, who, from their cover in the rear, watched the progress of the troops with admiration and surprise, were pealed forth as if in encouragement to the latter to proceed. But the American Commander had planned his defence with skill. No sooner had the several columns got within half musket shot, than a tremendous fire of musketry and rifles was opened upon them from two distinct faces of the stockade. Captain Cranstoun's division, being the nearest, was the first attacked, and suffered considerably without attempting to return a shot. At the first discharge, the two leading sergeants, and many of the men, were knocked down; but neither Cranstoun, nor Middlemore, nor Grantham, were touched.

"Foorward men, foorward," shouted the former, brandishing his sword, and dashing down a deep ravine, that separated them from the trenches.

"On, my gallant fellows, on!—the left column for ever," cried Middlemore, imitating the example of his Captain, and, in his eagerness to reach the ditch first, leaving his men to follow as they could.

Few of these, however, needed the injunction. Although galled by the severe fire of the enemy, they followed their leaders down the ravine with a steadiness worthy of a better result; then, climbing up the opposite ascent, under a shower of bullets, yet without pulling a trigger themselves, made for the ditch their officer had already gained.

Cranstoun, still continuing in advance, was the first who arrived on the brink. For a moment he paused, as if uncertain what course to pursue, then, seeing Middlemore close behind him, he leaped in, and striking a blow of his sabre upon the stockade, called loudly upon the axemen to follow. While he was yet shouting, a ball from a loop-hole, not three feet above his head, entered his brain, and he fell dead across the trench.

"Ha! well have you won your wager, my noble Captain!" exclaimed Middlemore, putting his hand to his chest, and staggering from the effect of a shot he had that instant received. "You are indeed the *better* man," (he continued excited beyond his usual calm by the circumstances in which he found himself placed, yet unable to resist his dominating propensity, even at such a moment,) "and deserve the palm of honor this day. Forward, men, forward: —axemen do your duty. Down with the stockade, my lads, and give them a bellyfull of steel."

Scarcely had he spoken, when a second discharge from the same wall-piece that had killed Cranstoun passed through his throat. "Forward," he again but more faintly shouted, with the gurgling tone of suffocation peculiar to a wound in that region, then, falling headlong into the ditch, was in the next instant trodden under by the advance of the column who rushed forward, though fruitlessly, to avenge the deaths of their officers.

All was now confusion, noise, and carnage. Obeying the command of their leader, the axemen had sprung into the ditch, and, with efforts nerved by desperation, applied themselves vigorously to the task allotted them. But as well might they have attempted to raze the foundation of the globe itself. Incapable from their bluntness of making the slightest impression on the obstinate wood, the iron at each stroke rebounded off, leaving to the eye no vestige of where it had rested. Filled with disappointment and rage, the brave and unfortunate fellows dashed the useless metal to the earth, and endeavored to escape from the ditch back into the ravine, where, at least, there was a prospect of supplying themselves with more serviceable weapons from among their slain comrades; but the ditch was deep and slimy and the difficulty of ascent great. Before they could accomplish it, the Americans opened a fire from a bastion, the guns of which, loaded with slugs and musket balls, raked the trench from end to end, and swept away all that came within its range. This was the first check given to the division of the unfortunate Cranstoun. Many of the leading sections had leaped, regardless of all obstacles, into the trench, with a view of avenging their slaughtered officers; but these, like the axemen, had been carried away by the discharges from the bastion and the incessant fire poured upon them from the loop-holes of the stockade. Despairing of success, without fascines to fill up the ditch, or a ladder to scale the picketing that afforded cover to their enemies, there was no alternative but to remain and be cut down to a man, where they stood, or to retire into the brushwood that lined the ravine. The latter was finally adopted; but not before one third of the column had paid the penalty of their own daring, and what the brave Cranstoun had sneeringly termed the "General's excellent arrangements," with their lives. The firing at this time had now almost wholly ceased between the enemy and the columns on the right and centre, neither of which had penetrated beyond the ravine, and at a late hour in the evening the whole were drawn off.

Meanwhile, steady at his post at the head of the division, Gerald Grantham had continued to act with the men as though he had been one of themselves. During the whole course of the advance, he neither joined in the cheers of the officers, nor uttered word of encouragement to those who followed. But in his manner there was remarked a quietness of determination, a sullen disregard of danger, that seemed to denote some deeper rooted purpose than the mere desire of personal distinction. His ambition appeared to consist, not in being the first to reach or scale the fort, but in placing himself wherever the balls of the enemy flew thickest. There was no enthusiasm in his mien, no excitement in his eye; neither had his step the buoyancy that marks the young heart wedded to valorous achievement, but was, on the contrary, heavy, measured, yet firm. His whole manner and actions, in short, as reported to his brother on the return of the expedition by those who had been near him throughout the affair, was that of a man who courts not victory but death. Planted on the brow of the ditch, at the moment when Middlemore fell, he had deliberately discharged his musket into the loop-hole whence the shot had been fired; but although, as he seemed to expect, the next instant brought several barrels to bear upon himself, not one of these had taken effect. A moment after and he was in the ditch, followed by some twenty or thirty of the leading men of the column, and advancing towards the bastion, then preparing to vomit forth its fire upon the devoted axemen. Even here, Fate, or Destiny, or whatever power it be that wills the nature of the end of man, turned aside the death with which he already seemed to grapple. At the very moment when the flash rose from the havoc-dealing gun, he chanced to stumble over the dead body of a soldier, and fell flat upon his face. Scarcely had he touched the ground when he was again upon his feet; but even in that short space of time he alone, of those who had entered the ditch, had been left unscathed. Before him came bellying along the damp trench, the dense smoke from the fatal bastion, as it were a funeral shroud for its victims; and behind him were to be seen the mangled and distorted forms of his companions, some dead, others writhing in acute agony, and filling the air with shrieks, and groans, and prayers for water wherewith to soothe their burning lips, that mingled fearfully, yet characteristically, with the unsubdued roar of small arms.

It was now, for the first time, that Gerald evinced any thing like excitement, but it was the excitement of bitter disappointment. He saw those to whom the preservation of life would have been a blessing, cut down and slaughtered; while he, whose object it was to lay it down for ever, was, by some strange fatality, wholly exempt.

The reflections that passed with lightning quickness through his mind, only served to stimulate his determination the more. Scarcely had the smoke which had hitherto kept him concealed from the battery, passed beyond him, when, rushing forward, and shouting—"To the bastion, men—to the bastion!" he planted himself in front of the gun, and not three yards from its muzzle. Prevented by the dense smoke that choked up the trench, from ascertaining the extent of execution produced by their discharge, the American artillerymen, who had again loaded, were once more on the alert and preparing to repeat it. Already was the match in the act of descending, which would have blown the unfortunate Gerald to atoms, when suddenly an officer, whose uniform bespoke him to be of some rank, and to whose quick eye it was apparent the rash assailant was utterly unsupported, sprang upon the bastion, and, dashing the fuze from the hand of the gunner, commanded that a small sally.

port, which opened into the trench a few yards beyond the point where he stood, should be opened, and the brave soldier taken prisoner without harm. So prompt was the execution of this order, that, before Gerald could succeed in clambering up the ditch which, with the instinctive dread of captivity, he attempted, he was seized by half a dozen long-legged backwoodsmen, and, by these, borne hurriedly back through the sally-port which was again closed.

CHAPTER IX.

Defeated at every point and with great loss, the British columns had retired into the bed of the ravine, where, shielded from the fire of the Americans, they lay several hours shivering with cold and ankle deep in mud and water; yet consoling themselves with the hope that the renewal of the assault, under cover of the coming darkness, would be attended with a happier issue. But the gallant General, who appeared in the outset to have intended they should make picks of their bayonets, and scaling-ladders of each others bodies, now that a mound sufficient for the latter purpose could be raised of the slain, had altered his mind, and alarmed, and mayhap conscience stricken at the profuse and unnecessary sacrifice of human life which had resulted from the first wanton attack, adopted the resolution of withdrawing his troops. This was at length finally effected, and without further loss.

Fully impressed with the belief that the assailants would not be permitted to forego the advantage they still possessed in their near contiguity to the works, without another attempt at escalade, the Americans had continued calmly at their posts; with what confidence in the nature of their defences, and what positive freedom from danger, may be inferred from the fact of their having lost but one man throughout the whole affair, and that one killed immediately through the loop-hole by the shot that avenged the death of poor Middlemore. When at a late hour they found that the columns were again in movement, they could scarcely persuade themselves they were not changing their points of attack. A very few minutes however sufficed to show their error, for in the indistinct light of a new moon, the British troops were to be seen ascending the opposite face of the ravine and in full retreat. Too well satisfied with the successful nature of their defence, the Americans made no attempt to follow, but contented themselves with pouring in a parting volley, which however the obscurity rendered ineffectual. Soon afterwards the sally-port was again opened, and such of the unfortunates as yet lingered alive in the trenches were brought in, and every attention the place could afford paid to their necessities.

An advanced hour of the night brought most of the American officers together in their rude mess-room, where the occurrences of the day were discussed with an enthusiasm of satisfaction natural to the occasion. Each congratulated each on the unexpected success, but commendation was more than usually loud in favor of their leader, to whose coolness and judgment, in reserving his fire until the approach of the enemy within pistol shot, was to be attributed the severe loss and consequent check they had sustained.

Next became the topic of eulogium the gallantry of those who had been worsted in all but their honor, and all spoke with admiration of the devotedness of the two unfortunate officers who had perished in the trenches—a subject which, in turn, led to a recollection of the brave soldier who had survived the sweeping discharge from the bastion, and who had been so opportunely saved from destruction by the Commandant himself.

"Captain Jackson," said that officer, addressing one of the few who wore the regular uniform of the United States' army, "I should like much to converse with this man, in whom I confess, as in some degree the preserver of his life, I feel an interest. Moreover, as the only uninjured among our prisoners, he is the one most calculated to give us information in regard to the actual force of those whom we have this day had the good fortune to defeat, as well as of the ultimate destination of the British General. Notes of both these important particulars, if I can possibly obtain them, I wish to make in a despatch of which I intend you to be the bearer."

The Aid-de-Camp, for in that capacity was he attached to the person of Colonel Forrester, immediately quitted the room, and presently afterwards returned ushering in the prisoner.

Although Gerald was dressed, as we have said, in the uniform of the private grenadier, there was that about him which, in defiance of a person covered from head to foot with the slimy mud of the trenches, and a mouth black as ink with powder from the cartridges he had bitten, at once betrayed him for something more than he appeared.

There was a pause for some moments after he entered. At length Colonel Forrester inquired, in a voice strongly marked by surprise :—

" May I ask, sir, what rank you hold in the British army ?"

" But that I have unfortunately suffered more from your mud than your fire," replied Gerald coolly, and with undisguised bitterness of manner, " the question would at once be answered by a reference to my uniform."

" I understand you, sir ; you would have me to infer you are what your dress, and your dress alone, denotes--a private soldier ?"

Gerald made no answer.

" Your name, soldier ?"

" My name !"

" Yes ; your name. One possessed of the gallantry we witnessed this day cannot be altogether without a name."

The pale cheek of Gerald was slightly tinged. With all his grief, he still was man. The indirect praise lingered a moment at his heart, then passed off with the slight blush that as momentarily dyed his cheek.

" My name, sir, is a humble one, and little worthy to be classed with those who have this day written theirs in the page of honor with their heart's blood. I am called Gerald Grantham."

"Gerald Grantham!" repeated the Commandant, musingly, as though endeavoring to bring back the recollection of such a name.

The prisoner looked at him stedfastly in return, yet without speaking.

"Is there another of your name in the British squadron?" continued Colonel Forrester, fixing his eye full upon his prisoner.

"There are many in the British squadron whose names are unknown to me," replied Gerald, evasively, and faintly coloring.

"Nay," said Colonel Forrester, "that subterfuge more than any thing betrays you. Though not answered, I am satisfied. How we are to account for seeing a gallant sailor attacking us in our trenches, in the humble garb of a private soldier, and so out of his own element, I cannot understand; but the name of Gerald Grantham, coupled with your manner and appearance, assures us we are making personal acquaintance with one to whose deeds we are not strangers. Gentlemen," addressing his officers, "this is the Lieutenant Grantham, whose vessel was captured last autumn at Buffalo, and of whose gallant defence, my cousin, Captain Edward Forrester, has spoken so highly. Lieutenant Grantham," he pursued, advancing, and offering his hand, "when I had the happiness to save your life this day, by dashing aside the fuze that would have been the agent in your destruction, I saw in you but the brave and humble soldier, whom it were disgrace not to have spared for so much noble daring. Judge how great must be my satisfaction to know that I have been the means of preserving, to his family and country, one whose name stands so high even in the consideration of his enemies.

Poor Gerald! how bitter and conflicting must have been his feelings at that moment. On the one side, touched by the highest evidences of esteem a brave and generous enemy could proffer—on the other, annoyed beyond expression at the recollection of an interposition which had thwarted him in his fondest, dearest hope—that of losing, at the cannon's mouth, the life he loathed. What had been done in mercy and noble forbearance, was to him the direst punishment that could be inflicted :—yet how was it possible to deny gratitude for the motive which had impelled his preservation, or fail in acknowledgment of the appreciation in which he thus found himself personally held.

"It would be idle, Colonel Forrester," he said, taking the proffered hand, "after the manner in which you have expressed yourself, to deny that I am the officer to whom you allude. I feel deeply these marks of your regard, although I cannot but consider any little merit that may attach to me very much overrated by them. My appearance in this dress, perhaps requires some explanation. Prevented by the shallowness of the river from co-operating with the army in my gun-boat, and tired of doing nothing, I had solicited and obtained permission to become one of the storming party in the quality of volunteer, which of necessity induced the garb in which you now behold me. You know the rest."

"And yet, Colonel," said a surly-looking backwoodsman, who sat with one hand thrust into the bosom of a hunting frock, and the other playing with the richly ornamented hilt of a dagger, while a round hat, surmounted by a huge cockade, was perched knowingly over his left ear, covering, or rather shadowing, little more than one fourth of his head—"I reckon as how this here sort of thing comes within the spy act. Here's a commissioned officer of King George, taken not only in our lines, but in our very trenches in the disguise of a private soger. What say you, Captain Buckhorn?" turning to one somewhat younger and less uncouth, who sat next him habited in a similar manner. "Don't you think it comes within the spy act?"

Captain Buckhorn, however, not choosing to hazard an opinion on the subject, merely shrugged his shoulders, puffed his cigar, and looked at the Colonel as if he expected him to decide the question.

"As I am a true Tennessee man, bred and born, Major Killdeer," said the Aid-de-Camp Jackson, "I can't see how that can lie. To come within the spy act, a man must be in plain clothes, or in the uniform of his enemy. Now, Liftenant Grantham, I take it, comes in the British uniform, and what signifies a whistle if he wears gold lace or cotton tape, provided it be stuck upon a scarlet coat, and that in the broad face of day, with arms in his hand,—aye, and a devil of a desperation to make good use of them too"—he added, with a good naturedly malicious leer of the eye towards the subject of his defence.

"At all events, in my conceit, it's an attempt to undervally himself," pursued the tenacious Kentuckian Major. "Suppose his name warn't known as it is, he'd have passed for a private soger, and would have been exchanged for one, without our being any the wiser; whereby the United States' service, I calculate, would have lost an officer in the balance of account."

"Although there cannot be the slightest difficulty," observed Colonel Forrester, "in determining on the doubt first started by you, Major Killdeer, I confess, that what you have now suggested involves a question of some delicacy. In the spirit, although not altogether in the letter, of your suggestion, I agree; so much so, Mr. Grantham," he added, turning to Gerald, "that in violence to the inclination I should otherwise have felt to send you back to your lines, on parole of honor, I shall be compelled to detain you until the pleasure of my government be known as to the actual rank in which you are to be looked upon. I should say that, taken in arms as a combatant without rank, we have no right to know you as any thing else; but as I may be in error, I am sure you will see how utterly impossible it is for me to take any such responsibility upon myself, especially after the difficulty you have just heard started."

Gerald, who had listened to this discussion with some astonishment, was not sorry to find the manner of its termination. In the outset he had not been without alarm that the hero of one hour might be looked upon and hanged as the spy of the next; and tired as he was of life, much as he longed to lay it down, his neck had too invincible a repugnance to any thing like contact with a cord to render him ambitious of closing his existence in that way. He was not at all sorry, therefore, when he found the surly looking Major Killdeer wholly unsupported in his sweeping estimate of what he called the "spy act." The gentlemanly manner of Colonel Forrester, forming as it did so decided a contrast with the unpolished—even rude frankness of his second in command, was not without soothing influence upon his mind, and to his last observation he replied, as he really felt, that any change in his views as to his disposal could in no way effect him, since it was a matter of total indifference whether he returned to Amherstburg, or was detained where he was. In neither case could he actively rejoin the service until duly exchanged, and this was the only object embraced in any desire he might entertain of the kind.

"Still," added the Colonel, "although I may not suffer you to return yet into Canada, I can see no objection to according you the privilege of parole of honor, without at all involving the after question of whether you are to be considered as the soldier or the officer. From this moment therefore, Mr. Grantham, you will consider yourself a prisoner at large within the fort—or, should you prefer journeying into the interior, to sharing the privations and the dullness inseparable from our isolated position, you are at liberty to accompany Captain Jackson, my Aid-de-Camp, who will leave this within thirty-six hours, charged with dispatches for the Governor of Kentucky."

Gerald had already acknowledged to himself that, if any

thing could add to his wretchedness, it would he a compulsory residence in a place not only destitute itself of all excitement, but calling up, at every hour, the images of his brave companions in danger—men whom he had known when the sun of his young hopes shone unclouded, and whom he had survived but to be made sensible of the curse of exemption from a similar fate ; still, with that instinctive delicacy of a mind whose natural refinement not even a heavy weight of grief could wholly deaden, he felt some hesitation in giving expression to a wish, the compliance with which would, necessarily, separate him from one who had so courteously treated him, and whom he feared to wound by an appearance of indifference.

"I think, Mr. Grantham," pursued Colonel Forrester, remarking his hesitation, "I can understand what is passing in your mind. However I beg you will suffer no mere considerations of courtesy to interfere with your inclination. I can promise you will find this place most dismally dull, especially to one who has no positive duty to perform in it. If I may venture to recommend, therefore, you will accompany Captain Jackson. The ride will afford you more subject for diversion than any thing we can furnish here."

Thus happily assisted in his decision. Gerald said, "since, Sir, you leave it optional with me, I think I shall avail myself of your kind offer and accompany Captain Jackson. It is not a very cheering sight," he pursued, anxious to assign a satisfactory reason for his choice, "to have constantly before one's eyes the scene of so signal a discomfiture as that which our arms have experienced this day."

"And yet," said Colonel Forrester, "despite of that discomfiture, there was nothing in the conduct of those engaged that should call a blush into the cheek of the most fastidious stickler for national glory. There is not an officer here present," he continued, "who is not prepared to attest with myself, that your column in particular behaved like heroes. By the way, I could wish to know, (but you will use your own discretion in answering or declining the question, recollect,) what was the actual strength of your attacking force ?"

" I can really see no objection to a candid answer to your question, Colonel," returned Gerald, after a moment's consideration. " Each division was, I believe, for I cannot state with certainty, little more than two hundred strong, making in all, perhaps, from six hundred to six hundred and fifty men. In return, may I ask, the number of those who so effectually repulsed us ?"

" Why I guess only one hundred and fifty, and most all my volunteers," somewhat exultingly exclaimed Major Killdeer.

" Only one hundred and fifty men !" repeated Gerald, unable to disguise his vexation and astonishment.

" That ere's a poser for him," said the Major, turning and addressing Captain Buckhorn in an undertone, who replied to him with a wink from his nearest eye.

" Even so, Mr. Grantham," replied the Colonel. " One hundred and fifty men of all arms, save artillery, composed my force at the moment when your columns crossed the plain. To night we muster one hundred and forty nine."

" Good Heaven !" exclaimed Gerald warming into excitement, with vexation and pique, " what a disgraceful affair."

" Disgraceful, yes—but only in as far as regards those who planned, and provided (or rather ought to have provided) the means of attack. I can assure you, Mr. Grantham, that although prepared to defend my post to the last, when I saw your columns first emerge from the wood, I did not expect, with my small force, to have been enabled to hold the place one hour ; for who could have supposed that even a school boy, had such been placed at the head of an army, would have sent forward a storming party, without either fascines to fill a trench, or ladders to ascend from it when filled. Had these been provided, there can be no doubt of the issue, for, to repulse the attempt at escalade in one quarter, I must have concentrated the whole of my little force—and thereby afforded an unopposed entrance to the other columns—or even granting my garrison to have been sufficient to keep two of your divisions in check, there still remained a third to turn the scale of success against us."

"I can understand the satisfaction with which you discovered this wretched bungling on the part of our leaders," remarked Gerald with vexation.

"No sooner had I detected the deficiency," pursued Colonel Forrester, "than I knew the day would be my own, since the obstacles opposed to your attempt would admit of my spreading my men over the whole line embraced within the attack. The result, you see has justified my expectation. But enough of this. After the fatigues of the day you must require both food and rest. Captain Jackson, I leave it to you to do the honors of hospitality towards Mr. Grantham, who will so shortly become your fellow traveller, and if, when he has performed the ablutions he seems so much to require, my wardrobe can furnish any thing your own cannot supply to transform him into a backwoodsman, (in which garb I would strongly advise him to travel,) I beg it may be put under contribution without ceremony."

So saying, Colonel Forrester departed to the rude log hut that served him for his head quarters, first enjoining his uncouth second to keep a sufficient number of men on the alert, and take such other precautions as were necessary to guard against surprise—an event, however, of which little apprehension was entertained, now that the British troops appeared to have been wholly withdrawn.

Sick, wearied, and unhappy, Gerald was but too willing to escape to the solitude of retirement, to refuse the offer which Captain Jackson made of his own bed, it being his intention to sit up all night in the mess room, ready to communicate instantly with the Colonel in the event of any alarm. Declining the pressing invitation of the officers to join in the repast they were about to make for the first time since the morning, and more particularly that of Captain Buckhorn, who strongly urged him to "bring himself to an anchor and try a little of the Wabash," he took a polite but hasty leave of them all, and was soon installed for the night in the Aid-de-Camp's dormitory.

It would be idle to say that Gerald never closed his eyes that night—still more idle would it be to attempt a description of all that passed through a mind whose extent of wretchedness may be inferred from his several desperate, although unsuccessful, efforts at the utter annihilation of all thought. When he met Colonel Forrester and his officers in the mess room at breakfast, he was dressed, as had been recommended, in the hunting frock and belt of a backwoodsman; and in this, his gentlemanly figure looked to such advantage as to excite general attention—so much so indeed, that Major Killdeer was more than once detected in eying his own heavy and uncouth person, as if to ascertain if the points of excellence were peculiar to the dress or to the man. Sick and dispirited as he was, Gerald felt the necessity of an attempt to rally, and however the moralist may condemn the principle, there is no doubt that he was considerably aided in his effort by one or two glasses of bitters which Captain Buckhorn strongly recommended as being of his wife's making, and well calculated to put some colour into a man's face--an advantage in which, he truly remarked, Grantham was singularly deficient.

Accurate intelligence having been obtained from a party of scouts, who had been dispatched early in the morning to track their course, that the British General with his troops and Indians had finally departed, preparations were made about midday for the interment of the fallen. Two large graves were accordingly dug on the outer brow of the ravine, and into these the bodies of the fallen soldiers were deposited with all the honors of war. A smaller grave, within the fort, and near the spot where they so nobly fell, was considerately allotted to Cranstoun and Middlemore. There was a composedness on the brow of the former that likened him, even in death, to the living man; while, about the good-humoured mouth of poor Middlemore, played the same sort of self satisfied smile that had always been observable there, when about to deliver himself of a sally. Gerald, who had imposed upon himself the painful duty of attending to their last committal to earth, could not help fancying that Middlemore must have breathed his last with an inaudible pun upon his lips—an idea that inexpressibly affected him. Weighed down with sorrow as was his own soul, he had yet a tear for the occasion—not that his brave comrades were dead, but that they had died with so much to attach them to life—while he whose hope was in death alone had been chained, as by a curse, to an existence compared with which death was the first of human blessings.

On the following morning, after an early breakfast, he and Captain Jackson quitted the fort—Colonel Forrester, (who had appeared to remark that the brusque manner of his Aid-de-Camp was not altogether understood by his charge,) taking occasion at parting to assure the latter that, with all his eccentricity he was a kind hearted man, whom he had selected to be near him more for his personal courage, zeal, and general liberality of feeling, than for any qualifications of intellect he possessed.

The means provided for their transport into the interior were well assimilated to the dreariness of the country through which they passed. Two common pack horses, lean, galled by the saddle, and callous from long aquaintance with the admonitory influence both of whip and spur, had been selected by Captain Jackson as the best within the fort, and, as a first evidence of the liberality ascribed to him by his Commander, the fastest of these (if a choice there was) he selected for his own use. Neither were the trappings out of keeping with the steeds they decked. Moth eaten saddles, almost black with age, beneath which were spread pieces of dirty blanket to prevent further excoriation of the already bared and reeking back—bridles, the original thickness of which had been doubled by the incrustation of mould and dirt that pertinaciously adhered to them—stirrups and bits, with their accompanying buckles (the absence of curb chains being supplied by pieces of rope) covered with the rust of half a century—all afforded evidence of the wretchedness of resource peculiar to a back settlement population. Over the hard saddles, however, had been strapped the blankets which, when the travellers were fortunate enough to meet with a hut at the close of their day's ride, or, as was more frequently the case, when compelled to bivouac in the forest before the fire kindled by the industry of the hardy Aid-de-Camp, served them as their only couch of rest, while the small leather valisse tied to the pummel of the saddle, and containing their scanty wardrobe, was made to do the duty of the absent pillow. The blanket Gerald found to be the greatest advantage of his grotesque equipment—so much so indeed, that when compelled, by the heavy rains which took place shortly after their departure, to make it serve after the fashion of a backwoodsman as a covering for his loins and shoulders, he was obliged to own that his miseries, great as they were, were yet susceptible of increase.

Notwithstanding Captain Jackson had taken what, he considered to be, the best of the two Rosinantes for himself, Gerald had no reason to deny the character for kind-heartedness given of him by Colonel Forrester. Frequently, when winding through some dense forest, or moving over some extensive plain where nothing beyond themselves told of the existence of man, his companion would endeavour to divert him from the abstraction and melancholy in which he was usually plunged, and, ascribing his despondency to an unreal cause, seek to arouse him by the consolatory assurance that he was not the first man who had been taken prisoner—adding, that there was no use in snivelling, as "what was done couldn't be undone, and no great harm neither, as there was some as pretty gals in Kaintuck as could be picked out in a day's ride; and that to a good looking young fellow like himself, with nothing to do but to make love to them, *that* ought to be no mean consideration, enabling him, as it would, to while away the tedium of captivity." At other times he would launch forth into some wild rhapsody, the invention of the moment, or seek to entertain his companion with startling anecdotes connected with his encounters with the Indians on the Wabash, (where he had formerly served,) in the course of which much of the marvellous, to call it by the most indulgent term, was necessarily mixed up—not perhaps that he was quite sensible of this himself, but because he possessed a constitutional proneness to exaggeration that rendered him even more credulous of the good things he uttered than those to whom he detailed them.

But Gerald heard without being amused, and, although he felt thankful for the intention, was distressed that his abstraction should be the subject of notice, and his despondency the object of care. To avoid this he frequently suffered Jackson to take the lead, and following some distance in the rear with his arms folded and the reins loose upon his horse's neck, often ran the risk of having his own neck broken by the frequent stumbling of the unsure-footed beast. But the Captain as often returned to the charge, for, in addition to a sincere desire to rally his companion, he began at length to find it exceedingly irksome to travel with one who neither spoke himself nor appeared to enjoy speech in another; and when he had amused himself with whistling, singing, hallooing, and cutting a thousand antics with his arms, until he was heartily tired of each of these several diversions, he would rein in his horse to suffer Gerald to come up, and, after a conciliating offer of his rum flask, accompanied by a slice of hung beef that lined the wallet depending from his shoulder, (neither of which were often refused,) enter upon some new and strange exploit, of which he was as usual the hero. Efforced in a degree to make some return for the bribe offered to his patience, Gerald would lend--all he could--his ear to the tale; but long before the completion he would give such evidence of his distraction as utterly to disconcert the narrator, and cause him finally to have recourse to one of the interludes above described.

In this manner they had journeyed some days, when the rains suddenly commenced with a violence, and continued with a pertinacity, that might have worn out the cheerfulness of much less impatient spirits than those of our travellers, who, without any other protection than what was afforded by the blanket tightly girt round the loins, and fastened over the shoulder, in front of the chest, presented an appearance quite as wild as the waste they traversed. It was in vain, that in order to promote a more rapid circulation, they essayed to urge their jaded beasts out of the jog-trot in which they had set out. Accustomed to this from the time when they first emerged from colthood into horsehood, the aged steeds, like many aged senators of their day, were determined enemies to any thing like innovation on the long established customs of their caste; and although, unlike the said senators, they were made to bear all the burdens of the state, still did they not suffer themselves to be driven out of the sluggish habits in which sluggish animals, of every description, seem to feel themselves privileged to indulge. Whip and spur therefore were alike applied in vain, as to any accelerated motion in themselves; but with this advantage at least to their riders, that, while the latter toiled vigorously for an increase of vital warmth, through the instrumentality of their con-complying hacks, they found it where they least seemed to look for it—in the mingled anger and activity which kept them at the fruitless task.

It was at the close of one of those long days of wearying travel throughout a vast and unsheltered plain, (where only here and there rose an occasional cluster of trees, like oases in the desert,) that, drenched to the skin with the steady rain which, commencing with the dawn, had continued without a moment's intermission, they arrived at a small log-hut, situate on the skirt of a forest forming one of the boundaries of the vast savannah they had traversed. Such was the unpromising appearance of this apology for a human dwelling that, under any other circumstances, even the "not very d—d particular" Jackson, as the Aid-de-Camp often termed himself, would have passed it by without stopping; but after a long day's ride, and suffering from the greatest evils to which a traveller can well be subjected—cold, wet, and hunger—even so wretched a resting-place as this was not to be despised; and accordingly a determination was formed to stop there for the night. On riding up to the door, it was opened to their knock, when a tall man—apparently its only occupant, came forth—and, after surveying the travellers a moment with a suspicious eye, inquired "what the stranngers wanted?"

"Why, I guess," said Jackson, "it doesn't need much conjuration to tell that. Food and lodging for ourselves, to be sure; and a wisp of hay and tether for our horses.—Hospitality in short; and that's what no true Tennessee man, bred and born, ever refused yet. No, not even to an enemy, such a night as this."

"Then you must go further in search of it," replied the woodsman, surlily, "I don't keep no tavern, and ha'nt got no accommodation; and what's more, I reckon, I'm no Tennessee man."

"But any accommodation will do, friend. If you hav'nt got beds, we'll sit up all night, and warm our toes at the fire, and spin long yarns, as they tell in the Eastern sea-ports. Anything but turn a fellow out such a night as this."

"But I say, strannger," returned the man, fiercely and determinedly, "I a'nt got no room any how, and you shan't bide here."

"Oh, ho! my old cock, that's the ticket, is it? but you'll

see whether an old stager, like me, is to be turned out of any man's house such a night as this. I hav'nt served two campaigns against the Ingins and the British for nothing; and here I rest for the night."

So saying, the determined Jackson coolly dismounted from his horse, and unbuckling the girth, proceeded to deposit the saddle, with the valise attached to it, within the hut the door of which still stood open.

The woodsman, perceiving his object, made a movement, as if to bar the passage; but Jackson, with great activity, seized him by the wrist of the left hand, and, all powerful as the ruffian was, sent him dancing some few yards in front of the threshold before he was aware of his intention, or could resist the peculiar *knack* with which it was accomplished. The Aid-de-Camp, meanwhile, had deposited his saddle in a corner near the fire, and on his return to the door, met the inhospitable woodsman advancing as if to court a personal encounter.

"Now, I'll tell you what it is, friend," he said calmly, throwing back at the same time the blanket that concealed his uniform, and—what was more imposing—a brace of large pistols stuck in his belt. "You'd better have no nonsense with me, I promise you, or—" and he tapped with the fore finger of his right hand upon the butt of one of them, with an expression that could not be misunderstood.

The woodsman seemed little awed by this demonstration. He was evidently one on whom it might have been dangerous for one man, however well armed, to have forced his presence, so far away from every other human habitation; and it is probable that his forbearance then arose from the fact of their being two opposed to him, for he glanced rapidly from one to the other, nor was it until he seemed to have mentally decided that the odds of two to one were somewhat unequal, that he at length withdrew himself out of the door-way, as if in passive assent to the stay he could not well prevent.

"Just so, my old cock," continued Jackson, finding that he had gained his point, "and when you speak of this again, don't forget to say it was a true Tennessee man, bred and born, that gave you a lesson in what no American ever wanted—hospitality to a stranger. Suppose you begin and make yourself useful, by tethering and foddering old spare bones."

"I reckon as how you've hands as well as me," rejoined the surly woodsman, "and every man knows the ways of his own beast best. As for fodder, they'll find it on the skirt of the wood, and where natur' planted it."

Gerald meanwhile, finding victory declare itself in favor of his companion, had followed his example and entered the hut with his saddle. As he again quitted it, a sudden flash of light from the fire, which Jackson was then in the act of stirring, fell upon the countenance of the woodsman who stood without, his arms folded and his brow scowling, as if planning some revenge for the humiliation to which he had been subjected. In the indistinct dusk of the evening Grantham had not been able to remark more than the outline of the figure; but the voice struck him as one not unknown to him, although somewhat harsher in its tones than that which his faint recollection of the past supplied. The glance he had now obtained, momentary as it was, put every doubt to rest. What his feelings were in recognizing in the woodsman the traitor settler of the Canadas, Jeremiah Desborough, we leave to our readers to infer.

CHAPTER X.

THERE was a time when to have met his father's enemy thus, would have been to have called into activity all the dormant fierceness of Gerald's nature; but since they had last parted, a new channel had been opened to his feelings, and the deep and mysterious grief in which we have seen him shrouded, had been of so absorbing and selfish a nature, as to leave him little consideration for sorrows not his own. The rash impetuosity of his former character, which had often led him to act even before he thought, and to resent an injury before it could well be said to have been offered, had moreover given place to a self-command, the fruit of the reflective habits and desire of concealment which had made him latterly almost a stranger to himself.

Whatever his motives for outwardly avoiding all recognition of the settler, certain it is that, so far from this, he sought sedulously to conceal his own identity, by drawing the slouched hat, which formed a portion of his new equipment, lower over his eyes. Left to do the duties of the rude hostelry, Captain Jackson and he now quitted the hut, and leading their jaded, smoking, steeds a few rods off to the verge of the plain they had so recently traversed, prepared to dispose of them for the night. Gerald had by this time become too experienced in the mode of travelling through an American wilderness, not to understand that he who expects to find a companion in his horse in the morning, must duly secure him with the tether at night. Following, therefore, the example of the Aid-de-Camp, he applied himself, amid the still pelting rain, to the not very cleanly task of binding round the fetlock joints of his steed several yards of untanned hide strips, with which they were severally provided for the purpose. Each gave his steed a parting slap on the buttock with the hard bridle, Jackson exclaiming, "go ye luxurious beasts, ye have a whole prairie of wet grass to revel in for the night," and then left them to make the best of their dainty food.

While returning, Grantham took occasion to observe, that he had reason to think he knew the surly and inhospitable woodsman, by whom however he was not desirous of being recognized, and therefore begged as a favor that Captain Jackson would not, in the course of the night, mention his name, or even allude to him in any way that could lead to an inference that he was any other than he seemed, a companion and brother officer of his own; promising, in conclusion, to give him, in the course of the next day's journey, some little history of the man which would fully explain his motives. With this request Jackson unhesitatingly promised compliance, adding, good humouredly, that he was not sorry to pledge himself to any thing that would thaw his companion's tongue into sociability, and render himself, for the first time since their departure, a listener. Before entering the hut Gerald further observed in a whisper, that the better to escape recognition, he would, as much as possible, avoid joining in any conversation which might ensue, and therefore hoped his companion would not think it rude if he suffered him to bear the tax. Jackson again promised to keep the attention of the woodsman directed as much as possible to himself, observing, that he thought Gerald had already, to his cost, discovered he was not one easily tired out by conversation, should their host be that way inclined.

On opening the door of the cabin, they found that the woodsman, or more properly the settler as we shall again term him, making a virtue of necessity, had somewhat cheered its interior. A number of fine logs, sufficient to last throughout the night had been heaped upon the hearth, and these, crackling and fizzing, and emitting sparks in all the burly of a hickory wood-fire, gave promise of a night of comparative comfort. Ensconced in the farther corner of the chimney, the settler had already taken his seat, and, regardless of the entrance of the strangers, (with his elbows resting on his knees, and his face buried in his large palms), kept his eyes fixed upon the fire, as if with a sullen determination neither to speak nor suffer himself to be questioned. But the Aid-de-Camp was by no means disposed to humour him in his fancy. The idea of passing some eight or ten consecutive hours in company with two fellow beings, without calling into full play the bump of loquacity, with which nature had largely endowed him, was, in his view, little better than the evil from which his perseverance had just enabled him to escape. Making himself perfectly at home, he unbuckled the wet blanket from his loins, and spreading it, with that of Gerald, to dry upon the rude floor before the fire, drew forward a heavy uncouth looking table, (which, with two or three equally unpolished chairs, formed the whole of the furniture), and deposited thereon the wallet or haversack in which remained a portion of provision. He then secured the last vacant chair, and taking up a position on the right of the table which lay between himself and Gerald, let it fall upon the dry clay hearth, with a violence that caused the settler to quit his attitude of abstraction for one of anger and surprise.

"Sorry to disturb you, friend," he said; "but these chairs of yours are so curst heavy, there's no handling them decently; 'specially with cold fingers."

"Beggars, I reckon, have no right to be choosers," returned the settler; "the chairs is quite good enough for me—and no one axed you to sit on em."

"I'll tell you what it is, old cock," continued the Aid-de-Camp, edging his seat closer, and giving his host a smart friendly slap upon the thigh, "this dull life of yours don't much improve your temper. Why, as I am a true Tennessee man, bred and born, I never set eyes upon such a crab apple in all my life—you'd turn a whole dairy of the sweetest milk that ever came from prairie grass sour in less than no time. I take it, you must be crossed in love old boy, eh?"

"Crossed in hell," returned the settler, savagely. "I reckon as how it don't consarn you whether I look sour or sweet—what you want is a night's lodgin', and you've got it, so don't trouble me no more."

"Very sorry, but I shall," said Jackson, secretly congratulating himself that, now he had got the tongue of his host in motion, he had a fair chance of keeping it so. "I must trouble you for some bread, and whatever else your larder may afford. I'll pay you honestly for it, friend."

"I should guess," said the settler, his stern features brightening for the first time into a smile of irony, "as how a man who had served a campaign agin the Ingins and another agin the British, might contrive to do without sich a luxury as bread. You'll find no bread here I reckon."

"What, not even a bit of corn bread! Try, my old cock, and rummage up a crust or two, for hung beef is devilish tight work for the teeth, without a little bread of some sort for a relish."

"If you'd ha' used your eyes you'd ha' seen nothin' like a corn patch for twenty mile round about this. Bread never entered this hut since I been here. I don't eat it."

"More's the pity," replied Jackson, with infinite drollery; but though you may not like it yourself, your friends may."

"I *have* no friends—I *wish* to have no friends," was the sullen reply.

"More's the pity still," pursued the Aid-de-Camp, "but what do you live on then, old cock, if you don't eat bread?"

"Human flesh. Take that as a relish to your hung beef."

Scarcely had the strange confession escaped the settler's lips, when Jackson, active as a deer, was at the farther end of the hut, one hand holding the heavy chair as a shield before him, the other placed upon the butt of one of his pistols. The settler at the same moment quitted his seat, and stretching his tall and muscular form to its utmost height, burst into a laugh that sounded more like that of some wild beast than a human being. The involuntary terror produced in his guest was evidently a source of exultation to him, and he seemed gratified to think he had at length discovered the means of making himself looked upon with something like fear.

On entering the hut, Gerald had taken his seat at the opposite corner of the fire, yet in such a manner as to admit of his features being shaded by the projection of the chimney. The customs of the wilderness moreover rendering it neither offensive, nor even worthy of remark, that he should retain his hat, he had, as in the first instance, drawn it as much over his eyes as he conceived suited to his purpose of concealment, without exciting a suspicion of his design; and, as the alteration in his dress was calculated to deceive into a belief of his being an American, he had been enabled to observe the settler without much fear of recognition in return. A great change had taken place in the manner of Desborough. Ferocious he still was, but it was a ferocity, wholly unmixed with the cunning of his former years, that he now exhibited. He had evidently suffered much, and there was a stamp of thought on the heavy countenance that Gerald had never remarked there before. There was also this anomaly in the man, that while ten years appeared to have been added to his age—his strength was increased in the same proportion—a change that made itself evident by the attitude in which he stood.

"Why now I take it you must be jesting" at length exclaimed the Aid-de-Camp doubtingly, dropping at the same time the chair upon the floor, yet keeping it before him as though not quite safe in the presence of this self-confessed anthropophagos; "you surely don't mean to say you kill and pickle every unfortunate traveller that comes by here. If so I must apprehend you in the name of the United States Government."

"I rather calculate not Mister," sneered the settler. "Besides I don't eat the United States subjects; consequently they've no claim to interfere."

"Who the devil do you eat then," asked Jackson, gathering courage with his curiosity, and advancing a pace or two nearer the fire, "or is it all a hum?"

The settler approached the fire, stooped a little, and applying his shoulder to the top of the opening, thrust his right hand and arm up the chimney.

"I reckon that's no hum," he said, producing and throwing upon the table a piece of dark dry flesh, that resembled in appearance the upper part of a human arm. "If you're fond of a relish," he pursued with a fierce laugh; "you'll find that mighty well suited to the palate—quite as sweet as a bit of smok'd venison."

"Why you don't really mean to say that's part of a man?" demanded Jackson, advancing cautiously to the table, and turning over the shrivelled mass with the point of his dagger. "Why, I declare, its just the color of my dried beef."

"But I do though—and what's more, of my own killin' and dryin'. Purty naturist you must be not to see that's off an Ingin's arm."

"Oh an Ingin's only, is it?" returned the Aid-de-Camp, whose apprehension began rapidly to subside, now that he had obtained the conviction that it was not the flesh of a white man. "Well, I'm sure! who'd have thought it. I take it, old cock, you've been in the wars as well as myself."

"A little or so I reckon, and I expect to be in them agin shortly—as soon as my stock of food's out. I've only a thigh bone to pick after this, and then I'm off. But why don't you take your seat at the fire. There's nothin' so out of the way in the sight of a naked arm, is there? I reckon if you're a soger, you must have seen many a one lopped off in the wars."

"Yes, friend," said Jackson, altering the position of the table and placing it between the settler and himself; "a good many lopped off, as you say, and in a devil of a stew, but not exactly eaten. However be so good as to return this to the chimney, and when I've eaten something from my bag I'll listen to what you have to say about it."

"Jist so, and go without my own supper I suppose, to please you. But tarnation, while you're eatin' a bit of your hung beef I'll try a snack of mine."

So saying he deliberately took from the table the dried arm he had previously flung there, and, removing a large clasp knife from a pocket beneath his coarse hunting frock, proceeded to help himself to several thin slices, corresponding precisely in appearance with those which the Aid-de-Camp divided in the same manner.

Jackson had managed to swallow three or four pieces of his favorite hung beef with all the avidity of an appetite, rendered keen by the absence of every other stimulant than hunger; but no sooner did he perceive his host fastening with a degree of fury on his unnatural food, than, sick and full of loathing, his stomach rejected further aliment, and he was compelled to desist. During all this time Grantham, who, although he had assumed the manner and attitude of a sleeping man, was a watchful observer of all that passed, neither moved nor uttered a syllable, except on one occasion to put away from him the food Jackson had offered.

"Sorry to see your ride has given you so poor an appetite," said the settler, with a look expressive of the savage delight he felt in annoying his visitor. "I reckon that's rather unsavory stuff you've got there, that you can't eat it without bread. I say young man"—addressing Grantham, "can't you find no appetite neither, that you sit there snorin', as if you never meant to wake agin."

Gerald's head sunk lower on his chest, and his affectation of slumber became more profound.

"Try a drop of this," said Jackson, offering his canteen, after having drank himself, and with a view to distract attention from his companion. "You seem to have no liquor in the house, and I take it you require something hot as h–ll, and strong as d—n—n, after that ogre like repast of yours."

The settler seized the can, and raised it to his lips. It contained some of the fiery whiskey we have already described as the common beverage in most parts of America. This, all powerful as it was, he drained off as though it had been water, and with the greedy avidity of one who finds himself suddenly restored to the possession of a favorite and long absent drink.

"Hollo, my friend," exclaimed the angry Aid-de-Camp, who had watched the rapid disappearance of his "travellers best companion," as he quaintly enough termed it, down the capacious gullet of the settler—and snatching at the same moment the nearly emptied canteen from his hands. I take it, that's not handsome. As I'm a true Tenessee man, bred and born, it aint at all hospitable to empty off a pint of raw liquor at a spell, and have not so much as a glass of methiglin to offer in return. What the hell do you suppose we're to do tomorrow for drink, during a curst long ride through the wood, and not a house of call till nightfall along the road."

The settler drew a breath long and heavy in proportion to the draught he had swallowed, and when his lungs had again recovered their play, answered blusteringly, in a voice that betokened incipient intoxication.

"Roar me up a saplin' Mister, but you're mighty stingy of the Wabash. I reckon as how I made you a free offer of my food, and it war'nt no fault of mine if you did'nt choose to take it. It would only have been relish for relish after all—and that's what I call fair swap."

"Well, no matter," said Jackson soothingly; "what's done can't be undone, therefore I take it its no use argufying—however, my old cock, when next you got the neck of a canteen of mine, twixt your lips, I hope it may do the cockles of your heart good; that's all. But lets hear how you came by them pieces of nigger's flesh, and how it is you've taken it into your head to turn squatter here. You seem," glancing around, "to have no sleeping room to spare, and one may as well sit up and chat as have one's bones bruised to squash on the hard boards."

"It's a sad tale," said the settler gruffly and with a darkening brow, "and brings bitter thoughts with it; but as the liquor has cheered me up a bit, I don't much mind if I do tell you how I skivered the varmint. Indeed," he pursued savagely, "that always gives me a pleasure to think of, for I owed them a desperate grudge—the bloody red skins and imps of hell. I was on my way to Detroit, to see the spot once more where my poor boy Phil lay rottin', and one dark night (for I only ventured to move at night,) I came slick upon two Ingins as was lying fast asleep before their fire in a deep ravine. The one nearest to me had his face unkivered, and I knew the varmint for the tall dark Delaweer chief as made one of the party after poor Phil and me, a sight that made me thirst for the blood of the heathens as a child for mother's milk. Well, how do you suppose I managed them. I calculate you'd never guess. Why, I stole as quiet as a fox until I got jist atween them, and then holdin' a cocked pistol to each breast, I called out in a thunderin' voice that made the woods ring agin Kit-chimocomon, which you know, as you've been in the wars, signifies long knife or Yankee. You'd a laugh'd fit to split your sides I guess, to see the stupid stare of the devils, as startin' out of their sleep, they saw a pistol within three inches of each of'em. 'Ugh,' says they, as if they did'nt know well whether to take it as a joke or not. 'Yes, 'ugh' and be damn'd to you,' say's I: you may go and 'ugh' in hell next—and with that snap went the triggers, and into their curst carcasses went the balls. The one I killed outright but t'other the Delaweer chief, was by a sudden shift only slightly wounded, and he sprung on his feet and out with his knife. But I had a knife too, and all a disappinted father's rage to boot, so at it we went closin' and strikin' with our knives like two fierce fiends of the forest. It was noble sport sure*ly*. At last the Delaweer fell over the bleedin' body of his warrior and I top of him. As he fell the knife dropt from his hand and he could'nt reach it no how, while I still gripped mine fast. 'Ugh,' he muttered agin, as if askin' to know what I meant to do next. 'Ugh,' and be damn'd to you once more, say's I—and the pint of my long knife was soon buried in his black heart. Then, when I see them both dead I eat my own meal at their fire, for I was tarnation hungry, and while I was eatin' a thought came across me that it would be good fun to make smoked meat of the varmint, so when I had tucked it in purty considerably, what with hominy and dried bear's meat, moistened with a little Wabash I found in the Delaweer chief's canteen, I set to and regularly quartered them. The trunks I left behind, but the limbs I packed up in the blankets that had been used to kiver them, I reckon; and with them slung across my shoulders, like a saddle bag across a horse, I made tracks through the swamps and the prairies for this here hut, which I know'd no livin' soul had been nigh for many a long year. And now," he concluded with a low drunken laugh, "you've the history of the dried meat. There isn't much left but when all is gone I'm off to the wars, for I can't find no peace I reckon without my poor boy Phil." He paused a moment, and then, as if suddenly influenced by some painful recollection, he struck his hand with startling violence upon the table, and, while every feature of his iron countenance seemed worked up to a pitch of intensity, added with fearful calmness. "May God's curse light upon me if I don't have my revenge of them Granthams yet:—yes" he continued with increased excitement of voice and manner, while he kicked one of the blazing hickory logs in the chimney with all the savageness of drunken rage, causiug a multitude of sparks to spit forth as from the anvil of a smith,—"jist so would I kick them both to hell for having murdered my poor boy."

"Why, surely, Liftenant Grantham, he can't meant you?"

abruptly questioned the Aid-de-Camp, drawing back his chair and resting the palms of his hands upon his knees, while he fixed his eye keenly and inquiringly upon Gerald.

But Gerald had no time to answer him--Scarcely had the name escaped the lips of the incautious Jackson, when a yell of exultation from the settler drew him quickly to his feet, and in the next moment he felt one hand of his enemy grappling at his throat, while the fingers of the other were rapidly insinuating themselves into the hair that shadowed one of his temples, with the evident intention to "gouge" him. Weak and emaciated as he was, Gerald was soon made sensible of the disproportion of physical strength thus suddenly brought into the struggle, and as the savage laugh of the settler, as his fingers wound themselves closer and closer within the clustering hair, proclaimed his advantage, he felt that his only chance of saving the threatened eye was by having recourse to some sudden and desperate attempt to free himself from the gripe of his opponent. Summoning all his strength into one vigorous effort, he rushed forward upon his enemy with such force, raising himself at the same time in a manner to throw the whole weight of his person upon him, that the latter reeled backwards several paces without the power of resistance, and falling over the table towards which he had been intentionally propelled, sank with a heavy crash to the floor, still however retaining his firm hold of his enemy and dragging him after him.

Half throttled, maddened with pain, and even more bitterly stung by a sense of the humiliating position in which he found himself, the feelings of Gerald became uncontrollable, until his anxiety to inflict a mortal injury upon his enemy became in the end as intense as that of the settler. In their fall the table had been overturned, and with it the knife which Desborough had used with his horrid repast. As the light from the blazing fire fell upon the blade, it had once caught the unassailed eye of the officer, and was the next moment clutched in his grasp. He raised it with a determination, inspired by the agony he endured, at once to liberate himself and to avenge his father's murder, but the idea that there was something assassin-like in the act as suddenly arrested him, and 'ere he had time to obey a fresh impulse of his agony, the knife was forcibly stricken from his hand. A laugh of triumph burst from the lips of the half intoxicated Desborough, but it was scarcely uttered before it was succeeded by a yell of pain, and the hand that had contrived to entwine itself, with resistless force and terrible intent, in the waving hair of the youth, fell suddenly from its grasp, enabling its victim at length to free himself altogether and start once more to his feet.

Little more than a minute had been passed in the enactment of this strange scene. The collision, the overthrow, the upraising of the knife had followed each other in such rapid succession that, until the last desperate intention of Gerald was formed, the Aid-de-Camp had not had time to interpose himself in any way between the enraged combatants. His first action had been to strike away the murderous knife with the heavy butt of one of his pistols, the other to plant such a blow upon the "gouging" hand of the settler from the same butt, as effectually to compel him to relinquish his ferocious clutch. In both objects, as we have seen, he fully succeeded.

But although his right hand had been utterly disabled by the blow from Jackson's pistol, the fury of Desborough, fed as it was by the fumes of the liquor he had swallowed, was too great to render him heedful of aught but the gratification of his vengeance. Rolling rapidly over to the point where the knife had fallen he secured it in his left hand, and then, leaping nimbly to his feet, gathered himself into a spring upon his unarmed but watchful enemy. But before the bound could be taken, the active Aid-de-Camp, covering Gerald with his body and presenting a cocked pistol, had again thwarted him in his intention.

"I say now, old cock, you'd much better be quiet I

guess, for them sort of tantrums won't suit me. If this here Liftenant killed your son why he'll answer for it later, but I can't let you murder my prisoner in that flumgustious manner. I'm responsible for him to the United States Government, therefore just drop that knife clean and slick upon the floor, and let's have no more of this nonsense for the night."

But even the cocked pistol had not power to restrain the fierce—almost brutal—rage of the settler, whose growing intoxication added fuel to the fire which the presence of his enemy had kindled in his heart. Heedless of the determined air and threatening posture of the Aid-de-Camp, he made a bound forward, uttering a sound that resembled the roar of a wild beast rather than the cry of a human being, and struck over Jackson's shoulder at the chest of the officer. Gerald, whose watchful eye marked the danger, had however time to step back and avoid the blow. In the next moment the Aid-de-Camp, overborne by the violence of the collision, fell heavily backwards upon the rude floor, and in his fall the pistol went off lodging the ball in the sinewy calf of Desborough's leg. Stung with acute animal pain, the whole rage of the latter was now diverted from Gerald to the Aid-de-Camp, on whom (assuming the wound to have been intentional) he threw himself with the fury of a tiger, grappling as he closed with him at his throat. But the sailor in his turn now came to the rescue of his companion, and the scene for some time, as the whole party struggled together upon the floor in the broad red glare of the wood fire, was one of fearful and desperate character. At length after an immense effort, and amid the most horrid imprecations of vengeance upon them, the officers succeeded in disarming and tying the hands of the settler behind his back, after which dragging him to a distant corner of the hut, they secured him firmly to one of the open and mis-shapen logs which composed its frame. This done, Jackson divided the little that had been left of his "Wabash" with his charge, and then stretching himself at his length, with his feet to the fire, and his saddle for a pillow, soon fell profoundly asleep.

Too much agitated by the scene which had just passed, Gerald, although following the example of his companion, in stretching himself before the cheerful fire, was in no condition to enjoy repose. Indeed, whatever his inclination, the attempt would have been vain, for so dreadful were the denunciations of Desborough throughout the night, that sleep had no room to enter even into his thoughts. Deep and appalling were the curses and threats of vengeance which the enraged settler uttered upon all who bore the name of Grantham; and with these were mingled lamentations for his son, scarcely less revolting in their import than the curses themselves. Nor was the turbulence of the enraged man confined to mere excitement of language. His large and muscular form struggled in every direction, to free himself from the cords that secured him to the logs, and finding these too firmly bound to admit of the accomplishment of his end, he kicked his brawny feet against the floor with all the fury and impatience of a spirit, quickened into a livelier sense of restraint by the stimulus of intoxication. At length, exhausted by the efforts he had made, his struggles and his imprecations became gradually less frequent and less vigorous, until finally towards dawn they ceased altogether, and his deep and heavy breathing announced that he slept.

Accustomed to rise with the dawn, the Aid-de-Camp was not long after its appearance, in shaking off the slumber in which he had so profoundly indulged. The first object that met his eye as he raised himself up in a sitting posture from his rude bed, was Gerald stooping over the sleeping Desborough, one hand reposing upon his chest, the other holding the knife already alluded to, while every feature of his face was kindled into loathing and abhorrence of his prostrate and sleeping enemy. Startled by the expression he read there, and with the occurrences of the past night rushing forcibly upon his memory, the Aid-de-Camp called quickly out,

" Hold, Liftenant Grantham. Well, as I'm a true Tennessee man, bred and born, may I be most especially d—d, if I'd a thought you'd do so foul a deed. What! assassinate a sleeping drunken man?"

" Assassinate! Captain Jackson," repeated Gerald, raising himself to his full height, while a crimson flush of indignation succeeded to the deadly paleness which had overspread his cheek.

" Yes, assassinate," returned the Aid-de-Camp, fixing his eye upon that of his prisoner, yet without perceiving that it quailed under his penetrating glance. " It's an ugly word, I reckon, for you to hear, as it is for me to speak; but your quarrel last night—your fix just now—that knife,—Liftenant Grantham," and he pointed to the blade which still remained in the grasp of the accused. " Surely these things speak for themselves, and though the fellow has swallowed off all my Wabash, and be d—d to him, (making a fruitless attempt to extract a few drops from his canteen,) still I should n't like to see him murdered in that sort of way."

" I cannot blame you, Captain Jackson," said Gerald calmly, his features resuming their pallid hue. " These appearances, I grant, might justify the suspicion, horrible as it is, in one who had known more of me than yourself; but was assassination even a virtue, worlds would not tempt me to assassinate that man—wretch though he be—or even to slay him in fair and open combat."

" Then, I calculate, one night has made a pretty considerable change in your feelings, Liftenant," retorted the Aid-de-Camp. " You were both ready enough to go at it last night, when I knocked the knife out of your fist, and broke the knuckles of his gouging hand."

" I confess," said Gerald, again coloring, " that excessive pain made me wild, and I should have been tempted to have had recourse to any means to thwart him in his diabolical purpose. As you have said, however, the past night has effected a change in my feelings towards the man, and death from my hand, under any circumstances, is the last thing he has now to apprehend." Gerald sank his head upon his chest, and sighed bitterly.

"Well," said Jackson, "all this is queer enough; but what were you doing standing over the man just now with that knife, if it was not to harm him? And as for your countenance, it scowled so savage and passionate, I was almost afraid to look at it myself."

"My motive for the action I must beg you to excuse my entering upon," replied Gerald. "Of this, however, be assured, Captain Jackson, that I had no intention to injure yon sleeping villain. On the word of an officer and a gentleman, and by the kindness you have shown me on all occasions since our journey commenced, do I solemnly assure you this is the fact."

"And on the word of an officer, and a true Tennessee man, bred and born, I am bound to believe you," returned the American, much affected. "A man that could fight so wickedly in the field would never find heart, I reckon, to stick an enemy in the dark. No, Liftenant Grantham, you were not born to be an assassin. And now let's be starting—the day has already broke."

"And yet," returned Gerald, with a smile of bitter melancholy, as they hurried towards the spot where they had left their horses, "if any man ever had reason to act so as to merit the imputation of being such, I have. In that savage woodsman, Captain Jackson, you have beheld the murderer—the self acknowledged murderer of my father."

"God bless my soul!" cried Jackson, dropping the saddle which he carried, and standing still with very amazement. "A pretty fix I've got into, to be sure. Here's one man accuses another of murdering his son, and t'other, by way of quits, accuses him, in his turn, of murdering his father. Why, which am I to believe?"

"Which you please, Captain Jackson," said the sailor coolly, yet painedly; and he moved forward in pursuit of his horse.

"Nay, Liftenant Grantham," said the Aid-de-Camp, who had again resumed his burden, and was speedily at the side of his companion, "don't be offended. I've no doubt the thing's as you say, but you must make allowance for my ideas, never too much of the brightest, being conglomerated, after a fashion, by what I have seen and heard, since we let loose our horses last night upon this prairie."

"I am not offended, only hurt," replied Gerald, shaking the hand that was cordially tendered to him; "hurt that you should doubt my word, or attach any thing to the assertion of that man beyond the mere ravings of a savage and diseased spirit. Justice to myself demands that I should explain every thing in detail."

"Now that's what I call all right and proper," returned the Aid-de-Camp, "and should be done both for your sake and mine; but we will leave it till we get once more upon the road and in sight of a tavern, for its dry work talking and listening without even so much as a gum tickler of the Wabash to moisten one's clay."

They found their horses not far from the spot where they had been left on the preceding night, and these being speedily untethered and saddled, the travellers again pursued their route towards the capital of the State in which they found themselves. As they passed the hut, which had been the scene of so much excitement to both, the voice of Desborough whom they had left fast asleep, was heard venting curses and imprecations upon them both, for having left him there to starve, bound and incapable of aiding himself. Wretch as the settler was, Gerald could not reconcile to himself the thought of his being left to perish thus miserably, and he entreated the Aid-de-Camp to enter and divide the cords. But Jackson declared this to be impolitic, urging as a powerful reason for declining, the probability of his having fire arms in the hut, with which (if released,) he might follow and overtake them in their route, and sacrifice one or the other to his vengeance—an object which it would be easy to accomplish without his ever being detected. However, that the villain might have sustenance until some chance traveller should come later to his assistance, or he could manage to get rid of his bonds himself (which he might do in time) he consented to place within his reach all the dried meat that had been left of his Indian foes, together with a pail of water—the latter by way of punishment for having swilled away at his Wabash in the ungracious manner he had.

While Jackson was busied in this office of questionable charity, the rage and disappointment of the settler surpassed what it had hitherto been. Each vein of his dark brow rose distinctly and swelling from its surface, and he kicked and stamped with a fury that proclaimed the bitter tempest raging in his soul. When the Aid-de-Camp had again mounted, his shrieks and execrations became piercing, and for many minutes after they had entered into the heart of the forest in which the hut was situated, the shrill sounds continued to ring upon their ears in accents so fearful, that each felt a sensible relief when they were heard no more.

On the evening of the third day after this event, Jackson and our hero, between whom a long explanation on the subject of the settler had taken place, alighted at the door of the principal inn in Frankfort, the capital of Kentucky, which was their ultimate destination. To mine host Gerald was introduced by his escort with the formality usual on such occasions in America, and with the earnest recommendation to that most respectable personage that, as his own friend, as well as that of Colonel Forrester, every indulgence should be shown to the prisoner, that was not inconsistent with his position.

CHAPTER XI.

Few situations in life are less enviable than that of the isolated prisoner of war. Far from the home of his affections, and compelled by the absence of all other companionship, to mix with those who, in manners, feelings, and national characteristics, form, as it were, a race apart from himself, his recollections, already sufficiently embittered by the depressing sense of captivity, are hourly awakened by some rude contrast wounding to his sensibilities, and even though no source of graver irritation should exist, a thousand petty annoyances, incident to the position, are magnified by chagrin from mole-hills into mountains. Such, however, would be the effect produced on one only, who, thrown by the accident of war into the situation of a captive, should have no grief more profound, no sorrow deeper seated than what arose from the being severed from old, and associated with new and undesired ties; one to whom life was full of the fairest buds of promise, and whose impatience of the present was only a burning desire to enter upon the future. Not so with Gerald Grantham. Time, place, circumstance, condition, were alike the same--alike indifferent to him. In the recollections of the scenes he had so lately quitted, and in which his fairer and unruffled boyhood had been passed, he took no pleasure, while the future was so enshrouded in gloom that he shrank from its very contemplation. So far from trying to wring consolation from circumstances, his object was to stupify recollection to the uttermost. He would fain have shut out both the past and the future, contenting himself as he might with the present, but the thing was impossible. The worm had eaten into his heart, and its gnawings were too painful, not poignantly to remind him of the manner in which it had been engendered.

Upwards of a fortnight had elapsed since his arrival, and yet, although Captain Jackson, prior to his return to Sandusky, had personally introduced him to many highly respectable families in Frankfort, he uniformly abstained from cultivating their acquaintance, until at length he was, naturally enough, pronounced to be a most disagreeable specimen of a British officer. Even with the inmates of the hotel, many of whom were officers of his own age, and with whom he constantly sat down to the ordinary, he avoided every thing approaching to intimacy—satisfying himself merely with discharging his share of the commonest courtesies of life. They thought it pride—it was but an effect—an irremediable effect of the utter sinking of his sad and broken spirit. The only distraction in which he eventually took pleasure, or sought to indulge, was rambling through the wild passes of the chain of wooded hills, which almost encircles the Kentuckian capital, and extends for a considerable distance in a westerly direction. The dense gloom of these narrow vallies he had remarked on his entrance by the same route, and feeling them more in unison with his sick mind than the hum and bustle of a city, which offered nothing in common with his sympathies, he now frequently passed a great portion of the day in threading their mazes—returning however, at a certain hour to his hotel, conformably with the terms of his parole.

On one occassion, tempted by the mellow beauty of the season (it was now the beginning of October) he had strayed so far, and through passes so unknown to him, that when the fast advancing evening warned him of the necessity of returning, he found he had utterly lost his way. Abstracted as he usually was, he had yet reflection enough to understand that his parole of honor required he should be at his hotel at an hour, which it would put his speed to the proof to accomplish. Despairing of finding his way by the circuitous route he had originally taken, and the proper clue to which he had moreover lost, he determined, familiar as he was with the general bearings of the capital, to effect his return in a direct line across the chain of hills already alluded to. The deepening shadows of the wild scene, as he proposed to ascend that immediately before him, told that the sun had sunk beneath the horizon, and when he gained its summit, the last faint corruscations of light were passing rapidly away in the west. Still, by the indistinct twilight he could perceive that at his feet lay a small valley, completely hemmed in by the circular ridge on which he stood. This traversed, it was but to ascend the opposite section of the ridge, and his destination would be gained. Unlike the narrow rocky passes, which divided the hills in every other direction, in which he had previously wandered, this valley was covered with a luxuriant verdure, and upon this the feet of Gerald moved inaudibly even to himself. As he advanced more into the centre of the little plain, he thought he could perceive, at its extremity on the right, the dark outline of a building—apparently a dwelling house—and while he yet hesitated, whether he should approach it and inquire his most direct way to the town, a light suddenly appeared at that point of the valley for which he was already making. A few minutes sufficed to bring him to the spot whence the light had issued. It was a small circular building, possibly intended for a summer-house, but more resembling a temple in its construction, and so closely bordering upon the forest ridge, by a portion of the foliage by which it had previously been concealed, as to be almost confounded with it. It was furnished with a single window, the same through which the light now issued, and this narrow, elongated, and studded with iron bars, was so placed as to prevent one even taller than our hero from gazing into the interior, without the aid of some elevation. But Gerald, independently of his anxiety to reach the town in time to prevent comment upon his absence, had no desire to occupy himself with subjects foreign to his object. Curiosity was a feeling dead within his bosom, and he was preparing, without once staying his course, to ascend the ridge at the side of the temple, when he fancied he heard a suppressed groan, as of one suffering from intense agony—Not the groan, but the peculiar tone in which it was uttered, arrested his attention, and excited a vague yet stirring interest in his breast. On approaching closer to the temple, he found that at its immediate basement the earth had been thrown up into a sort of mound, which so elevated the footing as to admit of his reaching the bars of the window with his hands. Active as we have elsewhere shown him to be, he was not long in obtaining a full view of the interior, when a scene met his eye which rivetted him, as well it might, in utter astonishment. Upon the rude uncarpeted floor knelt a female, who, with clapsed and uplifted hands, had her eyes fixed upon a portrait that hung suspended from the opposite wall--her figure, clad in a loose robe of black, developing by its attitude a contour of such rich and symmetrical proportion as might be difficult for the imagination to embody. And who was the being upon whom his each excited sense now lingered with an admiration little short of idolatry ? One whom, a moment before, he believed to be still far distant, whom he had only a few months previously fled from, as from a pestilence, and whom he had solemnly sworn never to behold again, yet whom he continued to love with a passion that defied every effort of his judgment to subdue, making his life a wilderness—Matilda Montgomerie—And if her beauty had *then* had such surpassing influence over his soul, what was not its effect when he beheld her *now*, every grace of womanhood exhibited in a manner to excite admiration the most intense!

It would be vain to describe all that passed through the mind of Gerald Grantham, while he thus gazed upon her whose beauty was the rock on which his happiness had been wrecked. His first impulse had been to fly, but the fascination which rivetted him to the window deprived him of all power until eventually, of all the host of feelings that had crowded tumultuously upon his heart, passion alone remained triumphant. Unable longer to control his impatience, he was on the point of quitting his station, for the purpose of knocking and obtaining admission by a door which he saw opposite to him, when a sudden change in the attitude of Matilda arrested the movement.

She had risen, and with her long and dark hair floating over her white shoulders, now advanced towards the portrait, on which her gaze had hitherto been so repeatedly turned. This was so placed that Gerald had not previously an opportunity of remarking more than the indistinct outline, which proved it to represent a human figure ; but as she for a moment raised the light with one hand, while with the other she covered it with a veil which had been drawn aside, he distinctly saw that it was the portrait of an officer dressed in the American uniform ; and it even occurred to him that he had before seen the face, although, in his then excited state he could not recollect where. Even had he been inclined to tax his memory, the effort would have been impracticable, for another direction was now given to his interest.

On the left, and close under the window, stood a rude sofa and ruder table, the only pieces of furniture which Gerald could observe within the temple. Upon the former Matilda now reclined herself, and placing the candle upon the table at her side, proceeded to unfold and peruse a letter which she had previously taken from her pocket book. The same unconsciousness of observation inducing the same unstudiedness of action, the whole disposition of the form bore a character of voluptuousness, which the presumed isolation of her who thus exhibited herself, a model of living grace, alone could justify. But although the form was full of the eloquence of passion, one had but to turn to the pale and severe face, to find there was no corresponding expression in the heart. As heretofore, the brow of the American wore a cast of thought—only deeper, more decided—and even while her dark eyes flashed fire, as if in disappointment and anger at sundry passages in the letter over which she lingered, not once did the slightest color tinge her cheek, or the gloom dissipate itself from that cold brow. Emotion she felt, for this her heaving bosom and occasionally compressed lip betokened. Yet never was contrast more marked than that between the person and the face of Matilda Montgomerie, as Gerald Grantham then beheld her.

On one who had seen her thus for the first time, the cold, calm countenance of the singular girl, would have acted as a chastener to the emotions called up by the glowing expression of her faultless form, but although there was now a character of severity on her features, which must have checked and chilled the ardent admiration produced by that form on a mere stranger, Gerald but too well remembered occasions when the harmony of both had been complete, and when the countenance, rich in all those fascinations, which, even in her hours of utmost collectedness, never ceased to attach to the person, had beamed upon him in a manner to stir his very soul into madness. There were other and later recollections too, that forced themselves upon his memory ; but these, even though they recalled scenes in which the voluptuous beauty of Matilda shone paramount, were as blots upon the fair picture of the past, and he fain would have banished them from his mind for ever.

The letter on which the American was now engaged, Grantham had recognized, from its fold and seal, to be one he had written prior to parting with her, as he had supposed, for ever. While he was yet dwelling on this singularity, Matilda threw the letter upon the table at her side, and leaning her head upon her hand, seemed as if musing deeply upon its contents. The contraction of her brow became deeper, and there was a convulsed pressure of her lips as of one forming some determination, requiring at once strong moral and physical energy to accomplish. A cold shudder crept through the veins of Gerald, for too well did he fancy he could divine what was passing in the soul of that strange yet fascinating woman. For a moment a feeling of almost loathing came over his heart, but when, in the next moment, he saw her rise from the sofa, revealing the most inimitable grace, he burned with impatience to throw himself reckless of consequences at her feet, and to confess his idolatry.

After pacing to and fro for some moments, her dark and kindling eye alone betraying the excitement which her colorless cheek denied, Matilda again took up the light, and having once more approached the portrait, was in the act of raising the veil, when a slight noise made by Gerald, who in his anxiety to obtain a better view of her, had made a change in his position, arrested her ear; and she turned and fixed her eye upon the window, not with the disturbed manner of a person who fears observation, but with the threatening air of one who would punish an intrusion.

Holding the light above her head, she advanced firmly across the room, and stopping beneath the window, fixed her eye steadily and unshrinkingly upon it. The mind of Gerald had become a chaos of conflicting aud opposing feelings. Only an instant before and he would have coveted recognition, now his anxiety was to avoid it; but cramped in his attitude, and clinging as he was compelled, with his face close to the bars, his only means of doing so was by quitting his position altogether. He therefore loosened his hold, and dropped himself on the mound of earth from which he had contrived to ascend, but not so noiselessly, in the unbroken stillness of the night, as to escape the keen ear of the American. In the next moment Gerald heard a door open, and a well known voice demand, in tones which betrayed neither alarm nor indecision.

"Who is there?

The question was repeated in echo from the surrounding woods, and then died away in distance.

"Who of my people," again demanded Matilda, "has dared to follow me here in defiance of my orders?

Another echo of indistinct sounds, and all again was still.

"Whoever you are, speak," resumed the courageous girl. "Nay," she pursued more decidedly, as having moved a pace or two from the door, she observed a human form standing motionless beneath the window. "Think not to escape me. Come hither slave that I may know you. This curiosity shall cost you dear."

The blood of Gerald insensibly chilled at the harsh tone in which these words were uttered, and had he followed a first impulse he would at once have retired from the influence of a command, which under all the circumstances, occurred to him as being of prophetic import. But he had gazed on the witching beauty of the syren, until judgment and reason had yielded the rein to passion, and filled with an ungovernable desire to behold and touch that form once more—even although he should the next moment tear himself from it for ever —he approached and stood at the entrance of the temple, the threshold of which Matilda had again ascended.

No exclamation of surprise escaped the lips of the ever-collected American; and yet, for the first time that night, her cheek was suffused with a deep glow, the effect of which was to give to her whole style of beauty a character of radiancy.

"Gerald Grantham!"

"Yes, Matilda," exclaimed the youth, madly heedless of the past, while he rivetted his gaze upon her dazzling loveliness with such strong excitement of expression as to cause her own to sink beneath it, "your own Gerald—your slave kneels before you," and he threw himself at her feet.

"And what punishment does not that slave merit?" she asked, in a tone so different from that in which she had addressed her supposed domestic, that Gerald could scarcely believe it to be the same. "What reparation can he make for having caused so much misery to one who loved and cherished him so well. Oh! Gerald, what days, what nights of misery, have I not passed since you so unkindly left me." As she uttered the last sentence, she bent herself over the still kneeling form of her lover, while her long dark hair, falling forward, completely enveloped him in its luxuriant and waving folds.

"You will be mine, Matilda," at length murmured the youth, as he sat at her side on the sofa, to which on rising he had conducted her.

"Yours, only yours," returned the American, while she bent her face upon his shoulder. "But you know the terms of our union."

Had a viper stung him, Gerald could not have recoiled with more dismay and horror from her embrace. Again the features of Matilda became colorless, and her brow assumed an expression of care and severity.

"Then, if not to fulfil that compact, wherefore are you here?" and the question was put half querulously, half contemptuously.

"Chance, Destiny, Fate,—call it what you will," cried Gerald, obeying the stronger impulse of his feelings, and clasping her once more to his beating heart. "Oh! Matilda, if you knew how the idea of that fearful condition has haunted me in my thoughts by day, and my dreams by night, you would only wonder that at this moment I retain my senses, filled as my soul is with maddening—with inextinguishable love for you."

"And do you really entertain for me that deep, that excessive passion you have just expressed," at length observed Matilda, after some moments of silence, and with renewed tenderness of voice and manner, "and yet refuse the means by which you may secure me to you for ever?"

"Matilda," said Gerald, with vehemence, "my passion for you is one which no effort of my reason can control; but let me not deceive you—it is *now* one of the senses."

An expression of triumph, not wholly unmingled with

scorn, animated the features of Matilda. It was succeeded by one of ineffable tenderness.

"We will talk of this no more tonight, Gerald, but tomorrow evening, at the same hour, be here: then our mutual hopes, and fears, and doubts shall be then realized or disappointed, as the event may show. Tomorrow will determine if, as I cannot but believe, Destiny has sent you to me at this important hour. It is very singular," she added, as if to herself, her features again becoming deadly pale—"very singular, indeed!"

"What is singular, Matilda?" asked Gerald.

"You shall know all tomorrow," she replied; "but mind," and her dark eye rested on his with an expression of much tenderness, "that you come prepared to yield me all I ask."

Gerald promised that he would, and Matilda, expressing a desire to hear what had so unexpectedly restored him to her presence, he entered into a detail of all that had befallen him from the moment of their separation. She appeared to be much touched by the relation, and, in return, gave him a history of what she too had felt and suffered. She, moreover, informed him that Major Montgomerie had died of his wound shortly after their parting, and that she had now been nearly two months returned to her uncle's estate at Frankfort, where she lived wholly secluded from society, and with a domestic establishment consisting of slaves. These short explanations having been entered into, they parted—Matilda to enter her dwelling, (the same Gerald had remarked in outline,) in which numerous lights were now visible, and her lover to make the best of his way to the town.

CHAPTER XII.

Morning dawned, and yet no sleep had visited the eyes of Gerald Grantham. The image of Matilda floated in his mind, and, to the recollection of her beauty, he clung with an aching eagerness of delight that attested the extent of its influence over his imagination. Had there been nothing to tarnish that glorious picture of womanly perfection, the feelings it called up would have been too exquisite for endurance; but alas! with the faultless image, came also recollections, against which it required all the force of that beauty to maintain itself. One ineffaceable spot was upon the soul of that fascinating being; and though, like the spots on the sun's disk, it was hidden in the effulgence which surrounded it, still he could not conceal from himself that it *did* exist, to deface the symmetry of the whole. It was his knowledge of that fearful blemish that had driven him to seek in drunkenness, and subsequently in death, a release from the agonizing tortures of his mind. Virtue and a high sense of honor had triumphed so far, as not merely to leave his own soul spotless, but to enable him to fly from her who would have polluted it with crime; yet, although respect and love—the pure sentiments by which he had originally been influenced—had passed away, the hour of their departure had been that of the increased domination of passion, and far from her whose beauty was ever present to his mind, his imagination had drawn and lingered on such pictures, that assured as he was they could never be realized, he finally resolved to court death wherever it might present itself.

Restored thus unexpectedly to the presence of her who had been the unceasing subject of his thoughts, and under circumstances so well calculated to inflame his imagination, it cannot appear wonderful that Gerald should have looked forward to his approaching interview with emotions of the intensest kind. How fated, too, seemed the reunion. He had quitted Matilda with the firm determination never to behold her more, yet, by the very act of courting that death which would fully have accomplished his purpose, he had placed himself in the position he most wished to avoid. Presuming that Major Montgomerie, who had never alluded to Frankfort as his home, was still with his niece a resideut in the distant State in which he had left them—he had gladly heard Colonel Forrester name the Kentucky capital as the place of his destination ; for, deep and maddening as was his passion for Matilda, no earthly considerations could have induced him voluntarily to have sought her. Even since his arrival in Frankfort, it had been a source of consolation to him to feel that he was far removed from her who could have made him forget that, although the heart may wither and die, while self-esteem and an approving conscience remain to us, the soul shares not in the same decay—confesses not the same sting. Could he even have divined that in the temple to which his curiosity had led him, he should have beheld the being on whose image he doted, even while he shunned it, he would have avoided her as a pestilence.

The result of this terrible struggle of his feelings was a determination to see her once more—to yield up his whole soul to the intoxication of her presence, and then, provided she should still refuse to unite her fate to his, unhampered by the terrible condition of past days, to tear himself from her for ever.

Strong in this resolution, Gerald, to whom the hours had appeared as days since his rising, and who quitted Frankfort about his usual time, and, in order to avoid observation, took the same retired and circuitous route by which he had reached the valley the preceding evening. As he descended into the plain, the light from the window of the temple was again perceptible—In a few minutes he was in the room.

"Gerald—my own Gerald," exclaimed Matilda, as carefully closing the door after her lover, she threw herself into his embrace. Alas, weak man! Like the baseless fabric of a dream, disappeared all the lately formed resolutions of the youth.

"Yes! Matilda, your own Gerald. Come what will henceforth, I am yours."

A pause of some moments ensued, during which each felt the beating of the other's heart.

"Will you swear it, Gerald?" at length whispered Matilda.

"I will—I do swear it."

There was a sudden kindling of the dark eye of the American, and an outswelling of the full bust, that seemed to betoken exultation in the power of her beauty; but this was quickly repressed, and sinking on the sofa at the side of her lover, her whole countenance was radiant with the extraordinary expression Gerald had, for the first time, witnessed while she lingered on the arm of his uncle, Colonel D'Egville.

"Gerald," she said tenderly, "confirm the oath which is to unite us heart and soul, in one eternal Destiny. Swear upon this sacred volume, that your hand shall avenge the wrongs of your Matilda—of your wife. Ha! your wife, think of that," she added with sudden energy.

Gerald caught the book eagerly to his lips. "I swear it, Matilda—he shall die."

But scarcely had he sworn, when a creeping chill passed through his frame. His features lost all their animation, and throwing away the book on which the impious oath had been taken, he turned away his face from Matilda, and sinking his head upon his chest, groaned and wept bitterly.

"What! already Gerald, do you repent? Nay, tell me not that one thus infirm of purpose, can be strong of passion. You love me not, else would the wrongs of her you love arm you with the fiercest spirit of vengeance against him who has so deeply injured her. But, if you repent, it is but to absolve you from your oath, and then the deed must be my own."

The American spoke in tones in which reproach, expostulation, and wounded affection, were artfully and touchingly blended, and as she concluded, she too dropped her head upon her chest and sighed.

"Nay, Matilda, you do me wrong. It is one thing to swerve from the guilty purpose to which your too seductive beauty has won my soul, another to mourn as man should mourn, the hour when virtue, honor, religion, all the nobler principles in which my youth has been nurtured, have proved too weak to stem the tide of guilty passion. You say I love you not!" and he laughed bitterly. What greater proof would you require than the oath I have just taken?"

"It's fulfilment," said Matilda, impressively.

"It shall be fulfilled," he returned quickly, "but at least deny me not the privilege of cursing the hour when crime of so atrocious a dye could be made so familiar to my soul."

"Crime is a word too indiscriminately bestowed," said Matilda, after a momentary pause. "What the weak in mind class with crime, the strong term virtue."

"Virtue! what, to spill the blood of a man who has never injured me; to become a hired assassin, the price of whose guilt is the hand of her who instigates to the deed? If this be virtue, I am indeed virtuous."

"Never injured you!" returned the American, while she bent her dark eyes reproachfully upon those of the unhappy Gerald. "Has he not injured *me;* injured beyond all power of reparation, her who is to be the partner of your life?"

"Nay, Matilda," and Gerald again passionately caught and enfolded her to his heart, "that image alone were sufficient to mould me to your will, even although I had not before resolved. And yet," he pursued, after a short pause, "how base, how terrible to slay an unsuspecting enemy.

Would we could meet in single combat—and why not? Yes it can—it shall be so. Fool that I was not to think of it before. Matilda, my own love, rejoice with me, for there is a means by which your honor may be avenged, and my own soul unstained by guilt. I will seek this man, and fasten a quarrel upon him. What say you, Matilda—speak to me, tell me that you consent." Gerald gasped with agony.

"Never, Gerald," she returned, with startling impressiveness, while the color, which during the warm embrace of her lover had returned to it once more, fled from her cheek. "To challenge him would be but to ensure your own doom, for few in the army of the United States equal him in the use of the pistol or the small sword; and, even were it otherwise," she concluded, her eye kindling into a fierce expression, "were he the veriest novice in the exercise of both, my vengeance would be incomplete, did he not go down to his grave with all his sins on his head. No, no, Gerald, in the fulness of the pride of existence must he perish. He must not dream of death until he feels the blow that is aimed at his heart."

The agitation of Matilda was profound beyond any thing she had ever yet exhibited. Her words were uttered in tones that betrayed a fixed and unbroken purpose of the soul, and when she had finished, she threw her face upon the bosom of her lover, and ground her teeth together with a force that showed the effect produced upon her imagination, by the very picture of the death she had drawn.

A pause of some moments ensued. Gerald was visibly disconcerted, and the arm which encircled the waist of the revengeful woman dropped, as if in disappointment, at his side.

"How strange and inconsistent are the prejudices of man," resumed Matilda, half mournfully, half in sarcasm; "here is a warrior—a spiller of human life by profession; his sword has been often dyed in the heart bloop of his fellow man, and yet he shudders at the thought of adding one murder more to the many already committed. What child-like weakness!"

"Murder! Matilda; call you it murder to overcome the enemies of one's country in fair and honorable combat, and in the field of glory?"

"Call *you* it what you will—disguise it under whatever cloak you may—it is no less murder. Nay, the worst of murders, for you but do the duty of the hireling slayer. In cold blood, and for a stipend, do you put an end to the fair existence of him who never injured you in thought or deed, and whom, under other circumstances, you would perhaps have taken to your heart in friendship."

"This is true, but the difference of the motive, Matilda? The one approved of heaven and of man, the other alike condemned of both."

"Approved of man, if you will; but that they have the sanction of heaven, I deny. Worldly policy and social interests alone have drawn the distinction, making the one a crime, the other a virtue; but tell me not that an all wise and just God sanctions or approves the slaying of his creatures because they perish, not singly at the will of one man, but in thousands and tens of thousands at the will of another. What is there more sacred in the brawls of Kings and Potentates, that the blood they cause to be shed in torrents for some paltry breach of etiquette, should sit more lightly on their souls than the few solitary drops, spilt by the hand of revenge, on that of him whose existence is writhing under a sense of acutest injury?"

The energy with which she expressed herself, communicated a corresponding excitement to the whole manner and person of Matilda. Her eye sparkled and dilated, and the visible heaving of her bosom told how strongly her own feelings entered into the principles she had advocated. Never did her personal beauty shine forth more triumphantly or seducingly than at the moment when her lips were giving utterance to sentiments from which the heart recoiled.

"Oh Matilda," sighed Gerald, "with what subtlety of argument do you seek to familiarize my soul with crime. But the attempt is vain. Although my hand is pledged to do your will, my heart must ever mourn its guilt."

"Foolish Gerald," said Matilda; "why should that seem guilt to you, a man, which to me, a woman, is but justice; but that unlike me you have never entered into the calm consideration of the subject. Yes," she pursued with greater energy, "what you call subtlety of argument is but force of conviction. For two long years have I dwelt upon the deed, reasoning, and comparing, until at length each latent prejudice has been expelled, and to avenge my harrowing wrongs appeared a duty as distinctly marked as any one contained in the decalogue. You saw me once, Gerald, when my hand shrank not from what you term the assassin's blow, and had you not interfered then, the deed would not now remain to be accomplished."

"Oh, why did I interfere? why did my evil Genius conduct me to such a scene. Then had I lived at least in ignorance of the fearful act."

"Nay, Gerald, let it rather be matter of exultation with you that you did. Prejudiced as you are, this hand (and she extended an arm so exquisitely formed that one would scarce even have submitted it to the winds of Heaven) might not seem half so fair, had it once been dyed in human blood. Besides who so proper to avenge a woman's wrongs upon her destroyer, as the lover and the husband to whom she has plighted her faith for ever? No, no, it is much better as it is; and fate seems to have decreed that it should be so, else why the interruption by yourself on that memorable occasion, and why, after all your pains to avoid me, this our final union, at a moment when the wretch is about to return to his native home, inflated with pride and little dreaming of the fate that awaits him—Surely, Gerald, you will admit there is something more than mere chance in this?"

"About to return," repeated Grantham shuddering. "When, Matilda?"

"Within a week at the latest—perhaps within three days. Some unimportant advantage which he has gained on the frontier,has been magnified by his generous fellow citizens into a deed of heroism, and, from information conveyed to me, by a trusty and confidential servant, I find he has obtained leave of absence, to attend a public entertainment to be given in Frankfort, on which occasion a magnificent sword, is to be presented to him. Never, Gerald," continued Matilda her voice dropping into a whisper,while a ghastly smile passed over and convulsed her lips, "never shall he live to draw that sword. The night of his triumph is that which I have fixed for mine."

"An unimportant advantage upon the frontier," asked Gerald eagerly and breathlessly. "To what frontier, Matilda, do you allude ?

"The Niagara," was the reply.

"Are you quite sure of this ?"

"So sure that I have long known he was there," returned Matilda.

Gerald breathed more freely—but again he questioned:

"Matilda, when first I saw you last night, you were gazing intently upon yon portrait, (he pointed to that part of the temple where the picture hung suspended,) and it struck me that I had an indistinct recollection of the features."

"Nothing more probable," returned the American, answering his searching look with one of equal firmness. You cannot altogether have forgotten Major Montgomerie."

"Nay, the face struck me not as his. May I look at it?"

"Assuredly. Satisfy yourself."

Gerald quitted the sofa, took up the light, and traversing the room raised the gauze curtain that covered the painting. It was indeed the portrait of the deceased Major, habited in full uniform.

"How strange," he mused, "that so vague an impression should have been conveyed to my mind last night, when now I recal without difficulty those well remembered features." Gerald sighed as he recollected under what different circumstances he had first beheld that face, and dropping the curtain once more, crossed the room and flung himself at the side of Matilda.

"For whom did you take it, if not for Major Montgomerie?" asked the American after a pause, and again her full dark eye was bent on his.

"Nay I scarcely know myself, yet I had thought it had been the portrait of him I have sworn to destroy."

There was a sudden change of expression in the countenance of Matilda, but it speedily passed away, and she said with a faint smile.

"Whether is it more natural to find pleasure in gazing on the features of those who have loved, or those who have injured us?"

"Then whose was the miniature on which you so intently gazed, on that eventful night at Detroit?" asked Gerald.

"That," said Matilda quickly, and paling as she spoke—"that was *his*—I gazed on it only the more strongly to detest the original—to confirm the determination I had formed to destroy him."

"If *then*," returned the youth, "why not *now*—may I not see that portrait Matilda? May I not acquire some knowledge of the unhappy man whose blood will so shortly stain my soul?"

"Impossible," she replied. "The miniature I have since destroyed. While I thought the original within reach of my revenge, I could bear to gaze upon it, but no sooner had I been disappointed in my aim, than it became loathsome to me as the sight of some venemous reptile, and I destroyed it." This was said with undisguised bitterness.

Gerald sighed deeply. Again he encircled the waist of

his companion, and one of her fair, soft, velvet hands was pressed in his.

"Matilda," he observed, "deep indeed must be the wrong that could prompt the heart of woman to so terrible a hatred. When we last parted you gave me but an indistinct and general outline of the injury you had sustained. Tell me now all—tell me every thing," he continued with energy, "that can infuse a portion of the hatred which fills your soul into mine, that my hand may be firmer—my heart more hardened to the deed.

"The story of my wrongs must be told in a few words, for I cannot bear to linger on them," commenced the American, again turning deadly pale, while her quivering lips and trembling voice betrayed the excitement of her feelings. The monster was the choice of my heart—judge how much so when I tell you that, confiding in *his* honor, and in the assurance that our union would take place immediately, surrendered to him *mine*. A constant visitor at Major Montgomerie's, whose brother officer he was, we had ample opportunities of being together. We were looked upon in society as affianced lovers, and in fact it was the warmest wish of Major Montgomerie that we should be united. A day had even been fixed for the purpose, and it wanted, but eight and forty hours of the time, when an occurrence took place which blasted all prospect of our union for ever.

"I have already told you, I think," resumed Matilda, "that this little temple had been exclusively erected for my own use. Here however my false lover had constant ingress, and being furnished with a key, was in the habit of introducing himself at hours when, having taken leave of the family for the evening, he was supposed by Major Montgomerie and the servants to have retired to his own home. On the occasion to which I have just alluded, I had understood from him some business, connected with our approaching marriage, would detain him in the town to an hour too advanced to admit of his paying me his usual visit. Judge my surprise, and indeed my consternation, when at a late hour of the night I heard the lock of the door (from which I had removed my own key) turn, and my lover appear at the entrance.

There was a short pause, and Matilda again proceeded.

" Scarcely had he shown himself when he had again vanished, closing the door with startling violence. I sprang from the sofa and flew forth after him, but in vain. He had already departed, and with a heart sinking under an insurmountable dread of coming evil, I once more entered the temple, and throwing myself upon the sofa, gave vent to my feelings in an agony of tears."

" But why his departure, and whence your consternation?" asked Gerald, whose curiosity had been deeply excited.

" I was not alone," resumed Matilda, in a deep and solemn voice. " When he entered I was hanging on the neck of another.

Gerald gave a half start of dismay, his arm dropped from the waist of the American, and he breathed heavily and quickly.

Matilda remarked the movement, and a sickly and half scornful smile passed over her pale features. " Before we last parted, Gerald, I told you, not only that I was in no way connected with Major Montgomerie by blood, but that I was the child of obscure parents."

" What then ?"

" The man on whose neck I hung was my own father."

" It was Desborough !" said the youth, with an air and in a voice of extreme anguish.

" It was," returned Matilda, her face crimsoning as she reluctantly acknowledged the parentage. " But how knew you it ?"

" Behold the proof," exclaimed Gerald, with uncontrollable bitterness, as he drew from his bosom the portrait of a child which, from its striking resemblance, could be taken for no other than her to whom he now presented it."

"This is indeed mine," said Matilda, mournfully. "It was taken for me, as I have since understood, in the very year when I was laid an orphan and a stranger at the door of that good man, who calling himself my uncle, has been to me through life a more than father. Thank God," she pursued with greater animation, her large dark eyes upturned, and sparkling through the tears that forced themselves upwards, "thank, God he at least lives not to suffer through the acts of his adopted child. Where got you this, Gerald?" she proceeded, when after a short struggle she had suceeded in overcoming her emotion.

Gerald, who in his narrative of events, had purposely omitted all mention of Desborough, now detailed the occurrence at the hut, and concluded what the reader already knows, by stating that he had observed and severed from the settler, as he slept heavily on the floor, the portrait in question, which, added to the previous declaration of Matilda as to the obscurity of her birth, connected with other circumstances on board his gun boat, on his trip to Buffalo, had left an impression little short of certainty that he was indeed the father of the woman whom he so wildly loved."

For some minutes after this explanation there was a painful silence, which neither seemed anxious to interrupt—at length Gerald asked.

"But what had a circumstance, so capable of explanation, to do with the breaking off of your engagement, Matilda, or, did he, more proud—perhaps I should say less debased—than myself, shrink from uniting his fate with the daughter of a murderer?"

"True," said Matilda, musingly; "you have said, I think, that he slew your father. This thirst for revenge then would seem hereditary. *That* is the only, because it is the noblest, inheritance I would owe to such a being."

"But your affair with your lover, Matilda—how terminated

that?" demanded Gerald with increasing paleness, and in a faltering tone.

"In his falsehood and my disgrace. Early the next morning I sent to him, and bade him seek me in the temple at the usual hour. He came, but it was only to blast my hopes—to disappoint the passion of the woman who doated upon him. He accused me of a vile intercourse with a slave, and almost maddened me with ignoble reproaches. It was in vain that I swore to him most solemnly, the man he had seen was my father; a being whom motives of prudence compelled me to receive in private, even although my heart abhorred and loathed the relationship between us. He treated my explanation with deriding contempt, bidding me either produce that father within twenty-four hours, or find some easier fool to persuade that one, wearing the hue and features of the black could, by human possibility, be the parent of a white woman. Again I explained the seeming incongruity, by urging that the hasty and imperfect view he had taken was of a mask, imitating the features of a negro, which my father had brought with him as a disguise, and which he had hastily resumed on hearing the noise of the key in the door. I even admitted, as an excuse for seeing him thus clandestinely, the lowly origin of my father, and the base occupation he followed of a treacherous spy who, residing in the Canadas, came, for the mere consideration of gold, to sell political information to the enemies of the country that gave him asylum and protection. I added that his visit to me was to extort money, under a threat of publishing our consanguinity, and that dread of his (my lover's) partiality being decreased by the disclosure, had induced me to throw my arms, in the earnestness of entreaty upon his neck, and implore his secrecy; promising to reward him generously for his silence. I moreover urged him, if he still doubted, to make inquiry of Major Montgomerie, and ascertain from him whether I was not indeed the niece of his adoption, and not of his blood. Finally I humbled myself in the dust and, like a fawning reptile, clasped his knees in my arms, entreating mercy and justice. But no," and the voice of Matilda grew deeper, and her form became more erect; "neither mercy nor justice dwelt in that hard heart, and he spurned me rudely from him. Nothing short of the production of him he persisted in calling my vile paramour, would satisfy him; but my ignoble parent had received from me the reward of his secrecy, and he had departed once more to the Canadas. And thus," pursued Matilda, her voice trembling with emotion, "was, I made the victim of the most diabolical suspicion that ever haunted the breast of man."

Gerald was greatly affected. His passion for Matilda seemed to increase in proportion with his sympathy for her wrongs, and he clasped her energetically to his heart.

"Finding him resolute in attaching to me the debasing imputation," pursued the American, "it suddenly flashed upon my mind, that this was but a pretext to free himself from his engagement, and that he was glad to accomplish his object through the first means that offered. Oh, Gerald, I cannot paint the extraordinary change that came over my feelings at this thought; much less give you an idea of the rapidity with which that change was effected. One moment before and, although degraded and unjustly accused, I had loved him with all the ardour of which a woman's heart is capable: *now* I hated, loathed, detested him; and had he sunk at my feet, I would have spurned him from me with indignation and scorn. I could not but be conscious that the very act of having yielded myself up to him, had armed my lover with the power to accuse me of infidelity, and the more I lingered on the want of generosity such a suspicion implied, the more rooted became my dislike, the more profound my contempt for him, who could thus repay so great a proof of confidingness and affection."

"It was even while I lay grovelling at his feet," pursued Matilda, after a momentary pause, during which she evinced intense agitation, "that this sudden change (excited by this most unheard of injustice) came over my mind—I rose and stood before him; then asked, in a voice in which no evidence of passion could be traced, what excuse he meant to make to Major Montgomerie, for having thus broken off his engagement. He started at my sudden calmness of manner, but said that he thought it might be as well for my sake to name, what I had already stated to him, in regard to the obscurity of my birth, as a plea for his seceding from the connexion. I told him that, under all the circumstances, I thought this most advisable, and then pointing to the door, bade him begone, and never under any pretext whatever again to insult me with his presence. When he had departed, I burst into a paroxysm of tears, but they were tears shed not for the loss of him I now despised, but of wild sorrow at my umerited degradation. That conflict over, the weakness had for ever passed away, and never since that hour, has tear descended cheek of mine, associated with the recollection of the villain who had thus dared to trifle with a heart, the full extent of whose passions he has yet to learn."

There was a trembling of the whole person of Matilda, which told how much her feelings had been excited by the recollection of what she narrated, and Gerald, as he gazed on her beautiful form, could not but wonder at the apathy of the man who could thus have heartlessly thrown if from him for ever.

"Had the injury terminated here," resumed Matilda, "bitter as my humiliation was, my growing dislike for him who had so ungenerously inflicted it, might have enabled me to endure it. But, not satisfied with destroying the happiness of her who had sacrificed all for his sake, my perfidious lover had yet a blow in reserve for me, compared with which his antecedent conduct was mercy. Gerald," she continued, as she pressed his arm with a convulsive grasp, "will you believe that the monster had the infamy to confide to one of his most intimate associates, that his rupture with me was occasioned by his having discovered me in the arms of a slave--of one of those vile beings communion with whom my soul in any sense abhorred? How shall I describe the terrible feeling that came over my insulted heart at that moment. But no, no--description were impossible. This associate—this friend of his—dared, on the very strength of this infamous imputation, to pollute my ear with his disrespectful passion, and when, in a transport of contempt and anger, I spurned him from me, he taunted me with that which I believed confined to the breast, as it had been engendered only in the suspicion, of my betrayer. Oh! if it be dreadful to be falsely accused by those whom we have loved in intimacy, how much more so it to know that they have not had even the common humanity to conceal our supposed weakness from the world. From that moment revenge took possession of my soul, and I swore that my destroyer should perish by the hand of her whose innocence and whose peace he had blasted for ever."

"Shortly after this event," resumed Matilda, "my base lover was ordered to join his Regiment then stationed at Detroit. A year passed away, and during that period, my mind pondered unceasingly on the means of accomplishing my purpose of revenge; and so completely did I devote myself to a cool and unprejudiced cxamination of the subject, that what the vulgar crowd term guilt, apeared to me plain virtue. On the war breaking out, Major Montgomerie was also ordered to join the Regiment at Detroit, and thither I entreated him, to suffer me to accompany him. He consented, for knowing nothing of the causes which had turned my love into gall, he thought it not improbable that a meeting with my late lover might be productive of a removal of his prejudices, and our consequent reunion. Little did he dream that it was with a view to plunge a dagger into my destroyer's false heart, that I evinced so much eagerness to undertake so long, and so disagreeable a journey."

"Little more remains to be added," pursued Matilda, as she fixed her dark eyes with a softened expression on those of

Gerald, "since, with the occurrences at Detroit you are already sufficiently acquainted. Yet there is one point upon which I would explain myself. When I first became your prisoner, my mind had been worked up to the highest pitch of determination, and in my captor I at first beheld but an evil Genius who had interposed himself between me and my just revenge, when on the very eve of its consummation. Hence my petulance and impatience while in the presence of your noble General."

"And whence that look Matilda, that peculiar glance, which you bestowed upon me even within the same hour?"

Because in your frank and fearless mien I saw that manly honor and fidelity, the want of which had undone me; besides it flashed across my mind that daring, such as I have witnessed yours in the capture of our boat, might, if enlisted in my behalf, securely accomplish my revenge.

"Then, if so, why the cold, the mortifying reserve, you manifested when we met at dinner at my uncle's table?"

"Because I had also recollected that, degraded as I was, I ought not to seek the love of an honorable man, and that to win you to my interest would be of no avail, as, separated by the national quarrel, you could not, by possibility, be near to aid me in my plans."

"Then," said Gerald reproachfully, "it was merely to make me an instrument of vengeance that you sought me. Unkind Matilda!"

"Nay, Gerald,—recollect, that then I had not learnt to know you as I do now—I will not deny that when first I saw you, a secret instinct told me you were one whom I would have deeply loved had I never loved before; but betrayed and disappointed as I had been, I looked upon all men with a species of loathing—my kind, good, excellent, more than father, excepted—and yet, Gerald, there were moments when I wished even him dead." (Gerald started)—"yes! dead—because I knew the anguish that would crush his heart if he should ever learn that the false brand of the assassin had been affixed to the brow of his adopted child." Matilda sighed profoundly, and then resumed. "Later however, when the absence of its object had in some degree abated the keenness of my thirst for revenge, and when more frequent intercourse had made me acquainted with the generous qualities of your mind, I loved you Gerald, although I would not avow it, with a fervor I had never believed myself a second time capable of entertaining."

Again the countenance of Matilda was radiant with the expression just alluded to by her lover. Gerald gazed at her as though his very being hung upon the continuance of that fascinating influence, and again he clasped her to his heart.

"Matilda! oh my own betrothed Matilda!" he murmured

"Yes your own betrothed," repeated the American highly excited, the wife of your affection and your choice, who has been held up to calumny and scorn. Think of that, Gerald; she on whose fond bosom you are to repose your aching head, she who glories in her beauty only because it is beauty in your eyes, has been, betrayed, accused of a vile passion for a slave; yet he—the fiend who has done this grievous wrong—he who has stamped your wife with ignominy, and even published her shame—still lives. Within a week," she resumed, in a voice hoarse from exertion. "Yes, within a week, Gerald, he will be here--perhaps to deride and contemn you for the choice you have made."

"Within a week he dies," "exclaimed the youth. "Matilda, come what will, he dies. Life is death without you, and with you even crime may sit lightly on my soul But we will fly far from the habitations of man. The forest shall be our home, and when the past recurs to me you shall smile upon me with that smile--look upon me with that look, and I will forget it all. Yes" he pursued, with a fierce excitement snatching up the holy book, and again carrying it to his lips—" once more I repeat my oath. He who has thus wronged you, my own Matilda, dies—dies by the hand of Gerald Grantham—of your affianced husband."

There was another long embrace, after which the plan of operations was distinctly explained and decided upon. They then separated for the night—the infatuated Gerald with a load of guilt at his heart, no effort of his reason could remove, returning by the route he had followed on the preceding evening to his residence in the town.

CHAPTER XIII.

Leaving the lost Gerald for a time to all the horrors of his position, in which it would be difficult to say whether remorse or passion (each intensest of its kind) predominated, let us return to the scene where we first introduced him to the reader, and take a review of the Military events passing in that quarter.

After the defeat of the British columns at Sandusky, so far from any renewed attempt being made to interrupt the enemy in his strong holds, it became a question whether the position on the Michigan frontier could be much longer preserved. To the perseverance and promptitude of the Americans, in bringing new armies into the field, we have already had occasion to allude; but there was another quarter in which their strength had insensibly gathered, until it eventually assumed an aspect that carried apprehension to every heart. Since the loss of their flotilla at Detroit, in the preceding year, the Americans had commenced with vigour to equip one at Buffalo, which, in number and weight of metal, was intended to surpass the naval force on Lake Erie; and so silently and cautiously had they accomplished this task, that it was scarcely known at Amherstburg that a squadron was in the course of preparation, when that squadron (to which had been added the schooner captured from Gerald Grantham the preceding autumn) suddenly appeared off the harbour, defying their enemies to the combat. But the English vessels were in no condition to cope with so powerful an enemy, and although many a gallant spirit burned to be led against those who so evidently taunted them, the safety of the

Garrisons depended too much on the issue, for that issue to be lightly tempted.

But misfortune was now beginning to overcast the hitherto fair prospects of the British arms in the Western District of the Canadas; and what the taunts of an enemy, triumphing in the consciousness of a superior numerical force, could not effect, an imperative and miserably provided for necessity eventually compelled. Maintaining as we did a large body of wild and reckless warriors, together with their families, it may be naturally supposed the excesses of these people were not few; but it would have required one to have seen, to have believed, the prodigal waste of which they were often guilty. Acknowledging no other law than their own will, following no other line of conduct than that suggested by their own caprice, they had as little respect for the property of the Canadian inhabitant as they would have entertained for that of the American enemy. And hence it resulted, that if an Indian preferred a piece of fresh, to the salted meat daily issued from the Commissariat, nothing was more common than for him to kill the first head of cattle he found grazing on the skirt of the forest; secure the small portion he wanted; and leave the remainder to serve as carrion to the birds of prey of the country. Nay, to such an extent was this wanton spoliation carried, that instances have repeatedly occurred wherein cattle have been slain and left to putrify in the sun, merely because a warrior found it the most convenient mode by which to possess himself of a powder horn. All this was done openly—in the broad face of day, and in the full cognizance of the authorities; yet was there no provision made to meet the difficulties so guilty a waste was certain eventually to entail. At length the effect began to make itself apparent, and it was shortly after the first appearance of the American fleet that the scarcity of food began to be so severely felt as to compel the English squadron, at all hazards, to leave the port in search of supplies.

At this period, the vessel described in the commencement of our story, as having engaged so much of the interest and attention of all parties, had just been launched and rigged. Properly armed she was not, for there were no guns of the description used on ship board wherewith to arm her ; but now that the occasion became imperative, all nicety was disregarded in the equipment ; and guns that lately bristled from the ramparts of the fort were soon to be seen protruding their long and unequal necks from the ports. She was a gallant ship, notwithstanding the incongruity of her armament, and had her brave crew possessed but the experience of those who are nursed on the salt waves of ocean, might have fought a more fortunate fight (a better or a braver was impossible) than she did. But in the whole of the English fleet there could not be counted three score able or experienced seamen ; the remainder were children of the Canadian Lakes, warm with the desire to distinguish themselves in the eyes of their more veteran European companions, but without the knowledge to make their enthusiasm sufficiently available. The Americans, on the contrary, were all sons of the ocean.

It was a glorious day in September, the beautiful September of Canada, when the gallant Commodore Barclay sailed with his fleet, ostensibly in fulfilment on the mission for which it was dispatched, but in reality under the firm expectation of being provoked to action by his stronger and better disciplined enemy. To say that he would have sought that enemy, under the disadvantages beneath which he knew himself to labor, would be to say that which would reflect little credit on his judgment; but, although not in a condition to hold forth the flag of defiance, where there was an inferiority in all but the skill of the leader and the personal courage of the men, he was not one to shun the battle that should be forced upon him. Still to him it was an anxious moment, because the fame of other days hung upon an issue over which no efforts of his own could hold mastery, and as he gazed at his armless sleeve, he sighed for the presence of those whose agency had coupled the recollection of past victory with that mutilated proof of honorable conduct. He knew, moreover, the magnitude of the stake for which he was thus compelled to play, and that defeat to him would be the loss of the whole of the Western District. While the British ascendancy could be maintained on the Lake, there was little fear, lined as the forests were with Indian warriors, that the Americans would push any considerable force beyond the boundaries they had assigned themselves at Sandusky and on the Miami; but a victory once obtained by their fleet, there could be nothing to oppose the passage of their army in vessels and boats across the Lake.

Such were the thoughts that filled the mind of the Commodore (in common with all who calmly reasoned on the subject) as he crossed the bar that separated him from his enemy; but neither in look, nor word, nor deed, was there aught to reveal what was passing in the inward man; and when later the hostile fleet was signalized as bearing down upon them, he gave his orders to prepare for action, in the animated voice of one who finds certain victory within his reach, and exultingly hastens to secure it.

The events of that day the page of History has already recorded in terms alike flattering to the conqueror and the conquered. Let it suffice that the Americans triumphed. What the issue would have been, independently of all the disadvantages under which the English Commodore labored, had the latter not been borne severely wounded to his cabin early in the action, it is impossible to say; but as the final defeat was owing to his two principal vessels getting foul of each other, without being able to extricate themselves, it is not unfair to presume that his presence on deck would have done much to remedy the confusion produced by the accident.

One incident only connected with this action, and in which two individuals with whom our readers have made partial acquaintance, were the principal performers, we will venture to relate. It will be recollected that at the dinner table at Colonel D'Egville's on the day of the capture of Major Montgomerie, and his party, among the guests were the chiefs Split-log and Walk-in-the-Water, the former distinguished by a huge bulbous excrescence miscalled a nose, and exquisitely slit ears that dangled gracefully upon his shoulders, at every movement of his Memnon-like head: the latter by his striking resemblance to the puritans of the days of the Commonwealth. Now it so happened that Messieurs Split-log and Walk-in-the-water were filled with an unconquerable desire to distinguish themselves at sea, as they had often done on *terra firma*, and they accordingly proffered their services in the forth-coming struggle. We hope we shall not be considered as detracting in the slightest degree from the courage of these chiefs, when we state that the position chosen by them on board the Commodore's ship, was one where they apprehended the least danger to themselves—namely in the tops; for although an Indian will scorn to shrink from a rifle bullet or tomahawk, it by no means enters into his code of bravery that he is to submit himself to the terrible ordeal of being battered to a jelly by a huge globe of solid iron. With an alertness not common to the habits and corpulence of these celebrated chiefs, and fully calculating on exemption from danger while they plied their rifles successfully themselves, they ascended to the main top long before the action commenced. But they had counted without their host, for no sooner did the enemy begin to suffer from their fire, and perceive the quarter whence it came, when a swivel gun, loaded with grape, was brought to bear upon the point where they lay concealed. They had provided themselves with a breast work against small arms, but no breast work could resist the shower of iron hail that was directed towards them; and in proportion as the splinters and shot flew about their ears, so did their desire to distinguish themselves oze forth from the palms of Messrs. Split-log and Walk-in-the-Water;

in so much so indeed that, without waiting to descend the rigging in the usual manner, each abandoning his rifle, slid down by the first rope on which he could lay his hands ; nor stayed his course until he found himself squatted, out of all reach of danger in the lowest hold, and within the huge coils of a cable where already lay ensconced a black bear, the pet of one of the sailors. In this comfortable hiding place were Messrs Split-log and Walk-in-the-Water found, when at the close of the action they became, in common with those with whose fortunes they had identified themselves, prisoners of the Americans.

The action between the adverse fleets had been witnessed by many of the inhabitants of Amherstburg, and by the officers of thc Garrison who, at the first sounds of conflict, had ridden along the banks of the lake to be as near spectators of the event as the distance of the combatants, and the thick smoke in which they speedily became enveloped, would allow. High in hope, and strong in the reliance they placed upon the skill and experience of the English Commodore, each had looked forward with confidence to the overthrow of the enemy, even with the limited means and unequal resources placed at his disposal. Great therefore was the disappointment of all, when after the firing, which raged for two hours without intermission, had finally ceased, they found the English squadron lay a mere wreck upon the waters, and in the very act of being towed by their more fortunate enemies into the harbour they had but recently quitted to engage them. But on none did the disappointment of that hour sit more heavily than on Tecumseh. He had watched the whole conflict with an anxious eye and a swelling heart, for he well knew what important results to himself and kindred hung upon the issue ; but filled with enthusiastic admiration as he was of the Naval Captain, he had believed that personal devotedness and heroism alone were sufficient to compensate for the absence of advantages he had heard named, without fully comprehending either their import or their influence upon the chances of victory. The event painfully undeceived him, and although his generous heart warmed with the same love for him whose valour, profitless even though it proved, was sufficiently attested by the shattered condition of almost every vessel of his little Squadron, he read in the downfall of him in whose aid he had so much confided, the annihilation of the English power in that remote region of the Canadas, and the consequent destruction of all his hopes of retrieving his race from the hated thraldom of American tyranny and American usurpation. Such was the first feeling of that noble Warrior, but his was not a soul to despoud under the infliction of even a worse trial than that just recorded, and in proportion as the danger and difficulty increased, so rose his energy and his desire to surmount them.

The result of the unlucky contest was, as had been anticipated, to open a free passage across the lake to the American armies, whose advance by land had been so repeatedly and effectually checked on former occasions, as to leave them little inclination for a renewal of an attempt in that quarter. Now however that they could forward a fleet of boats, under cover of the guns of their Squadron, to the very outworks of Amherstburg, the difficulty was at once removed; and an overwhelming army of not less than ten thousand men, were speedily assembled near Sandusky, with a view to the final invasion of Amherstburg and consequent recapture of Detroit.

Under these disheartening circumstances—the want of provisions being daily more and more felt by the troops and inhabitants—it became necessary to hold a council of war, to determine upon the course that should be pursued. Accordingly the whole of the chiefs and officers of the Garrison met in the hall already described in the beginning of our narrative, when it was proposed by General Proctor, at the conclusion of a speech in which the increasing difficulties and privations of the garrison were emphatically enumerated, that the fortifications should be razed to the ground, the dock yards and other public works destroyed, and the allied forces of English and Indians make the best of their way by land to join the centre division of the army on the Niagara frontier.

The indignation of Tecumseh, at what he conceived to be a base and cowardly abandonment of a position which stout hearts and willing hands might yet make available against any force the enemy should push forward for its reduction, was excessive and appropriately expressed. Filled with esteem as he was for the character and courage of General Brock, while a no less sincere admiration of the gallant but unfortunate Commodore Barclay animated his noble and generous heart, he could ill disguise his contempt for the successor of the former. Little familiarized as he was with the habits of European warfare, it could not escape the penetrating observation of such a mind, that the man who now proposed giving up his command without a struggle in its defence, was the same who, at French town, had suffered his troops to be cut to pieces, through mere nervousness to attack with the bayonet; and who, later at Sandusky, had through grossest neglect and ignorance, not only lost the means of securing a certain victory, but occasioned the most shameful waste of human life; neither had it escaped his observation that on almost every occasion wherein the hostile armies were brought in contact, he who called himself a leader was invariably a follower, and a follower at a most respectful distance—a mode of heading an army, so differing from Tecumseh's own view of the duties of a great chief, that he could not understand by what perversion of the judgment of his really brave fellows, who were erroneously called his followers, he had been suffered to continue in his command so long.

Under this impression of feeling towards the General, it may readily be supposed that Tecumseh was not sparing of his censure on the mode of proceeding which had been suggested by that officer—nay, he even carried his contempt and indignation so far, as to term him the coward he believed him to be; and had this merit, that he told, in plain and unvarnished language, what many of the English officers most religiously believed also, although their tongues dared not of course give utterance to the thought. He threw additional force into his spirited and exciting speech, by instituting a comparison between him to whom he addressed himself, and the gallant but unfortunate officer whose defeat had driven them to the necessity of debating the unworthy question of flight—a comparison which tended but to show how high the one had been raised, how low the other had been sunk, in the estimation of the truly brave; and concluded by a vivid expression of his determination to remain with his warriors and maintain the contest alone.

The animated delivery of the Warrior had communicated to the lesser chiefs an enthusiasm of approbation that carried them wholly beyond the bounds of the quiet and grave demeanor, so usually distinguishing their deliberative assemblies; and like the wild outburst of a fitful storm, rose the clamorous yells that told how responsively the heart of each excited chief beat to that of his great leader. There was a moment during that wild and tumultuous expression of the common feeling, when the British officers looked as if they expected some more serious results of the General's proposition than the mere utterance of the dissatisfaction it had created. But the apprehension soon passed away, for a sudden and commanding movement of the proud Tecumseh stayed the tempest his own powerful eloquence had raised,—and the quiet and order of the scene were restored, with a promptitude not inferior to that with which it had been interrupted.

The result of the proceedings of the day, was a compromise of the views of the two parties; and it was decided, that although the defences of Amherstburg and Detroit should be destroyed, and those forts evacuated, a final stand should be made near the Moravian village, on the banks of the narrow river Thames, on the line of communication with the Niagara frontier. If the opportunity permitted, and the Americans suffered them to remain unmolested, fortifications were to be constructed on this spot, and a rallying point for the numerous tribes of dispersed Indians finally preserved.

A few days later, and the work of destruction was entered upon and soon completed. The little British Army, scarcely excèeding eight hundred men of all arms, commenced its march at night, lighted by the flames of the barracks which had given them shelter for the last time. As they passed the fort of Detroit the next day, dense columns of smoke and flame were to be seen rising high in air, from the various public edifices, affording a melancholy evidence of the destruction which usually tracks a retreating army. Many an American inhabitant looked on at the work of destruction, as if he would fain have arrested the progress of an element which at once defaced the beauty of the town, and promised much trouble and inconvenience to those whom they knew to be at hand, for their final deliverance from the British yoke. But the Garrison continued stern spectators of the ruin they had been compelled to effect, until the flames had attained a power which rendered their suppression an impossibility; then and then only, did they quit the scene of conflagration, and embarking in the boats which had been kept in readiness for their transport, joined their comrades, who waited for them on the opposite bank. The two Garrisons thus united; the whole preceded by a large body of Indians, were pushed forward to the position which had been selected on the Thames, and both shores of the Detroit were left an unresisting conquest to the Americans.

Meanwhile, these latter had not been slow in profiting by the important advantages which had crowned their arms on the lake. On the third day after the retreat of the British Garrison from Amherstburg, a numerous fleet of large boats was discovered from the town pushing for Hartley's point, under cover of the united Squadrons. Unopposed as these were, their landing was soon effected, and a few hours later the American stars were to be seen floating over the still smoking ruins of the British fortress. Emboldened by the unexpected ease with which he had rendered himself finally master of a position so long coveted, the American General at once resolved to follow and bring his retreating enemy to action if possible. A force of five thousand men (fifteen hundred of whom were mounted rifles) was accordingly pushed forward; and so rapid and indefatigable was the march of these, that they came up with the retreating columns before they had succeeded in gaining the village, at which it was purposed that their final stand should be made. The anxiety of General Proctor to save the baggage waggons containing his own personnal effects, had been productive of the most culpable delay, and at the moment when his little army should have been under cover of entrenchments, and in a position which offered a variety of natural defensive advantages, they found themselves suddenly overtaken by the enemy in the heart of a thick wood, where, fatigued by the long and tedious march they had made under circumstances of great privation, they had scarcely time to form in the irregular manner permitted by their broken position, before they found themselves attacked with great spirit, and on all sides by a force more than quadruple their own. The result may easily be anticipated. Abandoned by their General, who at the very first onset, drove his spurs into the flanks of his charger and fled disgracefully from the scene of action, followed by the whole of his personal staff, the irregularly formed line of the little British Army, was but ill prepared to make effectual resistance to the almost invisible enemy by whom it was encompassed; and those whom the rifle had spared, were to be seen, within an hour from the firing of the first shot, standing conquered and disarmed, between the closing lines of the victorious Americans.

But although the English troops (sacrificed as they must

be pronounced to have been, by their incapable leader) fell thus an easy prey to the overwhelming force brought against them, so did not their Indian allies, supported and encouraged as these were by the presence of their beloved Chieftain. It was with a sparkling eye and a glowing cheek that, just as the English troops had halted to give unequal battle to their pursuers, Tecumseh passed along the line, expressing in animated language the delight he felt at the forthcoming struggle, and when he had shaken hands with most of the officers (we fancy we can feel the generous pressure of his fingers even at this remote period) he moved into the dense forest where his faithful bands were lying concealed, with a bounding step that proved not only how much his heart had been set upon the cast, but how completely he confided in the result. And who shall say what that result might not have been even notwithstanding the discomfiture of the English had the heroic Chieftain been spared to his devoted country! But this was not fated to be. Early in the action he fell by the hand of a distinguished leader of the enemy,* and his death carried, as it could not fail to do, the deepest sorrow and dismay into the hearts of his followers, who although they continued the action long after his fall, and with a spirit that proved their desire to avenge the loss of their noble leader, it was evident, wanted the directing genius of him they mourned to sustain them in the effort. For several days after the action did they continue to hang upon the American rear, as the army again retired with its prisoners upon Detroit; but each day their attack became feebler and feebler, announcing that their numbers were fast dispersing into the trackless region from which they had been brought, until finally not a shot was to be heard disturbing the night vigils of the American sentinels.

With the defeat of the British army, and the death of Tecumseh, perished the last hope of the Indians to sustain

* Colonel Johnson, now Vice-President of the United States.

themselves as a people against the inroads of their oppressors. Dispirited and dismayed, they retired back upon the hunting grounds which still remained to them, and there gave way both to the deep grief with which every heart was overwhelmed at the loss of their truly great leader, and to the sad anticipations which the increasing gloom that clouded the horizon of their prospects naturally induced.

CHAPTER XIV.

The interview so fatal in its results to Gerald's long formed resolutions of virtuous purpose was followed by others of the same description, and in the course of these, Matilda, profiting by her knowledge of the past, had the address so to rivet the chains which fettered the senses of her lover, by a well timed, although apparently unintentional display of the beauty which had enslaved him, that so far from shrinking from the fulfilment of the dreadful obligation he had imposed upon himself, the resolution of the youth became more confirmed as the period for its enactment drew nigher. There were moments when, (his passion worked up to intensity by the ever-varying, over-exciting picture of that beauty, would have anticipated the condition on which he was to become possessed of it for ever, but on these occasions the American would assume an air of wounded dignity, sometimes of deep sorrow; and alluding to the manner in which her former confidence had been repaid, reproach him with a want of generosity, in seeking to make her past weakness a pretext for his present advances. Yet even in the very moment she most denied him, she so contrived that the restrained fire should burn with tenfold fury within his heart—rendering him hourly more anxious for her possession, even as he became hourly less fastidious about the means of attainment.

At length the day arrived when Gerald—the once high, generous and noble minded Gerald,—was to steep his soul in guilt—to imbrue his hands in the life blood of a fellow creature. The seducer of Matilda had arrived, and even in the hotel in which Grantham resided, the entertainment was to be given by his approving fellow citizens, in commemoration of the heroism which had won to him golden opinions from every class. It had already been arranged that the assassination was to take place on the departure of their victim from the banquet, and consequently at a moment when, overcome by the fumes of wine, he would be found incapable of opposing any serious resistance to their design. The better to facilitate his close and unperceived approach to the unhappy man, a pair of cloth shoes had been made for her lover by the white hands of Matilda, with a sort of hood or capuchin of the same material, to prevent recognition by any one who might accidentally pass him on the way to the scene of the contemplated murder. Much as Gerald objected to it, Matilda had peremptorily insisted on being present herself, to witness the execution of the deed, and the same description of disguise had been prepared for herself. In this resolution the American, independently of her desire to fortify the courage of her lover by her presence, was actuated by another powerful and fearful motive, which will be seen presently.

The private residence of the officer was situated in a remote part of the town, and skirting that point of the circular ridge of hills where the lights in the habitation of Matilda had attracted the notice of Gerald, on the first night of his encounter. To one who viewed it from a distance, it would have seemed that the summit of the wood-crowned ridge must be crossed before communication could be held between the two dwellings which lay as it were back to back, on either side of the formidable barrier; but on a nearer approach, a fissure in the hill might be observed, just wide enough to admit of a narrow horse track or foot path, which wound its sinuous course from the little valley into the open space that verged upon the town, on gaining which the residence of the American officer was to be seen rising at the distance of twenty yards. It was in this path, which had been latterly pointed out to him by his guilty companion, that Gerald was to await the approach of the intended victim, who on passing his place of concealment, was to be cautiously followed and stabbed to the heart ere he could gain his door.

Fallen as was Gerald from his high estate of honor, it was not without a deep sense of the atrocity of the act he was about to commit that he prepared for its accomplishment. It is true that, yielding to the sophistry of Matilda's arguments, he was sometimes led to imagine the avenging of her injuries an imperative duty; but such was his view of the subject only when the spell of her presence was upon him. When restored to his calmer and more unbiassed judgment, in the solitude of his own chamber, conscience resumed her sway, and no plausibility of pretence could conceal from himself that he was about to become that vilest of beings—a common murderer. There were moments even when the dread deed to which he had pledged himself appeared in such hideous deformity that he fain would have fled on the instant far from the influence of her who had incited him to its perpetration, but when the form of Matilda rose to his mental eye, remorse, conscience, every latent principle of virtue, dissolved away, and although he no longer sought to conceal from himself that what he meditated was crime of the blackest dye, his determination to secure entire possession of that beauty, even at the accursed price of blood, became but the more resolute and confirmed.

The night previous to that fixed for the assassination was passed by the guilty Gerald in a state of dreadful excitement. Large drops fell from his forehead in agony, and when he arose at a late hour, his pale emaciated features and wavering step betrayed how little the mind or the body had tasted of repose. Accustomed however, as he had latterly been, to sustain his sinking spirits by artificial means, he was not long in having recourse to his wonted stimulants. He called for brandy to deaden the acuteness of his feelings, and give strength to his tottering limbs; and when he had drank freely of this, he sallied forth into the forest, where he wandered during the day without other aim or purpose than to hide the brand of guilt, which he almost felt upon his brow, from the curious gaze of his fellow men. It was dark when he returned to the hotel, and as, on his way to his own private apartment, he passed the low large room chiefly used as an ordinary, the loud hum of voices which met his ear, mingled with the drawing of corks and ringing of glasses, told him that the entertainment provided for his unconscious victim had already commenced. Moving hastily on, he gained his own apartment, and summoning one of the domestics, directed that his own frugal meal (the first he had tasted that day) should be brought up. But even for this he had no appetite, and he had recourse once more to the stimulant for assistance. As the night drew on he grew more nervous and agitated, yet without at all wavering in his purpose. At length ten o'clock struck. It was the hour at which he had promised to issue forth to join Matilda in the path, there to await the passage of his victim to his home. He cautiously descended the staircase, and in the confusion that reigned among the household, all of whom were too much occupied with the entertainment within to heed the movements of individuals, succeeded in gaining the street without notice. The room in which the dinner was given was on the ground floor, and looked through numerous low windows into the street, through which Gerald must necessarily pass to reach the place of his appointment. Sounds of loud revelry, mixed with laughter and the strains of music, now issued from these, attesting that the banquet was at its height, and the wine fast taking effect on its several participators.

A momentary feeling of vague curiosity caused the degraded youth to glance his eye through one of the uncurtained windows upon the scene within, but scarcely had he caught an indistinct and confused view of the company, most of whom glittered in the gay trappings of military uniforms, when a secret and involuntary dread of distinguishing from his fellows the man whom he was about to slay, caused him as instantaneously to turn away. Guilty as he felt himself to be, he could not bear the thought of beholding the features of the individual he had sworn to destroy. As there were crowds of the humbler citizens of the place collected round the windows to view the revelry within, neither his appearance nor his action had excited surprise; nor indeed was it even suspected, habited as he was in the common garments of the country, that he was other than a native of the town.

On gaining the narrow pass or lane, he found Matilda wrapped in her cloak, beneath which she carried the disguise prepared for both. The moon was in the last quarter, and as the fleecy clouds passed away from before it, he could observe that the lips and cheek of the American were almost livid, although her eyes sparkled with deep mental excitement. Neither spoke, yet their breathing was heavy and audible to each. Gerald seated himself on a projection of the hill, and removing his shoes, substituted those which his companion had wrought for him. He then assumed the hood, and dropping his head between his hands, continued for some minutes in that attitude, buried in profound abstraction.

At length Matilda approached him. She seated herself at his side, threw her arms around his neck, called him in those rich and searching tones which were so peculiarly her own —her beloved and affianced husband; and bidding him be firm of purpose, as he valued the lives and happiness of both, placed in his hand a small dagger, the handle of which was richly mounted in silver. Gerald clutched the naked weapon with a convulsive grasp, while a hoarse low groan escaped him, and again he sank his head in silence upon his chest.

Nearly an hour had passed in this manner, neither seeking to disturb the thoughts of the other, nor daring to break the profound silence that every where prevailed around them. At length a distant and solitary footstep was heard, and Matilda sprang to her feet, and with her head thrown eagerly forward, while one small foot alone supported the whole weight of her inclined body, gazed intently out upon the open space, and in the direction whence the sounds proceeded.

"He comes, Gerald, he comes;" she at length whispered in a quick tone.

Gerald, who had also risen, and now stood looking over the shoulder of the American, was not slow in discovering the tall figure of a man, whose outline, cloaked even as it was, bespoke the soldier, moving in an oblique direction towards the building already described.

"It is he, too well do I know him," continued Matilda, in the same eager yet almost inaudible whisper, "and mark how inflated with the incense which has been heaped upon him this night does he appear. His proud step tells of the ambitious projects of his vile heart. Little does he imagine that this arm (and she tightly grasped that which held the fatal dagger) will crush them for ever in the bud. But hist!"

The officer was now within a few paces of the path, in the gloom of which the guilty pair found ample concealment, and as he drew nearer and nearer their very breathing was stayed to prevent the slightest chance of a discovery of their presence. Gerald suffered him to pass some yards beyond the opening, and advanced with long yet cautious strides across the grass towards his victim. As he moved thus noiselessly along, he fancied that there was something in the bearing of the figure that reminded him of one he had previously known, but he had not time to pause upon the circumstance, for the officer was already within ten yards of his own door, and the delay of a single moment would not only deprive him of the opportunity on which he had perilled all in this world and in the next, but expose himself and his companion to the ignominy of discovery and punishment.

A single foot of ground now intervened between him and the unhappy officer, whom wine, or abstraction, or both, had rendered totally unconscious of his danger. Already was the hand of Gerald raised to strike the fatal blow—another moment and it would have descended, but even in the very act he found his arm suddenly arrested. Turning quickly to see who it was who thus interfered with his purpose, he beheld Matilda.

"One moment stay," she said in a hurried voice; "poor were my revenge indeed, were he to perish not knowing who planned his death;" then in a hoarser tone, in which could be detected the action of the fiercest passions of the human mind.—"Slanderer—villain—we meet again."

Startled by the sound of a familiar voice, the officer turned hastily round, and seeing all his danger at a single glance, made a movement of his right hand to his side, as if he would have grasped his sword—but finding no weapon there he contented himself with throwing his left arm forward, covered with the ample folds of his cloak, with a view to the defence of his person.

"Yes, Forrester," continued Matilda, in the same impassioned voice, "we meet again, and mark you," pulling back the disguise from Gerald, "'tis no vile slave, no sable paramour by whose hand you die—villain," she pursued, her voice trembling with excitement, "my own arm should have done the deed, but that he whose service I have purchased with the hand you rejected and despised, once baulked me of my vengeance when I had deemed it most secure. But enough! To his heart, Gerald, now that in the fulness of his wine and his ambition, he may the deeper feel the sting of death—strike to his heart—what! do you falter—do you turn coward?"

Gerald neither moved nor spoke; his upraised hand had sunk at his side, at the first address of Matilda to her enemy, and the dagger had fallen from his hand upon the sward, where it might be seen glittering in the rays of the pale moon. His head was bent upou his chest in abject shame, and he seemed as one who had suddenly been turned to stone.

"Gerald, my husband!" urged Matilda, rapidly changing her tone into that of earnest persuasion, "wherefore do you hesitate. Am I not your wife, your own wife, and is not yon monster the wretch who has consigned my fair fame to obloquy for ever—Gerald !" she added impetuously.

But the spell had lost its power, and Gerald continued immoveable—apparently fixed to the spot on which he stood.

"Gerald, Gerald !" repeated the officer, with the air of one endeavouring to recollect.

At the sound of that voice, Gerald looked up. The moon was at that moment unobscured by a single cloud, and as the eyes of the murderer and his intended victim met, their recognition was mutual and perfect.

"I had never expected to see Lieutenant Grantham figuring in the character of an assassin," said Colonel Forrester, in a voice of deep and bitter reproach, "still less to find his arm raised against the preserver of his life. This," he continued, as if speaking to himself, "will be a bitter tale to recount to his family."

"Almighty God ! have mercy !" exclaimed Gerald, as overcome with shame and misery, he threw himself upon the earth at his full length, his head nearly touching the feet of the officer. Then clasping his feet—"Oh ! Colonel Forrester, lost, degraded as I am, believe me when I swear that I knew not against whom my arm was to be directed. Nay, that you live at this moment is the best evidence of the truth of what I utter, for I came with a heart made up to murder. But *your* blood worlds could not tempt me to spill."

"I believe you," said the American, feelingly. "Well do I know the arts of the woman who seems to have lured you into the depths of crime ; yet low as you are fallen, Lieutenant Grantham—much as you have disgraced your country and profession, I cannot think you would willingly have sought the life of him who saved your own. And now rise, sir, and gain the place of your abode, before accident bring other eyes than my own to be witnesses of your shame. We will discourse of this tomorrow. Meanwhile, be satisfied with my promise, that your attempt shall remain a secret with myself."

While he spoke, Colonel Forrester made a movement as if to depart. Aroused by the apprehension of losing her victim, Matilda, who had hitherto been an impatient listener, called wildly upon Gerald, who had now risen, to fulfil his compact; but the youth turned from her with a movement of disgust, exclaiming with bitterness—"leave me, woman, leave me!"

Matilda looked after him for an instant with an expression of intensest scorn, then springing to, and snatching up the dagger, which lay glittering a few paces from the spot on which she stood, she advanced silently, but rapidly, upon her retreating enemy. Colonel Forrester had gained his threshhold, and had already knocked for admittance, when he heard the deep voice of Matilda at his ear, exclaiming in a triumphant tone,

"Think you twice then to escape your doom, traitor?"

Before he could make an attempt to shield himself, the fatal steel had entered deep into his side. Uttering a groan, he sank senseless on the steps, whither Gerald, who had watched the action of his companion, had flown in the hope of arresting the blow. Confused voices, mingled with the tramp of feet, were now heard within the hall. Presently the door opened, and a crowd of servants, chiefly blacks, appeared with lights. The view of their bleeding master, added to the disguise of Gerald, and the expression of triumph visible in the pale countenance of Matilda, at once revealed the truth. By some the former was borne to his apartment, while the greater portion busied themselves in securing the two latter, who however made not the slightest effort at resistance, but suffered themselves to be borne, amid hootings and execrations, from the spot.

The different groups we have described as being gathered together in front of the hotel, had dispersed with the breaking up of the party, which Colonel Forrester, in compliment to those who entertained him, had been one of the last to quit; so that on passing through the streets not an idler was found to swell the sable crowd that bore the wretched prisoners onward to the common prison of the town. Just as they had arrived at this latter, and a tall and muscular negro, apparently enjoying some distinction in his master's household, was about to pull the bell for admission, a man came running breathlessly to the spot, and communicated to the negro just mentioned, a message, in which the name of Colonel Forrester was distinctly audible to the ear of Gerald. A retrograde movement was the immediate consequence of this interruption, and the party, came once more upon the open space they had so recently quitted. Stupified with the excess of abjectness in which he had continued plunged, from the moment of his discovery of the identity of his intended victim, Gerald had moved unconsciously and recklessly whithersoever his conductors led; but now that he expected to be confronted face to face with the dying man, as the sudden alteration in the movement of the party gave him reason to apprehend, he felt for the first time that his position, bitter as it was, might be rendered even worse. It was a relief to him, therefore, when he found that, instead of taking the course which led to the residence of Colonel Forrester, the head of the party, of which Matilda and himself were the centre, suddenly immerged into the narrow lane which conducted to the residence of that unhappy woman. Instead, however, of approaching this, Gerald remarked that they made immediately for the fatal temple. When they had reached this, the door was unlocked by the tall negro above described, who, with a deference in his manner not less at variance with the occasion than with the excited conduct of the whole party on their way to the prison, motioned both his prisoners to enter. They did so, and the lock having been turned and the key removed, they silently withdrew.

CHAPTER XV.

HOURS passed away without either of the guilty parties finding courage or inclination to address the other. The hearts of both were too full for utterance—and yet did they acknowledge no sympathy in common. Remorse, shame, fear, regret, simultaneously assailed and weighed down the mind of Gerald. Triumphant vengeance, unmixed with any apprehension of self, reigned exclusively in the bosom of Matilda. The intense passion of the former, like a mist that is dissipitated before the strong rays of the sun, had yielded before the masculine and practical display of the energetic hate of its object, while on the contrary she, whose beauty of person was now to him a thing without price, acknowledged no other feeling than contempt for the vacillating character of her associate. In this only did they agree that each looked upon each in the light of a being sunk in crime—steeped in dishonor—and while the love of the one was turned to almost loathing at the thought, the other merely wondered how one so feeble of heart had ever been linked to so determined a purpose.

The only light admitted into the temple was through the window already described, and this was so feeble as scarcely to allow of the more distant objects in the room being seen. Gradually, as the moon sunk beneath the forest ridge, the gloom increased, until in the end the darkness became almost profound. At their first entrance Matilda, enshrouding herself in the folds of her cloak, had thrown herself upon the sofa; while Gerald continued to pace up and down the apartment with hurried steps, and in a state of feeling it would be a vain attempt to describe. It was now for the first time that, uninfluenced by passion, the miserable young man had leisure to reflect on the past, and the chain of fatality which had led to his present disgracefnl position. He recollected the conversation he had held with his brother on the day succeeding his escape from the storm ; and as the pledge which had been given in his name to his dying father, that no action of his life should reflect dishonor on his family now occurred to him in all its force, he groaned in agony of spirit, less in apprehension of the fate that awaited him than in sorrow and in shame that that pledge should have been violated. By a natural transition of his feelings, his imagination recurred to the traditions connected with his family, and the dreadful curse which had been uttered by one on whom his ancestor was said to have heaped injury to the very extinction of reason—and associating as he did Matilda's visit to the Cottage at Detroit, on the memorable night when he had unconsciously saved the life of Colonel Forrester, with the fact of her having previously knelt and prayed upon the grave that was known to cover the ashes of the unhappy maniac, Ellen Halloway, he felt a shuddering conviction that she was in some way connected with that wretched woman. In the intenseness of his new desire to satisfy his doubts—a desire which in itself partook of the character of the fatality by which he was beset—he overcame the repugnance he had hitherto felt to enter into conversation with her, and advancing to the couch, seated himself upon its edge at her side.

"Matilda" he said, after a few moments of silence, "by all the love you once bore me, I conjure you answer me one question while yet there is time."

" Fool," returned the American, " I never loved you. A soul like mine feels passion but once. Hitherto I have played a part, but the drama approaches to a close, and disguise of plot is no longer necessary. Gerald Grantham, you have been my dupe,—you came a convenient puppet to my hands, and as such I used you until the snapped wire proclaimed you no longer serviceable. No further."

Shame, anguish, mortification—all the most humiliating sensations natural to man, for a moment assailed the breast of the unfortunate and guilty Grantham, rendering him insensible even to the greater evil which awaited him. In the bitterness of his agony he struck his clenched hand against his forehead, uttering curses upon himself for his weakness, in one breath, and calling upon his God, in the next, to pardon him for his crime.

"This is good!" said Matilda. "To see you writhe thus, under the wound inflicted upon your vanity, is some small atonement for the base violation of your oath; yet what question would you ask, the solution of which can so much import one about to figure on the scaffold for a crime he has not even had the courage to commit?"

The taunting manner in which the concluding part of the sentence was conveyed, had the effect of restoring Gerald in some degree to himself, and he said with considerable firmness:

"What I would ask is of yourself,—namely, the relationship, if any, you bear to those who lie within the mound on which I beheld you kneeling, on the night of your first attempt on Colonel Forrester's life."

"The very recollection of that ill-timed intrusion would prevent me from satisfying your curiosity, did not something whisper to me that, in so doing, I shall add another pang to those you already experience," returned the American with bitter sarcasm.

"You are right," said Gerald hurriedly; "my miseries need but the assurance of your connexion with those mouldering bones to be indeed complete."

"Then," said Matilda eagerly, and half raising her head, "your cup of misery may yet admit of increase. My mother and my father's mother both sleep within that grave!"

"How knew you this?" demanded Gerald quickly. "Instinct could not have guided you to the spot, and by your own admission you were taken from the place of your home while yet a mere child."

"Not instinct, but my father Desborough, pointed out the spot, as he had long previously acquainted me with the history of my birth."

One question more—your grandmother's name?"

"Mad Ellen she was called, an English soldier's wife, who died in giving birth to my father—and now that you are answered, leave me."

"Almighty Providence," aspirated Gerald, in tones of inconceivable agony; "it is then as I had feared, and this woman has Destiny chosen to accomplish my ruin."

He quitted the sofa and paced up and down the room in a state of mind bordering on distraction. The past crowded upon his mind in all the confused manner of a dream, and amid the chaos of contending feelings by which he was beset, one idea only was distinct—namely, that the wretched woman before him had been but the agent of Fate in effecting his destruction. Strange as it may appear, the idea, so far from increasing the acerbity of his feelings, had the tendency to soften his heart towards her. He beheld in her but a being whose actions had been fated like his own, and although every vestige of passion had fled—even although her surpassing beauty had lost its subjugating influence, his heart yearned towards her as one who, wrecked on the same shore, had some claim to his sympathy and compassion. All that was now left them was to make their peace with God, since with man their final account would be so speedily closed, and with a view to impress her with a sense of the religious aid from which alone they could hope for consolation, he again seated himself at her side on the edge of the sofa.

"Matilda," he said, in a voice in which melancholy and sternness were blended, "We have been the children of guilt

—the victims of our own evil passions; but God is merciful, and if our penitence be sincere, we may yet be forgiven in Heaven, although on earth there is no hope—even if after this we could wish to live. Matilda, let us pray together."

There was no answer—neither did the slightest movement of her form indicate consciousness that she was addressed. "Matilda," repeated Gerald—still there was no answer. He placed his hand upon her cheek, and thought the touch was cold—he caught her hand, it too was cold and but for the absence of rigidity he would have deemed her dead.

Scarcely knowing what he did, yet with an indefinable terror at his heart, he grasped and shook her by the arm, and again, but with greater vehemence, pronounced her name.

"Who calls?" she said, in a faint but deep tone, as she raised her head slowly from the cushion which supported it. "Ha! I recollect. Tell me," she added more quickly, "was not the blow well aimed. Marked you how the traitor fell. Villain, to accuse the woman whose only fault was loving him too well, with ignominious commerce with a slave!"

"Wretched woman," exclaimed Gerald with solemn emphasis, "instead of exulting over the evil we have done, let us rather make our peace with Heaven, during the few hours we have yet to live. Matilda Desborough—daughter of a murderer; thyself a murderess—the scaffold awaits us both."

"Coward—fool—thou liest," she returned with suddenly awakened energy. "For one so changeling as thyself the scaffold were befitting, but know, if I have had the heart to do this deed, I have also had the head to provide against its consequences—see—feel—."

One of her cold hands was extended in search of Gerald's. They met, and a vial placed in the palm of the latter, betrayed the secret of her previous lassitude and insensibility.

Even amid all the horrors which environed him, and called so largely on attention to his own personal danger, Gerald was inexpressibly shocked.

"What! poisoned?" he exclaimed.

"Yes—poisoned!" she murmured, and her hand again sank heavily at her side.

Gerald dashed the vial away from him to the farther end of the apartment, and taking the cold hand of the unhappy woman, he continued:

"Matilda—is this the manner in which you prepare yourself to meet the presence of your God. What! add suicide to murder?"

But she spoke not—presently the hand he clasped sank heavily from his touch. Then there was a spasmodic convulsion of the whole frame. Then there burst a piercing shriek from her lips, as she half raised herself in agony from the sofa, and then each limb was set and motionless in the stern rigidity of death.

While Gerald was yet bending over the body of his unfortunate companion, shocked, grieved and agitated beyond all expression, the door of the temple was unlocked, and a man enveloped in a cloak, and bearing a small dark lantern, suddenly appeared in the opening. He advanced towards the spot where Gerald, stupified with the events of the past night, stood gazing upon the corpse, almost unconscious of the presence of the intruder.

"A pretty fix you have got into, Liftenant Grantham," said the well known voice of Jackson, "and I little calculated, when I advised you to make love to the Kentucky gals to raise your spirits, that they would lead you into such a deuced scrape as this."

"Captain Jackson," said Gerald imploringly; "I am sufficiently aware of all the enormity of my crime, and am prepared to expiate it; but in mercy spare the bitterness of reproach."

"Now as I'm a true Tenessee man, bred and born, I meant

no reproach, and why should I, since you could'nt help her doing it, (and he pointed to Matilda), yet you know its sometimes dangerous to be found in bad company. Every body might'nt believe you so innocent as we do.

"Innocent! Captain Jackson," exclaimed Gerald, losing sight of all other feelings in unfeigned surprise—"I cannot say that I quite understand you."

"Why, the meaning's plain enough, I take it. Others might be apt, I say, to think you had something to do with the thing as well as she, and therefore its just as well you should make yourself scarce. The Colonel says he would'nt, on any account, you shall even be suspected."

"The Colonel says--not suspected," again exclaimed Gerald with increasing astonishment--then, suddenly recollecting the situation of the latter—"tell me," he continued, "is Colonel Forrester in danger—is his life despaired of?"

"Worth a dozen dead men yet, or you would'nt see me taking the thing so coolly. The dagger certainly let the day light into him, but though the wound was pretty considerably deep, the doctors say its not mortal. He thinks it might have been worse if you had not come up, and partly stopped her arm when she struck at him."

Gerald was deeply affected by what he had just heard. It was evident that Colonel Forrester had, with a generosity to which no gratitude of his own could render adequate justice, sought to exonerate him from all suspicion of participation in the guilty design upon his life, and as he glanced his eye again for a moment upon the lifeless form of his companion, he was at once sensible that the only being who could defeat the benevolent object of his benefactor had now no longer the power to do so.

"She sleeps sound enough now," said Jackson, again pointing to the ill-fated and motionless girl, "but she'll sleep sounder still before long, I take it."

"She will never sleep sounder than at this moment, Captain Jackson," said Gerald, with solemn emphasis.

" Why, you don't mean to say she has cheated the hangman, Liftenant."

As he spoke, Jackson approached the sofa, and turning the light full upon the face, saw indeed that she was dead. Gerald shuddered as the rays from the lamp revealed for the first time the appalling change which had been wrought upon that once beautiful countenance. The open and finely formed brow was deeply knit, and the features distorted by the acute agony which had wrung the shriek from her heart at the very moment of dissolution, were set in a stern expression of despair. The parted lips were drawn up at the corners in a manner to convey the idea of the severest internal pain, and there was already a general discoloration about the mouth, betraying the subtle influence of the poison which had effected her death.

Gerald, after the first glance, turned away his head in horror from the view; but the Aid-de-Camp remained for some moments calmly regarding the remains of all that had once been most beautiful in nature.

" She certainly is not like what she was when Colonel Forrester first knew her," he said, in the abstracted tone of one talking without reference to any other auditor than himself; " but this comes of prefering a nigger to a white man. Such unnatural courses never can prosper, I take it."

" Captain Jackson," said Gerald, aroused by this remark, and with great emphasis of tone, while he laid his hand impressively on the shoulder of the other, " you do her wrong. Guilty she has been, fearfully guilty, but not in the sense you would imply."

" How do you know this?" asked the Aid-de-Camp.

" From her own solemn declaration at a moment when deception could avail her not. Even before she swallowed the fatal poison, her horror at the imputation, which drove her to the perpetration of murder, was expressed in terms of indignant warmth that belong to truth alone."

" If this be so," said Jackson, musingly, " she is indeed

a much injured woman, and deep I know will be the regret of Colonel Forrester when he hears it, for he himself has ever believed her guilty. But come, Liftenant Grantham, we have no time to lose. The day will soon break, and I expect you must be a considerable way from Frankfort before sunrise."

I—from Frankfort—before sunrise !" exclaimed Gerald, in perfect astonishment.

" Why, it's rather short warning to be sure; but the Colonel thinks you'd better start before the thing gets wind in the morning; for as so many of the niggers say you wore a sort of a disguise as well as the poor girl, he fears the citizens may suspect you of something more than an intrigue, and insult you desperately."

" Generous, excellent man !" exclaimed Gerald, " how can I ever repay this most unmerited service?"

" Why, the best way I take it, is to profit by the offer that is made you of getting back to Canada as fast as you can."

" But how is this to be done, and will not the very fact of my flight confirm the suspicion it is intended to remove?"

" As for the matter of how it is to be done, Liftenant, I have as slick a horse waiting outside for you as man ever crossed—one of the fleetest in Colonel Forrester's stud. Then as for suspicion, he means to set that at rest, by saying that he has taken upon himself to give you leave to return on parole to your friends, who wish to see you on a case of life and death, and now let's be moving."

Oppressed with the weight of contending feelings, which this generous conduct had inspired, Gerald waited but to cast a last look upon the ill-fated Matilda; and then with a slow step and a heavy heart for ever quitted a scene fraught with the most exciting and the most painful occurrences of his life. The first rays of early dawn beginning to develope themselves as they issued from the temple, Jackson extinguished his lamp, and leading through the narrow pass that conducted to the town, made the circuit of the ridge of hills until they arrived at a point where a negro (the same who had led the party that bore Matilda and himself to the temple) was in waiting, with a horse ready saddled and the arms and accoutrements of a rifleman.

The equipment of Gerald was soon completed, and with the shot-bag and powder-horn slung over his shoulder, and the long rifle in his hand, he soon presented the appearance of a backwoodsman hastening to the theatre of war.

When he had seated himself in the saddle, Jackson drew forth a well filled purse, which he said he had been directed by Colonel Forrester to present him with to defray the expences of his journey to the frontier.

Deeply affected by this new proof of the favor of the generous American, Gerald received the purse, saying, as he confided them to the breast of his hunting frock—

"Captain Jackson, tell Colonel Forrester from me, that I accept his present merely because in doing so I give the best evidence of my appreciation of *all* he has done for me on this trying occasion. In his own heart, however, he must look for the only reward to which this most noble of actions justly entitles him."

The frank-hearted Aid-de-Camp promised compliance with this parting message, and after pointing out the route it would be necessary to follow, warmly pressed the hand of his charge in a final grasp, that told how little he deemed the man before him capable of the foul intention with which his soul had been so recently sullied.

How often during those hours of mad infatuation, when his weakened mind had been balancing between the possession of Matilda at the price of crime, and his abandonment of her at that of happiness, had the observation of the Aid-de-Camp, on a former occasion, that he "was never born to be an assassin," occurred to his mind, suffusing his cheek with shame and his soul with remorse. Now, too, that conscious of having fallen in all but the positive commission of the deed, he saw that the unsuspecting American regarded him merely as one whom accident or intrigue had made an unwilling witness of the deadly act of a desperate woman, his feelings were those of profound abasement and self disesteem.

There was a moment, when urged by an involuntary impulse, he would have undeceived Captain Jackson as to his positive share in the transaction; but pride suddenly interposed and saved him from the degradation of the confession. He returned the pressure of the American's hand with emphasis, and then turning his horse in the direction which he had been recommended to take, quitted Frankfort for ever.

CHAPTER XVI.

WHILE the success of the British and American arms had been alternating (with eventual triumph to the latter) in the manner we have shown during the campaign of 1813, on the Western District of Upper Canada, some highly important operations had taken place in the army of the centre. Of these our space will admit but of a detail of one, and we thus travel out of the scene to which we have hitherto confined our labors, not only because it was the most dashing affair that occurred during the war, but because it offers a striking parallel to the enterprise and daring which destroyed the American power, at the outset of hostilities, and was productive of similar results.

Towards the close of May 1813, the Americans, after having hotly bombarded Fort George on the Niagara frontier, for two successive days, crossed the river and succeeded in establishing themselves in that post which was evacuated as untenable. The British loss on this occasion was considerable, and General Vincent, who commanded the army of the centre, retreated with much precipitation towards Burlington Heights, withdrawing at the same time the garrison from Fort Erie.

Emboldened by the absence of serious opposition, the American Generals (Winder and Chandler) pushed forward a force, exceeding three thousand men, as far as Stoney Creek, close to the position then occupied by the little British army, not more than one fifth of this number. Here they halted for the night, evidently to refresh their troops for the attack, which was meditated for the following morning.

The result of such attack, with so overwhelming a force,

upon a small body of men dispirited, by recent discomfiture, and destitute of supplies or reserves, could scarcely have been doubtful. Fortunately however for the honor of the British arms, Colonel Harvey, to whose conduct on this occasion allusion has been incidentally made in an early chapter of the present volume, had recently joined the centre Division from Lower Canada, and to his quick and comprehensive mind it immediately suggested itself, that if the attack of the American army should be awaited, the result, under the circumstances already alluded to, and in the position occupied by the British force (literally a Cul-de-Sac) must inevitably be attended by their utter discomfiture, if not annihilation. On the contrary, he felt persuaded that, even with the small force at the disposal of the British General, there was every probability that a bold and well concerted night attack would have the effect of restoring to the assailants that confidence in themselves, which had been weakened by a series of reverses, while it must necessarily, and in the same proportion, carry dismay into the ranks of the hitherto victorious enemy.

It was, we believe—indeed we have reason to know—a favorite military maxim with Colonel Harvey, and invariably acted up to whenever opportunity was afforded for its application, that defensive warfare, when the invading foe is greatly superior in number, is best carried on by a succession of bold and active offensive operations. The result of this theory was, in the instance under question, an offer to General Vincent to head a night attack and penetrate into the very heart of the enemy's encampment, as an only means of extricating the army from its perilous position, and restoring (if successful) to the victors that moral confidence which was necessary to the honor of the army, and the preservation of the country. Fortunately, we repeat, for the glory of the British arms, Colonel Harvey's proposal was accepted, although not without much doubt and indecision on the subject, and during the night of the 5th June the small band of heroes, destined to achieve so glorious a result, were silently got under arms for the disproportionate encounter. At the head of seven hundred and twenty bayonets Colonel Harvey dashed in upon his slumbering and unsuspecting enemy, amounting to more than quadruple his own force, and well provided with field artillery. So bold and unexpected was the attack, that the enemy fled, with the utmost precipitation, to a position called the forty mile creek, a distance of ten miles, leaving their Generals and a vast number of prisoners and military stores in the hands of the victors. Here they fell in with a reinforcement under General Lewis. So opportune however had been the blow struck by Colonel Harvey, and such the panic created by it in the American ranks, that even with this additional force, they, on the sudden appearance of the British fleet, with a small body of troops on board, after sustaining a short cannonade, continued their retreat to Fort George, leaving their tents standing, nor halting until they had gained their place of destination.

Thus, by this judicious and by far the most brilliant achievment of the war, was the centre District freed from the triumphant presence of the enemy, as the western had been, in the preceding year, by the bold and well timed movement of General Brock upon Detroit, with an equally inferior force.

The history of the war furnishes no similar enterprizes. Both were the results of a bold conception, and prompt and successful execution. Of the two, perhaps Stoney Creek was the most dashing and decided, since there the adverse armies actually came into collision.

In October of the same year,* a numerous body of Americans, principally troops of the line, had been collected under the orders of General Van Ransaellar, and advantage was taken of a dark night in October to push them across the river, with a view to the occupation of the commanding heights above the village of Queenston. In this, favored by circumstances, the enemy were eminently successful.—

* The anachronism referred to in the Preface. The events here described, occurred in 1812, and not in 1813.

They carried the batteries, and at day break the heights were to be seen covered with their battalions, before whom were thrown out a considerable body of tirailleurs, or riflemen. At the first alarm, the little detachment stationed at Queenston, marched out to dislodge them; but such was the impatient gallantry of General Brock, who had succeeded to the command on this line of frontier, that without waiting for the main body from Fort George to come up, he threw himself at the head of the flank companies of the Forty-Ninth, and moving forward in double quick time, soon came within sight of the enemy.

Among the General's Aides-de-Camps, was Henry Grantham, who having succeeded in making his escape at the fatal defeat of the Moravian Village, with a few men of his company, had in the absence of his Regiment, (then prisoners of war) and from considerations of personal esteem, been attached as a supernumerary to his staff. With him at this moment was the light hearted De Courcy, and as the young men rode a little in rear of their Chief, they were so rapt in admiration of his fine form and noble daring, (as he still kept dashing onward, far in advance even of the handful of troops who followed eagerly and rapidly in his rear,) that they utterly forgot the danger to which he was exposed.

On arriving at the ascent, the General for a moment reined in his charger, in order to give time to the rear to close in, then removing and waving his plumed hat,

"Hurrah, Forty-Ninth!" he exclaimed, in language suited to those he addressed. "Up these heights lies our road—on ourselves depends the victory. Not a shot till we gain the summit—then three cheers for old England—a volley—and the bayonet must do the rest!"

So saying, he resumed his hat, and wheeling his horse, once more led his gallant little band up the hill.

But it was not likely that the Americans would suffer the approach of so determined an enemy without attempting to check their progress in the most efficient manner. Distinguished from those around him by his commanding air, not less than by the military insignia that adorned him, the person of the General was at once recognized for one bearing high rank, and as such became an object of especial attention to the dispersed riflemen. Shot after shot flew past the undaunted officer, carrying death into the close ranks that followed noiselessly in his rear, yet without harming him. At length he was seen by his Aides-de-Camps, both of whom had kept their eyes upon him, to reel in his saddle. An instant brought the young men to his side, De Courcy on his right and Grantham on his left hand. They looked up into his face. It was suffused with the hues of death. A moment afterwards and he fell from his horse, with his head reclining upon the chest of Henry Grantham. There was a momentary halt in the advancing column; all were dismayed at the dreadful event.

De Courcy and Grantham, having abandoned their horses, now bore their beloved leader to the side of the road, in order to admit of the unimpeded progress of the men. Even in his last moments the General had no other thought but for the duty in which he was engaged.

"Bid them move on, De Courcy," he said in a faint voice, as he remarked the sudden check which had been given to the advance by his fall. Then, as if obedient to the command, they renewed the ascent, each man eyeing him as he past with a look in which deep sorrow and a desire to avenge his death were intimately blended. "Forty-Ninth, I have served with you from boyhood, and if ye would I die with honor this day—carry those heights."

There was a deep murmur through the ranks of both companies, that showed how each and all were affected by this appealing address of the dying officer. At that moment there arose a loud shout from the hill, as of triumph at the fall of him they mourned. They answered it with the fierce expression of men resolved to turn that shout of triumph into a cry of woe; and excited, maddened, infuriated, yet with a steadiness of movement that claimed the admiration even of their enemies, dashed, heedless of the galling fire of the riflemen, up the steep.

Left alone with the dying General, it became a first consideration with the young officers to convey him (provided he could bear removal) to some spot out of reach of the enemy's fire, where he might breathe his last moments in peace.

As Henry Grantham glanced his eye towards an old untenanted building, that lay some fifty yards off the road, and which he conceived fully adapted to the purpose, he saw the form of a rifleman partly exposed at a corner of the building, whose action at the moment was evidently that of one in the act of loading his piece. The idea that this skulking enemy might have been the same who had given the fatal death-wound to his beloved Chief, added to the conviction that he was preparing to put the *coup de grâce* to his work, filled him with the deepest desire of vengeance. As the bodies of several men, picked off by the tirailleurs, lay along the road, (one at no great distance from the spot on which he stood,) he hastened to secure the nearest musket, which, as no shot had yet been fired by the English, he knew to be loaded.

Leaving De Courcy to support the head of the General, the young Aid-de-Camp moved with due caution towards the building; but ere he had gone ten paces, he beheld the object of his pursuit issue altogether from the cover of the building, and advance towards him with his rifle at the trail. More and more convinced that his design was to obtain a nearer approach, with a view to a more certain aim, he suddenly halted, and raised the musket to his shoulder. In vain was a shout to desist uttered by the advancing man—in vain was his rifle thrown aside as if in token of the absence of all hostile purpose. The excited Henry Grantham heeded not the words—saw not the action. He thought only of the danger of his General, and of his desire to avenge his fall. He fired—the rifleman staggered, and putting his hand to his breast—

"My brother! oh, my unhappy brother!" he exclaimed, and sank senseless to the earth.

Who shall tell the horror of the unfortunate young Aid-de-Camp, at recognizing in the supposed enemy his long mourned and much loved Gerald—motion, sense, life, seemed for the instant annihilated by the astounding consciousness of the fratricidal act: the musket fell from his hands, and he who had never known sorrow before, save through those most closely linked to his warm affections, was now overwhelmed, crushed by the mountain of despair that fell upon his heart. It was some moments before he could so far recover from the stupor into which that dear and well remembered voice had plunged him, as to perceive the possibility of the wound not being mortal. The thought acted like electricity upon each stupified sense, and palsied limb; and eager with the renewed hope, he bounded forward to the spot where lay the unfortunate Gerald, writhing in his agony. He had fallen on his face, but as Henry approached him, he raised himself with one hand, and with the other beckoned to his brother to draw near.

"Great God, what have I done!" exclaimed the unhappy Henry, throwing himself in a paroxysm of despair upon the body of his bleeding brother. "Gerald, my own beloved Gerald, is it thus we meet again. Oh! if you would not kill me, tell me that your wound is not mortal. Assure me that I am not a fratricide. Oh, Gerald, Gerald! my brother, tell me that you are not dying."

A faint smile passed over the pale haggard features of Gerald: he grasped the hand of his brother and pressed it fervently, saying—

"Henry, the hand of fate is visible in all this, therefore condemn not yourself for that which was inevitable. I knew of the attempt of the Americans to possess themselves of the heights, and I crossed over with them under favor of this disguise, determined to find death, combatting at the side of our gallant General. Detaching myself from the ranks, I but waited the advance of the British column to remove from my concealment—you know the rest. But oh, Henry! if you could divine what a relief it is to me to part with existence, you would not wish the act undone. This was all I asked: to see you once more—to embrace you—and to die. Life offered me no hope but this."

Gerald expressed himself with the effort of one laboring under strong bodily pain; and as he spoke he again sank exhausted upon the ground.

"This packet," he continued, taking one from the breast of the hunting frock he wore, and handing it to his brother, who, silent and full of agony, had again raised his head from the ground and supported it on his shoulder; "this packet, Henry, written at various times during the last fortnight, will explain all that has passed since we last parted, in the Miami. When I am no more, read it; and while you mourn over his dishonor, pity the weakness and the sufferings of the unhappy Gerald."

Henry was nearly frantic, the hot tears fell from his burning eyes upon the pale emaciated cheek of his brother—and he groaned in agony.

"Oh, God!" he exclaimed, "how shall I ever survive this blow—my brother! oh, my brother! tell me that you forgive me."

"Most willingly; yet what is there to be forgiven? You took me for an enemy and hence alone your error. It was fate, Henry. A dreadful doom has long been prophesied to the last of our race. We are the last—and this is the consummation. Let it console you however to think that, though your hand had not slain me another's would. In the ranks of the enemy I should have found—Henry, my kind, my affectionate brother—your hand—there—there—what dreadful faintness at my heart—Matilda, it is my turn now—Oh, God have mercy, oh——"

While this scene was passing by the road side between the unfortunate brothers, the main body of the British force had come up to the spot where the General still lay expiring in the arms of De Courcy, and surrounded by the principal of the medical staff. The majority of these were of the Regiment previously named—veterans who had known and loved their gallant leader during the whole course of his spotless career, and more than one rude hand might be seen dashing the tear that started involuntarily to the eye. As the colors of the Forty-Ninth passed before him, the General made an effort to address some language of encouragement to his old corps, but the words died away in indistinct murmurs, and waving his hand in the direction of the heights, he sank back exhausted with the effort, and resigned his gallant spirit for ever.

For some minutes after life had departed, Henry Grantham continued to hang over the body of his ill-fated brother, with an intenseness of absorption that rendered him heedless even of the rapid fire of musketry in the advance. The sound of De Courcy's voice was the first thing that seemed to call him to consciousness. De Courcy had heard the cry uttered by the latter, on receiving the fatal shot, and his imagination had too faithfully portrayed the painful scene that had ensued. A friend of both brothers, and particularly attached of late to the younger from the similar nature of their service, he was inexpressibly shocked, but still cherishing a hope that the wound might not be attended with loss of life, he expected to find his anticipations realized by some communication from his friend. Finding however that the one rose not, and remarking that the general demeanour of the other was that of profound despair, he began at length to draw the most unfavorable conclusion, and causing the body of his Commander to be borne under cover of the building, until proper means of transport could be found, he hastened to ascertain the full extent of the tragedy.

The horror and dismay depicted in his friend's countenance were speedily reflected on his own, when he saw that the unfortunate Gerald, whose blood had completely saturated the earth on which he lay, was indeed no more. Language at such a moment would not only have been superfluous, but an insult. De Courcy caught and pressed the hand of his friend in silence. The unfortunate young man pointed to the dead body of his brother, and burst into tears. While these were yet flowing in a fulness that promised to give relief to his oppressed heart, a loud shout from the British ranks arrested the attention of both. The sound seemed to have an electric effect on the actions of Henry Grantham. For the first time he appeared conscious there was such a thing as a battle being fought.

"De Courcy !" he said starting up, and with sudden animation, "why do we linger here—the dead," and he pointed first to the body of the General in the distance—and then to his brother " the wretched dead claim no service from us now."

" You are right, Henry, our interest in those beloved objects has caused us to be mindless of our duty to ourselves.—See, too, how the flankers have cleared the brow of the hill for the advance of the main body. Victory is our own—but alas ! how dearly purchased !"

" How dearly purchased, indeed !" responded Henry, in a tone of such heart-rending agony as caused his friend to repent the allusion. " De Courcy keep this packet, and should I fall, let it be sent to my uncle, Colonel D'Egville."

De Courcy accepted the trust, and the young men mounted their horses, which a Canadian peasant had held for them in the mean time, and dashing up the ascent, soon found themselves where the action was hottest.

Burning with revenge, the flank companies had already succeeded, despite of a hot and incessant fire, in gaining the heights, and here for a considerable time they maintained the struggle unsupported against the whole force of the enemy. Already their bayonets had cleared for themselves a passage to the more even ground, and the Americans, dismayed at the intrepidity of this handful of assailants, were evidently beginning to waver in their ranks. A shout of victory, which was answered by the main body of the English troops, just then gaining the summit of the hill, completed their disorder. They stood the charge but for a moment, then broke and fled, pursued by their excited enemies in every direction. The chief object of the Americans was to gain the cover of a wood that lay at a short distance in their rear, but a body of militia with some Indians having been sent round to occupy it the moment the landing of the Americans was made known, they were driven back from this their last refuge upon the open ground, and with considerable loss.

Thus hemmed in on both sides—the rifles of the militia and Indians on one hand; the bayonets of the British force on the other—the Americans had no other alternative than throw down their arms or perish to the last. Many surrendered at discretion, and those who resisted were driven at the point of the bayonet, to the verge of the terrific precipices which descend abruptly from the Heights of Queenston. Here their confusion was at the highest—some threw down their arms and were saved, others precipitated themselves down the abyss, where their bodies were afterwards found, crushed and mangled in a manner to render them scarcely recognizable even as human beings.

It was at the moment when the Americans, driven back by the fire from the wood, were to be seen flying in despair towards the frowning precipices of Queenston, that De Courcy and Grantham, quitting their horses at the brow of the hill, threw themselves in front of the victorious and still leading flank companies. Carried away by the excitement of his feelings, Grantham was considerably in advance of his companion, and when the Americans, yielding to the panic which had seized them, flew wildly, madly, and almost unconcious of the danger, towards the precipice, he suddenly found himself on the very verge, and amid a group of irregulars, who arriving at the brink and seeing the hell that yawned beneath, had turned to seek a less terrific death at the hands of their pursuers. Despair, rage, agony, and even terror, were imprinted on the countenances of these, for they fought under an apparent consciousness of disadvantage, and utterly as men without hope.

"Forward! victory!" shouted Henry Grantham, and his sword was plunged deep into the side of his nearest enemy. The man fell, and writhing in the last agonies of death, rolled onward to the precipice, and disappeared for ever from the view.

The words--the action had excited the attention of a tall, muscular, ferocious looking rifleman, who, hotly pursued by a couple of Indians, was crossing the open ground at his full speed to gain the main body of his comrades. A ball struck him just as he had arrived within a few feet of the spot where Henry stood, yet still leaping onward, he made a desparate blow at the head of the officer with the butt end of his rifle. A quick movement disappointed the American of his aim, yet the blow fell so violently on the shoulder that the stock snapped suddenly asunder at the small of the butt. Stung with pain, Henry Grantham turned to behold his enemy. It was Desborough! The features of the settler expressed the most savage and vindictive passions, as with the barrel of the rifle upraised and clenched in both his iron hands, he was about to repeat his blow. Ere it could descend Grantham had rushed in upon him, and his sword still recking with the blood it had so recently spilt, was driven to the very hilt in the body of the settler. The latter uttered a terrific scream in which all the most infernal of human passions were wildly blended, and casting aside his rifle, seized the young officer in his powerful gripe. Then ensued a contest the most strange and awful; the settler using every endeavour to gain the edge of the precipice, the other struggling, but in vain, to free himself from his hold. As if by tacit consent, both parties discontinued the struggle, and became mere spectators of the scene.

"Villain!" shouted De Courcy, who saw with dismay the terrible object of the settler, whose person he had recognized—"if you would have quarter, release your hold."

But Desborough, too much given to his revenge to heed the words of the Aid-de-Camp, continued silently, yet with advantage, to drag his victim nearer and nearer to the fatal precipice; and every man in the British ranks felt his blood to creep as they beheld the unhappy officer borne, notwithstanding a desperate resistance, at each moment nigher to the brink.

"For Heaven's sake, advance and seize him" exclaimed the terrified De Courcy, leaping forward to the rescue.

Acting on the hint, two or three of the most active of the light infantry rushed from the ranks in the direction taken by the officer.

Desborough saw the movement, and his exertions to defeat its object became, considering the loss of blood he had sustained from his wounds, almost Herculean. He now stood on the extreme verge of the precipice, where he paused for a moment as if utterly exhausted with his previous efforts. De Courcy was now within a few feet of his unhappy friend, who still struggled ineffectually to free himself, when the settler, suddenly collecting all his energy into a final and desparate effort, raised the unfortunate Grantham from the ground, and with a loud and exulting laugh, dashed his foot violently against the edge of the crag, and threw himself backward into the hideous abyss.

A cry of horror from the lips of De Courcy was answered by a savage shout of vengeance from the British ranks. On rushed the line with their glittering bayonets, and at a pace which scarcely left their enemies time to sue for, much less obtain quarter—shrieks and groans rent the atmosphere, and above the horrid din, might be heard the wild and greeting cry of the vulture and the buzzard, as the mangled bodies of the Americans rolled from rock to rock, crashing the autumnal leaves and dried underwood in their fall, some hanging suspended by their rent garments to the larger trees encountered in their course—yet by far the greater number falling into the bottom of a chasm into which the sunbeam had never yet penetrated. The picked and whitened bones may be seen, shining through the deep gloom that envelopes every part of the abyss, even to this day.

THE END.

MONTREAL: JOHN LOVELL, PRINTER.

ERRATA.

VOLUME I.

In the inscription, for "500 men," read "720 men."

Page 4, line 33, for "adversify," read "diversify."

" 44, " 10, for "Brava," read "Bravo."

" 78, " 4, for "undisputable," read "indisputable."

" 81, " 29, for "sound of promise," read "word of promise."

" 138, " 17, for "unmeasurably," read "immeasurably."

" 144, " 17, for "in regard of," read "in regard to."

" 145, " 28, for "there is," read "there are."

" 166, " 32, for "Identlical," read "" Identical."

" 177, " 33, for "to saying," read "so saying."

" 185, " 9, for "last two files," read "last few files."

" 212, " 7, for "metamarphosed," read "metamorphosed."

VOLUME II.

Page 11, line 19, for "scuddling," read "scudding."

" 11, " 20, for "from these," read "from the noise."

" 44, " 5, for "vengeane," read "vengeance."

" 57, " 13, for "Buvouaced," read "Bivouacked."

" 58, " 30, for "in the bear skin," read "into the bear skin."

" 95, " 9, for "rerturn," read "return,"

" 160, " 5, leave out the word "then."

" 162, " 9, for resideut," read "resident."

" 165, " 35, for "bloop," read "blood."

" 166, " 14 and 17, for "heaven," read "Heaven."

" 170, " 17, for "surrendered," read "I surrendered."

" 175, " 24, for "if," read "it."

" 177, " 14, for "have," read "had."

" 182, " 24, for "on," read "of."

" 193, " 13, for "condition on which," read "the period when."

" 209, " 12, for "shall," read "should."

" 212 " 21, for "only reward," read "full reward."

LITERATURE OF CANADA

Poetry and Prose in Reprint
Douglas Lochhead, General Editor

1 *Collected Poems*, Isabella Valancy Crawford
Introduction by James Reaney

2 *The St Lawrence and the Saguenay and Other Poems, & Hesperus and Other Poems and Lyrics*, Charles Sangster
Introduction by Gordon Johnston

3 *Our Intellectual Strength and Weakness*, John George Bourinot
'English-Canadian Literature,' Thomas Guthrie Marquis
'French-Canadian Literature,' Camille Roy
Introduction by Clara Thomas

4 *Selections from Canadian Poets*, Edward Hartley Dewart
Introduction by Douglas Lochhead

5 *Poems and Essays*, Joseph Howe
Introduction by Malcolm G. Parks

6 *Rockbound: A Novel*, Frank Parker Day
Introduction by Allan Bevan

7 *The Homesteaders*, Robert J.C. Stead
Introduction by Susan Wood Glicksohn

8 *The Measure of the Rule*, Robert Barr
Introduction by Louis K. MacKendrick

9 *Selected Poetry and Critical Prose*, Charles G.D. Roberts
Edited with an introduction and notes by W.J. Keith

10 *Old Man Savarin Stories: Tales of Canada and Canadians*
E.W. Thomson
Introduction by Linda Sheshko

11 *Dreamland and Other Poems & Tecumseh: A Drama*, Charles Mair
Introduction by Norman Shrive

12 *The Poems of Archibald Lampman (including At the Long Sault)*
Archibald Lampman
Introduction by Margaret Coulby Whitridge

13 *The Poetical Works of Alexander McLachlan,* Alexander McLachlan
Introduction by E. Margaret Fulton

14 *Angéline de Montbrun,* Laure Conan
Translated and introduced by Yves Brunelle

15 *The White Savannahs,* W.E. Collin
Introduction by Germaine Warkentin

16 *The Search for English-Canadian Literature: An Anthology of Critical Articles from the Nineteenth and Early Twentieth Centuries*
Edited and introduced by Carl Ballstadt

17 *The First Day of Spring: Stories and Other Prose,*
Raymond Knister
Selected and introduced by Peter Stevens

18 *The Canadian Brothers; or, The Prophecy Fulfilled: A Tale of the Late American War,* John Richardson
Introduction by Carl F. Klinck

www.ingramcontent.com/pod-product-compliance
Lightning Source LLC
Chambersburg PA
CBHW050103120726
47904CB00004B/1202

* 9 7 8 0 8 0 2 0 6 2 6 4 2 *